MISTLETOE AND MAGIC FOR THE CORNISH MIDWIFE

JO BARTLETT

Boldwood

First published in Great Britain in 2022 by Boldwood Books Ltd. This paperback edition first published in 2023.

I

Copyright © Jo Bartlett, 2022

Cover Design: Debbie Clement Design

Cover Photography: Shutterstock

The moral right of Jo Bartlett to be identified as the author of this work has been asserted in accordance with the Copyright, Designs and Patents Act 1988.

Every effort has been made to obtain the necessary permissions with reference to copyright material, both illustrative and quoted. We apologise for any omissions in this respect and will be pleased to make the appropriate acknowledgements in any future edition.

A CIP catalogue record for this book is available from the British Library.

Paperback ISBN: 978-1-78513-793-8

Hardback ISBN: 978-1-80162-009-3

Ebook ISBN: 978-1-80162-012-3

Kindle ISBN: 978-1-80162-013-0

Audio CD ISBN: 978-1-80162-004-8

MP3 CD ISBN: 978-1-80162-005-5

Digital audio download ISBN: 978-1-80162-007-9

Digital audio MP3 ISBN: 978-1-80162-006-2

Large Print ISBN: 978-1-80162-010-9

Boldwood Books Ltd.

23 Bowerdean Street, London, SW6 3TN

www.boldwoodbooks.com

For my beautiful cousin, Viv, who always wants the best for others and grabs the joy from life, even in the midst of a challenge that would make most people crumble xx

1

Nadia glanced at the clock again. There were only thirty minutes left until pick-up from the after-school club at Port Agnes primary, but there was no hurrying a labour, not even this close to delivery. The baby would come when it was good and ready.

'What time did Ella say she'd get here?' Nadia whispered to Anna in between their patient's contractions. Unless it was unavoidable, there needed to be two midwives in the room when a baby was delivered.

Nadia should have left an hour ago, been to the supermarket and already be on the way to pick up her four-year-old son, Mo, from nursery before going to the school to get his sister, Remi. She also needed to pick up a couple of Halloween costumes from somewhere, because there was no way she'd have a chance to make them, even if she had the skill.

'She should be here by half five and then you can shoot off and get the kids.'

'Please don't go!' Agata Kowalski pulled a face. She'd been in labour since the start of Nadia's shift, and she was in no mood to change one of her midwives at this late stage. 'I don't want you to leave before I have this baby!'

'I'm not going anywhere.' Nadia exchanged a look with Anna. Unless this baby got a wiggle on, she was going to have to break that promise, but she didn't want Agata to worry about any of that. She'd seen the top of the baby's head with the last contraction and once she got near the end of the second stage of labour, Agata probably wouldn't realise if Nadia suddenly painted herself green, let alone which midwives were actually there to see her baby emerge into the world. For now, though, Nadia would just keep pretending she didn't need to be in two places at once.

'I can't do this!' Agata screamed as another contraction took hold.

'Of course, you can, *kotek*.' Agata's mother, Paulina, was her birthing partner. The identity of the baby's father was something Agata had chosen not to disclose, but based on what she and her mother *had* said, he had two other children already and was still married to their mother. In her twelve years as a midwife, Nadia had learned not to judge, but with two young children of her own and an estranged husband who'd also 'found comfort' elsewhere, she'd had to take a deep breath. This wasn't about her, and all that mattered was the health and welfare of both Agata and her baby.

Paulina had offered her daughter unwavering support throughout the labour. When Nadia had asked what the whispered endearment '*kotek*' meant, Paulina had explained that it translated to 'kitten', which had apparently been her nickname for Agata from the day she was born.

'Your mum's right: you can do this and, whatever happens, you know you've got her here holding your hand, so it's all going to be okay.' Nadia knew better than anyone how much support from their mothers meant to women in labour, and even more so once the babies arrived. Since her marriage had broken down, and she'd returned to Port Agnes from New Zealand, she couldn't even have managed to work without her mother's help and she wouldn't have had a roof over her head either. It might be cramped in Frankie's two-bedroom flat above The Cookie Jar café, but it had still proved to be a sanctuary after the pain of the marriage breakdown. Usually her mother would step in when there were childcare problems too, but today she was out on home visits as part of the plan to complete her own midwifery training. So it looked like Nadia would just have to accept being slapped with another late pick-up fine. At this rate, she'd be funding the renovation of the school hall all by herself.

'Damien should be here to see his son born. *Dupek*!' Agata shouted the last word and her mother laughed.

'My daughter. She barely speaks a word of Polish, despite me and her father speaking at our home all of the time, but of course she knows the bad words!' Paulina shook her head, before squeezing her daughter's shoulder. 'It's okay *kotek*, it will be over soon and it is that fool's loss not to be here.'

'The baby's crowning.' Nadia looked at Agata, locking eyes with her for a moment. 'This is it; it won't be long now.'

'Mama, why didn't you tell me it hurt this much?' Agatha clung to Paulina's arm, making the older woman smile.

'And what would good would that have done? I got through it three times and the baby has to come, if you like it or not!'

'I don't like it!'

'You're doing really well.' Nadia glanced at Anna, who nodded. 'But we want baby to come nice and slowly now.'

'I don't! I just want it out!'

'If the baby comes too quickly, it increases the risk of a tear.' Anna was the kindest of people, but as the most senior midwife she could still have a very authoritative tone when she needed one.

'When you get the next urge to push, I want you to take some shorter puff-puff type breaths to try and keep things nice and steady.' Nadia kept her voice as calm as she wanted Agata to be. All thoughts about rushing off for school pick-up were completely forgotten.

'Okay, okay, it's coming.' Agata did as instructed, her face screwing up with the effort.

'That's it *kotek*. You don't want to end up as I did with you, like one of *Babcia*'s patchwork blankets!'

'Mama!' Agata shook her head and attempted to puff-puff again through the next two contractions, which had exactly the desired effect.

'That's brilliant sweetheart, you've delivered baby's head now, so the next bit should be relatively easy.' Anna made it sound like it really could be.

'This time when you get the urge to push, I want you to go with it.' Nadia checked there was no sign of the baby's cord being wrapped around its neck as she spoke.

'I'll try.' Agata dropped her chin and grunted the words, going silent as she pushed hard.

'That's it, the baby's shoulders are out.' Nadia was close to tears, as she was at every delivery, but she had a job to do. 'One more good push and the rest of baby should follow.'

'Come on *kotek*, he's nearly here.' Paulina dropped a kiss on her daughter's forehead just before another contraction started.

'That's it, go on, you're doing so well.' Nadia took hold of the baby as the rest of him emerged, checking his airway and rubbing him with a towel, before lying him straight on his mother's chest. 'He's here and he's beautiful.'

'He really is, isn't he? Look Mama!' Agata leant into Paulina as they gazed down at the little boy, just as he greeted the world with a loud cry. 'He's got a good pair of lungs on him.'

'Like his mama.' Paulina brushed a strand of hair away from her daughter's head. 'Well done *kochanie*. He's perfect.'

'Oh no, I missed it!' Ella sounded breathless as she rushed into the delivery room. 'I got stuck behind a tractor on the road back from Port Kara. I'm really sorry Nadia, you're going to be so late.'

'It's okay, I wouldn't have missed it for the world.' Nadia touched Agata's shoulder. 'Congratulations again, you did an amazing job.'

'Thank you so much for staying.' Agata turned to look at Nadia, her eyes shining.

'It was my pleasure.'

'We were blessed to have you here to deliver my grandson.' Paulina's face was wet with tears as she gazed down at the baby.

'Your little boy is going to have so much love.' Nadia wanted to tell Agata how important Paulina was going to be, to both her and her newborn son, especially if she was raising him alone. But it wasn't the time, and she couldn't project her own experiences on everyone she met. She needed to get going anyway, otherwise the school would be calling social services thinking Remi had been abandoned altogether.

'Ella and I can handle the third stage, but thanks so much for staying on. You're a star.' Anna smiled.

Nadia had felt welcomed by the whole team, ever since she'd joined the Port Agnes midwifery unit just a couple of months before, and it was already hard to imagine being anywhere else.

'No problem. Right, bye everyone.' With a final wave, she rushed out of the room as quickly as Ella had come into it. She just hoped there wouldn't be any more tractors on the route between the unit and the school, because she was already horribly late.

* * *

Port Agnes primary school was a whitewashed, single-storey building, which looked down on the left-hand side of the harbour. Nadia had been so relieved that the tiny school had a place for Remi. For once, luck had been on her side and a family with three siblings had just left after moving out of Port Agnes. Remi seemed to have settled in almost instantly, making friends and talking non-stop about one little girl, Daisy, in particular. Nadia had promised to sort out a play date, but it was tricky when there was so little space in her mother's flat, and her job made it hard to arrange after-school activities, especially at this time of year, when the nights drew in so quickly.

It was long-dark by the time she arrived at the school and the lights were twinkling down in the harbour below, reflected in the inky, black water. Nadia had already racked up a fifteen-pound fine at the nursery, where the manager had added to her stress by tapping her watch and telling her that it was no good for Mo's confidence when his mother was late to pick him up. Her little boy was small for his age and quite shy compared to his big sister, and the worst part was Nadia knew the nursery manager was right. It wasn't as if she was late because she'd been out with her friends for some sneaky afternoon cocktails, though. She'd been working, and midwifery wasn't the sort of job where you could just pack up and walk out when the clock struck five – especially not in a rural unit like the one in Port Agnes.

Risking another telling off, Nadia parked in a space that was clearly labelled 'Reserved for the Headteacher' when she got to the school. If the head had any sense, she'd already be at home by now. Parking in that bay meant she could scoop Mo out of his car seat and dash straight into the building, instead of trying to find a space on the street and ending up several roads away.

'Come on sweetheart, let's go and get Remi.' Nadia picked up her son, who had fallen asleep and was a lot harder to manoeuvre than he'd been even a few months before.

As Nadia rushed to the gate at the far end of the school, she almost got knocked off her feet by a man hurtling towards the entrance. He was looking at his phone even while he was running, and it took all of Nadia's self-control not to shout at him. If she hadn't had Mo in her arms, she probably would have done. It had definitely been one of those days.

'Oh God, sorry, I wasn't looking where I was going.'

'No, you weren't.' Nadia looked up into the bluest eyes she'd ever seen. The tall man, who was illuminated by the security light outside the building, was attempting an apologetic smile, but she had no time for niceties. 'If you can just get out of the way please; I'm late to pick up my daughter.'

'Me too.' At least the mystery man wasn't a teacher. That would be just like Nadia, to upset someone who was going to spend at least a year teaching each of her kids, and who might well take their mother's rudeness out on them. Not bothering to acknowledge him, she darted through the door, with the mystery man hot on her heels.

'Ah Mrs Ennor, here you are. At last.' Miss Renfrew, who taught the year 2 class and took some shifts at the breakfast and after-school clubs sounded exasperated.

'I'm so sorry, there was a delivery at work and I couldn't—'

'Dr Spencer.' Miss Renfrew completely ignored Nadia and all but elbowed her out of the way as she spotted the mystery man. 'Don't forget what I said before: if you get caught up at the surgery, you only have to call and I'll always look after Daisy for you. I know you can't just clock off when you're a GP.'

'Thank you, but I couldn't possibly put you out, Fiona.' Those blue eyes not only had him on first name terms with Miss Renfrew, but they clearly got him the offer of unlimited late pick-ups too.

Maybe it wasn't the eyes. It could be the fact that the supervising teacher had referred to him as 'doctor'. But, looking at him again, Nadia would have put money on the eyes having a lot to do with it.

'I'm so sorry, my last patient was a toddler whose oxygen sats were so low I needed to call an ambulance. I didn't want to leave until the paramedics had him on board. The only downside of Port Agnes is that everything takes ages to get here, even ambulances. I would have asked Saffron to pick Daisy up, but she's already at the gym and she won't pick her phone up when she's in the middle of a workout.'

'That's fine, don't worry at all.' Fiona put a hand on his arm, clearly unfazed by the fact that his wife was probably some sort of gym bunny, with washboard abs and a size-six figure. If this was the same Daisy that Remi had spoken about almost constantly, she sounded perfect too, at least according to Nadia's daughter.

'Thank you and apologies again; you were talking to this lady before I barged in.' Dr Spencer had dimples in both cheeks when he smiled and Nadia might as well have been invisible for all the notice Miss Renfrew was taking of her.

'Thanks.' She had to physically position herself between Miss Renfrew and Dr Spencer to get the other woman to acknowledge her. 'Like I was saying, I was late because of a patient too.'

'Oh, you're a doctor as well?' Dr Blue Eyes held her gaze and she almost found herself nodding.

'Er no, I'm a midwife, but I had a lady who was really close to the end of her labour and she didn't want me to leave.'

'That's completely understandable.' He smiled again and despite wanting to dislike him for clearly having a perfect life, with an equally perfect wife and daughter, Nadia found herself returning his smile.

'The girls are in the cosy corner in classroom two with Miss Coleman.' Miss Renfrew directed a pointed look at Nadia. 'Remi was getting really tired, what with it being so late, so Miss Coleman offered to read them a story. I've got prep to do for tomorrow.'

'I'm sure Daisy was flagging just as much; we're both really sorry.' Dr Spencer was still smiling that irresistible, dimpled smile. 'I know you understand, though. Sick toddlers and newborn babies just don't have any respect for time. I'm so grateful that Daisy is in such good hands.'

'Well, yes, I understand it's difficult for you.' Miss Renfrew clearly still couldn't quite bring herself to direct the same under-standing towards Nadia.

'Mummy!' Suddenly Remi appeared at the door, looking more excited than tired, skipping into the room, hand in hand with a little girl who had golden blonde hair and the same bright blue eyes as her father. The name Daisy was perfect for her.

'Hello darling, I'm so sorry I'm late.' Nadia bent down and her daughter squeezed her tightly. Mo, who was still asleep and clamped to her side, didn't even stir when his sister let out an excited squeak.

'Can Daisy come to dinner? We want to play 'splorers.'

'We were reading *The Snail and the Whale*.' Miss Coleman, who had followed the children into the room, smiled. 'And the girls have decided they want to explore the world like the little snail.'

'Can she come, Mummy, pleeeaase?'

'Not tonight, darling, I'm sorry. It's already late.' Nadia felt her face colour. It wouldn't have mattered what time it was. There was no way she could invite any of Remi's friends home while they were crammed into the tiny flat over the café, and a mixture of guilt and embarrassment made Nadia go hot. Remi's downturned mouth and wobbling chin weren't helping either. 'How about if we pick Daisy up on Saturday and go exploring? There's a Halloween trail to follow through Port Agnes and if we solve all the clues there's even a prize at the end. Then we can get some cake or ice cream at The Cookie Jar afterwards.'

Nadia had seen the poster advertising the event pinned to the noticeboard in the reception area of the midwifery unit. She might be saving hard for the deposit to rent a place of her own, but Remi and Mo still needed the occasional treat. It wasn't the play date Remi wanted, but it would have to do for now. 'That's if it's okay with Daisy's mummy and daddy?'

'It sounds perfect to me.' Dr Spencer took his daughter's hand, an unreadable expression crossing his face as Daisy leant against him. He passed Nadia a card. 'If you want to text me, we can sort out the details and I'm sure I can get Saffron on board to return the favour at some point.'

'Great.' Nadia's smile felt tight. She hated the thought that it might be from bitterness, but there was no denying she disliked Saffron without even having met her. She couldn't imagine being friends with anyone who put their workout before picking up their daughter or who needed persuading to facilitate a play date for her child. Taking Dr Spencer's card, she stuffed it into her pocket. 'Come on then, sweetheart, let's get you home.'

'Bye, bye, Daisy-boo!' Remi waved at her little friend.

'Bye Remi-roo.' It was so cute the way the girls had instantly formed a friendship so strong that they already had nicknames for each other. It was the sort of thing that only children seemed capable of and Nadia would do whatever was needed to nurture that. Even befriend Saffron the gym bunny, if that's what it took.

'I'll be in touch then.' She turned to Daisy's father, whose killer smile was back in situ.

'Thank you; Daisy will love it.'

'No problem.' Forcing herself to turn away from those dimples, she looked towards the teachers. 'And apologies again for being so late.'

'Try not to let it happen again.' Miss Renfrew's tone hadn't softened, but all Nadia could do was nod. Not every child had a father willing to share the school pick-ups and Remi didn't even have one in the same hemisphere. Miss Renfrew really was wasting her breath, because Nadia already felt terrible about it. All by herself.

2

Working alongside Nadia was something Frankie had thought would never happen. She hadn't even let herself dream that her daughter would come back to the UK. The pain she'd felt when Nadia had got on that flight to emigrate to New Zealand had only been compounded when Frankie had slowly come to realise that her daughter and her family were never coming back. Her son, Harish, who everyone called Hari, had his own life in London, working long hours in the law firm where he was already a partner. Work had become his life fairly early on and his infrequent visits home had become even rarer once he'd got engaged to Uma, who was also a lawyer. They inhabited a world that was completely alien to Frankie and sometimes she found it hard to relate to them, even when she did get the chance to see them.

It had been different with Nadia. They'd always had so much in common and if Frankie had lived some of her dreams vicariously through her daughter when Nadia had become a midwife, it had just seemed to strengthen their bond. Looking back, having her daughter living just around the corner had been what had enabled Frankie to hold on in a marriage that had been limping along for years. But with Nadia gone, Frankie's relationship with her husband, Advik, had quickly reached breaking point and it had been a relief to move to the tiny flat she now called home.

Her friends had been supportive and even Advik and her children had seemed to accept the decision without too much drama, although Hari had taken it the hardest of the two. It was her elderly mother, Bhavna, who'd called her a fool and told her that she was ashamed of Frankie for acting like a silly teenager. She fired words like bullets that were fully intended to wound: *Don't you realise what you're throwing away, Firaki? Life isn't all about having fun!* It had taken all Frankie had not to tell her mother that she couldn't remember the last time she'd had fun, but that she was certain it hadn't been since before Nadia had left. Her mother still spoke to her as if she was and child and she was the only person who still called her Firaki, after a mispronunciation of her name had earned her the nickname Frankie when she was still at school. It felt like an indication of how well her mother knew her as a person. If she was an embarrassment to Bhavna, that was just something she was going to have to live with, because there was no going back.

Although leaving Advik had been a relief in the end, it hadn't done anything to lessen the empty feeling that had settled in Frankie's chest since her daughter had started a new life on the other side of the world. As soon as she'd scraped together enough money, she'd headed out to see them just after Mo was born. The last thing she'd expected to witness, on her second visit, was her daughter's marriage imploding too. It meant she'd ended up staying out there for much longer than planned – taking care of the children while Nadia went to work. Getting on the plane to eventually come home again had been one of the hardest things Frankie had ever done, and she hadn't dared hope that her daughter might follow on behind her.

Now, having Nadia and the children back was like a dream come true, but she still wished things had worked out between Nadia and Ryan. How could she do anything else when her daughter looked so broken, in between the painted-on smiles that only Frankie could see through.

'I don't think it's going to be long now before active labour starts and things really begin to progress.' Nadia had just examined Esther, the woman whose labour she was overseeing, with support from Gwen and Frankie. 'You're already at five centimetres.'

'Thank goodness for that; I'm not sure how long I can take the stress!' Esther's husband, Vince, looked a lot more panicked than his wife, who seemed to be coping with the whole thing with a serene calm. 'How long do you think it will be?'

'It could be as little as five hours based on the progress so far, but there are no guarantees unfortunately.' Nadia smiled, which had a way of putting everyone at their ease, and Frankie felt a surge of pride just watching her daughter.

'I'm not in any hurry for things to really kick in. Slow and steady works for me.' Esther's pink-streaked hair fanned out across the pillow. Frankie had always envied people whose hair was light enough to dye other colours. Her own was still almost completely black, despite the fact she was in her mid-fifties. Maybe when the greys really started to come in, she could finally rebel and have some streaks of pink too. That would give her mother something else to complain about.

'Either way, I don't think you'll be needing any assistance from me for a while.' Gwen, who'd popped in to see how things were going, looked towards Esther. 'I love your T-shirt by the way; now that's a diet I could get behind!'

The black oversized T-shirt had the words: *Breakfast, second breakfast, elevenses, luncheon, afternoon tea, dinner and supper*, emblazoned across the front.

'It's from *Lord of the Rings*.' Esther smoothed a hand over the T-shirt, the sensors for the heart monitor noticeable beneath the material tightly stretched across her bump. 'It seemed fitting as we met at a fan club event. It's also why we're calling the baby Arwen.'

'That's lovely and very unusual.' Frankie wasn't about to admit that she'd walked out of the cinema five minutes into the first *Lord of the Rings* film. She'd had smear tests that had been more enjoyable, but each to their own.

'I even asked her to marry me in Elvish.' Vince smiled at the memory.

'As Elvis?' Gwen looked completely confused and Frankie couldn't help laughing.

'No, in Elvish, the language from the *Lord of the Rings*.' Esther was laughing too. 'There were absolutely no rhinestone-covered jumpsuits involved!'

'That's a great story to tell Arwen when she's old enough to understand. In my experience, kids love knowing how their parents met.' Nadia had a wistful look on her face again and Frankie didn't need three guesses to work out what she was thinking about.

'She'll probably think it's completely tragic.' Esther rolled her eyes. 'And she wouldn't be the only one.'

'I think having a shared passion can only be a good thing.' Nadia's eyes met Frankie's for a split second, before she looked away again. From what her daughter had told her, the fact that Ryan had wanted to spend all his spare time playing the sports he loved had been the first wedge driven between them. The female golf pro he'd met had turned into a much bigger wedge, but when the affair had been revealed, Ryan had still blamed Nadia for not being interested in the things he was. Never mind that she was raising two young children and holding down a demanding job, the breakdown of their marriage was somehow still all her fault.

Frankie had tried her best to comfort her daughter, but Nadia was convinced she should have seen it coming. She'd admitted squashing the worries she'd had about how little they had in common when they'd first met, because she'd fallen head over heels in love with him and had assumed the rest would work itself out.

'I couldn't agree more that having something in common is a great starting point.' Gwen had a mischievous smile on her face. 'Maybe you should take some sort of class, Frankie. You might find your soulmate while you're reupholstering a chair or learning how to write place cards in calligraphy.'

'I think I'd rather just forget the whole idea. If I'm meant to meet someone I will.' The last thing Frankie wanted was to have a conversation about all of this right now, but Gwen seemed oblivious to boundaries of any kind. Frankie had kept her dating life quiet from everyone. It was early days with Guy, the father of Jess, one of the other midwives on the team, and she fully intended to continue to keep it quiet until there was something more to tell.

'What about you, Nadia? You could try a salsa class, or join the rock choir? My friend Maggie met her fourth husband there last year.'

'*Fourth* husband?' Nadia visibly shuddered. 'She's a brave lady. One ex is more than enough for me.'

'You shouldn't let that put you off forever.' Gwen was really pushing it, the way she often did. Even though Frankie knew it was with the best of intentions, she could tell it was making Nadia uncomfortable. It wasn't a conversation anyone wanted to have in front of strangers, much less one of their patients. It was definitely time for a change of subject.

'So when you go to these conventions' – Frankie turned towards Vince – 'do you wear costumes too?'

'Absolutely. The first time I met Esther, I was wearing a pair of rubber hobbit feet.'

'He had me at hairy toe!' Esther laughed again.

'Maybe I should go to one of these conventions. My Barry's always telling me I've got hobbit's feet, although thanks to the wonders of waxing I just about manage to keep the hairy toes in check.' Gwen winked. 'Well, most of the time!'

'I'm not quite sure how to respond to that.' Vince's face was a picture.

'The thought of all those hairy hobbit feet seems to have woken the baby up.' Esther grunted the words as another contraction took hold.

'I wish I could do something to take the pain away for you.' Vince clasped his wife's hand.

'Aside from the sort of drugs we're not able to offer here, there's only one thing that can take the pain away and that's the baby's arrival.' Nadia's tone was reassuring, but the wistful look was back on her face. 'Each contraction brings that a step closer. It's the most amazing thing the two of you will ever experience.'

'Tea might help too; I find it does with most things.' Frankie hoped she was right, because she'd recognised the look on her daughter's face. It seemed to appear so often lately, when she spoke about the children or her life with Ryan. Frankie had been there when Remi was born and she'd heard Ryan's declarations of love as Nadia had brought her into the world – his promise that nothing would ever change and that they'd always be a family. That promise of forever had turned out to be just one of the lies Ryan had told and it was incredibly hard to look at the sadness on her daughter's face. Making tea wasn't just for Esther's and Vince's benefit; Frankie needed a moment too.

'Like I said, it's going to be a while before you need me, so I'll give Frankie a hand.' Gwen was already halfway towards the door, thwarting any chance Frankie might have had of taking a moment for herself.

'I might even be able to rustle up some biscuits. They always work as a distraction for me.' Frankie smiled at Esther, whose latest contraction had now eased off. 'Hence why I've got hips like these. But at least I haven't got hobbit's feet.'

'So you say, but there could be anything hidden under those clogs!' Gwen waggled her finger. 'Come on, let's go and see if we can find the good biscuits for these two.'

Frankie followed her friend out into the corridor, unable to stop herself from emitting a huge sigh as she shut the door of the delivery room behind her.

'Come on, what's up?' Gwen blocked her path and any attempt to brush her off clearly wasn't going to work.

'I'm just worried about Nadia. I know she's sad about the break-up, but it's really hard that this is something I can't fix. When the kids were little, whatever problems they had, I was always able to find something to help. But this...' Frankie's words caught in her throat. 'It's broken her heart and there's nothing I can do about it.'

'I shouldn't have mentioned the dating.' Gwen's tone was uncharacteristically subdued. 'I suppose it's just my clumsy attempt to try to make things better. You and Nadia deserve to be happy and I hate seeing the two of you like this.'

'I don't think dating is the answer. I just want Nadia to be okay. That saying about you only being as happy as your unhappiest child is so true. If she was okay, I would be too, and none of that hinges on her meeting someone else. She just needs time to come to terms with what happened with Ryan and I've got to accept that nothing I can do will help to fast forward that.'

'You'll be helping her more than you realise.' Gwen gave

Frankie a quick hug. 'And I know where the chocolate-coated cookies are hidden too.'

'I thought they'd all gone.' The biscuits had been brought in by a grateful patient and all the midwives had agreed they were the best ones yet. 'How did you find out where someone had hidden them?'

'Because that someone was me!' Gwen might have no shame, but just this once Frankie was glad. She'd never needed the distraction of a good biscuit more than she did right now. She just hoped Nadia would be able to stop torturing herself over the end of her marriage soon, otherwise Frankie was going to need to go up a uniform size. Again.

3

One consequence Nadia had hoped there'd be from living above The Cookie Jar was that she might get so sick of the smell of freshly baked bread, cakes and biscuits that it would be like a kind of aversion therapy and she'd never want them again. Sadly, that hadn't happened yet. So when Gwen opened the lid of a box of pecan Danish pastries that she'd knocked up before work, Nadia's mouth was watering the moment the aroma filled the air.

'Come on you lot, dig in.' Gwen gave the order and most of them didn't even try to resist. 'I've put a couple into another box for you to take home, Bobby, so Toni doesn't miss out.'

'After the nightshift Izzy and I have just had, I'd only share them with someone I love as much as I love my wife.' Bobby was the only male midwife at the unit and his wife, Toni, who was also a midwife, was currently on leave after the birth of their daughter. 'Sharing Danishes with Toni is all part of married life, but after two back-to-back on call home deliveries, I'm still going to pick the biggest one.'

'That sounds fair enough to me, but then I always go for the biggest one!' Gwen never missed the chance to slip in an innuendo.

'Well, I know Nadia didn't eat this morning. She was too busy trying to persuade Mo to have some porridge before nursery.' Frankie raised her eyebrows.

The splatter of porridge oats that Nadia had wiped off the wall, so they wouldn't be concreted on by the end of the day, was testament to how Mo felt about the breakfast menu. She'd almost been tempted to cave in and give him whatever it was he'd eat, even if that was a bag of Pom-Bear crisps, just so he wouldn't go to nursery without having anything. But if she went down that route with someone as strong-willed as her son, there was no way of knowing where it might end.

'I have the same issues with Riley.' Jess rolled her eyes. 'It took him nearly half an hour to eat a piece of toast this morning, but every time I try and nag him, he starts giggling, and I get side-tracked all over again. He's too cute for his own good that one.'

'You'll have to sort a play date for the kids at some point.' Frankie looked from Jess to Nadia and back again. It made sense with Riley, Jess's stepson, being a similar age to Remi. 'Maybe at the soft play centre near Port Tremellien.'

'That would be great.' Jess picked up a Danish as she spoke and Nadia's stomach rumbled.

'We might have to take ours to go, Frankie.' Ella glanced at her watch. 'We've got a long list of home visits to get through, before you go to uni.'

'I get the results of my first assignment tonight, so I'm not sure I even want to eat!'

'You'll be fine, Mum, you've put so much work into it.' Nadia gave her mother's shoulders a squeeze. It had to be tough for her, having her daughter and two grandchildren land on her doorstep just when she'd decided to go back to university to complete her midwifery training. Frankie had worked as a midwifery care assistant for years, after dropping out of her midwifery training when she had children. Now this was her time. Nadia knew how much her mother loved having the three of them home, but there was no denying that trying to study in a crowded flat, with two young children, was an extra layer of challenge.

'I bet you'll do better than me.' Emily, the unit's other full time MCA, pulled a face. 'I had to drink half a bottle of wine just to face the prospect of sitting down to do the referencing. Who's going to care about the year some journal article is published when they're pushing a baby out?'

'It'll all be worth it in the end.' Anna, who'd previously headed up the unit, had recently returned to work after having twins and was now sharing the role with Ella. 'I think someone talking through the principles of Harvard referencing while I was having Kit and Merryn might have been a good diversion tactic.'

'I'm not sure it will catch on. If you want a distraction, there are a lot more exciting ones I can think of than that.' Gwen grinned. 'Idris Elba's always a good start.'

'Why does that not surprise me?' Frankie laughed. 'It's a good job you aren't in charge of the antenatal classes!'

'On that note, I'm going to grab a Danish and get sorted for clinics this morning.' The rumbling in Nadia's stomach was getting louder and she definitely needed to drown it out before she started any consultations.

* * *

Nadia's third patient of the day was a woman called Genevieve Bradshaw. It was such an unusual name, she couldn't help wondering if it was the same Genevieve she'd been at school with. Her surname had been Summers back then, and they'd been quite close until Genevieve had headed off to university in Scotland. As with a lot of her local friends, she'd lost touch with Genevieve over the years, especially as she'd never been keen on social media, even before having young children meant she didn't have the spare time to keep up with it all.

She glanced at the notes; Genevieve's year of birth was the same as Nadia's, so there was a good chance it could be her. If it was, she'd have to check whether Genevieve felt comfortable seeing her. Not everyone wanted someone they knew personally as their midwife.

'Come in.' Nadia responded to the knock at the door and, when the woman walked in, there was no question in her mind that it was the same Genevieve from school. She'd barely changed a bit. 'Hello! Long time no see.'

'Nadia! Oh my God, I'd heard you were back.' Genevieve looked delighted to see her. 'Can I give you a hug?'

'Of course.' Nadia stood up and embraced her old friend. Even her perfume brought back memories. Genevieve had regularly pinched bottles of her mother's Estée Lauder perfume when they'd been teenagers, liberally spritzing it around the sixth-form common room and for a moment Nadia felt seventeen again. 'It's really good to see you.'

'You too, but sorry if my bump crushed you, it's getting to the stage now where there are three of us in any hug.'

'It's a bonus as far as I'm concerned.' Nadia smiled. 'I just wanted to make sure that you're okay with me doing your checks today? Not everyone wants to be supported by a midwife they know and I promise not to take offence if that's the case.'

'Not at all. I've been meaning to get in touch, ever since I heard you were back.'

'I didn't realise you were living in Port Agnes again too.'

'I've been back a year now. I stayed up in Edinburgh after uni and that's where I met Freddie, but when we decided to start trying for a baby I wanted to come home to be close to Mum and Dad, especially after Mum was diagnosed with Parkinson's.'

'I'm really sorry to hear that.' Nadia couldn't even imagine how she'd feel if her mum was diagnosed with a serious illness. The heightened emotion of pregnancy must have made it even tougher.

'She's coping really well, but it's important to me that she gets to spend as much time as possible with this little one, so being close to her was my top priority.' Genevieve bit her lip. 'The news about the baby definitely helped her deal with her diagnosis. None of us can wait until she's here.'

'That's lovely and it will come around really quickly now you're thirty-one weeks.'

'I know. I've told Freddie he has to have the nursery finished by the end of November at the latest, in case the baby's a little bit early.' Genevieve sat down as she spoke.

'That's always a good idea, but everything is on track so far. All the tests from your twenty-eight week check came back clear. We'll test your blood pressure and urine again today, but you're looking really well. How are you feeling?'

'Yeah, yes, umm... I *feel* fine.'

'But?' Nadia looked at her old friend; there was definitely something else she wanted to say. Nadia had probably heard most things over the years, everything from disclosures of domestic violence to mothers-to-be who were in turmoil because they weren't sure whether their partner was really the father of their baby. Whatever it was, Nadia wanted Genevieve to know it was okay to share if she wanted to. 'You can tell me whatever it is that's worrying you. I've never had anyone say it didn't help to share a problem.'

'I've found a lump.' Four simple words that were so incredibly emotive. 'In my left breast, but it's probably nothing. When I googled it, the website said it's almost certainly a blocked milk duct.'

'That's more than likely.' Despite what Genevieve had said, Nadia could tell she was worried. 'But it's always worth getting these things checked, just to make sure. When did you notice it?'

'Just after my twenty-week scan.'

'Okay.' Nadia deliberately kept her tone light, but that was almost three months of missed opportunity to get this checked out and put Genevieve's mind at rest, so she could enjoy her pregnancy.

'I know what you're thinking, but getting an appointment to see the doctor is a nightmare. You have to ring at 8.30 a.m. on the day you want the appointment to even stand a chance and it's always about 8.45 before I remember.' That was an excuse for Genevieve to bury her head in the sand, if Nadia had ever heard one. If she'd mentioned the breast lump, the reception team would almost certainly have offered her an appointment for the following day, even if she'd called too late for a same day slot. So there was a good chance Genevieve was simply choosing to trust in Dr Google, rather than facing up to her fears. 'And with Mum's diagnosis, I just didn't want to make a fuss over something that's probably nothing.'

'Who's your doctor?'

'Dr Spencer, but the chances of getting an appointment with him are even less. Everyone wants to see him.' Nadia could imagine exactly how popular Dr Spencer was, just from Miss Renfrew's reaction to him.

'Let me give the surgery a quick try now.' She dialled the number on Genevieve's file before she had the chance to protest, putting it on speakerphone, but the automated voice just backed up her old friend's reason for not having had the lump checked.

Your call is very important to us. You are in a queue; please hold. Your position in the queue is currently number twenty-three.

'See what I mean?' Genevieve shook her head. 'It's fine, honestly. If the lump is still there after the baby arrives, I'll get it checked out then.'

'There's something else I can try. I've got Dr Spencer's mobile number.' Nadia grabbed her bag and fished out the card he'd given her. She'd put it in there, planning to text him about Remi and Daisy's play date. But when Remi had said she wanted to draw Daisy an invitation instead, with a picture of a pumpkin and a witch on the front, she'd been more than happy not to message him. Their lives were worlds apart and trying to strike up a friendship with Daisy's parents felt forced as a result. Not wanting to risk disturbing him in the middle of a consultation, Nadia fired off a quick text instead.

✉ Message to a number not in your contacts
Hi. It's Remi's mum, Nadia. We have a patient in common, Genevieve Bradshaw. She's 31 weeks pregnant and found a breast lump more than ten weeks ago, but hasn't been able to get an appointment to see you. Please can you let me know if you're able to see her?

'Okay, hopefully we'll get an answer soon, but if not, I'll give the surgery another call over lunch.' Nadia put her phone on the desk. 'Let's get you checked over in the meantime and see what your little one is up to.'

'Perfect. I never get bored of hearing her heartbeat.' Genevieve headed to the examination table and ten minutes later, the checks were all complete and the wonderful sound of the baby's heartbeat had sounded out loud and clear.

'Let me just check my phone before you head off.' Nadia picked up her mobile, not really expecting to have heard back from Dr Spencer so quickly, but there was already a reply.

✉ Message from a number not in your contacts
Hi Nadia. Thanks so much for letting me know. I'm really sorry to hear that Genevieve has had to wait so long. Please can you ask her if she can come into the surgery at 5 p.m. today and I'll see her after my last appointment. Thanks again, Hamish.

'That's great news, Dr Spencer said he can fit you in at the end of the day today.'

'What time?' Genevieve was biting her lip again.

'Five o'clock.'

'Can you come with me?' Genevieve clearly registered the look of surprise that must have crossed Nadia's face as she immediately shook her head. 'Sorry, I know it's a real cheek and you've probably got loads of stuff to do, but Freddie's away at the moment and I don't want to worry Mum with everything she's got going on. But I don't want to go on my own either. We've had far too much bad news from doctors lately and if he does think there's something wrong, the first thing I'm going to want to know is how it might affect the baby. Having you there would really help.'

'My last appointment is at three-thirty, so that should be fine.' Nadia crossed her fingers, trying to work out what to do about picking the children up. Her mum would be at uni until late, but she might be able to get her dad to come down, pick them up and take them out for a milkshake after school. As a freelance accountant, he seemed to spend most of his life holed up in his home office filing other people's tax returns. He'd mentioned picking the kids up one day, so hopefully he'd relish the opportunity, even if it was late notice.

'Thank you so much.' Genevieve hugged her again and Nadia suddenly had an image of them both in the sixth-form common room they'd left sixteen years before. Things had been so simple then and Nadia was silently praying that her old friend's life wasn't about to get a hell of a lot more complicated.

4

The moment Hamish got Nadia's message, a sick feeling settled in his stomach. A patient waiting ten weeks to get a lump checked out would never have sat well with him, but the fact that Genevieve was pregnant made in ten times worse. Even though the odds were that this would just turn out to be a blocked milk duct or even a cyst, he couldn't help picturing the worst-case scenario, after what had happened before Daisy was born. Either way, the sooner Genevieve got an answer – and hopefully the all-clear – the better.

Saffron was back in the mode of nagging him to eat more healthily and she'd insisted on packing him a lunch, even though he'd offered to do one for both of them when he'd been making Daisy's. There were carrot sticks and some hummus, a little pot of nuts and seeds and what looked like a whole bunch of grapes. She clearly didn't want him to go hungry, even if she wanted him to eat less rubbish. He'd have made the effort too, if his appetite hadn't disappeared the moment Nadia's text arrived. As it was, he was just clock-watching until 5 p.m.

Examining Genevieve could tell him a lot. If the lump felt smooth beneath the skin, like a grape, it was far more likely to be a cyst. A blocked milk duct would probably feel tender and warm to the touch. If the lump was firmer and rock-like, with angular edges, and didn't move around, there'd be more reason for concern. Whatever happened, Hamish would be referring her for further tests, but he wanted to do so when they'd almost certainly be able to confirm what he already hoped – that the lump was nothing to worry about.

His last appointment of the day had been a fairly routine consultation with a lady suffering from a host of symptoms which could all be menopause related. A blood test would tell them for certain, but he was able to reassure her that, regardless of the results, there'd be treatment options. It meant he was running to time for once and he'd be able to get Genevieve in without her having to wait. When there was a knock at the door, at exactly 5 p.m., and he called Genevieve in, the last thing he'd expected was for Nadia to be with her.

'Hi Genevieve. I was checking the last time I saw you and it's been more than six months.'

'I know. It was the appointment I made when I first found out I was pregnant.' She put a protective hand on her bump, her eyes flashing as she looked at Nadia and then back to him. It didn't take a mind reader to know how nervous she was.

'Come on in and take a seat, both of you.' Hamish looked at Nadia. She was watching Genevieve, and she reached out and touched her hand as they took their seats. He had no idea if they were friends, but he could see how much her midwife's support meant to Genevieve. 'I know you found a lump about ten weeks ago and the first thing to say is that the odds are it will turn out to be nothing to worry about. I'm going to examine you, but I need to ask you some questions first.'

'Okay.' Genevieve was stroking her bump again and Nadia's eyes still hadn't left her face.

'Where in your breast is the lump?'

'It's on the left breast, just beneath the nipple.'

'Is there any puckering to the skin or inversion of the nipple?'

'Well they've always been inverted, so it's tough to tell.' Genevieve looked at Nadia, who mouthed the words *It's okay*. It was obvious she genuinely cared about Genevieve and if Nadia had been a colleague, he'd have chosen to work alongside her because she clearly had the ability to put herself in her patients' shoes. She understood Genevieve's fears, he could see it in her eyes.

'And what does the lump feel like? Is it smooth or firm to the touch?'

'It's pretty hard, a bit like a piece of gravel, except it feels almost triangular.'

'Right.' Hamish had to concentrate hard to keep his expression neutral, as Genevieve listed another potential red flag. 'Any redness or heat to the touch?'

'No, nothing. Do you think it's a blocked duct? That's what Google says it probably is.' Hamish really wished he could just nod, tell her it was nothing and they could all go home, but it wasn't that easy.

'Let's just take a look first, but try not to worry. The vast majority of lumps won't be anything serious.' Hamish gave her what he hoped was a reassuring smile. 'Are you happy for Nadia to chaperone while I examine you?'

'Absolutely. I'd probably have done a runner if I hadn't brought her in with me. Ever since Mum's Parkinson's diagnosis, I find it hard to even walk into a consulting room. It's like my brain has decided it's going to be bad news before anyone even speaks. That's why I chose the midwifery unit – it feels a lot less medical somehow.'

'I get that.' Hamish had a better understanding than his

patients would ever realise and there'd been a time when he hadn't even been sure if he could do his job any more. Days like today, and patients like Genevieve, brought those feelings back.

'You're doing great.' Nadia had such a warm tone to her voice; she looked and sounded completely different from the stressed woman he'd met at the school the day before. There'd been something almost spikey about her then, but he couldn't blame her after how differently Miss Renfrew had treated the two of them. It might not be his fault, but he could understand why Nadia had directed some of her frustration at him. He just hoped it wouldn't affect Daisy's friendship with Remi. She'd been so much happier since Nadia's daughter had started at the school and he didn't want that to end.

'If you'd like to go behind the curtain. Remove your bra and top, get as comfortable as you can on the examination table and then let me know when you're ready.' As Hamish waited, he was still hoping the examination might be able to put all their minds at rest.

'Okay, I'm ready.'

'I'm sorry if my hands are cold, but just let me know if anything hurts at any point. I'm going to need to examine both breasts to compare what's normal for you, as some people just have lumpier breasts than others.'

'I'm one of those people.' Nadia immediately looked away as if she wished she'd kept the confession to herself, but she'd managed to make Genevieve laugh, which, in the circumstances, was nothing short of miraculous. There was something really special about her.

'If this turns out to be nothing, maybe we should start the lumpy boobs brigade.'

'It's a deal.' Nadia was smiling, but she still hadn't looked in his direction.

'Let's take a look then.' No one spoke as Hamish completed his examination, but he was having to fight the urge to release a string of expletives at the unfairness of it all. The lump in Genevieve's breast had far too many of the warning signs of cancer. 'Okay, if you pop your things back on, we can have a chat afterwards.'

'Is it bad?' Genevieve looked close to tears as she sat down opposite him again and Nadia reached out and took her hand, offering some words of comfort.

'Try not to panic. Remember: this is just an initial examination.'

'Nadia's right.' For a split second Hamish's eyes caught hers and he could tell she knew what was coming, but was doing her best to sound relaxed for Genevieve's sake, exactly like he was. 'I think you do need to see a specialist, so they can give you a mammogram and an ultrasound, but that doesn't mean it's cancer. I just can't completely rule it out.'

'Shit. I knew this was going to happen; that's why I didn't come before.' A single tear rolled down Genevieve's cheek. 'This is going to kill Mum.'

'You don't need to worry about any of that yet.' Nadia's tone was gentle but firm, all at the same time. 'Just take it a step at a time and even if the news isn't what you want to hear, there are so many options. You'll be surprised how strong you and everyone around you can be too. Just don't start dealing with the diagnosis before you even have one.'

'I know it's scary, but I couldn't have put it better myself.' Hamish blinked, trying not to picture the face that came into his head every time he had a consultation like this, or just how loaded the word *options* could be.

Genevieve looked at him. 'It is going to be all right, isn't it?'

'The best thing you can do is to get checked out properly.' He couldn't categorically promise her that everything was going to be okay, because the truth was he didn't think it would be. But even if the diagnosis brought the news that no one wanted, with advancements in treatment, the statistics were still in her favour and the last thing she needed right now was for him to sound uncertain.

'I need to call my husband and let him know what's going on.'

'I'm going to refer you to the hospital under the two-week-wait pathway and you should get an appointment within the next fortnight.'

'Thank you. Both of you.' Genevieve's voice still sounded shaky, but she had a more determined look on her face. 'I know I should have got this checked before, but there was part of me that didn't want to know. I've been such an idiot.'

'No you haven't.' Hamish and Nadia's responses matched word for word.

'I know I've already taken up far too much of your time.' Genevieve turned to Nadia. 'But can I ask you one last favour? Please can you wait for me until after I've spoken to Freddie?'

'Of course.'

'You're welcome to wait here until Genevieve's finished.' Hamish made the offer, despite the fact that Nadia could have waited in reception. He wanted the chance to talk to her on her own anyway. 'The nurse's room next door is empty now, if you want to make the call in there. That way, I can answer any questions Freddie might have before you leave.'

'Thank you both, I just hope he can be the strong one.' As soon as Genevieve left the consultation room, Nadia's shoulders slumped.

'Do you think it's cancer?' She was speaking in hushed tones and Hamish followed suit, neither of them wanting Genevieve to overhear anything that might upset her even more.

'If I was forced to guess, I'd say yes. But thankfully, I've been wrong more than once.'

'I really hope this is one of those times.'

'Me too.' Hamish sighed, not holding out nearly as much hope as he wanted to. 'I didn't know if you were friends, as well as her being your patient?'

'We knew each other at school, but I haven't seen her since we left at eighteen. Until today.'

'Not the reunion you'd have hoped for.' Hamish looked at Nadia as he spoke; she had dark corkscrew curls and the most perfect complexion he'd ever seen, with brown eyes that seemed capable of conveying every expression without the need for words.

'Definitely not and I feel like there's nothing I can do to help her.'

'You already are helping. When—' Hamish stopped himself from saying what he'd been about to. This was about how Nadia could help her friend; it wasn't his story. 'When I see people going through cancer scares and diagnoses, the support of the people around them makes all the difference, more than ever when it's a medical professional. Sadly, I've seen my share of medics whose empathy seems to have all but evaporated, if they even had any in the first place.'

'Me too. Remi had suspected meningitis when she was two and thankfully it turned out to be a virus, but the way one of the paediatricians spoke to us, I thought Ryan might actually punch him.'

'Is that your husband?'

'Yes, no, I mean I suppose technically yes.'

'Sounds complicated.' Hamish knew he should probably have left it at that, but for some reason he wanted to know more. He was already telling himself it was just because Daisy and Remi were good friends, but he'd never been a good liar, even when the only person he was trying to deceive was himself.

'It is. We're here and here's in New Zealand with his new girl-friend. So, like I say, technically we're still married, but it's been over for a while now.'

'I'm sorry.' As much as she was trying to be blasé, the expression in her dark eyes had given the game away again. What had happened with her husband had hurt her. A lot.

'At least it sounds like Genevieve will have the support she needs.'

It was a smooth change of subject and Hamish was more than happy to go with it. Otherwise she might start asking him about his own marriage and that was a can of worms he definitely didn't want to open.

'And I could still be wrong about the lump too.' Hamish cleared his throat, wishing that he found it easier to lie sometimes. 'When your text came through, I thought it was going to be about the play date.'

'Remi wanted to make Daisy a proper invitation. I asked the TA this morning if she could put in her book bag.'

'I'm sure Saffron will have found it by the time I get home and have it all written down on the fridge planner. She's trying to get me more organised.'

'I could do with a full time PA for the kids' appointments and school events.' Nadia smiled for the first time. She had a beautiful smile. 'I forgot to give Remi anything to bring in for the harvest festival, so when I got to school and saw everyone carrying in packets of pasta and tins of beans, I had to give her a three-pack of spearmint chewing gum that was in the car to take in.'

'Oh God, I can just imagine the look on Miss Renfrew's face when Remi handed that over!' Hamish laughed. It was nice to talk to someone who understood what it was like to try and juggle so much, but Nadia had twice as much on her plate with two young children. 'Maybe we should keep in touch with reminders about upcoming events at the school.'

'I'm sure Saffron has it all under control.' Nadia gave him an appraising stare, clearly trying to work out whether he had some ulterior motive for wanting to text her. The trouble was he suspected he might. 'I should probably liaise directly with her; it sounds like she manages Daisy's schedule.'

'She manages all of our schedules and I don't know how I'd manage without her.' Nadia looked as though she'd been about to answer when Genevieve came back into the room, bringing a rush of air in with her. Suddenly Hamish was right back where'd he'd been six years earlier, getting a phone call not a million miles away from the one Freddie had just received.

'He didn't answer and it was a difficult message to leave without sounding like I was completely freaking out.' Genevieve's face looked strained from the effort of trying to hope for the best and it was a look Hamish recognised far too well.

'If the two of you want to come in and talk to me about anything before the appointment comes through, just let me know.' He handed Genevieve one of the cards he'd promised his practice manager he'd stop giving out to patients. Sharing his personal mobile number might be a risk, but it was one he was willing to take. He hated the thought of Genevieve and her husband sitting at home, worried out of their minds, when he might be able to help allay at least some of their fears.

'Thank you, that's so kind.' Genevieve clutched the card to her chest, a tiny bit of the tension seeming to leave her face.

'It really is.' Nadia sounded as though she approved, despite the fact he was breaking protocol, and for some unknown reason it really mattered that she did.

5

Frankie had never eaten out as much as she had over the past couple of months. Ordinarily, she'd have cooked for Guy in her flat at least some of the time, but attempting to conduct a clandestine relationship, while sharing a flat with her daughter and grandchildren, meant that was an absolute no-no. It wasn't that Nadia would have objected to their relationship, Frankie was almost certain of that, but she didn't want to put her daughter in a difficult position. If it came out later that she'd known about Guy before Hari did, he might hold it against her. He was the main reason the relationship with Guy had to be kept quiet. He'd made it abundantly clear he wasn't ready to accept the prospect of either of his parents dating again after their divorce.

Hari was backed up by support from Frankie's mother, who was still mortified that her daughter was divorced. It was no surprise that Frankie always felt like she'd done something wrong when she was with her mother.

If Bhavna discovered she'd been dating Guy for the past two months, she'd be even more horrified than Hari. She regularly sent Frankie articles about divorced couples getting back together and freely quoted the statistic that 6 per cent of people who divorced remarried their original spouse. There was absolutely no chance of Frankie ever adding to that number; her only regret was that she'd waited so long to end a marriage that hadn't made either her or her ex-husband happy. They were both far better off now, but telling Bhavna that was like banging her head against a brick wall.

So as much as Frankie wanted a night in with Guy making dinner and settling down with a boxset and a cuddle on the sofa, it wasn't going to happen. Sometimes they hung out at Guy's place, but there was always the chance that Jess might drop by unexpectedly and even she didn't know quite how serious things were getting.

As it was, going out to dinner or lunch had become something Frankie did three or four times a week. If Nadia believed her excuse that she was going to the gym or the slimming group she'd been a member of, on and off, for years, she must have been wondering why Frankie was gaining weight, instead of losing it.

'What's up?' Guy reached out and touched her hand from across the table in Bello Mondo, a little Italian restaurant in neighbouring Port Kara which had fast become one of their favourite places to eat.

'Nothing, why?'

'Because you've pushed your food around your plate and back again, and you seem as though you're somewhere else tonight.'

'I was thinking about Advik.'

'If you're thinking about your ex-husband while you're out with me, then I'm obviously losing my touch.' Guy smiled. There was no tension in his tone, only concern, and Frankie's attempts to take things slowly were chipped away every time he showed her just how much he cared.

'I saw him walking along the road, holding hands with a

woman, when I was driving back from a home visit in Port Tremellien.'

'And does that bother you?' There was still no judgement in Guy's tone.

'Not at all. I wanted to get out of the car and high-five him.' Frankie sighed. 'I kept thinking to myself that if he's dating again, we could tell the kids together and Hari would have no choice but to accept it. He'll be able to see we're both okay and that we've moved on.'

'Why do I sense there's a but coming?' Guy's eyes searched her face and she sighed again.

'Because I'm scared of how Hari might react. I can't bear the thought of him hating me. He reacted much worse than Nadia to the divorce, but he finally seemed to come to terms with that as long as I didn't suddenly bring a new person into his life. We can't keep this a secret forever, though.'

'Forever; I like the sound of that.' Guy squeezed her hand again and she should probably have felt awkward for using that word, but the truth was she could already envisage a forever with him. What she couldn't envisage was having to choose between Guy and her son.

'Have you spoken to Advik about it?'

'I will, but with Hari's wedding coming up. I don't know... maybe I should wait.'

'It's not until next June is it?' Guy was always so reasonable, even though he had every right to be annoyed that she was effectively asking him to keep this secret for another seven or eight months.

'No and you're right, we can't keep doing this for that long.'

'I didn't say that.' Guy's gaze met hers. 'We can keep this the way it is for as long as you want to. The only thing I care about is being with you. I just don't want you to feel so pressured that you decide this – *us* – isn't worth it.'

'How could I ever look at that face of yours and think it isn't worth it?' Frankie smiled, some of the weight already lifting off her shoulders. When she'd thought about dating someone again, she'd expected to encounter the game playing and second guessing that seemed to go hand in hand with modern dating, but it had never been like that with Guy. From their very first date, at the cinema, watching one of the old movies they both loved so much, it was as if she'd finally found her other half. And the passion between them had surprised her too. Having been through the menopause, she hadn't expected to experience things she never had before, but Guy had awoken something in her that she hadn't even realised had been lying dormant her whole adult life. They hadn't actually said the L-word yet, but she was in love with him and she'd never felt this way before either.

'Good, because however difficult this might get, it will be more than worth it to me.' Guy squeezed her hand again and she breathed out. It was going to be okay, she just had to wait for the right moment. When the time arrived she'd be able to tell Hari the truth and after she did, she'd be ready to tell Guy that she loved him too. Until then, she just had to bide her time.

* * *

When Hamish had dropped Daisy off by the harbour, where Nadia had suggested they meet, he'd barely stopped the car. He'd apologised and said he needed to get back to take Saffron out for lunch and Nadia had been forced to bite her tongue. Her perception of Hamish had thawed considerably since his consultation with Genevieve, but seeing him rushing off so quickly to spend time with Saffron, who

Nadia had built up into a mystical figure – a cold woman, who cared more about her appearance and herself than her young daughter – made her re-evaluate him again. He'd been so gentle and kind in his consultation with Genevieve, and sharing his contact information so that he could give her and Freddie the support they needed was definitely beyond what most GPs would do. She was trying not to judge all men by the standards she judged Ryan – someone who dipped in and out of fatherhood when it suited him – but it was very hard not to when Hamish seemed so keen to dump his little girl with a virtual stranger, for a lunch date with his wife.

Daisy didn't seem to mind, though, and within seconds she was linking arms with Remi. With Mo clinging on to her hand, Nadia was ready to head to the start line of the Halloween trail and meet some of the others from the midwifery unit. Izzy, along with her boyfriend, Noah, had helped spread the word about the treasure hunt which was raising funds for the local hospice where Izzy's grandmother had been cared for before her death. Emily and Bobby had also been roped in to dress up as characters along the trail, and most of the rest of the team were coming along to support the cause. Jess and Ella were on call for home deliveries, but they'd be coming along anyway, in the hope that they made it to the end of the trail before any call-outs came in.

'Oh Nadia, I love the outfit!' Jess waved as she caught sight of them. Nadia was wearing a Maleficent costume that Frankie had insisted on buying her from an online store, but she hadn't put the headpiece with the horns on until after Hamish had dropped Daisy off. Remi had an Isadora Moon costume and for some reason Mo had insisted on coming as a lion.

'You all look great.' Nadia couldn't help smiling as she looked at her colleagues. There was a good selection of witches, zombies and vampires amongst the group, as well as a giant Cousin Itt, who resembled a mountain of discarded wigs, and she had no idea who was underneath. 'I've got to ask: who's in the Cousin Itt costume?'

'It's Brae.' Anna laughed. 'And I've never been more attracted to my husband than I am right now!'

'I get that; who wouldn't go for those long lustrous locks?'

'The only trouble is, I can't see where I'm going.' Brae shrugged his hairy shoulders. 'Which leaves Anna having to negotiate the trail with the double buggy and risking losing me in a hedge.'

'It's just an excuse for you to be able to hold on to Dan's arm and keep your bromance going.' Ella grinned. 'There has to be a reason why my fiancé is dressed as Lurch and you two can't pretend it's a coincidence. You definitely planned your costumes together.'

'You've caught us out.' Dan winked. 'But just wait until you hear what we've got planned for the stag do.'

'I don't want to know.' Ella shook her head. 'But whatever it is, it won't beat the time the two of you re-enacted the bike scene from *ET*.'

'I have to hear about this.' Nadia's shoulders relaxed as she glanced over to where Remi and Daisy were giggling about something with Jess's stepson, Riley. When she'd left Port Agnes for New Zealand it had felt huge, but coming home again she'd wondered if she could just slot back into the community where she'd grown up. She'd been a couple of years above Ella at the local secondary school, so she hadn't known her that well back then. But when they'd spoken about it since, she'd discovered they'd had some similar experiences, particular having lots of friends who'd ended up leaving the area. With her university friends scattered everywhere, she hadn't had the sense of coming home from that point of view either. Frankie had been the main draw, so finding out that the team at Port Agnes were as welcoming and friendly as they were had been a huge relief.

'It was when we were fundraising to save the Port Agnes lifeboat station and we recreated quite a few classic movie scenes.' It was weird to hear Brae's voice coming out from under his costume. 'It helped us get a bigger following on social media.'

'And of course there's the bonus of you being able to dress up.' Anna gave him a playful nudge.

'I wish my Barry would dress up, but it's always me who ends up wearing the outfits.' Gwen had brought two of her grandchildren along with her, but thankfully they'd already headed off to join the other kids.

'Dare we ask?' Toni, whose baby daughter Ionie was the cutest pumpkin ever, raised her eyebrows.

'I don't think we do. I'm too young for this conversation.' Her husband, Bobby, laughed. Even seeing a zombie with his hands clamped over his ears didn't seem to put Gwen off.

'The last one was a French maid's outfit, but his favourite was the bunny girl costume.'

'Thank God it isn't Easter, that's all I can say!' Frankie laughed as she joined the group in time to catch the tail end of the conversation.

'You should be so lucky.' Gwen grinned and Nadia couldn't help smiling too. She'd known Gwen for years, since she'd delivered Hari and had eventually persuaded Frankie to return to work as an MCA. Even so, it had taken Nadia a while to get used to Gwen's sense of humour at work, her pushiness when it came to trying to persuade both Nadia and Frankie to start dating, and a borderline obsession with talking about sex. It was all meant in good part, because Gwen was clearly still really happy with Barry after more than forty years together. She just wanted the same for everyone else, but didn't seem to realise not all of them wanted to do it her way. That didn't stop Gwen's 'sex tip of the week' becoming a standing joke in the staffroom, though, and she was probably never going to change.

'Shall we get going in case Izzy thinks we've all stood her up?' Nadia was keen for them to start the trail before Gwen could start asking her mum about her love life. She didn't mind the idea of Frankie dating again and both she and Jess had a good idea that her mother and Jess's father were seeing each other. Frankie admitted to going to the weekly cinema club with him, to watch an old film, but she was out and about quite a lot and her explanations of where she was going didn't always ring true. Still, if Frankie wanted to keep things quiet, that was fine with Nadia and infinitely preferable to listening to Gwen giving her mother the third degree about what was really going on and exactly how far things had progressed. That was the sort of information Nadia would never need to know.

* * *

The kids had loved every minute of the Halloween trail. It had taken almost an hour and a half to solve all the clues, and all the children got a prize at the end of the treasure hunt. Remi and Daisy had already eaten quite a lot of sweets by the time they got to The Cookie Jar, so there'd been more giggling than eating going on. The activity books from the prize bags had been a welcome distraction for Mo in particular and had made the whole thing a lot calmer than it might have been otherwise.

'I wish I had an Isadora dress.' Daisy gave Remi a soulful look as they walked up the hill in the direction of the address that Hamish had texted her. The house was in Ocean View, where a handful of properties looked out to sea from the private road. It was exactly what Nadia had expected.

'Mummy got mine and it was the last one in the shop.' Remi

grinned and Nadia felt a warm glow in the pit of her stomach. She couldn't give the kids everything they wanted, but sometimes she could still score a win and the look on Remi's face when she'd given her the outfit had been priceless.

'You're lucky. Saffy got mine from her 'puter.' Daisy frowned. 'But I didn't want to be Elsa.'

'You look beautiful, sweetheart.' Nadia's mind was working overtime. Saffron was either the sort of mother who insisted her child called her by her first name, or she was Daisy's stepmother. As much as Nadia hated to succumb to stereotypes, which were often ridiculous, it might explain a lot just this once. If Saffron was Hamish's second wife, it must be a fairly new thing, given Daisy's age, and maybe that was why he'd seemed so desperate to drop Daisy off and head back to meet up with her.

'Daisy's mummy can't buy her dresses, cos she's dead.' The matter-of-fact delivery of Remi's announcement took Nadia's breath away. In all the hundreds of times she'd mentioned her little best friend, she'd never once shared that piece of information before. It was almost as surprising that Daisy barely seemed to react to the harshness of Remi's words.

'Remi, that's not a very kind way to talk about what happened to Daisy's mummy and you need to be extra kind because it's very sad.' Nadia crouched down to look at Daisy. 'Are you okay sweetheart?'

The little girl nodded. 'My mummy died when I was a baby, but I've got Daddy, Saffy and George.'

'George?'

'He's Daisy's dog, Mummy, and he's sooooo cute.' Remi spread her arms out as widely as she could to demonstrate just how amazing George was. 'I wish we could get a puppy, if we can't have Lola back.'

'One day.' It was a phrase Nadia had used far too often since they'd got back from New Zealand, but adding a dog into the chaos of the flat above The Cookie Jar would have been nothing short of insanity; even if Remi wasn't the only one missing the Labrador they'd had to leave behind. 'Right, we'd better get Daisy home before it starts to get dark.'

'I'm tired.' Remi gave a huge yawn, seemingly determined to act out her every mood.

'I know darling, but the walk home will be much easier.' Sharing a car with her mother was getting trickier now that the MCAs were doing routine home visits too, but a car of her own was an expense she just couldn't afford yet. As soon as the divorce was finalised and she could get some equity back out of the house in New Zealand, she was going to sort it out. But for now, the priority was to get the money together to secure their own place to live. 'It's not far now anyway.'

Despite Remi's protestations, when they reached the top of the hill, she had more than enough energy to skip ahead with Daisy. White House, where Daisy and her family lived, at the end of a private road, was a sprawling art deco style building that wouldn't have looked out of place in a dramatization of an Agatha Christie novel. The towering electric gates at the end of the driveway were a thoroughly modern addition, however, and unfortunately Hamish appeared to have forgotten that Nadia would needed the code and she couldn't get a signal on her mobile to call him. There were two smaller properties to the right of Daisy's house which weren't hidden behind secure gates – the Lodge and the Gatehouse – but there were no lights on in either of them, so there wasn't even the option of knocking on a neighbour's door.

'Do you know what numbers to press to get in, Daisy?' The little girl shook her head solemnly in response. 'It's okay, it doesn't matter, I'll just press the intercom.'

'Yes.' It was amazing how sullen one word could sound, but the female voice that had responded to Nadia pressing the intercom achieved it.

'Oh hi, it's Nadia, Remi's mum, I told Hamish I'd bring Daisy back.'

'Okay.' If this was Saffron, she was living up to Nadia's expectations so far. Not even the hint of a thank you for bringing her stepdaughter back home, or for taking her out so that she could enjoy a child-free date with Hamish. Being friendly with her, for Remi's and Daisy's sakes, felt like more of a challenge with every passing moment. The gate slowly swung open as they were buzzed through.

The front door of White House was ajar as they walked up the drive and a young woman was standing in the doorway. A *very* young woman. If this really was Saffron, she barely looked more than eighteen. It couldn't be.

'Saffy!' Daisy broke into a run as soon as she spotted her, throwing herself into her arms when she reached the doorstep. Even if Saffron was a disturbingly young stepmum, Daisy was clearly very fond of her, which meant one of the stories Nadia had created had already been disproved.

'She's been an absolute joy to have. This is what's left of her prize from the treasure hunt.' Nadia handed the bag to Saffron.

'Say thank you for having me to Remi's mum.' Saffron gave the little girl the instruction, but she still hadn't cracked a smile herself, never mind offered to return the favour and invite Remi over for a play date, which would have meant the world to her. Saffron looked like she couldn't wait to get Nadia and her children off the doorstep.

'Thank you Nard-ya. I had the best time!' Daisy blew a kiss that made Nadia's heart contract. It didn't matter what Daisy's parents were like, she was a lovely little girl and it really had been a joy to take her out.

'You're welcome sweetheart.' Nadia painted on a smile and made eye contact with Saffron again. 'Is Hamish around?'

'He's visiting a patient of his at the hospital.'

'Oh right.' She wasn't sure what to say. She'd been hoping to ask him if he'd heard from Genevieve, but Saffron was still staring at her like Nadia was something she'd scraped off her shoe. 'Could you possibly ask him to give me a call when he's back?'

'Why?' Saffron tilted her head, her eyes never leaving Nadia's face. She didn't even seem to need to blink.

'It's just about a patient we share.'

'Good.' Saffron's face finally seemed to relax a tiny bit. 'Because despite what all the mums at Daisy's school seem to think, my dad isn't looking for a new wife.'

'Your dad...' Nadia seemed to have lost the ability to finish a sentence because she was still processing the information, but eventually she got there. 'Okay, well if you can just ask him to ring me please.'

'All right.' The words were released with a sigh and Nadia had no idea whether Saffron really would ask her father to call. What she did know for certain now was that she'd built up a completely false picture of Hamish's home life. If she'd made him feel judged in any way, then she owed him an apology.

6

'They're almost certain it's cancer.' Genevieve was waiting outside the unit when Nadia finished her shift. Despite Genevieve being so tall – Nadia would have guessed at least five feet ten – she suddenly looked tiny.

'I'm so sorry Genevieve. Do you want to come inside?'

'Yes please.' For once, Nadia didn't have to worry about picking up the children. Her mother and Guy were taking Remi, Mo and Riley to the soft play centre after school. Nadia had been planning to catch up on some housework and read through the latest exchange between her lawyer and Ryan's, but all of that could wait. By this time of day, the consultation rooms would be empty, so she'd be able to give Genevieve some privacy. Izzy and Ella were overseeing a delivery with Emily's support, but there were no classes running tonight, so the unit would be relatively quiet. Once they were inside, Nadia opened the door of the first consulting room and ushered Genevieve in.

'We'll use this room and you can tell me what happened at the hospital.' Nadia pulled out a chair. 'I think you should sit down; you look exhausted.'

'I've barely slept since I saw Dr Spencer. Somehow I just knew the doctors at the hospital were going to say what they did this morning. Freddie keeps insisting I should wait until we know for certain, but I just really needed to talk to someone who could tell me how all of this might affect the baby. That's what freaking me out the most.'

'I don't think many people would react any differently and I totally understand why you want to talk things through, even if the results of your tests aren't certain yet.' Nadia sat next to Genevieve, rather than at the desk. She wanted to be her friend, not just her midwife. 'What did the hospital actually say?'

'The consultant examined the lump and after I'd had the mammogram and ultrasound, they told me they were going to take a biopsy straight away. When I went back to see the consultant afterwards, he said it was definitely a tumour and the only question was whether it's benign or malignant.' Genevieve released a shuddering sigh. 'He said he was really sorry, but to him it had all the markers of being a malignant tumour. *Cancer*.'

Genevieve clutched her bump the whole time, as if wrapping her arms around the baby could somehow protect it from everything that was going on.

'Oh Ginny I'm sorry.' It had been almost half their lifetime since Nadia had called her that, but in that moment it felt right. She needed an old friend who had more than a professional interest in the outcome of her tests. 'Did they say how long it will be before you get the results?'

'I'll probably hear in three days. Freddie just keeps saying we don't know for sure yet and it might not be cancer, but I want to be ready. I want to know what my options are before I'm sitting in front of a consultant who's asking me to make decisions, when I've got the baby to think about.' Genevieve widened her eyes. 'I'm not agreeing to anything that will hurt her.'

'From what I understand, if it is cancer, the treatment they offer you will depend on what type of breast cancer it is.' Nadia had never cared for a mother-to-be with breast cancer before, but she'd done some research after Genevieve's appointment and she knew that the treatment would also depend on whether the cancer had started to spread. But that wasn't something she needed to bring up now.

'When I looked online, there was stuff about surgery, radiation and chemotherapy.' Genevieve was already shaking her head. 'I'm not having radiation; I don't care what they say.'

'Have you spoken to Hamish... Dr Spencer?' Nadia had barely been able to stop thinking about him since she'd dropped Daisy home and discovered that the tall, slim young woman who'd answered the door was his daughter, not his wife. He was a widower and even if there was someone new in his life, the only rushing off he'd done when he dropped Daisy off was to spend some quality time with his elder daughter. Nadia had to remind herself again that not everyone was like Ryan. Her ex had been due to FaceTime the children before they went to school, and she'd got them up and ready half an hour early in anticipation. When he hadn't called, she'd tried to reach him, but there was no answer and she'd been forced to lie to the children and tell them there was a problem with the internet connection. Lying to them had made her stomach churn, but having to look into their faces and admit that their father seemed to have forgotten his promise would have been so much worse.

'I did think about waiting for him at the surgery, but I don't know how much he'll understand about the baby.'

'If you like, maybe we could both ask to meet with him again? Because we definitely need his expertise when it comes to the treatments you might be offered, if it is cancer.'

'That would help so much.' Genevieve gave another shuddering sigh. 'I'm terrified, and if this was just me, I'd do whatever the consultant recommended. I know Freddie will want me to take all the treatment offered, but I need to go in there knowing enough to fight the baby's corner if I have to. I'm her mother and, even if she's not here yet, it's still my job to protect her.'

'Let me give Dr Spencer a call and hopefully he can see us before you go back in for your biopsy results.'

'Thank you so much Nards.' Genevieve seemed to be slipping into old habits too and she suddenly leant forward and hugged Nadia. 'I don't think I'd have coped if I didn't have you to talk to. I can't tell my sister, in case she mentions it to my mum and dad, and they've all been through so much already with Mum's diagnosis. I can't cope with the looks on my friends' faces either. I need someone calm like you, but who I know still cares what happens to me and the baby.'

'I promise I'll be here for you every step of the way.'

'Whatever happens?' Genevieve pulled away to look at her.

'Absolutely.' Suddenly, Ryan's flakiness as a father didn't matter any more. Things might be tough at times, but Nadia had the privilege of being there for her children whenever they needed her. It was something Ginny might not get and Nadia was never going to take it for granted again.

* * *

Hamish had offered to meet with Nadia and Genevieve the day after. When he'd texted back, he'd apologised for not being able to do it that same evening, but he was due at Saffron's sixth-form parents' evening. It seemed like he genuinely couldn't do enough to support his patients, so it was no wonder Genevieve had struggled to get an appointment with him.

Nadia had cleared it with Ella and Anna to use one of the

consulting rooms at the unit again. It was open late for the evening antenatal classes that Izzy and Jess were running, and thankfully Frankie had stepped in again to pick the children up from school.

'Is it cold in here? I can't seem to stop shivering.' Genevieve was visibly shaking as she spoke, but Nadia shook her head.

'I'm not cold and the heating is still on in the building because of the antenatal classes, but take this.' She handed Genevieve her black cardigan, wishing she could do more to help. It was almost certainly nerves that were making Genevieve shake, but there was nothing Nadia could do about those. She'd already taken Ginny's blood pressure and it was higher than she would have liked, but that was completely understandable too. In the next forty-eight hours, she'd be getting the results of her biopsy and the outcome could be life-changing. It was enough to make anyone shake.

'Thanks. Do you think Dr Spencer will be here soon?' Genevieve furrowed her brow. Hamish was already ten minutes late, but since he was coming straight from the surgery, Nadia would have been surprised if he'd made it on time. GP appointments almost always ran late and, from what she'd seen of Hamish, he wasn't the sort of doctor who'd hurry anyone who needed his help.

'Any minute now I should think.' She'd barely finished the sentence, before there was a knock at the door. 'Come in.'

'Hi, I'm so sorry I'm late.' Hamish smiled and Nadia found herself trying to work out how old he was. He had to be at least late thirties or early forties, with a daughter Saffron's age, but the dimples definitely helped to give him the sort of boyish good looks someone a decade younger might have.

'No problem at all, we're just glad you could fit us in before Genevieve's follow-up with the consultant.' Nadia felt like a bit of fraud taking the lead in the consultation. 'Take a seat, please. Can I get you a tea or coffee?'

'Maybe later.' Hamish smiled again and something that felt oddly like butterflies fluttered in her stomach, but that couldn't be happening. She wouldn't let it. 'How are you feeling Genevieve? I know the waiting is really tough.'

'If it was any more than three days I think my head might explode.'

'I think the trouble is you go through every possible scenario while you're waiting, don't you? The good news is that what you're imagining will almost certainly be worse than the reality.' Hamish had such a comforting way about him.

'I keep thinking, what if I don't live to see the baby take her first steps or say her first words?' Genevieve hadn't been able to stop her voice from cracking. 'But whatever happens, I'm not doing anything to risk the baby, because I had two miscarriages before I fell pregnant with her.'

'Was that on your records?' Nadia was certain she would have remembered something like that; she'd read through Genevieve's notes and she was sure they'd said this was her first pregnancy.

'It was before I got together with Freddie and he doesn't even know I tried for a baby with my first husband.' Genevieve shook her head. 'I wanted this to feel special, something we were going through together. I knew Freddie wanted kids almost from when we started dating and I was terrified that if I told him I'd lost two babies, he might think getting involved with me was too much of a risk. I lost the first two pregnancies so early on, I hadn't even made it to my booking-in appointments. I was planning to see my GP, to ask for a referral after I lost the second baby, but then I split up with David and I just pushed it to the back of my mind. I convinced myself it would be okay with a new partner, but that didn't stop me being terrified every single time I went to the loo that the bleeding would start again, just like it had with the other two. If it had, it would have been my fault for not telling Freddie about it, but it looks like this is my punishment instead. And I can take that, I really can, as long as the baby's okay.'

'This is not a punishment and you haven't done anything wrong.' Hamish took the words right out of Nadia's mouth, something he'd quickly developed a habit of doing.

'Your GP would probably just have told you to try again after two miscarriages, because most women who miscarry – even twice – have a successful pregnancy the next time around. It seems really hard, but referrals are only given for three consecutive miscarriages when they're as early on as yours were.' Nadia reached out and touched her arm. 'But that doesn't make them any less devastating, or the next pregnancy any less scary, and like Hamish said, none of this is your fault.' Nadia knew that feeling of being terrified every time the slightest twinge came in a pregnancy that followed miscarriage. She'd lost her first baby, the one she'd conceived six months before Remi, at almost nine weeks along, just two days after seeing its heartbeat in a scan at the Early Pregnancy Unit, when she'd had some spotting. They'd told her the heartbeat was a good sign, but that hadn't turned out to be the case. Experiencing a similar scare with Mo meant that whole first half of her pregnancy with him had felt like it was hanging by a thread. Despite having no idea what Genevieve was going through now, Nadia could understand how precious her pregnancy was and why she didn't want to do anything to risk it. Even if that meant risking her own life.

'Whatever happens, I want to be able to give Freddie the baby he's always wanted, even if I'm not here to raise it with him.' Despite her bravado, Ginny's eyes filled with tears.

'You will be.' Even though Nadia couldn't really make that promise, she was certain it was what Genevieve needed to hear and sometimes that was what mattered the most.

'Even in the absolute worst-case scenario, and this almost

certainly isn't that, there will be options for treatment.' Hamish clearly wasn't going to make any promises that might turn out not to be true, but every time he spoke it gave Nadia a bit more reassurance. She just hoped Genevieve felt the same. 'What worries me most is that you already seem to be shutting off the possibility of any treatment while you're still pregnant. If the doctors want you to start treatment straight away, I really think you should.'

'I can't take the risk.'

'They'll probably offer you surgery, as well as removal of some of your lymph nodes to make sure the cancer is contained in your breast.' Hamish held her gaze, but Nadia could tell Genevieve didn't want to listen to what he was saying.

'I don't what an anaesthetic. It says online that it isn't safe and there's a risk of affecting the baby's learning later on, or premature birth or even...' Genevieve clearly couldn't bring herself to complete the sentence.

'There are risks with every surgical procedure, but I promise you that at this stage in your pregnancy, any risk to your baby from having surgery is almost negligible.' Hamish sighed. 'Some of the online forums you'll find when you search these sorts of things aren't helpful. A one-off anaesthetic almost certainly won't affect your baby's development now or in the future. You'll be able to have chemo treatment safely too, if the doctors feel it's needed. It's just the radiotherapy that needs to be postponed.'

'How can pumping something that toxic into my body possibly be safe for the baby, when I'm not even allowed to have caffeine?'

'No one is saying it's ideal, but your baby is already developed, so the risk is minimal.' Nadia turned to Hamish. 'It would have been different earlier in Genevieve's pregnancy, wouldn't it?'

'Yes, chemo has more risk early on, but it's proven to be the best treatment alongside surgery for certain breast cancers at this stage of your pregnancy.' Hamish might be having to repeat himself, but his tone hadn't lost any of its gentleness as he took a document wallet out of his bag. 'Let me give you some things to read that might help you and Freddie have a better understanding of all of your options and please, whatever you do, don't make any decisions based purely on what you've read online.'

'Okay.' Genevieve looked at the wallet as though it might explode at any minute.

'And just call me if you or Freddie have any questions before or after your appointment. I might not know all the answers, but I've got a friend who's a consultant at the Royal Marsden and I'm sure she can give me any extra information you might need. I know how easy it can be to come out of appointments with an oncologist and not have asked the one thing you desperately want to know.'

'Thank you, that means a lot.' As Genevieve put the document wallet into her bag, Nadia couldn't take her eyes of Hamish's face. She was certain he was talking from personal experience and that his story would explain what had happened to Daisy's mother. Whatever he'd been through, he had to be hoping every bit as hard as Nadia was that Genevieve's story was going to end very differently.

* * *

'Thank you so much for taking the time to see Ginny. I'm sure it really helped.' Nadia caught up with Hamish as they crossed the car park after Genevieve had said her goodbyes.

'I wish I could be so sure.' Hamish sighed. 'I know she's terrified and that she's desperate for none of this to affect her baby, but I've seen the look she had on her face before. Where nothing you say to someone is getting through, because they've already made up their minds.'

'You're not talking about a patient, are you?' If Nadia had

thought about it beforehand, she probably wouldn't have had the guts to ask him. It was such a personal question, but his face had flickered a couple of times when he'd been talking to Genevieve, and she'd seen the naked emotion there. Cancer had robbed his child of the chance to grow up with her mother, she was sure of it.

'No, it was Sara, my wife.' Hamish turned to look at Nadia. 'Saffron was what you might euphemistically call a surprise baby. A bloody big shock is probably more accurate, given that we were both still studying.'

'That must have been a challenge.'

'It was, but we were certain we wanted to keep the baby and Saffy was born the day after our graduation ceremonies.' He laughed at the memory. 'She was a week late and I think Sara willed her into staying put so she could have that moment with her own parents before she became one too.'

'Was Sara a doctor as well?'

'She was a psychotherapist, but we were just at the beginning of our journeys when we had Saffy. I'd completed my five-year medical degree, but I had another five years to go before I could qualify as a GP. Sara had just finished her psychology degree, but she put the rest of her studies on hold while I finished my training, working two part-time jobs and doing the lion's share of raising Saffy. We got married just after Saffy's fifth birthday and it was finally Sara's turn to finish her training and go back to uni to do a master's. After that, she wanted to establish her career, so we didn't start trying for another baby until Sara was thirty and Saffron was coming up for nine. What we didn't anticipate was it taking over two years for us to get pregnant again. It seemed unbelievable when we'd been trying so hard not to have a baby first time around. But there we were, desperate to extend our family, and month after month nothing happened.'

'Did you have to get help?' The personal questions kept

coming, but Hamish clearly felt like opening up and Nadia wanted to know his story. She might be trying to tell herself that it was so she could understand more about Remi's best friend, but that was only part of it.

'We had two rounds of IVF and we found out we were expecting Daisy on my thirty-fifth birthday. It was the best present I've ever had and I honestly felt like the luckiest man in the world.' Hamish smiled again, but then he shook his head. 'When the sonographer told us at the twelve-week scan that the chances were we were having another girl, I was over the moon. I was going to be surrounded by my girls and I knew I'd die for every single one of them. But the last thing I'd expected was for Sara to have to make that choice too.'

'When she was still pregnant with Daisy?' Nausea swirled in Nadia's stomach. There were so many echoes between what had happened to Sara and what Genevieve was going through. It must have been incredibly hard for Hamish to relive that, but he'd never once made this about him. If Nadia hadn't asked him outright, she didn't think he'd have mentioned it.

'She was about sixteen weeks pregnant, but her morning sickness seemed to be getting worse instead of better. She was nauseous all the time and she couldn't face food. Then her balance started to go and her mood swings got way worse than they had with Saffy. I knew something wasn't right and I think she did too, but she just kept putting it all down to the pregnancy.' The tension in Hamish's jaw was visible. 'I finally managed to get her to go and see an old friend I'd gone to uni with, who's a neurologist. She was almost certain at first that it was a meningioma, a type of mostly benign brain tumour that can occasionally grow as a result of blood flow changes in pregnancy. Obviously it wasn't ideal, but we'd been told there was a very good chance of Sara living a normal life afterwards. Except it turned out to be much worse than that.'

'I'm so sorry.' Nadia might never have known Hamish's wife, but as a mother it must have been terrifying to face the prospect of leaving a young child behind following a cancer diagnosis. Facing up to that kind of thing while she was pregnant would have been completely devastating for Sara and Hamish.

'One of the worst things was that after ten years of training, there was absolutely nothing I could do.' Hamish let go of another long breath. 'Worse still was that there was almost nothing anyone else could do either, not if we wanted to save Sara and the baby. The MRI and brain biopsy resulted in the worst news possible; it was an advanced glioblastoma. Brain cancer.'

'Oh God.'

'We were told almost straight away that it was inoperable, but the best chance of giving her years instead of weeks was to start a concurrent course of chemo and radiation. She was nineteen weeks pregnant, and she refused to have any treatment that might risk ending the pregnancy or harming the baby. I'm ashamed when I look at Daisy now, but I begged her to take whatever treatment was offered and to end the pregnancy too, if that's what it took, but she wouldn't even consider it.'

'I can't even imagine how difficult that was for you.' Nadia was having to fight back tears. This wasn't her pain to stake any claim to, but the torture of what Hamish had been through was so obvious on his face it was hard not to feel it too.

'It was worse than anything I could ever have envisaged. We had to have counselling together and there was an ethics committee involved too, because Sara's consultant was saying she recommended a termination, but she just got more and more determined to keep the baby. When the twenty-week scan showed Daisy developing normally and I saw her kicking and waving her arms, with her little face in perfect profile, I knew I had to support Sara. She agreed to a low-dose chemo treatment, which we hoped would keep the tumour stable until Daisy had a fighting chance of survival, but by the time Sara was twenty-nine weeks pregnant, she was in ICU on ventilation. I signed the consent for Daisy to be delivered by Caesarean at thirty weeks and she was laid next to Sara for a few seconds before they took her down to the neonatal ward. They started the regime of chemo and radiotherapy they'd wanted to give Sara eleven weeks before, but the tumour didn't respond.'

'Was she able to see Daisy again?'

'Sara was back in ICU, but when Daisy was stable enough, I was allowed to take her down so Sara could see her. When Daisy reached what would have been thirty-six weeks they said I could take her home. By then, I knew her mother would never be coming home with us. She died a month later, just a few days after Daisy's original due date and I had absolutely no idea how to raise our two little girls without her.' There was such a haunted look in Hamish's eyes and Nadia felt an almost overwhelming urge to put her arms around him and tell him what an incredible job he'd done of raising the little girl who'd never got to know her mother. But the words alone would have to do.

'From what I can see, you've done brilliantly.' Everything Nadia had thought she'd known about Hamish had been turned on its head. He'd lost the one thing he'd wanted most in the world: a family life with Sara by his side.

'Saff can be a bit overprotective of me and Daisy at times, but at twelve years old she suddenly became this sort of mother figure and now she's talking about going to university locally too, because she can't leave Daisy. It's going to be a battle, but I can't let her give up any more rites of passage because she had so much responsibility so young. No way.' Hamish shook his head, as if Saffron was the one standing in front of him to see it. 'One thing I've never had to worry about is money, because of the life insurance Sara took out for both of us when Saffron was born. I feel guilty about that too, but it means she can go to university anywhere she wants and she can't use the excuse of saving money to stay local.'

'She just wants to be there for you and Daisy, that's all. It's obvious how important it is to her to look out for you both.' Saffron might have been frosty, but Nadia could totally understand why now, and she had huge respect for the young woman who was so willing to put her little sister's best interests first.

'I know. I hope she wasn't rude when you dropped Daisy home, by the way. She's got a tendency to be defensive and for some reason she thinks every woman who comes into our life, however briefly, has some kind of agenda to take her mother's place.' Hamish laughed at the ridiculousness of the idea. 'You'd think I had women beating down my door the way she acts. I've dated a grand total of three women since her mother died, but none of them have lasted long because they've always wanted more from me than I've got to give. The girls come first, second and third to me, with work after that and everything else even further down the list. It's not what any woman wants – to be number ninety-nine on the list of what their partner thinks is important. Two of the women I dated weren't asking for anything that most people wouldn't expect in a relationship, but me cancelling our plans last minute if one of the girls felt a bit poorly, or if they needed to be taken to an activity, became too much for them, especially when they saw it wouldn't change. The last person I dated didn't help with Saff's insecurities though.'

'Dare I ask?'

'At first Kate seemed the most understanding of them all and I'd begun to think maybe there was a tiny chance it could go somewhere, but she started dropping hints about good schools that I could put Daisy's name down for, once Saff went off to uni.'

'That doesn't sound too bad.' The expression on Hamish's face told Nadia there was a lot more to come.

'No, except they were all boarding schools and when I found out she'd gone as far as booking us in to view one of them, we had a huge row and Saffron overheard the whole thing. She knew Kate was clearing a path for herself and saw the opportunity of Saff leaving to push Daisy out of sight too. Saffron was so filled with rage that I had to hold on to her to stop her flying at Kate. She was just protecting Daisy and the truth was that I was every bit as angry as she was. For me, things were over with Kate the second I found out and I just wanted her gone so that it could just be me and my girls again. I promised Sara that Saff and Daisy would always be my priority and that's exactly what they'll always be.'

'No wonder Saffron thinks women are beating down your door, because if you're that kind of father, it means you're also a really good man.' The flush of heat washing over Nadia surprised her almost as much as the words she'd somehow said out loud.

'I'm just doing what anyone who loves their children would do.' Hamish turned to look at her. 'It must be hard for you too. Remi told Daisy that her father lives in New Zealand. With two young kids and a demanding job, that can't be easy.'

'It's nothing in comparison.' Nadia bit her lip. There might be challenges, but Hamish had to try and carry on after losing the sort of woman who'd give up her life for her child's. He clearly still loved her and that must make it even harder. All Nadia had to do was get over a man who'd started sleeping with a string of women before his wife had even recovered from delivering their son, and had eventually left the family home for one of them. There really was no comparison.

'Still, it must be hard, especially when you're shouldering all of the responsibility.' He touched her hand briefly in the darkness of the car park. She should have been cold – it was early evening in November – but the shiver in reaction to his touch had nothing to do with the weather. Even as she opened her mouth to answer him, she hadn't been planning to share anything personal, but it was the way he was looking at her; like he was capable of understanding just how hard it sometimes was.

'It's not the same for me, but there's a different kind of grief for the life I thought we'd have. But mostly I'm grieving for what the kids have lost and the father I thought they'd have. He doesn't keep his promises and when I see how much that hurts them, it breaks my heart. I can cope with him withholding money, because I just work all the overtime on offer to make up for that. But when he withholds his love from them, there's nothing I can do to make up for that, is there?' It had all just come spilling out in the end and she might have been embarrassed about being so open with a relative stranger, but there was so much kindness in his eyes that it was a relief to share it.

'I think you'll have done more than enough to make up for that and, from what I've seen, you're an amazing mum. As single parents we can beat ourselves up, but the truth is nothing about being a parent is easy.' He locked eyes with her and it was undeniable now, they understood each other on a whole new level. 'Maybe we should get together with the kids? Single parents unite and all that?'

'I'd like that.' She could have tried to play it cool, but her face would have given her away. So she tried to counter it instead. 'And the girls will love it.'

'Me too and I'm really glad Genevieve has got you to support her. It's not going to be easy for her and Freddie, but I just hope it'll be okay whatever they decide and I'll do anything I can to help.'

'They're lucky to have you.'

'They're lucky to have you too.' He touched her hand again and Nadia couldn't stop herself from picturing what it would be like to have someone like Hamish in her life. But that was never going to happen. Because, like him, her children would always come first. It was much easier staying single, even if there were other men like Hamish around. Although, from what she'd seen, he was a one-off.

7

One of the things Nadia liked best about working in community midwifery was the opportunity to build relationships with her patients. Every mother-to-be had at least seven antenatal appointments, ten if it was their first child, and more if there were additional factors involved with the pregnancy. Most of them took place in the unit, with the postnatal appointments more commonly taking place in the patients' homes. There were some patients who required antenatal visits at home too and Anne-Marie Hudson was one of those people. She was a mother of five already, with baby number six very much under construction, so getting to the unit for appointments was challenging to say the least.

Anne-Marie and her family ran a boarding kennel and cattery in a hamlet called Melynfow, which meant 'yellow cave' and local legend suggested it was the name given to the hiding place used by smugglers to store their contraband and stashes of gold. Whether it was true or not, there was a deep cave carved out of a hillside shrouded in woodland and you had to know it was there to find it, which added to the mystery of the place. Local guides offered tours and there was even a chance to do gold panning in the river that ran through the woodland. It was on Nadia's to-do list with the children at some point, although letting Mo loose in a cave – with all that potential for danger – probably wasn't the best idea she'd ever had. Nadia could still remember going there with Hari and their parents when they were young, and her father making up a story about a smuggler who'd travelled all the way from Sri Lanka to join a band of Port Agnes smugglers. Advik had told his children that the smuggler was their great-great-grandfather and that he'd hidden some treasure near Melynfow for them to find one day. They never had, of course, but part of her still wanted to believe it was a possibility and she knew Remi would love hearing the story too.

The house where Anne-Marie and her family lived looked like something from a painting on the lid of a biscuit tin. Although it had a thatched roof that dipped in the middle and was probably ten years on the wrong side of needing replacing. The leaded light windows at the front were like two eyes in a smiley face, though, and there was something innately welcoming about the place, despite it looking like it could do with a damn good haircut. There was a long single-storey extension on each side of the original cottage, making an elongated U-shape, which Anne-Marie told her had needed to be added to a total of three times over the years to accommodate her ever-growing brood. To the right of the house were the outbuildings housing the kennels and cattery and a chorus of dog barks greeted Nadia as she pulled her car up outside. A black Labrador gave her a hopeful look, pressing its nose up against the wire mesh and looking at her as if she was its last hope of release. She tried not to think about Lola, the chocolate Lab she'd been forced to leave behind when she'd come back from New Zealand. The fact she missed her canine companion more than she missed her husband said a lot about the state of their marriage by the time he left. Lola had been far more loyal for a start.

'Oh hi, come in, Mum's in the front room with her feet in the air.' The boy who opened the door to Nadia, who she guessed was probably in his late teens, sounded very matter-of-fact and she couldn't help smiling.

'She says her feet are aching from walking the dogs, but now she can't do any of the pooper-scooping duties, she's had to take the dog walking over from me so we could swap.' The boy screwed up his face. 'I'm supposed to be on a gap year and all my mates are in Thailand, but I've been roped into scraping dog poo up off the kennel floors instead.'

'Oh dear.' Nadia was trying not to laugh and, to his credit, the young lad didn't sound as if he really minded.

'Yeah, it's not ideal, but I can go over and catch up with my mates after Christmas, when Mum's had this latest one. I don't want to miss that, especially as I'm hoping this will be the last. Five siblings is enough for anyone.'

'It must be lovely to have so many brothers and sisters.'

'Yeah, I s'pose. I wasn't that keen at first, but I'm used to it now and it's dead quiet when I go to other people's houses and they've only got one brother or sister. It seems even weirder if they're an only child.' The young lad led the way down the hallway and into the front room as he spoke. 'Mum, the midwife's here.'

'Oh thanks Liam. Make us both a cuppa will you, love?'

Liam held his mother's gaze for a moment and then burst out laughing. 'All right, but make the most of it. You're not going to have butler service any more when I'm out in Thailand.'

'I'll try not to miss it too much.' Anne-Marie threw a cushion at him. 'Or the mountains of dirty washing I won't find on your bedroom floor any more!'

'Your washing machine must be on the go all the time with

seven of you.' Nadia smiled. 'Mine never seems to stop and I've only got two kids.'

'I get through at least one machine every two years. They always seem to die just after the warranty has run out, but it's hardly a surprise with what I put them through.' Anne-Marie returned her smile, swinging her legs round so she was in a sitting position. 'I'm still going to miss Liam like crazy when he's gone, though, washing and all. Sit yourself down, he'll be bringing that cuppa in soon, despite his protests.'

'Liam's your eldest, isn't he? It must be really hard to see the first one go.' Nadia did as instructed and took a seat opposite the sofa that Anne-Marie had been lying on.

'It's even harder than it probably would have been, because we've only really been this close for the last couple of years or so. He was ten when I first met his dad and he hated me on sight. It didn't help that his biological mum kept trying to stir up trouble and telling no end of lies about what had happened between them. They'd already been split up for two years by the time I met Greg, but the way she told it you'd think I broke up their marriage. She told Liam that too and I think that's why he hated me so much.'

'He clearly thinks the world of you now. He was telling me when I arrived that he didn't want to leave because he wanted to be here to see his younger brother or sister arrive.'

'It took a while, but when he started to see his birth mother for who she really is and decided that seeing her made him miserable, I could sense a thawing out in him. Last year, he asked if he could call me Mum. He said it was because he didn't want to confuse his younger siblings, but we both know there's more to it than that and I can honestly say it's still the sweetest sound in the world. Even when he delivers it with a typical teenage grunt!' Anne-Marie smiled. 'All the other kids call me Mum because it's the title I came with the moment they were born, but

I had to earn it from Liam and somehow that means so much more.'

'I love stories like that.' Even if Nadia couldn't envisage starting over again, she couldn't help hoping that her children would have new people come into their lives who could help fill the gap their father had left, at least in part. Maybe she was just trying to assuage her own guilt; after all, she'd been the one to bring the children here, to the other side of the world. The truth was, he'd left her no choice. According to Ryan, the rent on his apartment with the woman he'd left her for didn't leave enough for him to help out with the mortgage on their old family home. With no local support and Ryan's family backing off now that Nadia was the ex, she couldn't even work extra hours to make up the shortfall and pay for the childcare she'd need to cover the mortgage on her own. Frankie had stepped into the breech for a while, but once she'd gone back to the UK, it was clear Nadia was going to have to follow suit.

She'd rented out the family home to cover the mortgage. For her, it wasn't a wrench, it was a relief, but she had taken her children away from everything they knew and from their father, even if he was already letting them down at every turn. All of that meant she hoped they'd get closer to her own father and brother, and that maybe even Guy could become another grandfatherly figure at some point, if her mother ever admitted they were in a relationship. The more people who loved a child the luckier they were in Nadia's opinion, and she wanted Remi and Mo to be surrounded by love now that they were living in Port Agnes.

'The funny thing is, I always said I wanted six children when I was growing up and now I've got exactly what I wanted, even if I've only given birth to five of them. Liam has been working so hard in the business too, helping me and Greg out, and I couldn't be prouder of him.' Anne-Marie lay back against the cushions. 'I wish

I could wave a magic wand for him and make his birth mother add something positive to his life, because I know he still struggles with that, but sometimes you just have to do the best with what you've got. We haven't told him yet, but we're going to ask him to be godfather to the new baby when it arrives, because they couldn't have a better role model.'

'He might be putting off that trip to Thailand for a while then.'

'It's a bonus, not a cunning plan to keep him home for a little bit longer, I promise!' Anne-Marie laughed. 'Either way, this baby is definitely the last. Finding a bit of skin on my belly without a stretch mark on it is starting to become a challenge now.'

'I know that feeling and I've only got two kids.' Nadia gave her a wry smile. It was something else that had crossed her mind when Gwen had been nagging her to start dating again. The thought of getting naked in front of someone new would have been enough to send her over to the Sisters of Agnes Island, just off the coast of Port Agnes, begging them for a place at the convent... if it hadn't been turned into a hotel years before. 'How are you feeling in general?'

'Fat, knackered and as slow as hell.' Anne-Marie laughed. 'But fine. No swollen ankles this time and the sickness cleared up before I had the first scan, not like with Georgia. I think the fat and knackered bit would apply even if I wasn't pregnant; that's just life with five kids and running a business.'

'I think you're amazing. I'm sure the tiredness is just normal, but we'll do some bloods just to make sure you aren't anaemic or anything, then we can measure the baby's growth, take your blood pressure and test your urine too.'

'Not until I'm back outside in the cattery!' Liam pulled a face of utter disgust as he brought the promised tea into the room. 'If I'm going to be forced to deal with urine, I'd rather it was outside with a broom and a hosepipe, not in here.'

'Don't worry, love, I wasn't going to squat down and produce a sample in the middle of the front room.' Anne-Marie playfully chucked another cushion in his direction. 'Just let that be a lesson to you. If you aren't careful on your travels with the girls you meet, you could end up having to deal with all this first-hand.'

'That's it, you're now officially the most embarrassing mother in the world.' Liam grinned despite his words, before planting a kiss on the top of Anne-Marie's head. 'I'll be outside if you need me and then I'll go and get Lucas and Noah from Beavers.'

'Thank you, love, you're a star.'

'I know. You might be the world's most embarrassing mother, but I'm the world's best big brother. Willow told me that last night.' Liam winked.

'She isn't wrong,' Anne-Marie called after him as he disappeared outside to get on with his jobs, turning back to Nadia once he was gone. 'I just hope this little one gets a chance to really know Liam before he's off exploring the big wide world.'

'Letting them go is the hardest part sometimes, but you might well find he comes back home again before too long. I know it nearly broke my mum's heart when I moved to New Zealand, but the draw of home brought me back to Port Agnes and I can't imagine settling anywhere else now.'

'We're definitely lucky to live where we do.' Anne-Marie rolled up her sleeve, ready for her blood to be taken and Nadia nodded. She just hoped that settling down for good in this part of Cornwall was going to be an option. So far the cheapest place she'd found to rent in Port Agnes was still a couple of hundred pounds a month over her maximum budget. Her mother kept saying that something would turn up though, and all she could do was pray that mothers really did know best.

* * *

Frankie was trying to get ready for the house-warming Ella and Dan were hosting in the new house they'd bought about a mile to the east of Port Agnes. They'd moved out of their former fisherman's cottage in Mercer's Row, at the edge of the harbour, and were starting the renovation of what Ella had cheerfully declared would become their family home. Just the name, Crooked Cottage Farm, made Frankie smile. Ella had explained that it wasn't technically a farm any more, after most of the land had been sold off over the years, but there were still a couple of acres and it really did sound like it would make the perfect home, once the renovations were complete.

The fact that Dan was a property developer had to be a big help, but thankfully he'd turned out to be nothing like a lot of other developers in the area. He always offered lower prices to local buyers and he point-blank refused to sell to anyone who wasn't planning to be a permanent resident. He'd rescued Mercer's Row from demolition, and he rented out one of the other properties he owned in the terrace for a reduced rate to a local resident who couldn't have afforded to stay in the area otherwise. Ella had promised that Nadia would get first refusal on that cottage if it came up for rent again and Frankie couldn't help hoping that the current occupier would find a reason to move on.

Ella and Dan had decided to host the house-warming on a Sunday afternoon, and the children were invited too, now that so many of their friends from the midwifery unit had started families of their own. It meant that Frankie wasn't the only one trying to get ready for the party. Her attempts to have a shower had already been interrupted twice by Mo, who wasn't yet capable of waiting more than a minute or two when he needed the toilet. Then Remi had hammered on the door when she was mid-shower, asking Frankie if her Disney hair slides were in the bathroom. But Frankie had taken it all in her stride, despite Mo and Remi being hyped up with excitement at the prospect of a party and the chance to play with Riley again.

'Is Guy coming today?' Nadia held her mother's gaze and Frankie tried not to feel like a schoolgirl standing in front of a teacher who she was about to lie to.

'I've got no idea, I haven't seen him since Cinema Club last Monday night and there's never much of a chance to chat to the others who go, we're all too busy watching the film.' Frankie was just glad she didn't still have the same dead giveaway she'd always had when she'd lied as a child. Her right eyebrow had twitched involuntarily back then, but half a lifetime of suppressing how she really felt, during her marriage to Advik, seemed to have given her the ability to lie far more convincingly.

'I expect he'll be there. Ella was telling everyone to come and I think Dan's planning to do a few fireworks for the kids when it gets dark. He's got a load of stuff for them to make a guy, apparently, for the bonfire. Although not your Guy of course!'

'He's not *my* Guy.' Frankie's tone had been sharper than she'd intended, an unconscious decision that attack was the best form of defence.

'Why's Nanny shouting?' Remi skipped into the room, her chestnut curls swinging now that the Disney hairclips were firmly in place.

'It's called protesting too much.' Nadia blew her mother a kiss before turning to her daughter. 'Now, are you absolutely sure you want to wear a party dress? It's going to be quite chilly if you're playing outside with the other children and it'll be even colder by the time Dan lets off the fireworks.'

'Yes, I'm sure.' Remi did a twirl to prove just how perfect her dress was. 'Daisy's going to a party today too and she's wearing a dress made of diamonds!'

'Is she now?' Frankie exchanged a smile with her daughter.

'It's got millions and squillions of sparkles.'

'Whose party is it? Someone from your class at school?' Nadia was obviously trying to keep her tone casual, but she couldn't fool her mother. Frankie knew how worried Nadia had been about Remi being able to slot into a class who'd be joining their third year of primary school. Any indication that Remi might have been left out of a party would make Nadia worry, no matter how unnecessary that was when she'd clearly made such a good friend in Daisy.

'No, it's her daddy's friend, but she always buys Daisy lots of presents and Saffron said it's just cos she wants to marry Daisy's daddy.'

'And what does Daisy think?'

'About what?' Remi looked confused, her six-year-old mind already having wandered off to something more interesting.

'About the lady wanting to marry her daddy.'

'Dunno.' Remi shrugged. 'Can I wear my Elsa shoes?'

'Do you think that's a good idea if you're going to be playing outside?'

'Yes, because I love them!'

'Okay, but we'll have to take some wellies with us too, just in case.'

'I won't need to wear wellies.' Remi put her hands on her hips, suddenly looking so much like her mother had as a child.

'Well there's no harm in taking them. Go and find your Elsa shoes and we can get going to this party.' Remi followed her mother's instructions and Frankie turned to look at her daughter.

'Why are you so interested in what Daisy thinks about someone wanting to marry her father?'

'I'm not.'

'Yes you are. I saw the look on your face when Remi mentioned it.'

'I don't know what you're talking about.' There it was, that mirroring of her daughter, as Nadia put her hands on her hips. 'I was just asking a question, that's all.'

'Hmm, I think that's what they call protesting too much!' Frankie dropped the perfect wink and turned away from her daughter before Nadia could see the slow smile that had spread across her face. The question about Daisy's dad might mean nothing, but Frankie had heard from her daughter how wonderfully Dr Spencer had supported Genevieve. So if anyone could convince Nadia to think about dismantling the wall she'd been busy building up around herself since Ryan had walked out, then it could well be Hamish Spencer. And that would give Frankie a whole new reason to think he was wonderful.

8

Crooked Cottage Farm lived up to its name. It was built from traditional Cornish stone and according to Ella it had been through several lives in its history, right back to the 1500s, when it had been home to a group of monks. It was the undulating roof that gave the house its name and while Ella and Dan had some fairly major renovation plans for the smallholding they'd taken on, she'd told Nadia and the others that they wanted to retain many of the quirks of the farmhouse and some of the crooked charm that made it so unique.

For now, the two of them were living in a mobile home on site and the house-warming was really more of a garden-warming party. There were lights strung up between the trees and trestle tables set up close enough to the huge, roaring bonfire to make sure no one would get cold. There was a bar built out of scaffolding boards, where Ella had told everyone to help themselves to drinks. Dan and Brae were busy barbecuing, and for once Mo seemed more than happy to tuck into some vegetables when they came in the form of chargrilled corn on the cob. It was only six-thirty and he was already on his third helping.

'I've finally got these two to go to sleep and I reckon I've got just enough time for a rhubarb gin before the fireworks start.' Anna put her double buggy at the end of the trestle table and sat down hard.

'Luckily I've got you a drink ready and waiting.' Jess smiled and turned to Nadia. 'I think Riley and Remi will both sleep well tonight, but not as well as my dad and your mum!'

'I wish I had half their energy.' Frankie and Guy had been playing a very energetic game of tag with the children, whose squeals every time they got close to getting caught would probably drown out the sound of fireworks if they were still playing when Dan started to light them. The look on Frankie's face when Guy had caught up with her at one point, making her laugh as she tried and failed to evade being tagged, was priceless. Whatever was going on between her mother and Guy, it wasn't the casual friendship she made it out to be. Nadia couldn't remember ever seeing her mum smile like that in her father's company and it was lovely to see her looking so happy. Nadia knew why Frankie was trying so hard to keep it quiet, but she really didn't want her to feel like she had to sneak around for her benefit. Her parents had limped along as a couple until their children had left home and it was their time now. Whatever her brother or grandmother might think.

'You know why they've got so much energy don't you?' Gwen put down what looked like a vase of mulled wine, the steam coming off it carrying the aroma of cinnamon and orange into the air.

'I'm not sure we want to know, do we Nadia?' Jess grinned and Nadia shook her head in response.

'I won't tell you about the link between a good sex life and energy levels then.' Gwen shrugged and Nadia almost choked on her drink. Thank goodness Mo was still too engrossed in his corn on the cob to take in what was being said.

'Good, well that's another awkward moment avoided then.' Toni rolled her eyes, leaning into Bobby, who was cradling their sleeping daughter in the sling that was strapped to his chest. 'Where's Barry tonight?

'He'll be here soon. He had to play in the semis of a badminton tournament he's in.' Gwen raised her huge glass and winked. 'And I don't need to tell you where he gets the energy for that, do I?'

'You definitely don't!' Bobby shook his head, no doubt hoping that he could shake the image they all now had in their heads. Nadia was just grateful that her mum and Guy were no longer the focus of attention.

'How's Izzy holding up?' Nadia turned towards Anna. 'Do you think she'll feel up to coming tonight?'

'I hope so. She said being back at work is helping, but sometimes these things don't hit you all at once, do they?' Anna sounded like she was speaking from experience, but they'd all seen how hard losing her grandmother had hit Izzy. She'd been raised by her grandparents and it was obvious how much they meant to her. She'd never mentioned her father and the few times she'd spoken about her mother in the staffroom, it was clear they had never had the best of relationships. The fact that her grandparents had been able to fill that gap in Izzy's life so effectively had given Nadia hope that she wouldn't be damaging her children by separating them from their father, as long as they had enough other people in their lives showing them unconditional love.

The pain of loss was sometimes an unavoidable price of love, though, just like Izzy was experiencing now, and like Hamish and Saffron had done when Sara died. It was something no one could control, but Nadia could minimise the risk of her children having to deal with any more loss by keeping her circle small. One of her friends at school had been through three stepfathers by the time she'd left for university and she didn't want that for Mo and Remi.

Her marriage and her parents' marriage failing in such quick succession did nothing to help her feel optimistic about the odds of any future relationships working out. So she was more than happy to err on the side of caution.

'I think all sorts of losses can hit you again, when you least expect them.' Nadia kept her tone casual because the waves of grief that sometimes washed over her as a result of her marriage falling apart didn't compare to Izzy's loss. That didn't stop them hitting her hard, though. On the drive over to Crooked Cottage Farm, all it had taken was for the song from her first dance with Ryan to come on the radio and she'd had to pinch her leg hard to stop herself from crying. Her mother must have known because Frankie had switched stations before Nadia even had a chance to reach for the button. All those lyrics about finding the one to grow old with had felt like they were written for her and Ryan back then, but they hadn't even made it to the seven-year itch.

'I think Izzy's planning to come over with Noah later.' Emily ran a hand through her hair as she spoke. 'Apparently he's been in a meeting in Truro today to talk to his bishop about whether or not he's going to stay on as vicar of St Jude's.'

'That's a big decision for him to make.' Anna took another sip of her rhubarb gin as the twins slept on. 'Does Izzy know what his thinking is?'

'He's not even sure himself I don't think. He had a bit of crisis of faith, but he does so much good. I think it would be a real shame if he gave up being a vicar.'

'Me too.' Anna sighed. 'But I guess it's not the sort of job you can do unless your heart is a hundred per cent in it. I'm so glad he was here for Izzy though and they seem to be getting on really well.'

'It's like *The Thorn Birds*! Just imagining what might be under that cassock gets me all hot and bothered.' Gwen laughed at the sea of blank faces around the table and she turned towards Nadia. 'I need your mum over here; she'd know exactly what I mean.'

'I think you're going to have to fill the rest of us in. Is it a film?' For a moment Nadia felt like she was in a game of charades, but Gwen shook her head.

'No it was a TV series about a Catholic priest who had to choose between duty and love. It was seriously sexy. You know all that forbidden love is a real aphrodisiac.' Gwen looked all misty-eyed again. 'Although I reckon your mum is living her own fantasy at the moment. I just saw Guy pinching her bum.'

'Who's that with Ella and Dan?' Nadia would have leapt on any opportunity to change the subject, but the arrival of a new group of people to the party provided the ideal distraction. Ella and Dan were chatting with a man in a high-backed wheelchair whoseemed to be negotiating the rough terrain without any issues.

'It's Leo Cotton. He owns a big scaffolding firm and he's done a lot of work with Dan in the past from what he's told Brae, but he's been struggling to keep the business open since his accident at the beginning of the year.' Anna frowned. 'Some scaffolding he was erecting on a listed building collapsed, and now he's paralysed from the chest down.'

'However rough life might feel at times, it makes you realise that some people have to deal with so much more.' Nadia breathed out as Mo cuddled into her side, not caring in the slightest when he wiped his buttery cheeks all over her coat. Remi and Riley were still running around with Frankie and Guy, and Nadia felt some of the strain, which she hadn't even realised she'd been holding on to, leave her body. Her babies were happy and healthy, and her lovely mum was having more fun than she'd had in years. There was so much to be thankful for and she wasn't going to let Ryan's latest missed maintenance payment worry her. Tonight she was just going to be grateful for everything she did have, and from now on she was going to try her hardest to stop mourning a marriage that had only ever been an illusion of what she'd wanted it to be. She might already have moved back to Cornwall, but it was finally time to move on.

* * *

Daisy was flagging. She was desperately trying to pretend that she wasn't, but Hamish knew his daughter far too well. The promise of fireworks meant that she almost certainly wouldn't give in and admit that she was tired, but it was past nine o'clock now and Camilla, whose bonfire party it was, hadn't given any indication that the fireworks would be starting any time soon. So when Camilla had beckoned for him to follow her through to the kitchen, he was hoping she was going to ask for his help to get the fireworks started. If not, it was going to be a choice between upsetting Daisy now or dealing with her being overtired and miserable for the next twenty-four hours.

'Can you keep an eye on Daize for a minute, sweetheart?' Hamish smiled at his older daughter, who looked like she'd been sucking lemons. He'd been surprised when Saffron had agreed to come along to the party in the first place. She'd never taken to Camilla, despite her being Sara's best friend, but she'd insisted she wanted to join them. Hamish had made a joke that someone needed to tell her face that, which had gone down like a lead balloon. It was another reason he was keen to get home, because Saffron definitely wasn't enjoying herself.

'Where are you going?' His older daughter would have made a good interrogation officer. She had a way of narrowing her eyes and staring at him with an unflinching gaze that would have made him confess everything, if there'd been anything to tell.

'To give Camilla a hand with the fireworks, so we can get Daize home before she completely flakes out and misses all the fun.'

'Yeah cos there's so much fun to be had here.' Saffron rolled her eyes.

'It'll be over soon, Saff, I promise. Just keep an eye on Daisy, darling, okay?'

'Yeah, okay.' Saffron's lack of enthusiasm might know no bounds, but he knew she'd keep her promise to look after her sister. She'd put that at the top of her list every single time. Even when it came at her own expense.

Hamish followed Camilla through to the kitchen. He still couldn't go in there without expecting to see Sara leaning against the island, with a glass of wine in her hand, laughing with Camilla. Or comforting her best friend as Camilla confided her now ex-husband's latest misdemeanour. Except there was only an empty space where his wife used to stand.

'Do you want a hand with the fireworks? Oh, no thanks.' Hamish shook his head as Camilla held out a glass of champagne for him.

'Come on, just one won't hurt.'

'I'm driving the girls home after this.'

'One glass won't put you over the limit.' Camilla smiled and he noticed for the first time how different her face looked from the last time he'd seen her. He couldn't quite work out what it was, but something had changed and he'd put money on Botox being involved.

'I don't drink at all when I'm driving. I promised Sara when we brought Saffron home from the hospital that I'd never have even a sip when I had her in the car.'

'You promised Sara quite a lot over the years, didn't you?' Camilla put down the glass, her smile wavering for a moment. 'But

I knew her as well as anyone and she wouldn't have wanted this life for you.'

'What do you mean?' The muscles in Hamish's jaw were already tensing. Camilla had crossed the line once before, telling him that he needed to take a firmer line with Saffron and that Sara wouldn't have let her act the way she did. It had nearly put an end to his association with his wife's best friend, but he wanted the girls to have Camilla in their lives. They may not appreciate it now, but one day they might want to hear stories about what their mother had been like as a teenager, when she'd first met Camilla.

There was no doubting that Sara's best friend had stories to share that even Hamish didn't know. So he'd told her as respectfully as he could that he'd be raising his daughters his own way and since then she'd kept her counsel about Saffron. That didn't mean he hadn't seen the look on Camilla's face sometimes, and she was probably right. If Sara had still been around, she would have pulled their eldest daughter into line, but then there would probably have been no need to if Sara had survived the cancer. Saffron was who she was because her mother had died. Things would get better when she went to uni and she didn't feel the need to protect her little sister any more. He just had to convince her that she could go and that nothing would happen to Daisy.

'What I mean is that you promised Sara you'd put the girls first and there's no doubting you do that.' Camilla's voice was soft and he had to lean slightly closer to hear her over the noise drifting in from the room next door. 'But that doesn't mean you can't have a bit of a life for yourself too.'

'The girls are my life.' He was about to take a step back when she reached out and put a hand on his arm.

'Hamish, she wanted you to have someone else in your life. You know that.'

'When the girls are older.' He shook his head, already

dismissing the possibility. There was no point in him trying to deny what Camilla was saying, because she'd been there when Sara had said those very words – that she wanted Hamish to find someone after she'd gone. What she couldn't have known was that it would turn out to be impossible for him to do that and to truly put the girls first. Like he'd said to Nadia, nobody wanted to come as far down his list of priorities as he needed to put them. It was strange, because the moment his thoughts drifted to Nadia, the prospect of having someone in his life was something he could admit to wanting. The timing just wasn't right now and it probably wouldn't be until both of the girls had left home and had lives of their own. But Camilla seemed to have ideas of her own.

'So you're going to wait what, another ten years? Sara would have hated the thought of you wasting all that time.'

'Raising my daughters isn't a waste of my time.' Hamish's jaw muscles were tighter still as he flinched away from Camilla, but she was too quick for him.

'Oh Hamish, I didn't mean that and you know it.' She gripped his hand in hers, lifting it up to her chest. 'My heart was broken, too, when Sara died and then when I split with Edward, but there's no point in me pretending that it doesn't beat that little bit faster whenever I see you. I'm ready for this now and I think Sara would have loved it. She told me to keep an eye on you and to make sure you chose someone who wouldn't try to wipe her out of the girls' lives, but who better to keep her memory alive than her best friend?'

'Camilla, this is—' Before he could even get the words out of his mouth, she'd clamped hers over his.

'Dad! What the hell are you doing? You're disgusting, both of you!'

Hamish leapt away from Camilla as though she was on fire,

aware that he sounded like a cliché of a cheating husband. The truth was he felt like it too. 'Saffron, this isn't what you think.'

'You make me sick and she' – Saffron pointed a shaky finger at Camilla – 'is an old slag.'

'That's enough!' Guilt and anger made Hamish roar, but his daughter had already turned away and broken into a run. She was far more adept than he was at darting in and out of the throng of people in the next room, all still waiting patiently for the fireworks to start. 'Saffron, wait!'

He shouted after her again, but she didn't even look back and seconds later the front door had slammed with a resounding bang, the crowded room falling silent as they watched the spectacle unfold.

'Daddy, where's Saffy going?' Daisy looked up at him. She was rubbing her ear, the way she always did when she was really tired.

'Home, sweetheart.' Hamish was silently praying that he hadn't just lied to his younger daughter. 'And I think we should go too.'

'What about the fireworks?' Daisy's bottom lip was already trembling.

'We'll pick some up from Penhale's on the way home.' The general store stayed open until ten o'clock every night, selling everything anyone could ever wish for. They were bound to have a couple of rockets and a packet of sparklers, which would be enough to satisfy Daisy. He just had to hope that finding a solution to Saffron's troubles was going to be possible too, but not even Penhale's had an answer for a problem that big. Hamish had no idea how to help his older daughter and he blamed himself; he'd let someone come into his life – albeit temporarily – who'd left her feeling insecure and terrified of what might happen to her younger sister. It didn't seem to matter how many times he reassured her, she'd lost her trust in people and the worst of it was that she seemed to have lost her trust in her father too. Saffy didn't seem to think Hamish was capable of protecting Daisy as well as she was, and if he didn't find a way of convincing her that he'd give up his whole life to do that if he needed to then he'd have failed in everything he'd promised Sara. He had to find a way to make this right for his daughters, whatever it took.

9

'They think I'm going to need a mastectomy.' Genevieve's voice on the other end of the line quivered.

'Oh Ginny.' It was one of those moments when nothing Nadia said could help and all she wanted was to be able to give her friend a hug. 'What did the consultant say?'

'Because I can't have radiotherapy until after the baby's born, removing the whole best is probably the only chance of getting all the cancer out.' Genevieve gave a shuddering sigh. 'Every time I say the word mastectomy I want to scream. I'm too young for this, it isn't fair. I was getting ready to accept my boobs changing so I could feed my baby, and them probably ending up much droopier, but I couldn't wait for that to happen. Now I feel like one of them is trying to poison me.'

'I really wish you didn't have to go through all of this.'

'I'm not even going to be able to feed the baby with the one boob I'll have left am I?'

'Probably not.' It would be so easy for Nadia to tell her it didn't matter and that bottle-feeding didn't mean a woman's bond with her baby was reduced in any way. It might be the truth, but she knew how deeply it could affect women who had the choice taken away from them. 'Are you starting chemo?'

'If I have the op...'

'But you're still not sure?'

'I kept asking questions, but the oncologist and Freddie both treated it like it was already a done deal. I'm supposed to have my first dose of chemo as soon as I've recovered from the operation, but I don't think I can go ahead with any of it. Chemo has to stop a few weeks before the delivery anyway because it can cause complications during the birth and the oncologist mentioned the possibility of inducing me early instead. But I don't want that. They gave me some information about my options and they all carry some risks. There's even a risk of losing her with the surgery. I know it's tiny, but I still don't think I can take it.'

'Did the oncologist say anything about the possibility of postponing treatment?'

'She just said she didn't recommend it and then Freddie shut the conversation down.'

'Have you talked to him about the miscarriages?' If Freddie understood the reason why his wife was finding it so hard to believe the oncologist when she told her the risks were low at this stage of her pregnancy, he might be more willing to discuss the options. But if he still had no idea about the miscarriages, it was no wonder Freddie was trying to railroad Genevieve into making what seemed like the sensible decision.

'I keep opening my mouth to tell him, but then he turns and looks at me and tells me how much he loves me and that it's all going to be okay. And then I just can't say it. I don't want him to look at me differently.'

'He won't. All he wants is for the cancer to be behind you; nothing else is going to matter.'

'Even if I tell him, I don't think he'll really understand. No one does unless they've lost a baby themselves and I don't want any treatment that carries even the tiniest risk of that happening again.'

'Could you talk it through with Hamish? Maybe if you and Freddie sit down with him, you can both feel happier with what you decide.'

'I don't know. I get the feeling that Hamish will side with Freddie anyway.' Genevieve cleared her throat. 'But maybe if you were there too, you could support my side of the argument and help me protect the baby.'

'I'm sure Freddie and Hamish will want the best for the baby too, but they both just want to make sure you're okay first.'

'I know, but I need someone who understands from personal experience what it's like to lose a baby.' Genevieve paused for a moment. 'And you do, don't you?'

Nadia thought about Remi and Mo – the children she did have – to stop the ache from the baby she'd lost overwhelming her. The empty feeling had felt as though it would never be filled after her miscarriage, and it was a difficult place to go back to. 'How did you know?'

'I saw it on your face when I was talking about my miscarriages and I need someone to know how that changes you. *Please.*' There was so much desperation Genevieve's voice and Nadia couldn't have refused her, even if she'd wanted to.

'If you really think it will help.'

'I do. Thank you so much. I'll speak to Hamish and see if he's free one evening this week if that suits you best? I want to get it done before I have to give the consultant my decision.'

'Evenings are fine. Mum will have the kids, but I'm on call on Wednesday night, so it might be best to avoid that in case I get a call-out.'

'I'll ring Hamish now, and thank you again.'

'I haven't done anything.'

'But you will. I know I can rely on you and I really need a friend on my side right now Nards.' Genevieve cut off the call before she had a chance to respond. It was a hell of a lot of responsibility for Nadia to carry, when she had no idea what to do or say for the best. But if her old friend needed someone to help her present the other side of the argument, then she'd be there for Ginny, whatever she decided to do.

* * *

Genevieve had arranged for the four of them to meet on Tuesday evening. She'd told Nadia that Hamish hadn't been able to get a babysitter, so they were meeting at his house, at 8.30 p.m., after Daisy was safely tucked up in bed. Saffron was apparently away on a school trip, hence why he hadn't been able to leave Daisy with her. Nadia had been able to put Remi and Mo to bed before leaving them in the care of Frankie and Guy, who'd ordered in a takeaway and were planning to watch *Roman Holiday* on DVD. Her mother was still spinning the line that she and Jess's father were just friends, but they weren't fooling anyone any more, least of all Nadia.

'Hi, sorry, I was a bit worried about ringing the buzzer in case it woke Daisy.' Nadia wrapped her arms around her body as she stood at the end of Hamish's driveway talking to him on the intercom. 'But other than scaling the gate, I didn't have much choice.'

'Oh God, sorry, I meant to leave the gates open, but Daisy insisted on three chapters of *George's Marvellous Medicine* tonight and by the time I got downstairs, I'd forgotten all about them.'

'If you're reading to a child instead of doing something else it's always worth it.' When she'd first brought the children back to the UK, Ryan had made a handful of videos of himself reading bedtime stories to Remi and Mo because it was hard to coordinate FaceTiming with their bedtime routine. But much like the maintenance payments, the videos had quickly dwindled. Nadia had tried to fill in for Ryan, but Remi had got very upset. When Nadia attempted to get to the bottom of why she was so distraught, Remi had said it was because her mother had got the voices wrong, but it was obvious she just wanted her daddy to be the one reading her the story.

'I've got to admit it's one of my favourite times of the day, but I'm sure you don't want to stand out there any longer listening to me waffling on. Come on in, I'll buzz you in.' Nadia had got into the habit of comparing every man she met to Ryan, but it was as if he and Hamish came from completely different planets. They couldn't have been more opposite.

'Thanks.' It took a couple of minutes to walk up Hamish's driveway, but he was already waiting for her by the open front door.

'I'm so sorry about that. I've left it open for Genevieve and Freddie.'

'They're not here yet, then?' It was a pointless question, but Hamish shook his head anyway.

'She texted to say they're running twenty minutes late.'

'Oh. I can go away and come back again, if you like?' Nadia suddenly felt awkward. She didn't have a reason to be there without Genevieve and Freddie and she needed one. Otherwise she might get into another conversation with Hamish that got far too personal, far too quickly, just like it had before.

'Don't be silly. Come in. It will be nice to have some time on our own first.' For a moment she wondered what he was going to say. 'I feel like we might need a glass of wine before the conversation we're about to have, unless you're driving?'

'I walked up. I wanted to clear my head.' She hadn't meant to add that last bit, but she just seemed to blurt things out when Hamish fixed his blue eyes on hers.

'Everything okay?'

She was grateful when he turned away to head into the house, so he wasn't looking at her when she responded to his question. Letting someone like Hamish get close made her feel vulnerable because he'd want to help. It was just the way he was. But Ryan was her problem and she felt like a fool for ever believing he'd be worthy of his children. She didn't want to cry in front of Hamish because her husband had let their children down again. But she couldn't just ignore his question, so she took a deep breath and steadied her voice, concentrating on the facts.

'Just Ryan being Ryan again, that's all. He promised to get the kids an iPad for Christmas, so they can video chat with him more often, but he's missed his latest maintenance payment and I'm just bracing myself for the email saying he's got no money for presents. I'll find a way somehow, because there's no way I'll allow Santa Claus to let them down on Christmas morning, but it might mean another month or two before we can move out of Mum's flat. She's been brilliant, but four of us squeezed into a two-bed flat would test the strongest of relationships.'

'Ryan's an idiot.' Hamish turned to look at her again as they reached the kitchen, running a hand through his hair, and Nadia found herself wishing she'd fallen for someone like him. Someone who'd prioritise reading a bedtime story to his daughter over almost anything else.

'He is.' She laughed, her shoulders relaxing for the first time. She already felt better for getting it off her chest. 'He was the same when we were together, always saying he couldn't cover half the bills, but somehow finding money for nights out with the boys and golfing trips. I should have left long before I did, but leaving would have meant coming home and I didn't want to take the children away from him. In the end, he made the decision for me.'

'It's official. He's definitely an idiot.' Hamish smiled, looking at her in a way that made something in her chest flutter. Luckily he was distracted again, turning to open the fridge door. 'White or rosé? Or I can open a bottle of red if you prefer?'

'White's great, thank you.' She couldn't help smiling as she caught sight of the piece of paper attached to the fridge door with a magnet in the shape of a lobster. 'That's quite the list you've got there.'

'Yes and it's in block capitals thanks to Saff!' He laughed, taking the list off the door. 'She's left me a full set of instructions of all the things I mustn't forget while she's away and top of the list is the form for the nativity play, which seems ridiculously early. For a start it's only early November and secondly who ever heard of six-year-olds needing to put in a request for the parts they want to audition for?'

'That's exactly what I thought, but according to Miss Renfrew it means there are less arguments and upset.'

'Hmm.' Hamish looked doubtful. 'I'm even more stumped because Daisy is absolutely insisting she wants to audition to be one of the sheep.'

'I might be able to solve that particular riddle.' Nadia grinned at the look on his face. 'They're telling the story from the point of view of the animals to make it a bit more inclusive for children of other religions, or those with no religion at all. Miss Renfrew felt the need to hammer the point home to me. What she doesn't realise is any religion I might have had lapsed back with my parents, and only my grandmother ever goes to temple. But at least it explains why Remi is desperate to be the donkey and why Daisy is going after the role of one of the sheep, because I was wondering, too, before Miss Renfrew filled me in.'

'I'm really glad Daisy has a friend like Remi. She was so shy when she started at Port Agnes primary, but the two of them are as thick as thieves and since Remi started, Daisy can't want to get to school in the mornings.'

'Remi's the same. I was worried about her joining a class that had already been established in their first couple of years at school, but it's like she's found a little soulmate in Daisy.'

'It's incredible when that happens.' Hamish had the most expressive face, which seemed capable of conveying just how deep the loss of his own soulmate had been. But then he smiled again, pushing it down to the place where these things had to be kept if there was any chance of carrying on with some kind of life. 'We've just got to hope that our little sheep and donkey can pull it off, and not get stuck with bit parts like Mary or the Angel Gabriel!'

'I'm just praying they're not going to ask the parents to think about making the costumes again, which they apparently did last year.' Nadia pulled a face. 'Because a tinsel halo or a cardboard crown would be a heck of lot easier.'

'Well if they do, maybe we should get together and have a costume-making evening. I'll provide the wine and a takeaway, if you bring a sewing kit and a swear jar big enough to take all of the money I'm going to end up putting in it.'

'It's a deal.' Nadia had no idea if he was being serious or not, because they'd never done anything without the children or Genevieve before. But she had to admit that she liked the sound of an evening like that – even if it did mean trying to make costumes they clearly didn't have the skills for. It was nice having a friend who understood that as a single parent, all of that stuff only landed in one place. And it had absolutely nothing to do with the fact that Hamish Spencer was as beautiful on the outside as he was on the inside. Nothing whatsoever.

* * *

'I don't even know why we're here.' Freddie had the hollowed-out look of a man on the edge, the dark shadows under his eyes revealing just how long it must have been since he'd had a decent night's sleep. As soon as the introductions and greetings had been exchanged, he cut to the chase. 'Ginny needs the operation and the chemo to give her the best chance of eradicating all traces of cancer from her body, so what is there to even discuss?'

Nadia looked at Genevieve, whose eyes seemed to be pleading for her to answer, and she wasn't going to let her down. 'I think the main concern Genevieve has, is how the surgery is going to affect the baby.'

'The risks of the anaesthetic affecting the baby are much lower in the third trimester.' Hamish was taking the tack Nadia had expected him to. After all, he knew the price Sara had paid for waiting, even if a glioblastoma was vastly different to breast cancer. Nadia had read up about Sara's type of cancer after Hamish had told her his story and the chances were that she wouldn't have survived long even if she'd had the treatment straight away, but they might have had more time together. Back then, Hamish would probably have given anything for another year with his wife. Instead, Sara had taken a decision which they must have known would mean Hamish raising two young children alone. Freddie might not want to say the words out loud, but there was every chance he was wrestling with the prospect of raising a child by himself too.

'Low risk isn't no risk though, is it?' Genevieve gave Hamish an unblinking stare and he shook his head in response.

'No and there are two schools of thought on this. Some consultants recommend treatment straight away and they might even suggest you're induced. But sometimes they're happy to delay until after the baby's delivered, depending on the stage of the cancer. I think if you haven't already done so, you need to explore both options with your consultant.' Hamish looked directly at Freddie, which was just as well as Nadia's mouth had dropped open in surprise. This wasn't what she'd anticipated; she'd fully expected Hamish to support the idea of Genevieve starting the treatment as soon as possible, but he was taking a far more measured view.

'Look I don't want to lose the baby any more than Ginny does, but if I'm forced to choose between them, then I choose my wife.' Freddie folded his arms across his chest and Hamish nodded.

'I understand that, I really do, but I don't think the choice is as stark as that.'

'The pregnancy has been going great, there's been nothing to worry us until this.' Freddie turned to his wife. 'So I don't get why you won't have the treatment? We've been told that the risks of the operation are low and even an induction wouldn't be that big of a risk. It's not like this baby is only just hanging in there. She needs her mum and I want you to be there for her.'

'I do want to be there and I will, but I'm already her mum and I'm not doing anything that might hurt her.'

'Even if it hurts you not to, or worse still, kills you?'

'If I lose another baby it will kill me!' The words tumbled out of Genevieve's mouth and Nadia watched the other woman's eyes widen with shock at having said them aloud. Now it was all out there, laid bare, with none of the careful wording she'd no doubt practised in her head.

'What do you mean lose *another* baby?' Freddie, for his part, just looked confused and he was already reaching out to offer his wife some comfort, because it was obvious to every single person in the room how hard this was for her. Genevieve was visibly shaking and all the colour seemed to have left her face.

'Before this.' Genevieve placed a protective hand over her

bump, as her voice cracked. 'Before us, when I was with David. We tried for a baby.'

'And you lost one?' Freddie's voice was gentle. Whatever it was his wife had feared his reaction would be, it surely couldn't have been this.

'Not one. Two.' Genevieve couldn't even look in his direction any more, but he was still holding her arm and Nadia had seen the tears filling the other woman's eyes.

'Why on earth didn't you tell me any of this?'

'Because I knew how much you struggled with the fact that I'd been married to David before and that sometimes the things we did, that were new for you, weren't new for me. Like when we got engaged, and the wedding itself.' She gave a shuddering sigh. 'And I wanted you to think this was different, because it is different. What I've got with you is a million times better than what I'd settled for with David, but I didn't realise that until I met you. I wanted us having a child together to be exciting and not feel like it was tainted by anything that might have happened in the past.'

'You are daft sometimes.' Freddie cupped his wife's face in his hands so she had to look at him, and Nadia exchanged a brief look with Hamish. It was obvious this was getting to him too. 'Of course I'm jealous of David, because he had five years with you that I could have had if we'd met earlier, but none of what you went through with him changes what we've got. We've got the rest of our lives to experience things together that we've never done with anyone else. I can't believe you've carried all this worry about what could happen with the baby, instead of telling me so that I could try and take some of that burden off you.'

'It seems so stupid now, but it mattered so much at the time. Part of me thought if I didn't say anything about losing the babies it would mean it wasn't real and there'd be less chance of losing our little girl.' Genevieve turned towards Nadia, her eyes still glassy with the threat of tears. 'It's crazy when I say it out loud, but that's what was going on in my head.'

'It's not crazy; a lot of women go into denial about miscarriages and even medical staff sometimes write off early losses as though they were nothing much more than a late period.' Nadia shook her head. Having lost a baby of her own she knew just how wrong that felt to so many women, but it didn't mean it didn't happen. She'd seen the proof far too many times.

'I can also see why it would make you much more apprehensive about the risks of chemo and the operation itself.' Hamish's voice was even, somehow conveying understanding and reassurance all at the same time. 'I think the two of you probably need to talk this through again. It doesn't change my advice, but that doesn't mean you have to take it.'

'It's got to be Ginny's choice.' Freddie let go of a long breath. 'She's been through hell and back already, losing two babies and now this. None of it is fair, but whatever choice we make she's the one who's going to have to deal with the consequences more than me. I want my daughter *and* my wife to survive, but Ginny's who matters to me most right now.'

'The thing is, I don't think I'll survive either way if I lose this baby.' Genevieve's voice cracked on the words again and the first of the tears she'd been fighting rolled down her cheeks, but her tone was determined. 'She's my reason to keep going through all of this, when part of me just wants to curl up and ignore it. Whatever treatment I have to go through after she's here, I'll do it because she needs her mum, but I'm not sure I'll have the fight left without her.'

'If that's what you want, that's what we'll do.' Freddie folded his wife into his arms, as she started to sob. For a few seconds Nadia resisted the urge to look in Hamish's direction. When she did, he was looking straight back at her, glassy-eyed and his jaw taut with the effort of holding everything in. She wished there was something she could do to comfort him, the way he'd comforted her when she'd opened up about Ryan. It didn't explain the almost overwhelming urge she had to wrap her arms around him, because that wouldn't even begin to ease his grief. He'd been in this moment before, and Nadia knew he'd be praying every bit as hard as she was that this time the outcome would be different.

10

'You're not reading it right.' Remi's downturned mouth matched the sulky tone of her voice. She'd been grumpy ever since she got in from school, which Nadia had put down to the little girl being overtired. It was no surprise with a six-year-old doing a ten-hour day, with breakfast and after-school clubs tacked on to either end of their lessons. Guilt washed over Nadia, as it so often did these days, and she made an extra effort to get the voice right.

'Among the tallest, darkest trees, a shape was shifting in the breeze. "Come closer to me little one," said the witch in a voice that made Maddie run.'

'That's not how the witch speaks!'

'I'm sorry sweetheart, I can't remember how Daddy did the voice.' Another tidal wave of guilt was threatening to wash Nadia right off the end of Remi's bed. 'Why don't we read another story? This one's a bit scary anyway.'

'I'm not a baby.'

'I know, but Mo might not like it.'

'He's already asleep.' If Remi had added the word 'stupid' to the end of the statement, it would have fitted perfectly with her tone.

'And anyway, it's not scary because Maddie and her friends get rid of the witch cos they're very clever and Daddy says I'm very clever too.'

'That's true, darling, you are.'

'Good cos clever people earn loads and loads of money, like Daisy's daddy, and I want to have loads of money too.'

'Why's that?' Nadia braced herself for Remi to say something that would turn the tidal wave into a tsunami. She probably wanted the money so that she could escape from the cramped flat, sharing a room with the little brother she seemed to find increasingly annoying, not to mention Nadia. Or maybe she wanted to buy a stable full of ponies, or fly to the moon. Right now that felt like almost as likely as the prospect of them ever being able to leave the flat.

'Cos then I could fly back and see Daddy whenever I wanted.' Remi fixed her mother with a serious look. 'Every weekend probably and then he could read me *Maddie and the Witch Hunters* and do the proper voice.'

Nadia felt her daughter's words like a punch to the gut and a hand on her throat all at the same time. The guilt that she couldn't give her daughter what she wanted was crippling, but then came the second blow – the brutal truth that she wasn't enough for Remi and that given the choice, her daughter wanted to spend every weekend with her father. It took all Nadia had to answer in a way that didn't reveal just how heartbroken she was. 'I'm sorry you can't see Daddy, darling, but I promise I'll ask him to make some more videos so he can read you the rest of the story. And as soon as we get a place of our own, I'll start saving so that I can take you and Mo back to see Daddy, or maybe he can come here even sooner than that.'

'That will take forever and ever and I might be really old like Saffron is.'

'You won't be darling, I promise.' Just the hint of a smile tugged at the corners of Nadia's mouth as she responded to her daughter. It was almost impossible to believe that anyone could think an eighteen-year-old was as ancient as Remi did, but it was also a reminder of just how long a few months could feel in a child's life. 'Now try to get some sleep sweetheart. It's a big day tomorrow and you need to rest your voice as much as possible if you're going to do your best singing for Miss Renfrew and get the part of the donkey.'

'Hee-haw!' Mo suddenly piped up from the corner of the room, even though he'd been softly snoring a few minutes earlier.

'You're supposed to be asleep young man.' Moving across to tuck him in again, she dropped a kiss on her son's head.

'Cuddle Mummy?' He was far more astute than a four-year-old should be and he'd long since cottoned on to the fact that requests for cuddles could delay his bedtime quite significantly. But the truth was that Nadia wanted those cuddles every bit as much as he did. The last couple of weeks had been a stark reminder that not every mum had the chance to read their kids a bedtime story, or respond to their requests for a cuddle when they wanted one. Those opportunities had been ripped away from Hamish's wife and there was no knowing if Genevieve would have the chance by the time her daughter was Remi's age, or even Mo's. Who cared if bedtime took far longer than it should? She was trying really hard not to worry too much about what Remi had said either. If Ryan wanted to maintain regular contact with his children then it was up to him.

* * *

Something strange happened to the time between the middle of November and the arrival of Christmas Day. Hamish had never noticed it until the second Christmas after Sara had died. The whole of the first year after she'd gone had passed in a weird, torturous slow motion, with so many milestones he wished his family had never had. The first of the girls' birthdays without their mother to make a big fuss of them, the first wedding anniversary she hadn't been there to celebrate with him and suddenly he wasn't sure if he was even married any more. Did it count once you were a widower? Then there was that first Christmas, of course, when he hadn't been able to do anything more than just function, and making sure it was any sort of occasion for Saffron and baby Daisy had been down to his parents and in-laws, who themselves must have been struggling to put one foot in front of the other.

By the time they got to the second Christmas, Hamish's best friend, Charlie, had told him he needed to buck the hell up for his daughters' sakes, if nothing else. He hadn't been able to disagree; the girls needed him and he need to try and stop wallowing in the grief and self-pity that was threatening to swallow him up all together. The first step to acting on Charlie's advice had been to take over the Christmas shopping for his daughters' gifts. It was at that point that time had begun to speed up. With six weeks to get everything organised, it had felt like something even the most novice of stand-in Santa Claus figures could achieve. But gift shopping was such a tiny part of it. Saffron had seemed to have at least one school event every single day that he'd needed to organise something for – everything from buying what felt like the contents of Hobbycraft for Christmas decoration day, to trying – and failing – to make gingerbread men for the school's winter fair. Discovering that Jago Mehenick could knock up almost anything that was requested in his bakery by the harbour, had felt akin to discovering the Dead Sea Scrolls.

Five more Christmases down the line and each year seemed to hurtle towards the 'Big Day' even quicker than the last. It wasn't helped by the fact that Saffron was now almost impossible to buy for and, as easy as handing over an envelope of cash was, it had none of the magic of finding a gift that would be the perfect surprise on Christmas morning. That was the only thing that made the hell of gift shopping even vaguely worthwhile.

Daisy, on the other hand, was still slap bang in the middle of the magic and she had no concept of the fact that there might be a limit to what Santa Claus could deliver in his sleigh. It wasn't that she ever asked for anything expensive, it was just that almost everything at the top of her wish list was a living, breathing entity. This year she'd said she didn't mind what Santa wanted to bring her out of the top three things on her list, which comprised of a donkey, a giraffe or a giant house rabbit. The giraffe was obviously a no-no and although, according to Google, they technically had enough space to keep a donkey, they needed a hell of a lot of looking after.

All of which meant that Hamish had spent more time than he'd ever dreamt possible researching the care, and just as importantly, the expected lifespan of giant house rabbits. He'd even ended up having an *Alice in Wonderland*-esque nightmare featuring a huge rabbit, dressed not unlike the March Hare, which resolutely refused to make any room for him whatsoever on the sofa. He was already starting to regret his decision not to try and persuade Daisy to adopt a donkey instead. It was what he'd convinced her to do the year before, when she'd insisted that all she wanted was a baby goat. He'd managed to persuade her that a year's pass to Thunderhill Farm and sponsorship of one of the goats in their petting zoo, was a far better option. Especially as their dog George was afraid of his own shadow sometimes, never mind a belligerent goat. But even if he had tried to persuade her to do the same with the donkey, she probably wouldn't have gone for it again. So he'd just have to console himself with the knowledge that a rabbit hogging the sofa was better than a donkey, because knowing Daisy, she'd want to try and bring whatever pet she eventually got indoors.

Today was another big day in the Christmas calendar, at least where Hamish's younger daughter was concerned. It was the day that the children at Port Agnes primary school would discover what parts they'd be getting in the nativity play.

'Sara, see if you can't have a word with the man in charge – if there really is one – to make sure Daisy gets to be a sheep.' He did this every so often, speaking to Sara as if she was sitting in the seat next to him on the drive down to the primary school, instead of wherever she was. Or wasn't. If his wife had still been alive, they'd have laughed together about Daisy's desperate desire to be cast as a sheep, but there'd have been a hint of nervousness in Sara's laugh too. She'd always wanted everything to go right for Saffron and all through her primary school years, Sara had protected their elder daughter like the lioness she was. But she hadn't had the chance to patch up Daisy's grazed knees, or whisper words of comfort to her at the end of a bad day. Whatever the outcome, it was going to be down to Hamish to celebrate or commiserate with their little girl. It wasn't a big thing to anyone else, but it was the biggest thing in Daisy's life right now and it mattered to her. So it mattered to Hamish too. It was why he'd been determined to finish work early enough to be able to pick her up himself and not rely on Saffron to deal with the fall-out if things hadn't gone Daisy's way.

It was one of those grey wintry days where it had never seemed to get light and despite only being quarter past three, the cars that were queuing to try and bag a place close to the school gates all had their headlights on. Hamish managed to squeeze into the last space opposite the playground before the road snaked up the hill away from the school, and it took him a moment to register that it was Nadia getting out of the car in front of him. She was wearing a rainbow-striped woolly hat which clamped down her trademark corkscrew curls, the oversized pompom bouncing as she hurried across the road.

'Nadia!' He'd flung open his door and called out her name before he'd had the chance to think about it. She might be hoping for a quick pick-up, in and out of the school and heading back home without having to make conversation with any of the other parents. God knows it was what Hamish had silently wished for on almost every school run he'd ever completed, but not today. He wanted to speak to Nadia, even if that meant the conversation steering towards Genevieve, which was always tough because of the parallels to what had happened to Sara.

The truth was, when he was with Nadia, he didn't want Sara's face to immediately swim in front of his eyes. And the desire to talk to Remi's mother had nothing to do with their professional connection. Not this time. Nadia would understand exactly what it would be like to face his daughter's disappointment alone and not be able to do anything about it. Both Daisy and Nadia's children had already missed out on more than a part they wanted in the nativity play, but she was one of the few people who probably wouldn't think it was crazy that it mattered to him too, for that very reason. Ryan's decision to opt out as a father was just as out of Nadia's control as Sara's illness had been for Hamish. Their circumstances were worlds apart and yet he'd felt a connection to her that he hadn't felt in years, and told her things he hadn't told anyone else. It had happened in those shared moments of under-standing, talking about the children and supporting Genevieve. He'd let his guard down and Nadia had got inside his head in a way that left him thinking about her far more often than he was willing to admit.

'Hey, I don't usually see you here,' Nadia said, as he caught up with her. 'Although that might be to do with the fact that I hardly ever do pick-up unless it's from the after-school club. Bad mother alert, right there.'

'There's no way you're a bad mother.'

'How can you possibly know?' Her eyes sparkled when she smiled and he found himself wondering what it would be like to make her laugh.

'I can just tell. In my job you meet people all day long and after a while you just get this sort of sixth sense.' He shrugged, unable to stop himself from mirroring her smile, despite wondering if he sounded as much of a prat as he suspected he did. 'You must feel it too, especially in your job, when you see a new mum with her baby?'

'Actually it starts a lot sooner than that. Sometimes you can tell as early as a first antenatal appointment whether this is going to be a situation that needs outside support. The hardest ones are when the mother is never going to get to parent her child, even when you know it's for the best, and all you can do is try to make sure the baby is kept as safe as possible until it's delivered.'

'That must be really tough; does it happen much?'

'It was more common when I worked in city hospitals, but it happens everywhere. I haven't been in Port Agnes long enough to have to make one of those referrals, but nowhere is immune from situations like that. I keep reminding myself that while I might not be able to give Mo and Remi everything right now, I can keep them safe and let them know just how much I love them.'

'That's all kids really need in the end, isn't it?' Hamish held her gaze for a moment, and if it had been a movie, that would have been the moment they kissed, because he couldn't deny that he wanted to. In truth his brain had already fast-forwarded to thinking about what it would be like to kiss her. But then she laughed and the spell was broken.

'Well love *and* the part of a donkey or sheep in the school nativity play, of course!'

'Is it crazy that I'm so nervous about what the outcome might be? It's like my medical finals all over again.' It was Hamish's turn to laugh and Nadia shook her head.

'No, I've got butterflies too.' She caught his eye again and half a lifetime ago, he might have thought about trying to say something flirtatious. Not that he'd ever been any good at that, even before he'd got horribly out of practice. There was something reassuring about having the desire, though, because he couldn't remember the last time he'd felt it. He wasn't going to pretend he'd lived like a monk since Sara's death; that status had only lasted for the first two years. But he'd never wanted to make something happen, the way he did when he was with Nadia. The relationships he'd had, if you could call them that, had just seemed to happen with little effort on his part. As soon as the women had wanted more than that from him, he'd backed off, because none of them understood why he couldn't give them what they were asking for, if it robbed even a moment from Saffron and Daisy. Maybe that's why he felt so differently about Nadia, because Remi and Mo so obviously came first for her too.

'We'd better face the music then.' Hamish hesitated for a second, but then he said it anyway. 'Maybe we should take the girls to The Cookie Jar for one of their famous milkshakes. Either as a celebration or a commiseration?'

'I've got to get Mo from the nursery at five.' Nadia glanced at her watch. 'But that should give us the best part of an hour if they let the girls out quickly.'

'Brilliant.' Hamish felt better already. Whatever the outcome of the teacher's decision, it would be much easier to cheer the girls up if they had each other and a milkshake large enough to wash away even the biggest disappointment.

'I'm the donkey!' Remi came hurtling out of the classroom first and straight into her mother's arms.

'That's brilliant darling, what about Daisy?'

'She's one of the sheep! It's the bestest day ever.'

'It certainly is.' Nadia smiled in Hamish's direction and he put two thumbs up, immediately wishing he hadn't, positive that he looked like a prat this time. There was something about Nadia that made him feel like a desperately uncool teenager trying to impress the girl he liked. There was no time to overthink it, though, as a moment later Daisy had almost knocked him flying.

'I'm sheep number one, Daddy. That's the most important sheep there is!'

'Well it would be sweetheart, well done and well done to Remi too.' His words were muffled as his daughter clung to his neck like a koala bear. 'As a special treat to celebrate, we're all going to The Cookie Jar for milkshakes.'

'Remi and her mummy too?' Daisy sounded as if she could barely take any more good news.

'Yes, all four of us.' As he said the words a sudden image of Sara flitted into his mind. She'd kept saying the same thing over and over again after her diagnosis: *'One day all four of us will be out having fun together and we'll forget this ever happened.'* That day had never come, but maybe it was finally time to stop spending so much of his life wishing that it had. Suddenly 'all six of us' was something Hamish could see himself saying, but it was just his imagination outrunning logic again. They were going for milkshakes together, that was all, and for now that was more than enough.

11

Going out with Hamish had left Nadia wracked with guilt and it had nothing to do with the chocolate cookie dough milkshake she'd downed far too quickly. The guilt stemmed from wishing she'd met someone like Hamish instead of Ryan. Not that she owed Ryan a scrap of loyalty, and she didn't feel guilty about wishing him all kinds of karma to come down the line, but it had felt as if she was wishing away the life she had. Every time she was with Hamish, she couldn't help wondering what marriage would be like with a man who adored his children as much as he clearly did, or how lovely it would have been if the scene of family contentment they'd presented in The Cookie Jar had been real. But if she hadn't met Ryan, there'd be no Remi or Mo, and whatever he'd put her through in the past – and whatever was still to come – every single second of it was worth dealing with, a million times over for them.

When Hamish had offered for Remi to go back to his place for a play date with Daisy while she picked Mo up from the nursery, she'd been grateful for the time alone to clear the ridiculous thoughts out of her head. Her stupid fantasy had been just that, and even if they'd met before they'd had children, Hamish would never have looked twice at someone like her. Ryan had told her in the heat of one of their biggest arguments that no one else would want her. She was a nag who'd let herself go, and a control freak for wanting him to spend at least one day of the weekend with his family, instead of on the golf course. *Impossible to live with.* That's what Ryan had called her and he should know. It was why she'd made a promise to herself never to try and do that again, at least not while the children were living at home and might have to witness another break-up. She wouldn't put them through that. So even if Hamish had been interested, she'd have had to turn him down. It was just as well he wasn't, and thank goodness no one but her would ever know about the daydreams she couldn't stop from popping into her head. That would be almost as mortifying as being told, by the person who'd promised to love her for the rest of his life, that she was completely unlovable.

Hamish had been much easier to talk to than she'd imagined. There was nothing about him that suggested he thought he was better than her in any way, not because of where he lived or what he did for a living. He was just another single parent, able to laugh at how crazy they'd both become about the girls' roles in the nativity play. And when Daisy and Remi had been engrossed in their milkshakes, and completely oblivious to the conversation going on around them, they'd spoken about Genevieve, too, and how worried they both were about her. Every now and then, Hamish would get a wistful look on his face and Nadia could tell he was thinking about Sara, which must have made the whole situation so much harder for him.

But Nadia had to put worries about Genevieve and the effect that Ryan's prolonged silence was having on their children out of her mind the moment she got to work. The women coming to see her in clinic needed her full attention and she was grateful for the chance to give it to them.

Amber Trent was Nadia's eighth patient of the day and she puffed into the consultation room, carrying one of the largest refillable water bottles Nadia had ever seen. She just hoped Amber hadn't got confused, the way some of her patients in the past had, and thought she needed to come to the consultation with a bladder as full as they required at some of the scans. There was no point in any woman, pregnant or otherwise, putting herself through that for no reason.

'Hi Amber, how's it going?' Nadia gestured for her patient to take a seat and the other woman landed in the chair with a thump and an audible outtake of breath.

'Good, I think. Except for feeling like the side of a six-bedroom house. Am I supposed to be this big already?'

'We'll measure your bump in a bit, but at this stage in your pregnancy things can feel like they're suddenly changing very quickly.' Nadia smiled. 'The muscles in your abdomen start to lose the battle, but trust me, second time around they don't try nearly so hard to hold out this long.'

'Urgh, I'm not sure there'll be a second time the way I'm feeling and I don't think the muscles in my abdomen ever knew they were there in the first place!'

'Is there anything you're finding particularly difficult?' A lot of women said they were never getting pregnant again at this stage, or took the decision to only have one child, but Amber's tone suggested there was more to it than that.

'I just feel bleurgh a lot of the time. I can't stop peeing and I mean I *literally* cannot stop peeing sometimes. My mum warned me there was a risk of me wetting myself when I was near the end, but I'm only just over halfway through and it's already happened more than once.'

'Have you got any pain when you pass water? It could be an infection and I'll get you to do a sample to rule that out, but I couldn't help noticing you've got a huge water bottle with you. Are you drinking more than usual?'

'That's the thing, I tried to cut down a bit to make sure I didn't get caught short again but my mouth feels like the bottom of a bird cage all the time, really dry, like when you've got a stonking hangover. And I promise you, I haven't touched a drop of anything since I started trying for a baby.'

'Okay.' Nadia had a strong suspicion what was causing the symptoms, but she didn't want to cause Amber any panic. 'Can you remember if they offered you an extra blood test when you had your booking-in appointment? It's a glucose tolerance test.'

'That's the one for diabetes, isn't it?' Amber frowned as Nadia nodded.

'Your records don't say anything about it and you'd have been booked in for the test by now if they thought you needed it, but I just wondered if it had been mentioned?'

'My BMI was on the obesity borderline at twenty-nine, so she said I didn't need the test because I didn't have any other risk factors for diabetes.' Amber sighed. 'But I'd been dieting like mad to get to a healthy weight to conceive and before that my BMI was thirty-five. I should probably have mentioned that at the booking-in. Do you think it might be diabetes?'

'It's possible, but even if it is, we can manage it to reduce any risk to the baby. The chances are that gestational diabetes will go away once the baby's born, too.'

'I kept telling myself that I'd maintain the diet while I was pregnant, but in the early days the only thing that seemed to stop me feeling sick was to eat constantly and I knew I was putting on more than just baby weight. I'm a crap mum already.' Amber's voice broke on the last sentence and Nadia got up from her chair and crouched in front of the other woman, as Amber started to cry.

'No you're not. Dieting isn't easy and pregnancy makes that harder too. This might have happened regardless of any of that and I promise you that it isn't the end of the world. We just need to find out what we're dealing with and make sure it has as little impact on the baby as possible. I've looked after lots of women with gestational diabetes and they all delivered their babies safely. It's going to be okay.'

'What could it do to the baby?' Amber fixed her eyes on Nadia's face as she spoke.

'The main risks are a larger-than-usual birth weight and increased fluid around the baby, which can lead to premature delivery, but like I said, we should be able to reduce the risk of that by treating you. Occasionally the baby needs a slightly longer stay in hospital after delivery to treat jaundice, but that can happen even when the mother doesn't have gestational diabetes. And we don't even know if it is that yet.' Nadia didn't mention that in very rare cases gestational diabetes could cause stillbirth. Amber was already getting herself into a state and that wouldn't do the baby any good either.

'How can you tell if I've definitely got it?' As Nadia moved back to her chair, Amber rested her hand on her bump, her eyes still brimming with tears.

'I'll book you in for the oral glucose tolerance test. It's usually scheduled for women with risk factors at between twenty-four and twenty-eight weeks of pregnancy, so we're right in that window with you being at twenty-five weeks.'

'So it wouldn't have been any different, even if I'd admitted that my BMI had only just gone down?' Some of the tightness left Amber's face.

'No, but it's really important you feel able to tell us anything, because we just want to help. I've supported mums-to-be with BMIs well over forty in the past and everyone just wants the best for mum and baby.'

'I know it was stupid, but I think it comes from having a father who fat-shamed every person who was even a bit overweight the whole time I was growing up. He told me on my wedding day, just before he walked me down the aisle, that it was a pity I didn't manage to lose a bit more weight so the photos would look better.'

'That's awful, but you did the right thing getting as healthy as you could to conceive and we can give you as much help as you want from this point forward, but I know how hard this is and you've got nothing to feel guilty about.' Despite her promise to herself at the start of the clinic, Nadia couldn't stop her thoughts suddenly turning to Ryan and what he'd said to her at his sister's wedding, about what a state she'd let herself get into since having children. She'd felt so good about the way she'd looked, in a floaty summer dress that clung to the bits that flattered her and flared over the ones that didn't, but she couldn't compare to his size-eight sister and her equally tiny bridesmaids. She'd spent the rest of her sister-in-law's wedding day feeling uncomfortable and unhappy in equal measure, so she knew only too well what it felt like not to be able to live up to the expectations of someone who was supposed to love you. 'Do you think it might help you to talk through your relationship with your dad? I can make a referral for you to have some talking therapy if you feel it would be useful?'

'I've been having therapy for a while and I'm getting there. My husband, Nathan, looked into it for me. He said he wanted me to see myself the way he does, instead of the images my dad put in my head.'

'Nathan sounds great.'

'He is, but I know he'll be really worried about me and the

baby if I've got diabetes. Will I have to have insulin injections?' Worry was clouding Amber's face again.

'If you're diagnosed, we'll start by looking at whether changes to your diet and exercise can help and you can monitor that with a home-testing kit for your blood sugar levels. If that doesn't lower your levels, then there's medication you can take, but that could be in tablet form or via injections. There are different options, depending on your levels, but the main thing is to find out what we're dealing with and start treating it as soon as possible.' Nadia gave her what she hoped was another comforting smile. 'We'll run the other usual tests today and I can take your blood pressure and measure your bump, because that might give us some indication too, but we'll get this all sorted quickly, I promise.'

'Thank you.' Amber managed a weak smile in response. 'Will I be able to listen to the baby's heartbeat too, just so I know he or she is okay in there with all of this going on.'

'Of course. If you get onto the examination table we can do that first, so you can relax a bit.' The chances of Amber relaxing any time soon were almost zero and Nadia wished there was a way to reassure her that, just because she hadn't stuck to her diet, it didn't make her a bad mother. There were far too many people who didn't have anywhere near the concern Amber was demonstrating for the children they already had, and they were the ones who needed to feel guilty. The trouble was that deadbeat parents never did and it looked more and more like she was going to have to count her ex-husband among that number.

* * *

The end of the day – when all the clinics and home visits were over and there was a good chance of most of the team being at the unit – was something Frankie looked forward to. On busy days, there was barely the chance to catch up with her colleagues who, over the years, had become her closest friends, too. Nadia had already texted to say she'd headed off to collect the children, while Frankie had been doing some routine home visits as part of the new initiative to give MCAs a broader role. It had fired up her desire to complete the midwifery training she'd started before she'd had Nadia and Hari, and it was beginning to feel like she might finally get there one day, after all these years. She could have headed straight back to the flat after her last home visit, but she knew that some of the other midwives would be finishing their working day too and having a catch up in the staffroom. And it felt like ages since she'd done that.

Helping Nadia out with the children was an absolute pleasure, but it also meant that time to just hang out after work and chat was mostly a thing of the past these days. There was a second small team of midwives, who it suited – for various reasons – to work the overnight shifts at the unit, covering any deliveries in progress, or ladies who went into labour out of hours. It meant that, mostly, there were less unsocial hours than there might have been for everyone else, which was a good fit for Nadia as a single mum. Frankie needed to be available whenever her daughter was on call to cover childcare and despite Nadia joining the team, they were still at full stretch and relying on agency staff to cover some of the shifts. Sometimes Frankie wished she could fast-forward the completion of her training so she could fill in for the other midwives, but for now her daughter needed her even more than the unit did.

As Frankie headed down the corridor to the staffroom, she could hear music playing and a female voice loudly chanting what sounded like a dance count: 'Five, six, seven, eight!'

Reaching the open door, she almost got knocked back into the corridor by Gwen, who came twirling towards her like a whirling dervish before twirling back towards Bobby, who was holding her hand, and then dipping backwards over his arm like something out of Strictly.

'Wow, I wasn't expecting that!'

'You're just in time to catch the end of Gwen's demonstration and thankfully Bobby volunteered to stand in for Barry, otherwise I'd have had to try.' Anna laughed. 'I might be tall enough to take the man's role, but since I had the twins any heavy lifting definitely has risks of its own!'

'Who are you calling heavy lifting?' Gwen poked her tongue out. 'My Barry assures me I'm as light as a feather, but then if he values his life he wouldn't dare say otherwise.'

'True. But the question is, what's all this in aid of?'

'Our dance teacher, Nicky, has chosen me and Barry to represent the Port Agnes Quicksteppers in the Three Ports Dance Extravaganza and I was borrowing Bobby to demonstrate our routine.'

'Mighty impressive it is too.' Izzy raised her eyebrows as she spoke and it was lovely to see her looking more like her old self. She'd had an incredibly tough time over the autumn and everyone in the team had been worried about her.

'I've got a whole new respect for Barry.' Bobby looked at Gwen. 'I mean, we knew you kept him on his toes, but this is another level.'

'You know what I always say: trying something new never fails to spice things up and we've both got a lot bendier since we started Nicky's classes, which has all sorts of benefits, let me tell you!'

'Please don't tell us.' Jess pretended to put her hands over her ears and everyone laughed. There'd been more than enough of Gwen's stories over the years to leave them all in no doubt where the conversation was heading and sometimes Frankie could barely look at Barry when they met up.

'Okay, if you don't want to hear how good things can be in your sixties if you work at it, Jess, you can at least tell us what's going on with you?' Gwen's tone made it clear she wasn't in the least bit offended, although Frankie wasn't sure it would be possible to offend her if they tried. 'How's Dexter?'

'He's good and we're almost at the point of deciding to try IVF next year.' Jess made it sound so casual, but there was no pretending it had been a snap decision. Jess and her partner were already parents to his stepson, Riley, but it had been Jess's infertility that had been the reason her ex-husband had given for the breakdown of their marriage. The fact that he was a lying, cheating scumbag seemed to have escaped him, but Frankie knew the decision to go down the infertility treatment route wouldn't have been easy for Jess.

'Nicole said she'd been talking to you about it and it'll be great if you can support each other through it.' Izzy reached out and squeezed Jess's hand. Nicole was a former patient, whose baby had been stillborn during the summer. Frankie and the rest of the team had witnessed how much Izzy had done to help Nicole through it, even during the midst of her own grief. Nicole had already been through IVF to conceive baby Gracie, so trying again was going to be even more of an emotional rollercoaster.

'I'm hoping we can.' Jess smiled at Izzy and then looked towards where Bobby, Ella and Anna were standing. 'But a little birdie tells me I'm not the only one of the team who's going to be trying for a baby.'

'Don't look at me!' Ella widened her eyes. 'I've got the wedding to get through first and Mum is still trying to turn it into a much bigger event than either me or Dan want it to be. I can't even imagine what kind of overdrive she'd go into if I told her she was going to be a grandma.'

'Don't look at me either. The twins are more than enough for me and Brae, even if I wasn't as old as the hills.' Anna laughed and suddenly all eyes were on Bobby.

'Toni told you then?' He looked at Jess, who nodded. 'I know you're all probably going to say we're mad, given that we've only just had Ionie, but Toni wants to have another baby before she gets to forty. So we're going to try next year because she doesn't want to come back to work and then go off on maternity leave straight away.'

'She did talk to me and Ella about it, but we obviously wouldn't have said anything until you guys did.' Anna turned to Bobby. 'Toni knows there'll always be a place for her here, if and when she decides it's time to come back to work.'

'It sounds like Noah might be very busy with christenings next year.' Izzy smiled and Emily clapped her hands together.

'He's decided to stay on as the vicar of St Jude's then? That's great news.'

'For a while he wasn't sure, but over the last two weeks he's got more and more certain that it's where he wants to be and what he wants to do.'

'There's so much going on, I knew I was long overdue an end-of-the-day catch-up with you lot.' Almost as soon as the words were out of Frankie's mouth, she wished she hadn't said them, especially when Gwen turned towards her.

'I was about to say the same, but we haven't had any update from you or Emily yet.'

'Same old same old here.' Emily shrugged. 'I'm studying hard at uni, going on disappointing Tinder dates and working with you guys, so nothing new to report sadly.'

'Nothing new to report here either.' Frankie tried to keep her tone neutral, but Gwen knew her far too well, and the expression on her friend's face told her she'd been rumbled. As casual as she was trying to pretend things were with Guy, and as much as they'd tried to hide the progress of their relationship from both of their daughters, there was no fooling Gwen.

'Well something's putting a spring in your step and making you hum cheerful little tunes all the time.'

'It's having Nadia and the kids home, that's all.'

'Hmm. If you say so.' Gwen gave her a knowing look. 'I'm counting on all of you to come and cheer me and Barry on at the dance competition by the way.'

'Absolutely.' At that moment Frankie would have agreed to have her head shaved, if it meant they could change the subject, and the rest of the team seemed happy to agree to witness Gwen's big moment too. Whatever happened, with Gwen taking centre stage, it was bound to be entertaining.

'That's a date then.' Frankie added the event to the calendar on her phone, just as a text popped up.

✉ Message from Guy

Hello gorgeous. Hope you've had a great day. I know we weren't due to meet tonight, but I wondered if you fancied a walk around the harbour and a quick drink somewhere? We can pick up a takeaway for you and Nadia on the way home xxx

Frankie wasn't going to risk replying with Gwen liable to peer over her shoulder at any moment, but she already knew she'd be saying yes as soon as she got the chance. Guy wanting to spend as much time with her as he did was lovely, but the fact he was always thinking about what Nadia and the children might need too made him all the more special. And, whatever she might try to pretend to Gwen and the others, she'd already fallen for Jess's dad, hook, line and sinker.

12

There were rows of Christmas lights strung between the narrow streets around the harbour in Port Agnes already, but they wouldn't be illuminated until the Christmas light switch-on in December. Every time Frankie took the children home from school, or they passed anywhere near the harbour where the big Christmas tree had already been sited, Remi would ask how many days were left until the lights were switched on. Even though she'd spent her first two Christmases in England, she obviously had no recollection of them and Frankie was almost as excited as she was to share all of Port Agnes's Christmas traditions with her grandchildren.

Gwen had been spot on when she'd said that Frankie seemed happier than she'd been in years. Despite the overcrowding in the flat, having Nadia and her grandchildren home was worth every queue for the bathroom and every broken night's sleep. And walking hand in hand around the harbour with Guy, looking out to the lights twinkling in the hotel on the Sisters of Agnes Island, life felt pretty perfect. She probably wouldn't have risked holding his hand in public if it hadn't been a cold evening that seemed to be keeping all the locals huddling by a fireside somewhere, either at home or in one of the cosy local pubs.

'Are you bringing Riley to see the lights get switched on?' They'd stopped to look up at the big Christmas tree as Frankie spoke. She'd have loved to arrange with Nadia to meet up with Guy and his family for the illumination, and she was almost certain neither of their daughters would object, but it wasn't them she was worried about. Hari and Bhavna were still dropping unsubtle hints about Frankie and Advik getting back together one day. It was like her mother had a sixth sense that something was going on, and just the night before, Bhavna had left her a voicemail filled with unwelcome advice.

'I'm ringing to see whether you've come to your senses yet, Firaki?' As soon she heard the first part of her mother's voicemail, she should probably have deleted the rest, but she couldn't seem to stop herself from listening to it, even though she already knew what was coming.

'It's not too late to make things right with Advik, but it will be if you leave it much longer. You've made some ridiculous decisions in your time, but this is definitely the worst and Hari thinks so too. You're too old for all this and as for going back to university... Words fail me.' It was at that point that Frankie hit the key to delete the message. But just because it wasn't there any more, it didn't mean she had any chance of silencing her mother. She'd keep on about her favourite subject until there was no breath left in her body. Frankie could have coped with all of that without worrying about it too much – after all she'd spent more than half a lifetime being a permanent disappointment to her mother – but it was the fact that Hari agreed with Bhavna that caused her so many sleepless nights. Being a disappointment to her son hurt Frankie far more than her mother's harsh words ever could.

'Yes, we'll all be here.' Guy's words brought her back to the present and she pushed her worries about Hari to the back of her mind. 'Jess has got so many plans for Riley this Christmas and I think she's even more excited than he is. I was wondering if we could do something together with all the kids too?'

'Is there any room in Riley's schedule for that?' Frankie looked up at him as she spoke and her stomach did the loop the loop thing it always seemed to do when he smiled back at her, his eyes twinkling with a mischief that made her feel thirty years younger.

'Well one thing she seems to have forgotten is a pantomime and they're putting *Jack and the Beanstalk* on at the Tom Thumb Theatre in Port Kara. It only seats about sixty people, so we'll need to book seats soon if we're going to have any hope of getting some.'

'It sounds good to me. Everyone needs a fairy tale at Christmas.'

'I've already got mine.' Guy laughed as she rolled her eyes and nudged him in the side.

'I suppose you think that's a smooth line, do you?'

'No, I knew it was embarrassing even before I said it, but I don't care, because it's true.'

'Oh, you old romantic.' Frankie couldn't help laughing too. It was probably what she liked best about Guy, the fact they could laugh together so easily. She might even have said she loved that about him, but she wasn't ready to admit that yet. Her head said it was far too soon, even if her heart said otherwise. Instead, she lifted her heels off the floor and reached up to kiss him, the loop the loop in her stomach going up another gear. For a moment, the rest of the world disappeared, but then she heard it: a sharp voice cutting through the cold night air.

'Mum! What the hell do you think you're doing?' Before she even turned around, she knew it was Hari. When she finally looked at him, horror was written all over his face.

'It's not... It isn't...' The words wouldn't come out because nothing she could say was going to change the way Hari was looking at her. Pretending what he'd witnessed was anything other than it seemed would just make things worse. 'Please, just let me explain.'

'There's nothing to explain.' Hari's lip curled and a muscle was going in his cheek. 'At least a lot of stuff makes sense now. I suppose he's the reason you threw away everything with Dad and broke up the family. Nani said there'd be something behind all of this. How could you be so selfish?'

'You can't talk to your mother like that.' Guy's tone was firm but icily calm, and Frankie reached out to put a hand on his arm.

'Don't you dare tell me what I can do!' Hari almost spat the words in their direction. 'I didn't want to believe what Nani said was true. I could accept you splitting up, at least I tried to, but now I know this has been going on for God knows how long behind my father's back... I can't even look at you.'

'Hari, stop it, this is all getting out of hand. Let's sit down and talk about it.'

'You can forget about me sitting down and talking to you about anything.' Hari's lip was still curling. 'I was coming to surprise you, but it was me who got the surprise, wasn't it?'

'Hari please, just wait, I don't want you going off like this.' Frankie was pleading with him now.

'We don't always get what we want do we, Mother?' Hari was already walking away from her and she knew, even if she ran after him, he still wouldn't listen. She just hoped that there'd come a point when he'd be ready. Because if her son refused to talk to her, there was no chance of her ever being happy again, let alone having Guy's fairy tale ending.

* * *

Nadia had finally got Mo off to sleep. He'd been in one of his clingy moods and she couldn't afford to let him work through it, because if he kicked off about her leaving the room, there was no chance of Remi getting to sleep either. Instead, she had to squeeze up next to him on the bottom bunk, her own single bed just an arm's reach away. Creeping out once he was finally asleep, without disturbing either him or Remi, was another challenge and she'd had to stuff a hand into her mouth to stifle a scream when she'd trodden on a small metal aeroplane on the way out.

Pouring herself a glass of rosé before she tackled the washing up felt like a treat well-earned. Her mother had texted to say she was doing a bit of late-night shopping in Port Kara after work, but that she'd pick up a takeaway on the way home. There was a good chance Nadia and her mum would finish off the bottle of wine when she got in.

The one upside about her marriage falling apart, and Ryan's decision to increasingly pretend he didn't have two young children, was that she'd been able to come home to Cornwall. Her mum had been brilliant about accommodating the three of them, and had bent over backwards to help out with school runs. Nadia was busy thinking up ways to say thank you as she washed up the kids' dinner plates, when she heard a voice behind her which made her jump so suddenly that the plate she'd been holding slipped out of her hands and smashed against the tiled floor.

'Bloody hell!' Putting her hands on top of one another on her chest, as if she was clutching her heart from the outside, she turned and saw her mum. 'You nearly killed me.'

'Sorry love—' Frankie had barely got the words out before she started to cry and Nadia put her arms around her mother, ignoring the shards of broken plate on the floor. Something bad had to have happened.

'Is it Nani?'

'No, yes, no.' Frankie started to cry again, her sobs strangling the words she was trying to get out and Nadia still had no idea what the problem was.

'It's all right, Mum, just sit down and I'll get you some water. Then you can try again, but whatever it is, I'm here. Okay?'

'I'm sorry, I'm sorry.' Even when Frankie's words started to make sense, all she seemed to be offering was an apology, over and over again, but Nadia still had no idea why.

'What for?' She crouched in front of her mother, one hand over Frankie's. 'Whatever it is, I'm sure we can sort it out.'

'Not with Hari, he's never going to forgive me.' Frankie shook her head. 'The look on his face... He was horrified, but I didn't plan any of this and I definitely didn't expect to have those sort of feelings for someone.'

'You're talking about Guy? Hari's found out about you and Guy?' Nadia could have wept too. Except it would have been with relief. All sorts of scenarios had run through her head, from her mother making a life-changing mistake at work to a family member being gravely ill, and everything in between. This was nothing, but her mother was staring at her open-mouthed.

'You know about Guy?'

'Of course I do.' Nadia smiled and squeezed one of her mother's knees. 'We live in a shoebox-sized flat together. How the heck did you think you'd manage to keep a secret like that?'

'I thought you'd believe that we were just friends.'

'Hmm, but I've got eyes and ears and so has Jess.' She smiled again. 'It's okay, Mum, I'm pleased for you, I really am. Guy's great and Jess is over the moon about it.' Her mother's frozen expression was evidence of how little impact Nadia's words were having on her. 'How did Hari find out?'

'He saw us kissing.' Frankie couldn't meet her eyes and for a split second Nadia had the urge to laugh. Frankie was like a

teenager who'd been caught smoking behind the bins. But
however ridiculous Hari's overreaction might have been, her
mother definitely didn't consider it a laughing matter.

'Hari's just being Hari. You know how he is. If things don't go
exactly the way he thinks they should, he makes it into a big
drama. He's got a bit too much of Nani in him and the two of them
wind each other up. Sometimes I don't know how Uma puts up
with him.' Nadia sighed. 'But he always gets over it in the end.'

'He thinks Guy's the reason why I split up with your father.'
Frankie sniffed.

'That's ridiculous. I love you both, but you and Dad were
completely wrong for each other. Even if you had left him for
someone else, I think I'd have cheered. You're much better apart.
Both of you.'

'I know that and I'm certain your dad does too, but Nani has
never given up on us getting back together and neither has Hari.'
Frankie shivered. 'I dread to think what your grandmother is going
to say once Hari's spoken to her. She already thinks I'm a disgrace
to the family and a total let-down as a daughter.'

'You could never be a let-down. Nani just lives in a different
world sometimes. I'm so glad I've got a mother like you instead of
her, because whatever cock-ups I've made, I've always known you
had my back and that you just wanted me to be happy.' Nadia
squeezed her knee again. 'That's exactly what I want for you, too,
and so should Hari, and Nani come to that.'

'Your brother wouldn't even look at me and every time I try to
call him, it goes straight to voicemail. I can live with my mother
ignoring me, but not Hari.'

'Do you want me to talk to him? And Nani?' Nadia would do it
in a heartbeat, even if trying to reason with her grandmother was
as likely as the artificial grass in her back garden suddenly starting
to grow. Hari was a different matter, though. He was her little

brother and she was capable of putting him in his place if needs be. Right now was definitely one of those times. If Hari tried to stop Frankie being happy, just because he'd rather his parents were still unhappily married, then it was time for him to get a short, sharp lesson in reality from his big sister.

'I don't know if it would help.' Frankie's eyes met hers. 'But I can't leave things like this and I can't give up seeing Guy either.'

'Why the hell should you!' The skin on Nadia's scalp prickled at the thought that her mother had even considered it. She'd respected her mum's decision not to want to shout about the relationship, but it had been obvious how happy Guy made her. Her mother had spent her whole life putting other people first and she was still doing it now, but there was no way Nadia was going to stand by and watch her sacrifice her relationship with Guy just to fit in with what her brother and grandmother thought was right. 'You light up every time you talk about Guy, that's why it's so obvious. What does Hari expect you to do, get back with Dad just because that would suit him best? As for Nani, nothing either you or I have ever done has impressed her, because it's always been Hari from the moment he was born.'

'She wanted a boy, but she got me and she never tires of telling me how the trauma of giving birth meant she'd never have another child. So she couldn't even try again and get it right second time around.'

'But she thinks you did.' Nadia caught her mother's eye, the look silently acknowledging the truth. It was why her grandmother had always thought her son-in-law was more important than her daughter. Just because Bhavna was a woman, it didn't mean she wasn't capable of misogyny.

'I knew from the moment I held you in in my arms that I'd got everything I ever wanted.' Frankie's eyes went glassy again as she looked at Nadia. 'But I love Hari too and I can't bear the thought that he feels I've betrayed him in some way. I wanted to be honest, but with the wedding coming up, I thought it was better to wait, because I knew he wouldn't take it well.'

'He needs reminding that the world doesn't revolve around him, even if Nani has spent his whole life telling him it does. I doubt very much he'll have gone straight back to London, so he'll probably be staying at Dad's. If I go over early tomorrow, I should catch them before Dad leaves for work or Hari goes home.' Nadia was on call for home deliveries from noon until midnight, but she had plenty of time to give Hari a piece of her mind before then.

'Are you sure? I don't want to put you in an awkward position.'

'You won't be, because I'm on your side for this and everything else.'

Frankie leant forward and put her arms around Nadia. 'I'm so happy you're home, darling, and I'm so sorry I'm causing you all this hassle on top of everything else you're dealing with.'

'You causing me hassle?' Nadia moved back slightly so she could look at her mother. 'I think we can safely say it's the other way around. You've been brilliant ever since I came home.'

'You might not think I'm brilliant when I tell you what else I've got to confess.'

'What is it?' Nadia widened her eyes and Frankie finally managed a half-smile.

'I forgot all about the takeaway.'

'Now that's a game changer.' Nadia paused for a moment. 'At least it would be if Chopsticks didn't have a promise on their website to deliver within thirty minutes of placing an order.'

'If only everything was as easily solved.'

'We'll get it all sorted with Hari, I promise, but for now I'm going to pour you a glass of wine and give the takeaway a ring, because there's nothing in the world that isn't improved with a cold glass of rosé and a plate of prawn crackers.'

'How did my little girl get so wise?'

'I learned from the best.' Nadia smiled again as Frankie stroked her hair, and for a few seconds it was as if she was eight years old again, when her mother had seemed capable of solving anything. This was Nadia's chance to return the favour and she was already praying she could pull it off.

13

Nadia loved her father, but there was no pretending it wasn't a different sort of love to what she felt for her mum. She loved Advik because he was her dad, but there'd always been a slightly unbridgeable distance between them, as if he was somehow holding her at arm's length. It wasn't that he didn't do the things fathers were supposed to do. He'd prided himself on providing well for his family and he'd been there for the major events in her life, and had seemed to revel in fulfilling his role as father of the bride when she'd married Ryan. But they'd never been the sort to just sit down and really talk, the way she'd always been able to with her mum.

If Frankie hadn't been her mother, and they'd met through work instead, Nadia was certain they'd have been close friends anyway. They just seemed to get each other, in a way that didn't necessarily happen just because you were mother and daughter. She'd seen how some of her friends struggled with those kinds of relationships and Izzy's mother in particular sounded like a complete nightmare. But the thought of what Nadia's childhood would have been like if she'd been raised by Nani instead of

Frankie made her shiver. She'd never stop being grateful for being her mother's daughter and it was about time Hari started appreciating how lucky he was too.

Pulling up outside the house she'd grown up in, and knowing that there was no longer any trace of her mother inside, still felt odd. Whatever twisted notion Nani and Hari had got into their heads about the way they thought her mother had ended her marriage, not even they could say she hadn't been more than fair in terms of how she'd handled the financial side of things. Advik had been given the opportunity to remortgage the house to give Frankie a small pay-off and would keep a far more sizeable chunk of equity and his pensions intact. But as far as Nadia knew, her father still hadn't finalised the remortgage and perhaps her mother had been too soft on him, too.

Even if her brother and grandmother didn't appreciate how fair Frankie had been, at least her father seemed to and it meant that her parents' relationship was more cordial than it might be otherwise. Nadia knew how important that had been to her mother, for her and Hari's sake as much as anything. Frankie even seemed willing to accept Advik's attempts to keep control of everything related to Hari's wedding. Advik liked to do things the way he thought they should be done and he was the reason Hari had ended up studying law, when he'd originally planned to go into property management with his best friend. Despite not being related, her father and grandmother were very alike in lots of ways too, and small doses were the best solution Nadia had found of dealing with them both. She loved her brother dearly, but when she heard her father's or grandmother's words coming out of his mouth, she had to bite her tongue. Maybe that was the problem. She and her mother had been biting their tongues for far too long.

'*Beta*, what are you doing here?' Her father's hair was still sticking up on one side when he answered the door, even though his burgundy pyjamas looked as if they'd been freshly ironed. *Beta* was a term of affection he sometimes used. Even if she had got him out of bed, he clearly wasn't upset about it. Despite still having a key to the house, she wouldn't dream of using it now that her mother no longer lived there, which was telling in itself.

'Is Hari here?' Nadia cut to the chase as her father ushered her over the threshold. She had no doubt the two of them had been talking about her mother and she didn't want them labouring under any illusion that she was going to tolerate that. It was a weird feeling, a bit like when she'd had to march into Remi's school, when they were still in New Zealand, to meet with the teachers about two other little girls who'd been picking on her daughter and making her life a misery. It had brought out the tigress in Nadia and the situation with her mother was doing the same.

'He is, but he's still asleep. We had a bit of a night of it last night.'

'I bet you did.' Nadia was more than ready to tip a bowl of cold water over her brother's head to give him the wake-up call he deserved, in more ways than one.

'Your mother told you about him catching her with her fancy man then?'

'Fancy man?' Nadia couldn't help laughing. 'God you're even more like Nani than I thought you were. I suppose Hari was straight on the phone to her, too?'

'He called her on the way over here. She wasn't impressed.'

'It's none of her business and, given that you're divorced, it's none of your business any more either.' Nadia was still bristling.

'Your brother and grandmother seem to think it's why she left.' Her father had followed her down the hallway and into the kitchen.

'And is that what you think?' Turning to look at him, she tried to work out what was behind his expression and whether it would bother him if what Hari had suggested was true.

'It doesn't matter any more; she left either way.' Advik shrugged. 'Coffee?'

'I think it would matter to me.' Nadia gritted her teeth. She'd never had this sort of conversation with her father before, but they were having it now whether he liked it or not. 'In fact, I know it would, because it *did* matter to me why Ryan left. If his feelings for me had just changed, like he said they had, it still would have hurt like hell. But the fact there was someone else involved, almost since the moment our plane touched down in Auckland, makes me wonder if he ever really loved me. So I can't believe you don't care and I can't believe you don't know Mum better than that, after all the years you spent together.'

'It's not my job to defend your mother; she's made her own choices.' Advik shifted from foot to foot, looking distinctly uncomfortable.

'She's been really fair to you, Dad, and you know it. The least you can do is be fair to her too.'

'I don't want your brother falling out with me as well.' Advik turned away from her, putting a pod into the coffee machine despite the fact she hadn't said she wanted a drink.

'That's a cop-out and if you don't say something, there's a good chance he'll end up falling out with me as well as Mum. I suppose that's not your problem either, is it?'

'You and your mother have always been as thick as thieves. Hari knows that as well as I do.'

'What's that supposed to mean?' The volume of Nadia's voice had increased considerably, and her father's unwillingness to take any responsibility for setting Hari straight wasn't helping her efforts to stay calm.

'What he means is that you'd cover for our mother whatever

JO BARTLETT

was happening. In fact, you probably have been for years.' Hari suddenly appeared in the doorway of the kitchen, looking like a younger version of their father, even down to the hair flattened on one side.

'I'm not covering anything up because there's nothing to cover. Mum's been seeing Guy for a few months, that's all. She didn't leave Dad for him or anyone else for that matter. They just weren't any good for each other, surely you must be able to see that? They're both happier now and I'm glad Mum had the courage to make that happen.'

'Oh, you can bet she's happier, she's got exactly what she wanted and left Dad with nothing.'

'Are you for real?' Nadia could barely believe she was hearing the words that were coming out of Hari's mouth. He was in his early thirties; quite where he'd got his Victorian morality from would have been a mystery, if he hadn't been so clearly influenced by Nani. 'Mum left Dad with more than 80 per cent of what they owned together and he's kept the house and his pensions. She's the one starting again in her fifties and going back to uni on top of everything else.'

'That was her choice!' Hari's was shouting now and Nadia was having to fight to stop herself from mirroring him.

'So what, you'd rather they stayed together and were much unhappier, just to fit in with what suits you, or what Nani thinks is the done thing?'

'She thinks people give up on marriage far too soon these days and do you know what, I think she's right. When I make the promises I'm going to make to Uma, I'll mean them and I won't be looking for an easy route out a few years down the line.' Whether or not Hari's comments were directed at Nadia, they hit her straight in the chest, and for a moment or two neither of them said anything. 'I wasn't talking about you, I just—'

'That's the thing. Whether you realise it or not, you *were* talking about me, because if you're judging Mum, you're judging me too.' Nadia had to bite her lip to stop herself from crying and when Hari tried to reach out to her, she flinched away. 'Come and tell me how easy all of this is when you've been married at least ten years, but I've no doubt you'll do it all perfectly Hari, because you always do.'

'Don't be like that, I don't want us falling out.'

'Unless you apologise to Mum, we already have.'

'Why should I apologise when she's the one who was lying?' Hari was straight back up on his high horse again. 'I'm not even sure if I want her at the wedding, not if it makes things awkward for Dad or Nani.'

'Are you going to stand by and let him do this to Mum?' Nadia jaw was so tense it was hard to even speak. But when her father shrugged again, her decision was made. 'Okay, I wasn't going to say this now, but if Hari's going to be as blind to what's going on here as he seems to be, then I've got no choice.'

'What are you talking about?' Even as Hari asked the question, the realisation seemed to hit her father.

'Did you not see the cups next to the coffee machine?' Nadia gestured towards the *I'm Yours* and *He's Mine* mugs on the kitchen counter. 'Or the silk scarves hanging off the coat rack in the hallway, or that teddy with the love-heart T-shirt next to the cookbooks? Are you really that blinkered, Hari? Because just in case you need me to explain it to you in the simplest of terms: Dad's seeing someone too. That's right, isn't it?'

'That's not the point.' Her father's foot shifting was in danger of turning into a dance routine. 'I didn't meet Caroline until this spring; she had nothing to do with the marriage ending.'

'Neither did Guy!' Nadia had finally lost the battle not to shout.

'And if you don't want Mum at the wedding, you can cancel my place too.'

Whatever it was Hari said in response, she didn't hear him, because she was already slamming the kitchen door behind her and ten seconds later she was wheel-spinning off the driveway. Tears of anger and frustration were streaming down her face before she even reached the end of the road. Rowing with her father and brother hadn't been in the plan, but it felt as though things had changed irrevocably between them. Worse than that, she'd let her mum down and probably made things even worse between her and Hari than they'd been already. If Hari left Frankie out of the wedding, it would break her heart, and all Nadia had done was make that more likely.

* * *

The day after her confrontation with Hari and her father, Nadia volunteered to help out at the winter fair at the school. A combination of guilt at not being as involved in school events as a lot of the other mums were and the steely gaze of Miss Renfrew as she sought out volunteers, meant Nadia was doing one of the first shifts. Frankie had offered to take Mo with her to Sunday lunch at Gwen and Barry's, but Remi would be coming to the fair – the five pounds of pocket money her grandmother had given her burning a hole in her pocket.

Nadia had been grateful for the two back-to-back home deliveries she'd got when she was on call the day before. It meant she didn't have much chance to talk to Frankie about what had happened with Advik and Hari. All she'd admitted to was giving them both some things to think about and she hadn't mentioned that her father was dating someone too. Advik had tried to phone her a couple of times, but she'd let it go to voicemail, too exhausted to deal with any of it. The wedding was still over six months away and there was plenty of time for everyone to calm down. Hari would come to his senses long before then and give Frankie the apology she deserved; at least, that's what Nadia was trying to convince herself.

Stifling a yawn, she headed through the gates into the playground, with Remi clutching her hand. The home births the day before might have provided a welcome distraction from what was going on in her own family, but that didn't mean she wasn't exhausted.

The PTA mums, who had an uncanny knack of making Nadia feel woefully inadequate even when they weren't trying to, were wearing matching angel outfits and handing out the assignments to other volunteers as they entered the school hall. It was nowhere near big enough to comfortably accommodate the fair and the crowd of people they were expecting to attract. As a result, the stalls were so close together there was barely room to squeeze between them to get around the back.

'Ah, Remi's mum.' The tallest of the PTA 'angels' addressed her by the title they all used, none of them seeming to know or care that she had a name of her own, or proffering their own names in response. 'We've put you on the trash and treasure stall.'

'Okay, no problem. Is there anything I need to know?'

'Emma Collins is supposed to be coming to run it, and you'll just need to help out with whatever she wants, but she's not here yet.' Angel number one glanced down at her clipboard, before looking up at Nadia again and giving her a tight smile. 'I'm sure you can cope, though. It's just a case of getting people to part with as much money as you can for the donated stuff Emma has been collecting. You'll be surprised what people will pay out for boot sale rejects, especially the kids.'

'Tell me about it. Remi's got five pounds to spend and I can only imagine what we'll end up carting home.' Nadia's daughter had already broken off from her and was standing about ten feet away, with her face pressed up against the 'guess the number of jelly beans' jar, as if she might be able to work out the answer if she looked closely enough.

'Hmm, yes, well I wouldn't want any of it in my house, but you know, each to their own.' Angel number one handed Nadia a Tupperware box, filled about a third of the way with change.

'I'll try to leave some of the stock for other people. Come on Remi.' Nadia painted on a smile and took the box over to the trash and treasure stall, grabbing her daughter's hand on the way past. She couldn't help smiling at the sight of three *World's Best Teacher'* mugs stacked next to each other, obviously donated by staff members who were probably inundated with the things at the end of every academic year. To be fair to Angel number one, the rest of the stuff on the stall was more trash than treasure, although Remi had already spotted something Nadia had a horrible feeling would end up coming home with them. It was a porcelain figurine of a girl clutching a kitten under one arm and a puppy under the other, in the sort of muted washed-out colours that still somehow clashed with everything. It was hideous and just the sort of thing she'd envisaged her daughter choosing.

An hour later, it was becoming increasingly clear that Emma Collins wasn't going to turn up and take over the running of the stall, even before one of the PTA angels stopped by to inform Nadia that Emma had texted saying she had a sickness bug. Half an hour after that, one of the other mums had kindly offered to take Remi to do a circuit of the stalls, after the little girl had announced loudly for about the fifteenth time, that standing behind the stall was boring.

By the time Remi came back, every penny of the five pounds had been spent and she was clutching a plastic snake she'd picked out of the lucky dip and a box of luxury Christmas crackers she'd apparently won on the tombola.

'I thought you wanted to buy the ornament?' Nadia put her arm around her daughter's shoulders after she'd thanked the mum who'd taken Remi around the fair and watched her walk away to freedom. There was still another hour left to go before Nadia could follow suit.

'Please can you get it for me?' Remi turned the puppy-dog eyes she used to such good effect towards her mother, delivering the line they both knew would seal the deal if that didn't work. 'Daddy always buys me things.'

Irritation made Nadia's scalp tingle. Whether she was conscious of it or not, Remi had learned that she could manipulate her mother's guilt to her benefit and Nadia was determined to get more of a balance so that her daughter didn't turn into a tiny version of her Uncle Hari. She'd learned a long time ago to bite back the urge to respond with *'Well, Daddy isn't here!'*. It just upset them both. Everything she'd read told her to take a calm approach and ignore the attempts at manipulation, rather than giving in every time or letting it make her angry. Distraction and rewarding good behaviour was what the self-help sites recommended. Thankfully she'd had the foresight to bring a colouring book, which meant there might be a small chance of keeping Remi occupied until the fair ended. 'If you colour in two of the pictures in your book I'll get the ornament for you.'

'Okay. I'll do the Rudolf one for you Mummy.' Remi leant against her for a moment, seeming to sense that she needed some affection, but suddenly she tore herself away from her mother's side. 'Daisy!'

'Remi!' The two little girls called out to each other as if they hadn't seen one another in months, rather than since the afternoon before at school.

'You look like you had enough at least an hour ago.' Hamish smiled and despite the warmth of his tone, Nadia felt instantly self-conscious. Her hair had a habit of becoming more and more unruly over the course of the day if she didn't pay attention to it, which was just one more thing Ryan had found to criticise about her.

'I'm cultivating a dragged-through-the-garden-hedge-back-wards look, as an antidote to the PTA angels.' Nadia pulled a face, but Hamish was shaking his head.

'You look great, just worn-out that's all. Are you running the stall on your own?'

'The woman I was supposed to be helping isn't well and I was on call until half-past two this morning.' Nadia glanced at her watch. 'Only fifty-three minutes left to go now though.'

'Not that you're counting down!' Hamish laughed. 'I can cover for the rest of the fair if you want to call it a day.'

'I might as well see it through to the end. I don't want the angels thinking I can't stick it out.'

'Do you really care what they think?' Hamish's eyes searched her face and she was glad of the opportunity to look towards their daughters, to see if they were listening. But Remi was busy explaining to her best friend exactly why the figurine she wanted to buy was so precious.

'I don't, but I do want them to include Remi in things. She had a tough time at her first school in New Zealand and I want things to be different this time. If that means doing a three-hour stint on the trash and treasure stall, that's fine with me.'

'I don't think there's any danger of Remi being left out this time, not with Daisy wanting to be glued to her side all the time, but I get what you mean.' Hamish leant in closer and her pulse quickened as he lowered his voice. 'And talking of being judged, have you heard about the nativity play?'

'Do I want to know?' He was standing so close that Nadia could smell the citrusy scent of his aftershave. Thank God they were in an overcrowded school hall, otherwise her body might have responded in a way that she'd never have lived down with the PTA mums. Not to mention making things very awkward with Hamish.

'They've decided we're all handmaking the kids' costumes again and this time, they're not just suggesting it, it's compulsory. No one's allowed to buy them! I was relying on Amazon Prime to sort out Daisy's sheep costume.'

'They're making it an actual *rule* that we aren't allowed to buy them?' Nadia turned her head to look at him and if they'd been a few inches closer, her lips might have made contact with his skin. Luckily the thought of having to hand-sew a donkey costume was enough to kill off any inappropriate thoughts.

'Apparently, it's more authentic, not to mention environmentally friendly. According to Saskia, who chairs the PTA, people can make the costumes with stuff they find lying around the house.' He grinned. 'But I must have put my sheep's fleece material away somewhere very safe, because I can't find it anywhere.'

'Poor Remi. Never mind looking like a donkey, she's definitely going to look like an ass if I try to sew her costume. If I can't fix something with Wonderweb and safety pins, it's a write-off in my house.'

'Maybe we should do what you said before and get together to see what we can come up with. I've already ordered an industrial-sized carton of fabric glue, so I'm sure we can do it if we pool our resources.'

'Gluing a costume together is something I can get behind.' Nadia's body relaxed slightly, as Hamish pulled away. Being that close to him was disconcerting and it felt much safer this way. 'When were you thinking of?'

'One night after work? I could get Saffron to babysit for Daisy, or you could come to me if your mum can have Remi and Mo.'

'Let me speak to her and we can take it from there, but I'm sure we can work something out.'

'You don't know how much I've been hoping you'd say that.' Her pulse started racing again in response to his words. 'I couldn't face the thought of trying to do that on my own. What are friends for, if not to get each other through the hell of school events?'

'I'm glad you asked.' Nadia looked down at the stall, shifting the two remaining '*World's Best Teacher*' mugs six inches to the left for no reason at all. Hamish couldn't have made it clearer that what he was looking for was friendship, something that suited him while his daughter was at school. It was just as well, because there was something about him that made Nadia forget she'd sworn off even considering another relationship. And given that she was even worse at keeping relationships going than she was at being a seamstress, that was definitely for the best.

14

The first Sunday in December was promising to be a busy one. It was also Barry and Gwen's big day at the Dance Extravaganza and even the children were invited to go along and watch.

The leaflets Gwen had brought in and handed to everyone like they were personal invitations, detailed the activities that would be running at the Guildhall in Port Tremellien. As well as a range of competitions between dance schools from the Three Ports area, there would be taster sessions for both children and adults. Remi had been saying for the last few weeks that she wanted to be a dancer when she grew up, and had become obsessed with *Strictly Come Dancing* after Frankie had let her stay up later than usual to watch an episode. If Nadia could get Mo interested in dancing too, that would be even better. Anything that helped her children use up their excess energy outside of the confines of the flat held huge appeal.

'Are you ready sweetheart? We need to get going.' Nadia opened the door of the bedroom and couldn't help smiling. Remi was wearing stripey pale pink and fuchsia tights, her sparkly silver party dress and a feather boa, which her grandmother had worn to a 1920s themed party at Gwen's house earlier in the year.

'Wow, you really do look like you're on *Strictly*.' Nadia knew that was absolutely the right thing to say, even before a smile lit up her daughter's face.

'Nanny's feathers are so pretty, Mummy.'

'They are darling and it was very kind of her to let you have them.'

'She's the best nanny in the whole wide world.' Remi's grin got broader still as she opened her arms to demonstrate just how wide that was. 'And I want to live with her forever.'

'Do you?' Nadia held her breath for a second. It had been almost a week since Remi had last mentioned Ryan, and Mo seemed to have forgotten about him altogether.

'Yes, because I love Nanny and if I wake up in the night, I can have a cuddle with you. And I can see Daisy every day and they sell cookies downstairs, and milkshakes, and yummy brownies.' Remi sounded as if she could go on listing the benefits of living in her grandmother's flat above The Cookie Jar forever. It was great that she seemed so much happier, but Nadia couldn't help worrying that there'd be another wrench to come for her children when they eventually moved out of Frankie's flat. But that was a problem for another day. Today was all about the Three Ports Christmas Dance Extravaganza and Remi was more than ready to go.

Forty minutes later, they'd finally found a parking spot within a walkable distance to the Guildhall. Frankie had lent Nadia her car, and Guy had taken her out for breakfast before they both headed over to the dance competition. She was putting a brave face on the situation with Hari, who still wasn't taking her calls or responding to her texts. But Nadia could tell from how often her mother checked her phone that she was desperately hoping he'd break his silence soon. She was just glad her mother hadn't had a knee-jerk reaction and called things off with Guy, because he was such a nice man and clearly head over heels in love with her mother. How they thought they'd ever keep that quiet when he looked at her the way he did, was beyond Nadia.

Jess had mentioned her past relationship with Guy had not always been what it could have been. But whatever problems they'd had, he clearly adored his daughter, and he was great with Riley, Remi and Mo as well. Nadia was hoping that Guy's experience with Jess would help Frankie keep things in perspective too. She needed to stop panicking and thinking she had to choose between Guy and her son, because Hari had already had things his own way for far too long. Every time Nadia thought about his reaction, and the things he'd said to their mother, she could feel the heat rising up her neck. Hamish's older daughter clearly struggled with the idea of her father dating again, but she was only eighteen, still living at home, and protective of her younger sister. Hari was a thirty-two-year-old man with a life of his own, who didn't seem to realise that his mother was entitled to one too. He needed to grow the hell up.

'Mummy, hurry up!' Remi tugged on her hand as they reached the Guildhall, bringing Nadia's thoughts back to the present. Mo was on his scooter. He'd decided in the last couple of weeks that walking any significant distance was fundamentally against his principles and had insisted the scooter was put in the boot of the car. There was no reasoning with a four-year-old and some battles just weren't worth fighting. They'd just have to hope it would still be outside the building when the competition was over.

'Okay darling, but don't worry, we've got plenty of time.' Music with a samba beat was drifting out of the Guildhall by the time they reached the steps, and the moment they went inside the building Remi had stepped into her idea of heaven. There were dancers in all sorts of outfits, including a group in Celtic costumes, whose shoes tap-tapped as they walked across the wooden floor of the foyer, and another group of children dressed like cats, in black leotards with furry ears attached to their headbands and long tails which looked in danger of taking out the Christmas trees on either side of the desk where the dancers were completing their registration forms.

The Guildhall was a stunning building, with a large main space and a number of other rooms which made it the perfect venue for the event. The crypts beneath the building had been set aside for the competitors to change and prepare for the competition, the old library was being used for the taster sessions and children's activities, and the main hall was hosting the competition itself. There were lots of categories but only one Nadia really couldn't miss – the rumba, which Gwen and Barry were competing in. The rest of the day would be led by whatever caught Remi and Mo's attention. She'd already prebooked them into a tap taster class starting in ten minutes time, and she had a feeling Mo was going to love stomping about and making lots of noise.

'I didn't expect to see you in the taster sessions.' Nadia had barely got the words out when Gwen pulled her into a tight hug.

'Nicky's asked me to help out with some of the classes and it turns out I'm a natural at tap.' Gwen did a couple of step heel taps as she released Nadia, to demonstrate her point, before blowing a kiss in Remi's direction. 'Although I can't begin to compete with Remi's beautiful outfit.'

'I don't think anyone can, but she's going to have to remove the wellies if she wants to join in.' Nadia exchanged a smile with Gwen, as Remi reluctantly pulled off the glittery wellington boots, which she'd insisted completed her outfit. Admittedly, they were the most sparkly items of footwear her daughter owned.

'Right everyone, it's time to get started. My name's Nicky Kirby-

Jones and I'm so excited to have you all here for the first taster session. I can already tell that we're going to have lots of fun.' Gwen's dance teacher was one of those people who radiated the sort of infectious enthusiasm that could make even the most reticent person want to join in. But with a room full of kids keen to try out tap shoes, the atmosphere soon reached fever pitch. For a least ten minutes after the session ended, Nadia could still hear ringing in her ears. The kids loved it though, and after three more twenty-minute sessions, they'd also tried out ballet, street-dance and jazz. Gwen and Nicky had slipped away after the second taster session to prepare for the competition, and one of the teachers from a dance school in Port Kara had taken over for the jazz session.

'What's next Mummy?' Remi was still raring to go, but Mo had sat down several times during the jazz class and he was definitely ready for a break.

'There's less than an hour until Auntie Gwen and Uncle Barry do their dance competition. So how about we go and get a drink and a snack and watch some of the other dancers while we wait for their competition to start and then you can come back and try out a few more things later?'

'Okay. I hope Auntie Gwen is going to win.' Remi had made her own score card, with a number ten drawn on the front and lots of stickers all around the edge, to hold up after Gwen and Barry's dance. It was folded carefully into Nadia's bag.

'Me too darling, but as long as she has fun that's all that matters.' Thankfully the queue for refreshments wasn't too long and a few moments later, Remi was happily munching on a cookie in the shape of a Christmas tree. But Mo's eyes had started to droop before he even got his. Finding a space at the end of one of the rows of seating in the main hall, Nadia pulled him onto her lap, and folded her coat up on Remi's seat for her to sit on so that she'd get a good view. It wasn't long before they spotted the other midwives and their families dotted around the audience. The whole team were out to support Gwen, exactly as they'd promised. There was no sign of Frankie and Guy yet, though, and just as Nadia reached for her phone, a text pinged through.

✉ Message from Mum

Can't find anywhere to park. We'll be there as soon as we can, but whatever you do don't admit to Gwen that I didn't make it in time if I don't get there! Hope Remi and Mo are loving the dancing, see you soon. Love you xxxx

'Daisy!' Remi shot up with excitement at the sight of her best friend, nearly knocking the phone out of Nadia's hand.

'Can we sit with Remi please Daddy?' Daisy had stopped at the end of their row and was staring up at her dad with a look that suggested her entire day would be ruined if he said no.

'I'm sorry angel, I don't think there's any room.' Hamish looked more disappointed than relieved and if someone had put thumb-screws on Nadia, she'd have to admit she felt the same.

'Remi can squeeze on my lap with Mo to watch the competitions, I need to wake him up so he doesn't miss Gwen anyway. If you do the same with Daisy we should just about be able to squash in.' Nadia forced a deliberate shrug. 'But no worries if you'd be more comfortable on the other side, there are a lot more spare seats over there.'

'I don't think I could drag Daisy away from here if I wanted to. If you're sure you don't mind, we'd love to squeeze in with you.'

'Yay!' Remi's reaction sealed the deal, but squeezing in turned out to be an apt description. Nadia's thigh was pressed up against Hamish's and she couldn't have moved it away even if she'd wanted to. There was something everyday but intimate about it all at the same time. Maybe it was because she hadn't had that sort of causal intimacy in such a long while, but either way it felt nice.

'Interpretive dance next. Adult category.' Hamish pulled a face as he looked up from his programme. 'I remember once, in GCSE drama, our teacher making us all pretend to be trees in a forest during a violent storm. I kept getting told off for not *being the tree*. I mean I admire anyone who can let their inhibitions go to that extent, but I've got to admit I don't really get it.'

'You mean you don't use interpretative dance as a way to work through your emotions?' Nadia raised her eyebrows, but she couldn't stop the smile tugging at the corners of her mouth.

'No, but I'd definitely pay for a ticket to see you do that.'

'You couldn't afford a ticket to that particular show.' It had been such a long time that she could barely remember, but this was starting to feel a lot like flirting.

'I'll start saving my money then, but for now we'll just have to see which of the Three Ports is Cornwall's hotbed of interpretive dance.'

'That should do wonders for house prices.' She laughed. 'So it's bound to be a hard-fought competition.'

The first two dance troupes were from Port Agnes and Port Tremellien. Nadia might have been biased, as well as knowing next to nothing about interpretive dance, but in her opinion Nicky's troupe definitely had the edge over the other one. There were plenty of people in the crowd who clearly took it very seriously and the atmosphere was hushed when the final group, from Port Kara, came on to the floor. The lights were lowered and a second later the six members of the dance troupe unfurled light-up butterfly wings. It was an impressive start, but when the lights came back on, it started to go downhill. The lead dancer was wearing a black leotard along with her butterfly wings; it was at least three sizes too small and left nothing to the imagination, particularly when it came to how tightly it fitted around the crotch area. She was clearly relishing taking centre stage and several times when the troupe unfurled their wings as the song reached a key change, she managed to whack one of her fellow dancers in the face.

'Blimey, what's the interpretation? The attack of the killer camel toe?' When a man sitting in front of them presented his summary of what they were watching, Nadia caught Hamish's eye and she knew she was going to laugh. Once she started, she couldn't stop and it seemed to be catching because neither could Hamish. The more she tried to get control of herself, the more she laughed and by the time the lead dancer tried to do the splits, but stopped a good eighteen inches away from reaching her goal, there were tears streaming down her face and several people had turned to look at her. Including a woman on the far side of Hamish.

'It's all right.' His face was now perfectly deadpan. 'She's just overcome with emotion.'

'My sister's in the troupe and I completely understand. I was moved to tears the first time I saw them rehearse.' The woman smiled, more than satisfied by Hamish's response, and Nadia was forced to bury her head in his shoulder to stop herself from laughing out loud.

'No wonder you're so popular with your patients, you could convince them of anything.' She'd finally managed to regain her composure, so it was safe to lift her head off his shoulder, whispering the words to avoid offending anyone. 'Sorry, but that was the funniest thing I've seen for a long time.'

'Don't be sorry.' Hamish's voice was low too, extending the intimacy of sitting so close to him. 'It was hilarious and watching you trying not to laugh made it even better. Your whole face lights up when you laugh.'

'I couldn't help myself.' She had no idea how to respond, so it was easier just to ignore his comment.

'I'm glad. Maybe we could go out together and watch some more interpretive dance, if it has that effect on you?'

'You want to go out and watch more of this?'

'If you like, or we could go out and do something else.'

'I—' Nadia hesitated. She still couldn't work out how to respond. Her heart was screaming at her to grab the chance with both her hands, but her head was already listing all the reasons why that would be a stupid idea. Luckily fate intervened before she was forced to give him an answer.

'Thank you to the interpretive dance teams from all three troupes.' The compère took to the centre of the floor with a microphone in one hand and clipboard in the other. 'The points are in and the winners of that section of the competition are the Port Agnes Quicksteppers, which puts them at the top of the leader board! Now we're going straight into the rumba competition and the first couple are Gwen and Barry Jones from the leading troupe. Let's see if they can keep the winning streak going or whether the teams from Port Kara or Port Tremellien can claw back some of the points.'

'It's Auntie Gwen!' Remi's reaction would have wiped out any response that Nadia might have tried to give Hamish at that point and she was bouncing up and down on her mother's lap, almost pushing Mo off in the process. It was no surprise to discover that Gwen and Barry were step-perfect, or that Gwen had capitalised on what she'd informed the rest of the midwives was by far the sexiest dance of the whole competition. But if Nadia could lift her leg half as high as Gwen by the time she was in her sixties, she'd very impressed. And if she had a partner who adored her half as much as Barry clearly adored his wife, she'd be happier still. The kids might be her sole focus for now, but if she pretended she wanted to go through the whole of her life without ever having that connection to someone – a connection she'd never really come close to with Ryan – then she'd only have been lying to herself.

Two rumbas later and it was another win on the board for the Port Agnes Quicksteppers, with the compère announcing that it was time for the solo ballet section of the competition.

'This is one of Saffron's dances.' Hamish squeezed Daisy's hand. 'Let's hope it's another win for Port Agnes.'

'Saffron's definitely going to win. She can do spins and everything, and she's got a room made of mirrors. I saw it in Daisy's garden.' Remi's voice was filled with wonder.

'She's got a little dance studio in the garden, with mirrors on one wall.' Hamish seemed keen to play it down. 'I was just so thrilled that she kept up her dancing instead of getting as stressed about her A levels as I thought she would. Despite all our jokes about interpretive dance, ballet has definitely been a good outlet for Saffy's emotions.'

'That can only be a good thing.' Nadia whispered the response as the music started and within seconds she was mesmerised. Saffron's dancing wasn't just a good outlet for her emotions, she had a gift. It was impossible for Nadia to take her eyes off Hamish's daughter and the audition erupted into the loudest applause of the day when Saffron's routine finally came to an end. So it was no surprise to hear that Nicky's dance school had got the highest score in the solo ballet section of the competition too.

When Mo started to get too fidgety to watch any more of the competition, it took all of Nadia's negotiation skills to persuade Remi to go back to the old library for a couple more taster sessions. She had to promise they'd be back in the main hall in time to watch Saffron's second dance, which was also the final performance of the competition. Nadia had managed to catch up with

Frankie, who'd come down to watch the children taking part in the taster sessions after she had thankfully got to the Guildhall just in time to see Gwen perform.

Daisy sat on their vacated chair to save it for their return, and after two more sessions, along with another snack, Mo was happy to curl up on Frankie's lap on the other side of the hall. Meaning it wasn't quite such a squeeze for Nadia, Hamish and the girls this time around.

'You're not allowed to leave again.' Hamish fixed her with an intense look as she retook her seat and Daisy hopped back on to her father's lap.

'Why's that?' In the few seconds it took him to respond, an entire make-believe scene played through her head about how Hamish was going to answer that question, but his response was simple.

'Because you must be the lucky charm. Port Agnes haven't won another section of the competition since you left. We keep swapping places with the Port Tremellien Twirlers, but poor old Port Kara seemed to peak with that unique interpretive dance. We need to win the grand finale to win the competition overall.'

'What sort of dance is it?'

'Each of the groups have chosen one of their own and Saffron said the only rule is that they've got to feature Christmas somehow, but she wouldn't even tell me what the Quicksteppers are doing.'

'Ooh exciting.'

The Port Kara troupe was first out and chose ballet, performing part of *The Nutcracker*. Next were the Quicksteppers' big rivals from Port Tremellien, who jived to 'Rocking Around the Christmas Tree'. Finally it was Nicky's troupe, with both Saffron and Gwen among their number. It was essentially a tap routine, but it was more like a scene from a West End show, with some of the dancers playing the roles of Santa's reindeer and others moving in a motion that made it look like they were part of the sleigh itself. Saffron was the star of the performance again, playing the part of Rudolph.

'If Port Agnes doesn't win, we've been robbed.' Nadia would never have believed she could get so invested in a dance competition, but nerves fluttered in her stomach as she waited for the compère to make an announcement. Remi and Daisy would both be really disappointed if Gwen and Saffron's troupe didn't win, but Nadia knew how important it would be to Hamish's older daughter too, and to him as a result.

'We're collating the final scores and we'll be making an announcement very soon about which dance school is the winner of this year's Christmas extravaganza, so get ready!' After the compère made the announcement, some of the supporters started to join the troupes on the dancefloor to await the result.

'Shall we take the girls down to Saffron and Gwen?' Nadia could see some of the other midwives already standing with Gwen, ready to cheer on their resident glitter ball winner whatever the outcome.

'Yes Daddy, let's go!' Daisy didn't even give her father the chance to answer before running on to the floor with Remi close enough behind to be her shadow. She also spotted Frankie heading towards the dance floor with Mo, and by the time they got there too, the Port Agnes Quicksteppers were busy working out exactly how many points they needed to win the competition.

'Come back up here for a cuddle my gorgeous boy, you still look very tired.' Frankie let go of Mo's hand and lifted him into her arms.

'How are you feeling?' Nadia squeezed Gwen's shoulder. 'You were brilliant by the way.'

'Thank you, but if we don't win after I high-kicked so hard that I chafed my unmentionables, there'll be trouble.'

'What's unmentionables?' Remi furrowed her brow and the tension was broken, as everyone laughed.

'Ladies and gentlemen, we have a decision! And the winner is...' The compère had obviously undergone the same training as all competition presenters, and there was an overly long pause before the result was finally announced. 'The Port Agnes Quicksteppers!'

What followed wasn't all that dissimilar to the moments after the clock strikes midnight on New Year's Eve. Everyone was cheering and hugging, and the dance troupe members were chanting Nicky's name. So when Nadia found herself face-to-face with Hamish, it would have seemed odd not to kiss him on the cheek, the way everyone else seemed to be doing. The fact that it felt completely different from the other celebratory kisses was neither here nor there. Or so she thought.

'I knew you were just like all the others.' Saffron's tone was every bit as vicious as her grip on Nadia's arms. But she was hissing the words, so at least in the furore of the celebrations not everyone could hear what she had to say. 'He's not looking for a girlfriend; why can't you desperate old cows get that into your heads? It's bad enough that my mum's best friend made an embarrassment of herself, but now you're doing it too. I suppose that's why you tried so hard to get your kid to be friends with Daisy.'

'Saffron!' Hamish peeled his older daughter away from Nadia's side, but even without looking she knew Saffron would have left the imprint of her fingertips on her arm. It wasn't that making her eyes fill with tears though and the last thing she wanted was for Hamish to make a scene that would draw more attention to them.

'We were just celebrating your win, everyone was.' Nadia's attempt to make light of things had resulted in her voice taking on a weird sing-song tone and she could see a few people starting to look in their direction, despite her best efforts to brush off Saffron's reaction. After what Hamish's older daughter had gone through with his ex, she could understand why Saffron was so angry. What was sad was that she didn't seem to realise that he'd always choose his daughters. None of that made the moment any less uncomfortable, but for once fate seemed to be on Nadia's side and before Saffron could take things any further, suddenly all eyes were on someone else.

'I think I'm going to faint,' one of the other dancers, a girl who looked to be about the same age as Saffron, called out. All the colour drained from her face and Nadia caught her elbow just before she fell.

'Let's get you to where you can sit down. What's your name?' She could tell from the way the girl's face twisted in pain that this wasn't a just a dance injury.

'Beth.' She'd barely got the word out before she bent double. 'It feels like someone's trying to tear my insides out!'

'It's going to be okay Beth; my name's Nadia and I promise we'll find out what's causing this and sort it out.' She turned to Frankie. 'Can you keep an eye on the kids for a bit?'

'Of course, darling.'

'I'll give you a hand.' Hamish moved to the other side of the girl.

'Dad, you're not going with *her,* are you?' Saffron attempted to block his path, but Hamish had finally had enough.

'Beth's one of your friends, Saff, and she needs me *and* Nadia to help her. I'll let you know what's happening as soon as we've checked her out, but I want you to look after Daisy for a little while.'

'Yeah, because that's all I'm good for.'

'Not now, Saffron.' Nadia had no idea if it was the way Saffron's father was looking at her, or the fact that Beth was now groaning loudly, but even she seemed to realise this wasn't the time to try and cause any more drama, and she finally moved out of the way.

'We'll find out what the problem is and do something about the pain as soon as we can.' Beth was pulling down on Nadia's arm as she spoke, as though she was finding it hard to support her own weight.

'I'll give your mum a ring Beth, don't worry,' Nicky called out. 'And if you need anything else I'll get it sorted.'

'I'm really sorry I've ruined the celebration.' There were tears running down Beth's face and as Nadia put her arm around the younger woman's waist to give her more support, she had a feeling she might have solved the mystery of what was causing Beth's pain. But she wasn't about to announce that in front of the watching crowd. If there was going to be a new member of the Port Agnes Quicksteppers welcomed into the world, then it would be up to the baby's mother to share that news. Especially as there was a chance that Beth didn't even know that herself yet.

15

With the taster classes over, Hamish, Nadia and Beth were able to commandeer the old library. Everything seemed to have dissolved into chaos since the Port Agnes Quicksteppers had been announced as the winners and Hamish was still reeling from Saffron speaking to Nadia the way she had. Maybe he'd been too soft on her, because he knew when she behaved like this it came from a place of wanting to protect Daisy and because she missed her mum. Saffy had lost so much when Sara had died and as she moved through each phase of her life, it was as if that grief was renewed. When she'd lost her mother as a twelve-year-old girl, she hadn't known what the young adult version of herself would miss out on by not having Sara there when she went off to university and took the first steps towards independence. But none of that excused her being so terribly rude to someone as lovely as Nadia. If he'd believed in mind-reading, he might have understood Saffron's reaction. The truth was he'd wanted to kiss Nadia more than once in the past and what he'd pictured hadn't been a peck on the cheek in the middle of a crowd. But Saffron couldn't read his mind and her reaction had been ridiculous. He was going to give his older daughter a serious talking-to, but right now Beth was everyone's priority.

'Do you think you can sit down, or I can grab some coats to put on the floor and you can lie down if that's easier. Just while we check you over?' Nadia's voice was gentle and Beth, who was being supported on both sides by her arms, muttered a response.

'I think I can sit.'

'Okay sweetheart, here we go.' Nadia took the lead, as they manoeuvred Beth into a chair.

'Are you on any medication?' He sat next to her, but she didn't look at him even when she answered.

'No.'

'Okay. Have you been diagnosed with any medical issues in the past that might be causing this sort of pain?'

'No.' Tears had started rolling down Beth's face and Hamish turned to look at Nadia, raising his eyebrows and silently asking a question he hoped she'd understand. When Nadia nodded, it was obvious they were thinking the same thing.

'Beth, sweetheart.' Nadia took hold of one of the girl's hands. 'Do you think there's any chance you could be pregnant?'

'Mum and Dad are going to hate me for this.' Beth's silent tears turned into noisy sobs, echoing around the walls of the old library.

'Try not to worry about that at the moment. All that matters right now is making sure that you and the baby are safe so we need to get you checked over properly.' Nadia had a gift for making it sound simple. 'Have you got any idea how far along you might be?'

'I haven't had any periods since before the summer.' Beth sniffed, her eyes fixed on Nadia.

'And were you on the pill or anything?'

'Yeah, the mini pill and at first I tried to convince myself that's why I wasn't having periods any more.' Beth screwed up her face and closed her eyes, as if that might make this all go away. 'I wasn't getting sick or anything, but then I started to feel it move.'

'When was that sweetheart?' Watching Nadia, Hamish felt pretty useless. She was the one Beth needed and all he could do was marvel at how much calmer the young woman was already. He wished Saffron could see it too, so she'd understand how wrong she was about Nadia.

'It was when we went back to school in September, but I just kept telling myself I couldn't be pregnant, even though I knew I was. My belly was getting bigger, but I still managed to hide it. I even suggested we dress as reindeers for the competition, so no one would be able to tell.' Beth started crying again.

'It's okay. Just focus on what's happening now; there's nothing that can't be sorted out. How long have you been having these pains?'

'Since we finished the first half of the competition. It comes and goes but it feels like it's getting stronger and with that last one I really thought I was going to pass out.'

'How often do you think the pain is coming?'

'About every fifteen minutes. I was praying I'd get through the final dance and I just about made it.'

'You're doing brilliantly, Beth.' Nadia turned to Hamish. 'I think we need to take her straight to hospital rather than the unit, so she can get checked out properly because I can't do it here. It'll probably be quicker to drive straight there, rather than wait for an ambulance, especially as I'm pretty sure this is the early stages of labour.'

'I can drive, if you can come with me to take care of Beth. You're far more qualified to support her than I am, if anything unexpected happens en route.'

'Are you sure? I thought you might need to stay with Saffron and Daisy.' There was no judgement in her tone, so if Saffron had upset her, she wasn't letting it show.

'They'll understand and Nicky will make sure they get home safely. If I tell them they can order in whatever takeaway they want, it'll more than make up for me not being there.' Hamish smiled. Even if Saffron wasn't okay with it, she'd just have to suck it up. It was time she started to realise that she couldn't act however the hell she wanted to.

* * *

Thankfully the journey to the hospital had been uneventful. Frankie and Guy had been more than happy to take Mo and Remi with them, and Nadia had given her mum the keys to the car. Hopefully Hamish would be able to give her a lift back from the hospital, but if not, she'd work it out somehow. Beth was clinging to her the whole way to Truro and there was no chance of Nadia leaving until she was certain Beth was okay and had the support she needed. That was the thing with being a midwife, you couldn't turn it off just because you weren't supposed to be working that day, especially not with someone as vulnerable and frightened as Beth was.

'They're going to fully assess her and put her on monitoring to see how close the contractions are as soon as they've cleared one of the rooms, and she wants me to be there.' Nadia came out to the waiting area outside the entrance to the maternity ward, where Hamish had been sitting since she'd gone to get Beth checked in. 'I don't know how long it's going to take or whether she'll want me there after that, but don't worry if you need to shoot off.'

'I'm waiting for you.' Hamish's response didn't allow any room for argument. 'Nicky's just texted me to say she dropped the girls off and everything's fine there. She also said Beth's parents are on their way here.'

'How much has she told them?'

'Not a lot, I don't think.'

'She's terrified.' Nadia furrowed her brow. 'I just hope they don't react as badly as she thinks they might.'

'If it was Saff and I was rushing over here, not knowing what was wrong, I'd just be glad she was going to be okay. Nothing could upset me once I knew that the prospect of losing her was gone.'

'I've seen this happen a few times and most parents think the same as you, but some of them still react really badly. I think it's shock a lot of time, and whatever Beth decides about the future for her and her baby, their lives are never going to be the same again. We've got to give them some leeway, but if I can shield Beth from some of that I will.'

'You're amazing, do you know that?' Hamish seemed to be waiting for a response, but she just shook her head. 'I'm so sorry about the things Saffron said and I'm going to talk to her about it. I should have said something a long time ago, but going easy on her because of losing her mum got out of hand somewhere along the line.'

'I've been the same with Remi. I think it comes from feeling guilty, but I don't want her to turn into my brother, Hari, or even worse, to be as selfish as Ryan. As hard as it is, I've finally started putting my foot down and enforcing some boundaries with her.' Nadia breathed out. 'I was terrified that she might hate me, but I think it's actually made her feel safer. She knows how far she can push me and she knows I'll love her even if she does act up, but she's also realised I care enough to take action when her behaviour starts to spiral.'

'I really need to do that with Saff and you're so right, I think she's pushed the boundaries because deep down she's scared there's something she could do that would make me stop loving her. She's wrong, but I need to show her that. Is there anything you aren't brilliant at?' He smiled and it had been on the tip of her tongue to say relationships, but for some reason she needed him to believe she could hold a relationship down.

'I better get back. Thanks for waiting.' Holding up a hand to stop him from saying anything else, she headed back into the maternity department. Frankie had told Nadia more than once that she was brilliant at seeing the best in everyone except for herself, and sometimes she had to admit that focusing on people's good sides had cost her dearly. But it was much easier to see the good in some people than others and seeing that side of Hamish was dangerously simple.

* * *

Beth's examination confirmed that she was only three centimetres dilated and the contractions were still about fifteen minutes apart. But because she hadn't had any antenatal care, and was finding the pain difficult to manage, the hospital midwifery team decided against sending her home until her labour had progressed. Nadia didn't have the option of staying for the delivery unless Beth wanted her to be a designated birthing partner. To act as a midwife at the hospital, she'd have had to seek permission from the Trust and there was no time to get that sorted.

'Can you stay until my parents get here?' Beth's eyes were like saucers as she turned to look at Nadia.

'Of course. Do you want me to be here when you tell them?'

'Can you tell them for me when they arrive? Please. Before they come in?' Beth was pleading with her, but her parents were almost certainly going to put two and two together when they turned up at the main reception of the hospital and got directed to the maternity unit.

'Have they texted you?'

'Yes, but I haven't replied. The last one said they were fifteen minutes away.' Beth bit her lip.

'When was that?'

'About five minutes ago.'

'Okay.' Nadia took a deep breath. 'Text them back and say you're okay, but that I'll meet them in the main reception to let them know where you are and what the hospital staff have said.'

'Thank you.' Beth had already snatched up her phone, the prospect of not having to tell her parents herself overriding any other worries at least for the moment.

'Are you going to be okay if I head down there now?' Nadia touched Beth's arm and the young woman nodded, lying back against the pillows as soon as she'd sent the text.

'I just want this all to be over.'

'I know you do, sweetheart.' Nadia squeezed her hand. This had only just begun for Beth, but all she could do was take it a step at a time and one big hurdle to get over was telling her parents. If Nadia could help with that before she left Beth in the capable hands of the hospital midwifery team, then she would. But there was no way of knowing how it would go.

* * *

'Have you met Beth's parents before?' Nadia was standing with Hamish in front of the hospital's main reception, suddenly wondering if she should have asked Beth to describe what she looked like to them. She didn't want to think how that might have gone.

'I've seen them at some school events. Beth's in the same year as Saffron. So I should recognise them.'

'I keep thinking how best to word it, but there's no way to sugarcoat it, is there?'

'Not really, because there'll be no more hiding the baby after today.' Hamish looked towards the doors as a couple rushed in. 'I'm almost certain this is them.'

'Are you Beth's parents?' In the end, there was no time to hesitate.

'Yes, are you Nadia?' Beth's mum looked like she was on the verge of tears already.

'Yes and this is Hamish, Saffron's dad; we brought her in from the dance competition.'

'Do you know what's wrong? I've been imagining every worst-case scenario on the drive over, but Beth didn't answer my texts and then she just said you'd explain when we got here.'

'She's okay.' Nadia swallowed and looked directly at Beth's parents. 'But this is probably going to come as a shock. She's pregnant, full-term based on the midwives' assessment, and she's already in established labour.'

'She's *what*?' Beth's father's roar made a porter almost swerve a wheelchair and its occupant into the wall of the corridor. 'Where the hell is she?'

'Simon, don't.' Beth's mother caught hold of her husband's arm before he could charge off in search of their daughter. 'I should have known she was lying when I asked her.'

'You knew about this?' There was a vein bulging on Simon's forehead as he yanked his arm away from his wife.

'I could see her stomach was getting bigger, but she said it was just bloating. She even said she'd been to see one of the other doctors at your surgery about it.' Beth's mother turned to Hamish. 'And that they'd said it was down to IBS.'

'I think she was terrified of facing the truth, let alone telling you.' Hamish looked at Nadia. 'From what she told us, it sounds like she was ignoring it as much as possible.'

Nadia could see a whole gamut of emotions crossing Beth's mother's face, everything from anger to guilt. 'She probably kept hoping that it might somehow turn out not to be true, until she couldn't ignore it any more.'

'She's ruined her future, Claire. You do realise that, don't you?' Simon's face was getting redder by the minute. 'The school have been saying she can have her pick of universities, but now she's gone and done this. How can someone so intelligent do something so stupid?'

'Have you forgotten we weren't exactly planning Beth when we found out we were expecting her?' Beth's mother was already on her daughter's side and Nadia felt some of the tension leaving her spine. The chances were that Simon would calm down at some point too, but even if he didn't, Beth's mother would do her best to protect her. Just like Frankie had always done for Nadia, and the way Hamish was doing for his daughters. Having two parents who were there for their child was amazing, but having one who was in your corner – whatever happened – was enough. And Nadia would make sure she was enough for Remi and Mo too.

'I think the best thing you can do is to go and see Beth. I know she'll feel better when you're there. She's in the maternity unit; it's all signposted from here – you just need to press the buzzer and let them know when you've arrived.'

'Are you coming with us?' Claire sounded hopeful, but Nadia shook her head.

'It's you she wants there, but she's got my number if you need me and, if you get a moment to let me know how she is later on, that would be great. She'll be fine.' Nadia exchanged a look with Claire that needed no words and the other woman nodded.

'Thank you. Come on, Simon, Beth needs us.' Grabbing her husband's arm again, she started off in the direction of the maternity unit and within seconds they were out of sight.

'Can we go outside for a minute? It's so stuffy in here.' Nadia had a strong suspicion that her face was every bit as red as Beth's dad's had been and she needed some air before her own emotions started to get to her.

'Of course.'

'Do you think Simon's going to shout at Beth?' Nadia turned to Hamish when they got outside. 'I'm still shaking.'

'If he does, I think Claire will chuck him out. When she mentioned that thing about Beth not being planned either, I saw the look in his eyes. He might be angry, but I think that's just disguising his fear that she's taken away her choices in life.' Hamish sighed. 'Things will be difficult, I know that from when we had Saff, but we always thought of her as a wonderful surprise, never a mistake. If Beth decides to bring up the baby herself, I'm sure Simon and Claire will come to think like that too, in time. You handled it brilliantly by the way.'

'I just didn't want to make things worse, but thank you for what you did.'

'What did I do?'

'You said all the right things.' She leant forward, with every intention of kissing him on the cheek again, but at the last moment something happened and even afterwards she wasn't sure if it was her or Hamish who'd moved their head. Suddenly he was kissing her and she was kissing him back as if they were in their own little world, instead of standing in a hospital car park. It was everything she'd imagined, all the time she'd been trying to pretend to herself that she wasn't. Her body had taken over, responding to the sensation of his lips on hers, drowning out any hope her brain had of telling her to hold back. If they'd been truly alone she didn't think she'd have been able to stop and she wouldn't have wanted to, but fate had other ideas.

'That's my phone, sorry.' It had only taken two rings for him to pull away and as he looked at the screen, his face clouded over. 'I wouldn't answer it, but it's the girls.'

'Of course, don't worry.' It was as though Saffron had caught them in the act again and heat flushed Nadia face as she stood awkwardly listening to Hamish's conversation with his elder daughter.

'Hi Saff, what's up?' Hamish paused for a moment. 'Okay, put her on the sofa with a blanket and a bowl and whatever film she wants. I'll be home as soon I can.' There was another brief pause. 'Okay darling, thank you.'

'Is Daisy ill?' Nadia dreaded those sorts of phone calls, feeling like you were a million miles away from your child when they needed you, and she could tell Hamish felt exactly the same.

'She's been sick. Saff thinks she might just have had too much ice cream when they got back from the competition, but she's asking for me.'

'I can get a bus back, just go.'

'Don't be silly, I'm going back to Port Agnes and I'm virtually passing your door.'

'I know, but I want to hang around for a bit in case Beth needs me.'

'I thought you told Claire you weren't staying?' Hamish searched her face.

'I won't stay long, but you need to get off. I'll be fine.'

'Are you sure? I'd stay too, but Daisy...'

'I promise it's not a problem.' Hamish almost certainly had no idea it took about two hours to get from Truro to Port Agnes on the bus, or that she might have to wait ages for the next bus on a Sunday, and she wasn't going to tell him. Suddenly it seemed worth it to avoid having to sit next to him during the journey back home. She'd crossed a line when she'd kissed him that she couldn't uncross, and the worst part of all was she didn't want to.

16

When Nadia had phoned her mother to say she was getting the bus home from Truro, Guy had insisted on paying for a taxi to bring her back to Port Agnes. He'd been too quick for protests and had booked and paid for it before Frankie or Nadia could argue. When Frankie had tried to pay him back, he'd refused to even entertain the idea. It was just one thing, on an increasingly long list, that was making Frankie fall in love with him a little bit more every day. Nadia had looked completely exhausted by the time she got home, so it had been just as well she hadn't come on the bus. When they'd got up the next day, a text had come through on Nadia's phone to say that Beth had safely delivered a 7lb 1oz baby boy. It must have been one hell of a shock for Beth and her parents, but in Frankie's experience, babies almost always brought their own love and the family would soon be making Beth's son the centre of their world.

Frankie could remember being told, when Nadia was expecting Remi, that there was no love like a grandparent had for their grandchildren, but the force of it had still blown her away. When Ryan had decided he was taking his family back to New Zealand, it was as though a part of Frankie was being ripped away from the rest of her body and it hurt every bit as much. Her own mother had always favoured Hari over Nadia and she'd definitely made the most of having a grandson. That had been compounded when Nadia had married someone Bhavna thought wasn't good enough for her, but Frankie had to give her mother credit for that one, because she'd been right. Ryan was nowhere near good enough for Nadia or their children.

Bhavna's face had twisted almost in on itself, as if she was sucking on the world's bitterest lemon, when she'd been told about Nadia and Ryan's marriage breaking down. She'd blamed Frankie, telling her that she'd set her daughter the worst possible example by walking away from her own marriage. But if that had helped Nadia to finally accept she was fighting a losing battle with Ryan, then Frankie would go through with the trauma of ending her own marriage a hundred times over. Except now it looked like she'd lost Hari and all of her messages to him were listed as being unread. The silence was deafening.

The day after the dance competition was Frankie's last day of university before the Christmas break, but she'd found it almost impossible to concentrate on anything and every five minutes she checked her phone to see if there was anything from Hari. The last message she'd sent him had been a knee-jerk reaction to the silence and a desperate attempt to provoke a response. Now she was wishing she'd deleted it, before he'd seen it, but it was too late and now she was terrified of what his response would be.

✉ Message to Hari

I know I've upset you and I'm very sorry for that, but not talking to me won't help us to sort this out. I love you more than you'll ever under-stand and I know you find it tough that I'm no longer with your dad. I don't want those feelings to spoil your wedding day for you, so if you don't want me there at least tell me that. It'll break my heart, but even that's better than you just ignoring me.

She was expecting a message any moment telling her that he didn't want her at the wedding and she had no idea how she'd deal with that. She'd considered messaging Hari to promise she wouldn't see Guy any more, but she wasn't sure it was a promise she was capable of keeping. The truth was, she loved them both and she couldn't bear the thought of having to choose between them. If she'd spoken to any of her friends at uni about it, or the other midwives at the unit, she knew what they'd have said: that Hari needed to grow up and accept that his mother had a life of her own. She'd have said exactly the same to any of her friends in the same circumstances, but when it came to the prospect of her son not wanting to see her, it wasn't so cut and dried.

'I wasn't expecting to see you here.' Frankie caught her breath as she looked up to see Guy descending the last few steps that led down from the entrance to her flat. He smiled, the way his eyes crinkled in the corners reminding her how often they laughed when they were together. She'd never had that before and the thought of letting it go made her want to cry instead.

'You weren't supposed to see me.' He shrugged, still smiling. 'I thought you might be exhausted after uni and you mentioned that Nadia and the kids were going to see your mum tonight, so I thought it would be nice if you came home and could just put your feet up. I got a moussaka, a lemon tart and some other bits and pieces from the deli and I've left them in a box by your front door.'

'You're not staying?' The urge to cry was almost overwhelming now and there was no denying what she needed most was for Guy to give her a cuddle.

'I thought you might want some space. I know it's been tough and I don't want to put any pressure on you.'

'That's why I love you.' Frankie clapped her hand over her mouth as soon as the words were out, widening her eyes as she tried to read Guy's expression, but the smile hadn't left his face. It was broader than ever.

'You do?' He took hold of one of her hands and pulled her towards him, still on the steps outside the flat.

'Uh huh.' She could barely look at him. The heat flooding her body had nothing to do with the joys of menopause for once. He'd made her forget about getting older since the moment they'd met and all the things she'd dreaded about hitting middle-age had disappeared. It was like starting over again, in the best possible way, but she still had her family to consider.

'I've almost said that to you at least twenty times.' He gently tilted her chin up with his other hand, so she had no choice but to stop staring at her shoes. 'That first ever date we had to the cinema, I thought I'd suddenly developed Tourette's because I had this almost overwhelming urge to shout out *I love Frankie* in the middle of the film. But I knew any sensible person would say it was crazy. That's the thing isn't it? Love doesn't make you sensible.'

'It definitely doesn't.' Frankie tried to blink back the tears that had filled her eyes, but it was no use. The more she blinked, the faster they came.

'Hey, what's wrong?'

'I should be so happy.' Looking up at him, she couldn't even make out his features any more, they were so blurred. 'I never dreamt I was going to find something like this and the truth is I thought I might live my whole life without ever really being *in love*. I love the kids and my grandchildren so much, and I thought that was enough, but then I met you and now it feels like I'm having to choose.'

'No you're not.' She might not be able to see Guy clearly, but even Frankie could tell he wasn't smiling any more. 'I love you and

I want this to work, but I'm not going to be the one who puts pressure on you to choose me, because you'll never be happy if Hari isn't happy too.'

'What are you saying?' It suddenly felt like she'd forgotten how to swallow.

'I'm saying that I'm here for you whenever you're ready and I really do love you, but if it comes to having to choose between me and Hari, I can't let you do that, because you'll never forgive me.' Guy sighed heavily. 'I've been selfish in the past, Jess will tell you that, but I know how important having a second chance with my daughter was to me. I can't stand the thought of not seeing you but hurting you by being selfish and making you choose would kill me.'

'So what do we do, just wait to see if Hari comes round?' This time, when she blinked back the tears, they weren't immediately replaced. Suddenly another emotion was taking over.

'If that's what it takes.'

'No!' The force of her reply shocked even Frankie and if Guy hadn't still been holding on to her, she might have fallen down the steps.

'No what?'

'No, I'm not waiting for Hari to decide if it's okay for me to be happy. All I've ever done is put the kids first and do what other people thought was right, especially my mother, even when that made me miserable. But this is something I want just for me and I'm not giving up the chance to be happy for anyone. Not even Hari.' If someone had told Frankie ten minutes before that she'd be saying those words, she'd have told them they were mad. But standing on those steps, it was like a light had been switched on. Hari had his own life and he made tiny pockets of time in it for Frankie every now and then when it suited him, exactly the way most adult children did. She wouldn't expect him to make decisions to suit her and nothing made her happier than seeing him make his own choices and flourish, but it was finally time she was allowed to do the same thing.

'Are you sure?'

'Never more certain.' Looking at him again, she reached up and put a hand on either side of his face. 'But are you? Because this can't be a casual thing for me any more.'

'If you wanted me to promise you forever, I could do that.' There wasn't even a hint of doubt in his voice.

'I'm not asking for that, but I do need to know where you see this going.'

'Right to the end.' He put his hands over hers and if Hari had witnessed that moment, he'd probably have exploded in anger. But this was her time, and her son was just going to have to learn to live with it. She still couldn't bear to think about what would happen if he didn't, but right now she was making a choice – a choice to be happy. No one could deny her that, not even Frankie herself.

* * *

Nadia's attempts to reason with her grandmother had gone exactly the way she'd expected them to. Badly.

As far as Nani was concerned, Hari's response had been justified. But what shocked Nadia the most was how her grandmother had reacted when she'd told her Advik was dating too.

'That's your mother's fault. If she'd stuck with her marriage, none of this would be happening!' She'd had no idea how to respond after that. If Hamish thought Saffron was overreacting to the prospect of him dating again, he should try being related to Nani and Hari. Saffron was eighteen, while Nani and Hari had well over a hundred-and-ten years' life experience between them and no one had tried to pack Hari off to boarding school to get him out of the way. Although Nadia was starting to think her mother had missed a trick.

It was almost like a holiday to go back to work, with all the drama going on at home. Nadia spent the day in clinic and it had gone really smoothly. None of her patients had had major concerns and, aside from one water infection and one mother-to-be with low iron levels, there hadn't been anything to worry Nadia either. There was a chance that the status quo was all about to change, though, because the next patient she was due to see was Genevieve.

'Hi Ginny. It's good to see you.' Nadia rose to her feet to give her old school friend a hug as she came into the consulting room. They'd exchanged several texts every day, and quite a few phone calls since the last time they'd seen one another. Nadia would have been happy to answer twenty texts a day if it gave Ginny the reassurance she so badly needed, but it was so good to meet up with her in person and to see for herself that she was doing as well as she could in the circumstances. As Nadia had suspected, Ginny had decided not to have the operation or any other treatment until the baby arrived and everyone was trying to support her as best they could.

'It's good to see you too.' Ginny attempted a smile, but the strain and sleeplessness was evident on her face, along with the dark shadows underneath her eyes.

'How has your back pain been?' The last few texts Nadia had received from Ginny had been about pains in her back and when they'd spoken on the phone, it had been obvious that she was terrified the cancer had somehow spread to her bones since her scans, and it was that causing the pain she'd been feeling. Nadia had done her best to convince Ginny that it was far more likely to be sciatica, but she'd suggested she speak to Hamish or her oncologist, if only to give her some extra peace of mind.

'A bit better, but Hamish said the same as you and that it probably won't ease off completely until Neviah arrives.'

'You've settled on a name then?'

'Originally I wanted to wait until we saw her for the first time, but I decided we needed a name that meant something.' Ginny lowered herself gingerly into the seat next to Nadia's desk, a combination of the late stage of her pregnancy and her back pain making her much slower than she might have been otherwise. 'It means someone who can see the future and I wanted her to have a name that was all about looking ahead, to a time when all of this will be over.'

'It's lovely and I've never heard it before, which is quite unusual for me. The longer I'm a midwife, the more I start to think that all the baby names will be used up before I retire.'

'That would be some list!' For a moment Ginny's face seemed to relax, but the pinched expression soon came back. 'I didn't want to leave Freddie to have to pick the name by himself. Just in case.'

'That's not going to happen.' Nadia shook her head; this was nothing like the situation with Hamish's wife.

'It's not the cancer.' Ginny sighed so hard it was almost as if she'd sucked half the air out of the room. 'Well at least not directly, but I never dreamt I'd be diagnosed with breast cancer at this age. That sort of thing happens to other people. It's shown me this is something that can happen to anyone, including me. So I'm not taking it for granted that I won't be the million-to-one case where something terrible happens during the delivery either. If I'm not here for Neviah, I want her to know that I loved her and I chose her name because I want her to have the most amazing future, one where she gets to make all her own choices. Because right now I feel like that's been taken away from me.'

'I understand that, but I really think you'll be able to tell her all of those things yourself.'

'I hope so and I try hard not to feel bitter about everything this has robbed me of, when there are other people who've got much worse to contend with.'

'You don't have to justify your feelings. No one can say you aren't going through an incredibly tough time and you've got a right to feel however you do about it.' Nadia just hoped no one had been thoughtless enough to even suggest to Ginny that her fears weren't valid, because it was a ridiculous idea when she was going through so much.

'I know it shouldn't bother me when I should just be focussed on getting rid of the cancer, but I'm so angry that it's come along and ruined my only pregnancy, when this is all I've wanted for years.' Ginny screwed up her face. 'I wanted to cherish every moment of this with Freddie and now all we're doing is wishing it away, so I can get the operation. I'm never going to be pregnant again and I don't even get to enjoy this one.'

'Are you saying there won't be another pregnancy because of the miscarriages? Because the problems you had before might have been caused by DNA fragmentation in your ex-husband's sperm, which can lead to miscarriage. The fact that you've had a successful pregnancy this time around means there's a good chance you will again in the future.'

'Would you call this a successful pregnancy? Because it doesn't feel like it.' Ginny shook her head. 'As awful as the miscarriages were, I'd still be willing to risk going through that again if it meant I'd be able to have another child. What I'm not willing to risk is leaving another child without their mother. I've got no choice with Neviah, but how could I try for another baby when I know there's a chance the cancer could come back?'

'I'm probably the wrong person to talk to about this, because I can't claim to even begin to understand what that feels like, but have you thought about speaking to other new mums who've been through a similar experience? I'm sure the Macmillan team could put you in touch with a support group. There'll be people who'll understand everything you're saying and some of them have probably made that decision, but there might be others who've made different choices and can talk to you about that too.'

'I guess it would be good to talk to other people who don't feel they've got to tell me everything's going to be okay.' Ginny held up her hand. 'I'm not counting you in that number, but I've had it from Freddie, both our families and lots of friends. I know it's because they want it to be true, but they're not the ones sitting in the nursing chair in Neviah's nursery, staring into the darkness at two o'clock in the morning and holding on to a Babygro that I can't be sure I'll ever get to see her wear, or a story book that I might never be able to read to her.'

'I think talking to others who've been through it can only help.' Nadia had been through her share of sleepless nights. Nothing that could compare to Ginny's, but when she'd discovered Ryan's string of affairs and experienced what could only be described as ghosting from his family, the only thing that had stopped her doing something crazy was talking to other people who understood. Complete strangers in online forums at 3 a.m. could be surprisingly insightful and supportive. Of course, some of them were probably just there to get off on other people's misery, and there were others whose advice was dubious at best and definitely bordered on the illegal at times. But those forums had stopped her feeling alone and helped her to believe she could find a solution and come out the other side. Like Ginny's family and friends, Nadia's had been too biased to be able to tell her what she needed to hear, instead of what she wanted to hear. And she'd always be grateful to those women who were up in the early hours just like her, nursing themselves and strangers through the pain of a bitter break up.

'I'll ask Heather, my Macmillan nurse, but I'm not going to be greedy.' Ginny looked into Nadia's eyes and somehow managed to convey just how scared she was. 'I might have had it all planned out once. Three kids, a nice big four-bedroom house and a husband who adores us all. But all I want now is to be with Freddie and get to see Neviah grow up. That's everything to me.'

'I think that makes you just about the wisest woman I've ever met.' Nadia barely resisted the temptation to echo Ginny's family and friends and promise it would all be okay. None of them could know that for sure, but all they could do was hope it would turn out to be true. Her thoughts turned to Hamish, as they so often did these days. He'd understand everything Ginny was feeling, because of what had happened to Sara, but that wasn't Nadia's story to share. Either way, she knew she needed to speak to him again as soon as she could, however awkward things might have got between them at the hospital. They were in this together, part of Ginny's team, and she was just going to have to put the uncomfortable feelings she had for him to one side.

17

Nadia had picked up the phone to text Hamish at least three times since her consultation with Ginny. But she didn't want to put him in an awkward position, especially he was also Genevieve's GP. She'd tried to find a chance to talk to Ella or Anna about it, to ask their advice, but Gwen had been holding court in the staffroom, giving the other midwives a demonstration of the latest dance class she'd taken. If the routine itself wasn't enough to grab everyone's attention, Gwen's accompanying description of how effective belly dancing was for building stamina in the bedroom would definitely have done the job.

It was probably just as well, because Nadia had no idea what she'd have said to Hamish anyway. She could hardly ask him to share intimate details with Ginny of how Sara felt when she was diagnosed, unless he decided to himself. She wasn't even sure that would be an appropriate thing him to do, but at times like this it was impossible to stay strictly professional.

The conversation with Ginny had invaded her dreams and she'd woken up at just after 3 a.m. She couldn't help wondering whether Ginny was sitting in her baby's nursery at that moment, just as she'd described, and imagining every worst-case scenario over and over again. Glancing across at Mo and Remi, both sleeping peacefully in the bunk beds Frankie had bought them, it was suddenly incredibly easy to count her blessings. She couldn't think of anything worse than having to face up to the prospect of leaving them, but Ginny was having to do that before she'd even held her baby in her arms.

Nadia had found it impossible to get to sleep again after waking up and she'd ended up searching the internet for houses to rent, hoping that something she could actually afford might suddenly pop up. She knew she shouldn't head over to Instagram, but she couldn't help it. Ryan's girlfriend had a public account, a necessary element of her ambitions to get more work as a sports model, which was a sideline to her career as a golf pro. Clicking on her latest reel, Nadia tortured herself watching Delilah showing off her workout routine in an outfit she claimed had been sent to her by a company who wanted her to represent them. It was so tiny Remi could probably have worn it, but there wouldn't have been any of the toned abs on display if she had.

If that wasn't bad enough, Delilah pulled Ryan in at the end of the video, using him much like she might have used a wall to demonstrate exactly how high she could stretch her leg. He was wearing tight yoga pants too and, knowing him as she did, Nadia could be a hundred per cent certain that the bulge in the front was at least seventy per cent man-made. Watching the two of them posturing and posing, she started to really laugh and she had to put a hand over her mouth to make sure she didn't wake either of the kids up. This was definitely progress. A month or so before, she'd have been analysing the video frame by frame, trying to work out if Ryan was really as deliriously happy with Delilah as he claimed to be, or whether there was any way in which she could come off favourably in a comparison with her husband's girlfriend.

The answer had always been no, but suddenly she didn't want to compete. Ryan looked ridiculous, trying so hard to pretend to be something he wasn't. If there'd been even a shadow of a doubt, she knew it for certain now: she was definitely over her ex. She wasn't just trying to convince herself any more, it was completely genuine. Unlike whatever it was he had stuffed down the front of his yoga pants.

The problem with a sleepless night, even one that had brought a welcome epiphany, was that by four o'clock the next day, she was seriously flagging. A round of home visits meant lots of driving around country lanes and she'd had to open the windows to make sure there was no risk of her dropping off and ending up in a ditch.

Her next visit was to Anne-Marie Hudson, the mother of five who lived in the very rural hamlet of Melynfow and whose sixth baby was due in a month. Given how busy she was, running the kennel and cattery, alongside taking care of five children, Nadia was amazed at how incredibly Christmassy the front of Anne-Marie's house looked. It was getting dark and the icicle lights strung all along the bottom edge of the roof of the thatched cottage were already illuminated. There was a whole herd of light-up reindeer grazing in the front garden and a Santa Claus hanging from a ladder that was fixed to the top of the chimney. Someone had been very busy decorating the house and, at eight months pregnant, it couldn't have been Anne-Marie. At least Nadia hoped not.

Getting out of her car, she was greeted by some of the Hudson family's menagerie of animals. Amongst the group of five dogs, there was an ancient black Labrador, who had telltale greying fur on its face and the sort of stiff-legged walk that only arthritis could cause. Nadia still found it hard to look at dogs, especially Labradors, when she missed Lola as much as she did. The chocolate Lab she'd been forced to leave behind in New Zealand had been like her shadow, especially during those seemingly endless nights in the early days after Ryan had left, when she'd thought she might never get over the pain of her marriage breaking up. In the end, getting over Ryan had been easier than she'd imagined because of what a total arse he'd turned out to be, but getting over Lola was proving impossible. The kids might think they could replace their beloved dog with a giant house rabbit, an aim which seemed to be the result of collusion between Remi and Daisy, but Lola had been a member of the family and she couldn't just be replaced.

'Hello, aren't you all lovely?' Nadia bent down to pet the dogs when they rushed up to greet her. The old Labrador's head felt like velvet and Nadia was going to have to force herself to carry on walking towards the house instead of staying with the dog. In the end the decision was taken away from her.

'Come on you lot! Leave Nadia alone, she doesn't want to get covered in dog slobber.' Anne-Marie came to the doorway, shaking a silver bowl that sounded suspiciously like it might contain dog biscuits. The canine welcoming committee obviously thought so too, and went hurtling in her direction with the old Labrador at the back, moving as quickly as its stiff-legged gait would allow. 'Poor old Margo's starting to walk like she's heavily pregnant too, bless her.'

'She's really lovely.' Nadia smiled as she followed the dogs towards the front door.

'Margo's been the best dog ever with the kids. They still dress her up, even now, and she always seems quite happy. This year Willow and Noah are insisting she's got to have some felt reindeer antlers to go with her Christmas jumper.'

'It's looks like you've got Christmas completely under control here.' Nadia gestured towards the lights. 'I've got to say I'm very impressed, especially with everything else you've got going on.'

'That's all down to Liam. Greg's been rushed off his feet with running this place and doing his training to set up our dog grooming business. I didn't even have to ask Liam to sort it out, though, and you should see inside. He let all the kids help with the big tree and it looks like an explosion in a tinsel factory.'

'That sounds brilliant. My two have been angling to put the decorations up since just after the October half-term and I think I'm going to have to finally give in. Although it won't be anything on this scale. The kids would love this.'

'You'd be welcome to bring them up any time.'

'That's lovely of you, but you've got enough children to look after. The last thing you need is me adding to your workload by turning up with my two.'

'It's always been a case of the more the merrier for me.' Anne-Marie laughed. 'After all, you don't have six kids if you don't like being surrounded by noise and chaos. The neighbours all say I'm the old woman who lived in a shoe! Come on in and you can see the tinsel-fest for yourself.'

'If I brought the kids here they'd probably try to sneak a couple of the dogs out with them too.' Nadia followed Anne-Marie down the hallway.

'That would probably do me a favour, but you might not be too pleased.' Anne-Marie grinned and did a passable impression of a magician's assistant when they reached the lounge. 'Ta da! This is Liam's pièce de résistance. There is a Christmas tree under all that lot, I promise. You just can't see it for all the baubles and tinsel.'

'It looks brilliant; the whole room does.' Even if that many decorations might not exactly be to Nadia's taste, the row of eight Christmas stockings hanging from the mantelpiece above the fire-place depicted Anne-Marie's family perfectly. The stockings were a mix of styles and sizes, but they were all handmade, with each family member's name lovingly embroidered on to the top. There was even one for Anne-Marie's unborn child, which for now just had the word *Baby* stitched on to it. 'Santa Claus obviously remembers everyone in this house, even the ones who haven't yet been born.'

'She does and she couldn't resist buying a few things for the baby, just in case.' Anne-Marie laughed. 'I wouldn't dare say this out loud if the younger children were at home, but thank goodness the online elves deliver to the door these days. Otherwise I'd have had to rope poor old Liam in for that too.'

'Even with help it must be exhausting. Are you still feeling okay?'

'I'm so tired, I feel like I've got somebody else's eyeballs in.' Anne-Marie sank down onto the sofa as she spoke. 'I'm half hoping they'll keep me in hospital for a few days after I've had this one, so I can get some proper rest. But at least Greg finishes his training this week, so he and Liam should be able to handle the boarders between them. The trouble is, it gets busier again at this time of year because a lot of people go away for Christmas. I'm grateful for the money, don't get me wrong, but the thought of going away for Christmas and putting Margo into kennels would be like leaving a family member behind during the one time of year when you most want to spend it together. Thankfully not everyone thinks like me or we'd be bankrupt!'

'I know what you mean, dogs really do make a house a home. Are you having specific problems sleeping, or just finding it hard to get into a comfortable position this late on?' Nadia was trying to concentrate on the job in hand, checking on her patient, but it was hard for her thoughts not to keep drifting towards Lola when Margo was gazing at her with those soulful eyes all Labs seemed to have. It was difficult to imagine a Christmas without Lola waiting expectantly under the table for one of the children to drop a roast potato, which she'd snatch up before there was any chance of Nadia getting to it first. What was even harder to imagine was Ryan choosing not to be with his children for Christmas. Guilt had got the better of her again during another sleepless night two days before and she'd texted, offering to pay for his flights from New Zealand and back, if he wanted to come over and spend Christmas and New Year with the children. It would make a big dent in the money she'd been saving, but the years when Christmas was as magical for the children as it was right now were fleeting. The thought of Remi and Mo missing their dad more than ever, at a time of year when every other family on TV and in real life seemed to be spending the holiday period together, was even more of a motivator. But it was up to him now.

Her father had offered up the use of his house for Nadia and the children over Christmas. It was almost certainly a gesture to assuage Advik's guilt about his recent double standards and because he'd no doubt be spending Christmas with Caroline, but it meant that Ryan coming over didn't need to cost any more than the flights. The old family house had four good-sized bedrooms, and more than enough space for Nadia and Ryan to stay out of one another's ways when they weren't putting on a united front for the children. Despite all of that, and the fact that Ryan always got two weeks off work over Christmas, the text that Nadia had sent to suggest he visit had been met with a continued wall of silence so far. And she was desperately hoping that Anne-Marie wouldn't start asking about her plans for Christmas, because she didn't want to think about them. Even trying to help Anne-Marie to do the impossible and get a good night's sleep this late into her pregnancy seemed infinitely more doable than giving her children the Christmas they deserved.

'I'm getting quite a lot of Braxton Hicks and I seem to feel them more when I finally get a chance to lie down. I'm getting up to pee at least three times a night too. Greg's almost as bad as me these days and it wakes me up every time he gets up. We've both said it's a sign we're definitely too old for any more after this one.'

'It might be worth me doing a pelvic examination once I've done your blood pressure and urine checks and we've measured baby's growth. Just to see if you're starting to get some softening of the cervix. Although I don't have to if you'd rather not; it all sounds pretty normal to me.'

'I gave up being shy about letting people look at my hoo-hah when I had my first baby. And after this many, I should think there's a good proportion of medical professionals in the South West who wouldn't recognise me with my clothes on!' Anna-Marie's ready laugh rang out again.

'It won't take long, and once we've done all your checks, I can go through the information about the vitamin K injection and the tests the hospital will run on the baby once he or she arrives. I don't suppose a lot has changed since you had Willow.'

'I can barely remember what happened after any of my babies were born, so I definitely need reminding. I must be the only woman looking forward to a pelvic examination, just so I get the chance to lie down for a few minutes.'

'I must admit my patients aren't usually quite this keen!' Nadia took out the blood pressure monitor, so she could get Anne-Marie's check-up started and was pleased to see that her blood pressure was right in the middle of the normal range. Her fundus height, and the baby's size, was spot on for the expected due date, and the urine test was clear too. The pelvic examination had revealed something, though. It was nothing to worry about, but Nadia needed to let Anne-Marie know that there was a small chance of things progressing more quickly than she was expecting.

'Everything looks fine, but you're already two centimetres dilated.'

'Does that mean I've started to go into labour?'

'No, it's not that unusual for women to be two centimetres dilated for a few weeks before active labour starts, but it can sometimes mean things could start fairly soon. You're thirty-six weeks now, so if it doesn't start for another week you'd be considered full-term anyway.'

'I'd better get my hospital bag sorted then.' Anne-Marie widened her eyes. 'Will it be a problem if the baby does arrive early?'

'At thirty-seven weeks the baby would only have the same risk of needing special care as any other full-term delivery. So there's no need to worry about anything other than being all packed and ready to go once labour finally starts.'

'Will the Braxton Hicks bring the labour on early, do you think?'

'They don't cause dilation, it's just your body doing a few things to get ready and maybe giving you a timely warning that babies don't wait for anyone or anything. Sometimes not even for their mum to pack a hospital bag.'

'Oh blimey, could you imagine if hanging around to pack my bag meant I couldn't make it to the hospital? We're struggling to come up with names for this one, but I don't fancy Greg suggesting we call it lay-by or minivan after the place it was delivered. I'm definitely going to get organised now, so we can leave straight away if we need to.'

'That sounds like a good plan and at least if the baby comes a bit early you won't have to worry about going into labour in the middle of your Christmas dinner.'

'No, especially as Greg and Liam are doing all the cooking this year. I can't believe how much effort Liam is putting into everything and I think it's because he knows he won't be around in the same way next year, so he doesn't want to miss out on doing anything with the younger kids.'

'You've raised a lovely young man there.' Nadia smiled, but she couldn't help experiencing a twinge of dread at the thought of how quickly Christmas was approaching. Anne-Marie's family were putting in the effort to make it special, whereas Nadia's so-called husband couldn't even be persuaded to spend time with his children when it was all handed to him on a plate, and it was only a matter of time before Remi started asking whether she'd get to see her dad over Christmas. There was every chance that would be another thing on her children's wish list that Nadia couldn't grant and, all of a sudden, the idea of getting a giant house rabbit didn't seem so crazy after all.

* * *

Twenty-four. That's how many unread WhatsApp messages Frankie had sent her son since he'd seen her kissing Guy. She knew because she'd counted them and it was exactly double the number of voicemail messages her mother had left her telling her how unacceptable her behaviour was. She couldn't bear the thought of talking to Bhavna and it broke her heart that Hari obviously felt the same way about her. She was dreading the first contact being a message telling her that missing the wedding was fine by him.

'I forgot to tell you, I've found a buyer for this place,' Guy called out from the kitchen, where he was busy making what would no doubt turn out to be another delicious meal.

'Really? That was quick.' Frankie put her phone face down on the table so she wouldn't be tempted to check it, at least for a little while, and wandered through to the kitchen-diner where gorgeous smells were already making her mouth water.

'Yes, it was a young couple looking for their first place and this suited them perfectly. There's no chain, so it should go through pretty quickly. I just need to find somewhere else to buy now.'

'Places are going so fast. My landlord keeps making threats about selling the flat while the market's hot, as she puts it, or having to put my rent up when my tenancy is renegotiated next month to *compensate* her for not selling it. I should probably have given Advik a deadline to get the money together to buy me out of our old place, but I didn't want to be the bad guy in every respect and it's one thing he seems to appreciate. We agreed we'd give both kids some money from the sale, too, just as a little nest egg they can invest for the future, but he doesn't seem to realise how desperately Nadia needs that right now. So I can't help thinking that maybe I should start to push it. I don't want to be enemies with someone I was married to for over thirty years, but the constant fobbing off I'm getting from him, and the silent treatment he seems happy for Hari to give me, makes it hard to just keep taking it all.'

'You shouldn't have to.' Guy shut the oven door and turned away from the stove, pulling her into his arms and immediately making the world feel like a better place. 'You know, I could rent for a while when the buyers move in here. It might take me some time to find what I'm looking for anyway and it could be a great opportunity for us to see how we get on living together.'

'You want me to move in to a rented place with you?' Frankie's eyes shot open, as she pulled away to look at him.

'Not really, because that's only a six-month commitment. What I really want is for us to make a much more permanent commitment than that and have a mortgage and a marriage, the whole works. But I know it's far too soon for you to think about that, so renting somewhere for six months could get us further down that line, and it might mean you feel ready to make a longer-term commitment.'

'Or it might split us up.'

'It might, but I don't think it will. Even if it does, all that means is that we know sooner where this is going. I've waited half my life to fall in love again and now that I have I don't want to waste time. If we could be living together in two months instead of two years, that gives me all that extra time with you.' Guy stroked the side of her face. 'But just because it's what I want, it doesn't mean you have to want it too. I'm not going anywhere. You can take this as slowly as you like, but I'd never forgive myself if I didn't at least ask you to think about it.'

'If I moved in with you, what would happen to Nadia and the kids?'

'I don't want you to think I'm trying to corner you, but there's a place on the edge of town that's up for rent. It's been let as two separate Airbnbs, but it came off the site when the owner decided to sell it after he moved to Spain. The sale fell through really late, after the exchange of contracts, so now he's looking to rent it out on a six-month tenancy until the start of next summer. He can't complete a new sale or start offering holidays before then, because he's suing the company who were supposed to be buying it for breach of contract. The smaller house has plenty of room for the two of us, and the main property has three bedrooms, which could suit Nadia and the kids perfectly.'

'It sounds great, but I don't know if Nadia could afford her share of a place like that, or whether I could, come to that.'

'I know the owner from way back and he offered me a really good deal. He's come back from Spain to stay for a month over Christmas and New Year, but after that it'll just be sitting empty again. He wants someone living there who'll be happy to put up with viewings when the property goes back on the market and who won't suddenly refuse to leave when the tenancy ends. He needs someone he trusts, so he wants to rent it to someone he knows and it's a great price for that reason.' Guy took a deep breath. 'I don't want you to take this the wrong way either, or for it to make you think I'm trying to take over, but you and Nadia wouldn't need to worry about paying for anything if we took this place on. It could give you both the breathing space you need.'

'We couldn't let you do that.' Even as Frankie said the words she could picture the relief on Nadia's face knowing she had more time to sort out the sale of the house in New Zealand, instead of taking a tenancy on the first thing she could afford. If Advik released Frankie's share from the old house, it might even be enough of a deposit for Nadia to buy somewhere instead.

'Steve, the guy who owns it, has phoned me twice already today to ask me to move in by the end of January, because he's worried about it being empty in the new year. If I take it, I won't be paying any more than I would to rent a flat in Port Agnes, so there'd be no need for you and Nadia to contribute.'

'It sounds too good to be true.'

He laughed at the expression that must have crossed her face. 'I know, I know, it's too much. Not everything has to be difficult, but unfortunately it usually is and it could be perfect timing for us and for Nadia. The only difficult bit is how Hari and your mum will take it, and I can understand if Nadia doesn't want to be seen to be taking sides.'

'She just wants the best for her kids.' A thousand thoughts were racing through Frankie's mind. 'And so do I, which means I'd be an absolute idiot to say no to this.'

'Well no one could accuse you of that.'

'If I say yes, I want to split the rent with you and pay the bigger share to cover Nadia's place.'

'We can argue about that later. Do you want to go and see the place before I tell Steve we'll do it?'

'Has it got heating and running water?'

'Are you just after me for my utilities?' Guy grinned. 'It's got all mod cons and even an inside toilet! There's a lovely garden and great views too, which was why it was so popular as an Airbnb. Do you think Nadia will be okay with the idea?'

'She'll be over the moon. The flat's so cramped and the kids desperately need some more space. They're always asking when they're going to see you again, so I know they'll love it and if there's outside space they'll love it even more.' She was already thinking about some of the things on Remi's Christmas list, almost all of which required a garden – from the trampoline to the long list of pets she'd told Santa he could pick from. Apparently even just one would do.

'The garden's huge and part of the deal with Steve is that I'll keep it in check. I'll even get you your own rake for when we have to sort out the leaves in the spring.'

'Well that seals it then; after all, what more could a girl want?' She pretended to flutter her eyelashes and he spun her around.

Guy's smile was even broader than before. 'So I can tell Steve it's definite?'

'Uh huh.' The butterflies were back and doing somersaults in her stomach, but it had nothing to do with nerves about moving in with Guy. She might not be ready to admit it yet, but she'd thought about the future a lot too and taking the plunge of a long-term commitment didn't scare her at all, despite how her marriage to Advik had ended. Guy was completely different and so was she.

'What about your mum and Hari?'

'I've been a disappointment to my mum from the moment I popped out without the right anatomy, so I learned to live with that a long time ago.'

'And Hari?'

'He's already ignoring me, so I haven't got much to lose.' Frankie shook her head, determined not to spoil the moment by crying, despite the ache that seemed to have permanently settled in her chest from not hearing from her son. 'I stayed with Advik for a lot longer than I should have, because I thought that was best for Nadia and Hari, but it would probably have been easier for Hari to accept if I'd done it years ago. I know for certain it would have been better for me and Advik. If that's taught me anything, it's that I can't live my life trying to please other people, because there's a good chance they won't like the choices I make anyway.'

'So you'd be moving in with me because you want to, not just for my utilities?' He was teasing her now and a little bit of the heaviness in her chest lifted.

'Absolutely.' She reached up to kiss him and her body responded in a way she hoped would make her forget everything, even for a little while. If Hari was determined to keep punishing her for having a life of her own, then she was just going to have to hope he'd eventually get over it. If he didn't, not even being able to grant Remi's wish of getting a pet would save Christmas. Nothing could.

18

The Christmas light switch-on in Port Agnes had over an hour's build up. The lights themselves would be illuminated at five o'clock, to make sure it was fully dark, but there was plenty to keep the children entertained up until then. Hamish had texted Nadia to ask if they could meet by the artificial ice rink that had been set up on the piece of land behind Mehenick's Bakery and the other shops and cottages on that side of the harbour. There was a wooden cabin there, too, which had been erected overnight, and was now decked out ready for Santa to use as his grotto. It would also be the starting point for the parade, where Santa would board an old wooden boat that had been mounted on wheels, and be pulled up King's Street and down the high street, handing out small gifts to the children lining the parade route.

Santa would turn on the Christmas lights once he reached the harbour and the parade would continue, with groups of local performers joining Santa on the next leg of his tour. Lots of the children dressed up and joined the end of the parade with their families, and Remi and Mo were no exception. Unlike the nativity play, there'd been no pressure on Nadia to handmake the costumes. Mo was dressed as a snowman and Remi was a ginger-bread girl, in outfits from an online fancy dress store that hadn't broken the bank. Although with Ryan still not responding to the offer to pay for his flights, Nadia had decided to go all-out for the kids at Christmas and try and make it as special as possible, despite the absence of their father.

When Frankie had told her about the property Guy was getting for a peppercorn rent, and his offer for Nadia and the children to take the larger of the two properties on the plot, she'd been gobs-macked. Here was a man who'd only been a part of their lives for a matter of months and yet he was doing all he could to make life easier for them. She still hadn't come to terms with the fact that he wouldn't accept any contribution towards the rent and she was determined to find a way around that, but the kids would be so much happier with a bit of the outside space they'd been used to in New Zealand. Even better was the fact that her mother had finally decided to put herself first. It was obvious how much Frankie loved Guy, and there was no doubting he felt the same. Nadia had been worried that her mother might throw away her chance of happiness to keep the peace with Nani and Hari and she'd been ready to rope Gwen into an intervention if necessary. Thankfully it hadn't come to that and as soon as Nadia had saved enough to finally put a deposit down on a place for her and the children, she'd be giving Frankie and Guy the space they needed too. If Hari hadn't come to his senses by then, she'd be getting Gwen on the case for that too and her little brother wouldn't stand a chance.

'I love the wings!' Hamish called out, as Nadia and the children walked towards the ice rink. She'd added a costume for herself to the online basket at the last minute. Dressing as an angel didn't seem too daring, especially as the only choices left in her size and price range were between that and a Christmas pudding. She hadn't seen Hamish since the kiss at the hospital and there'd been no mention of it in the texts they'd exchanged. It had obviously been a heat of the moment thing, otherwise he'd definitely have brought it up. The fact that Nadia had found herself thinking about it several times a day was just something she was going to have to get over. Having Hamish as a friend was really important to her and he completely understood what it was like to take on the role of both parents. She wasn't going to jeopardise that for a fantasy, no matter how tantalising it might be.

'Wings are surprisingly difficult to control! I managed to knock about six packets of sweets off the shelf in the newsagent's with them. I don't think Doris Myklow was very amused.'

'I reckon it was worth it; you look fabulous.' Hamish gave her an appreciative look. Mo was already chasing the two girls around, threatening to turn them into snowballs. According to him, snowmen had the power to do that, and the squeals from Daisy and Remi suggested they believed it too.

'Are you hiding anything under your coat?' As soon as the words were out of Nadia's mouth she realised how suggestive they sounded. It was almost as bad as blurting out just how many times she'd thought about that kiss. 'That didn't come out right; what I meant to say was... are you hiding a fancy dress costume under there?'

She deliberately didn't look at him when he answered, but she could tell he was smiling by the tone of his voice. 'No, sadly just an embarrassing Christmas jumper. If I venture onto the ice there's a danger I could humiliate myself without adding in the prospect of doing it dressed as an elf, and I don't want to end up in A&E wearing red and white stripey tights.'

'I think you could carry them off.' She hadn't meant to say that either, but given how good he looked in jeans, it was a safe bet he could get away with wearing tights too.

'Maybe I should dress like that for the party after the nativity play. Did you see the email from the PTA suggesting the parents dress up too, to get into the spirt of things?'

'The only spirit I'll be getting into is a very large gin.' Nadia couldn't stop her face from falling at the thought of the nativity play.

'I know what you mean. I've still got no idea how I'm going to turn the pile of fabric I've bought into a sheep costume for Daisy, but don't forget you promised to help.'

'It's not that.' Nadia had been determined not to think about Ryan on a day when she was supposed to be concentrating on having fun with the kids, but it was impossible. 'I haven't heard from Ryan about coming over for Christmas to see the kids, despite offering to pay for his flights. I even offered to video chat him when the nativity is on instead, so he can see Remi's big moment.'

'And he still hasn't answered?' Hamish's eyebrows knitted together, as if he was finding it impossible to understand Ryan's attitude. He wasn't the only one, but he didn't know the half of it.

'Oh no, I finally got a response. He said he's too busy to come over for Christmas and that he can't guarantee to be available to watch the nativity play either. So I replied asking if he wanted me to video it and if we could arrange a few times for him to FaceTime the kids over the Christmas break too. And now we're back to silence. I don't know what to do. I've got no idea if he's even got them any presents. I've bought some extra things just in case and I'll put a label on them pretending they're from Ryan, but I can't believe they can mean so little to him.'

'I know it probably doesn't help, but it's his loss. He's an idiot if he doesn't realise what he's missing.' Hamish gestured towards the children, who were now throwing imaginary snowballs at one another. 'Just look at those kids. Sara would have done anything to be here to see this.'

'Oh Hamish, I'm so sorry. Here I am whingeing on about how useless Ryan is and worrying about how it'll affect the kids, when this time of year must be so hard for you and the girls. Just tell me to shut up.'

'I'd never do that.' He smiled and she couldn't help wishing for the thousandth time that she'd chosen someone like him to be her children's father. Remi and Mo deserved better and so did she. Hamish made it easy to imagine what a different life could be like and she was starting to think she might not want to rule that out altogether after all. When she'd told Remi and Mo they were meeting up with Daisy and Hamish to go skating, they'd been so excited and it wasn't just because the girls were such good friends. Remi had said she hoped Hamish would go skating with them because he was really funny, and every time Nadia met up with him his kindness shone through. 'You don't whinge on at all. Ryan is a word I can't use with so many children about, and he doesn't appreciate how lucky he was to have the kids, or you. It must be so hard to accept that someone can do that. One day he's going to regret it more than he can ever imagine, and you're going to be glad he made the choices he did. I promise.'

'I hope so.' She had to drop her gaze, otherwise there was a very real danger of her making a move that would embarrass them both. 'I just hope his choices don't make the kids sad, even when they're older.'

'They look like they're doing pretty well to me.' Hamish smiled as another peal of laughter drifted across from where the children were playing. 'And that's all down to you.'

'Thank you, that means a lot and it so nice having someone I can talk to about all of this.'

'Any time. But right now, I think we need to go and strap our skates on and get shown up by the kids on the ice. I've already got my eye on one of the penguin things that are meant to help preschoolers learn to skate; Mo's just going to have to take his chances if there's only one.' Hamish grinned and held out his hand. 'Or we could just hold on to each other and hope we stay upright, because me going it alone could be dangerous for everyone.'

'Well I wouldn't want you to face danger alone.' Nadia took his hand, her reaction to such a simple touch proving beyond all doubt that she was already in danger of something far scarier than slipping on the ice. But there were just some things she couldn't control.

* * *

Spending time with Nadia and her children was the most fun Hamish had had in a very long time. Remi and Mo were lovely kids, and Daisy radiated happiness when she was around them. But he'd have been lying if he said spending time with them was all about making Daisy happy. Nadia was the first person since Sara he'd felt he had a chance of developing strong feelings for. She was totally different from any of the women he'd previously dated. It couldn't be clearer that her children came first for her and he loved that about her. There were other things he loved too, like the way she supported Genevieve with such empathy, and the shy smile she'd use to try and detract from things when she felt a bit vulnerable. He pictured that look even when he wasn't with her, the way she'd tuck some of her hair behind her ear and look down at the ground, somehow making her smile even more beautiful.

He'd wondered whether the kiss would change things between them and he'd definitely wanted it to, at least at first, but he'd known he needed to leave the ball in her court when it came to taking things further. When she hadn't mentioned it, he'd been tempted to go against his instincts and bring it up, but there was a good chance that could make her back off altogether and her friendship meant a lot to him. Losing that, and risking Daisy's relationship with Remi, wasn't worth it. Not when the chances were that things between him and Nadia wouldn't work out, even if they decided to give it a try. Some things were better left to the imagination. At least that was what he kept telling himself.

It was so nice to watch the children's faces when Santa handed them each a gift, and to watch their eyes light up when the Christmas tree did. It was obvious how much joy watching them brought Nadia, too, and if they'd been a family it would be a memory they'd have talked about for years to come.

'I think someone's ready for bed.' Nadia smiled as Mo yawned so hard he was in danger of dislocating his jaw. The two girls were back on the ice rink after the parade, but Nadia was clearly going to need to head home as soon as they'd finished.

'It's been a lovely afternoon; thanks for letting us hang out with you.' Hamish had been about to suggest meeting up again, when he got cut off.

'Nadia! We were looking out for you in the parade.' Anna, who Hamish had met a few times through work, was pushing a double buggy, closely followed by Gwen and a younger woman.

'I'm sorry we missed you.' Nadia scooped up Mo, who was clinging to her side like a limpet, his eyes already opening and closing as he desperately tried to pretend he wasn't tired. 'But I think this is the biggest crowd I've ever seen for the switch-on.'

'Me too and it was quite the workout with the double buggy, I can tell you. Brae had to shoot off after the lights were turned on to open up the restaurant. We met up with Toni and Jess, too, so we were only missing you to have the whole gang together. Although you probably did well to avoid walking too close to me in the parade; I think I bruised a few ankles with this thing!' Anna smiled at Hamish. 'It's lovely to see you again.'

'You too, and I can't believe how much the twins have grown.'

'I know, it's costing us a fortune! That's why Brae had to go and open the restaurant; we need to sell as many fish and chips as we can to keep up with what these two need.' Anna laughed and turned towards the blonde woman on her left. 'Have you met Izzy before? She's one of the newer midwives on the team. Hamish is a GP at the surgery.'

'I don't think we have met, have we?' Hamish smiled as Izzy shook her head. 'It's great to meet you and I'm sorry I kept Nadia all to myself.'

'No you're not!' Gwen, who was dressed as Mrs Claus, wagged a finger at him. He was trying to think of a comeback that wouldn't betray the truth when he was cut off for the second time.

'Hamish, this is where you've been hiding! I spotted Daisy on the ice rink just now and Portia insisted on joining her, but I've been trying to spot you all afternoon.' Saskia, who ran the PTA, enveloped him a heavily perfumed embrace before he even had a chance to respond.

'I definitely haven't been hiding. Nadia and I even braved the ice rink. It's been great fun and we're already planning on getting together to try and finish the challenge you've given us of making the kids' costumes for the nativity play.' Hamish looked towards Nadia and smiled when Saskia finally released him. It was a relief to breathe fresh air again.

'I must admit I didn't expect to see you here, Nadia. I didn't think you'd celebrate Christmas.' Saskia was still smiling, but her tone was almost as tight as the expression on her face.

'Oh really, why's that?' Nadia raised her eyebrows.

'Well you know, you guys have your own celebrations, don't you? So I didn't think this would be your sort of thing. I was a bit surprised that Remi was taking part in the nativity play, too, and I was shocked that Miss Renfrew gave her a main part when there were other children, like Portia, who the nativity means a lot more to.'

'I didn't realise you were such a committed Christian, Saskia?' Gwen really did seem to know everyone. 'I remember your mum saying how much she wanted you to get married in St Jude's, but that you were absolutely insistent on having the ceremony at Tregenna Castle.'

'I, er—' For once in her life Saskia seemed to be lost for words, but the midwives weren't done yet.

'Yes, and it's funny that I've never seen you at any of the services at St Jude's. I've been going to a lot of them since my partner, Noah, took over as vicar there.' Izzy was fixing Saskia with a look that would have put a headteacher to shame.

'Well, we go to all the important ones. You know, like at Christmas and...'

'So just Christmas then?' Izzy shook her head. 'I'll have a word with Noah and see if he can get you booked into the Sunday school that some of the regular members of the congregation are setting up. It's a bit of an early start, but I'm sure you won't mind that, given that the nativity story is so important to your daughter. It'll give you both the chance to learn about more of the bible stories too, especially as they're looking for more volunteers to help run it.'

'Look, I wasn't being funny, I just thought that because Remi has her own celebrations, it was a bit odd she was given one of the main parts in the nativity, that's all.' Saskia at least had the good grace to look embarrassed.

'And what celebrations do you think those are?' Gwen's gaze was as direct as her question.

'I don't know, Diwali and Ramadan, isn't it?'

'For a start, one's a Muslim festival and the other one is a Hindu celebration, but either way my religious credentials are about as solid as yours. So here I am, celebrating Christmas with everyone else, because anything that gives my kids a reason to have fun is worth celebrating in my book.' Nadia shrugged. 'I'm sorry if Portia was disappointed about the nativity play, but you're not seriously expecting me to ask Miss Renfrew to give Remi's role to her instead?'

'Of course not.' Saskia's laugh was hollow and her eyes were darting from side to side, looking for an excuse to get out of there as quickly as she could. 'Right, well, it was lovely to see you all, but I think Portia has had enough of skating now, so we're going to head home.'

'We'll see you at the nativity play, if we ever manage to get the costumes sorted.' Hamish almost felt sorry for Saskia, who'd definitely got more than she'd bargained for taking on the sisterhood of the Port Agnes midwives.

'Yes, see you then.' Saskia almost broke into a run as she headed over to force poor little Portia to leave.

'If I know Saskia, she's probably already tried to persuade the teacher to drop Remi from the nativity in favour of her daughter.' Gwen pulled a face. 'She's been a little madam ever since she was old enough to open her mouth. Even her mum thinks she's hard work.'

'I almost felt sorry for her,' Nadia echoed Hamish's thoughts as Mo's head lolled on her shoulder. The little boy had managed to sleep through the whole exchange. 'Until she started suggesting that Remi shouldn't be in the nativity play.'

'She'll be a brilliant donkey.' Gwen laughed. 'And if either of you need any help with those costumes, you know where I am. I've got pretty good at it since I started with the Quicksteppers and had to start sewing sequins into parts of costumes I wouldn't have dreamt sequins could go!'

'We'll bear that in mind.' Hamish exchanged a look with Nadia.

'It's all right, I saw that. You two *want to be alone*.' Gwen attempted a Garbo-esque accent. 'That's going to upset Saskia even more than the role her daughter has been assigned in the nativity play.'

'Well, I think I'd better get my two home before my arm goes completely dead from carrying Mo.'

Hamish shouldn't have been as pleased as he was that Nadia hadn't tried to brush off Gwen's comments, but he couldn't help it. 'I'll come with you. Daisy won't want to stay without Remi and I can take a turn carrying Mo, if he gets too heavy.'

'You two.' Gwen shook her head, giving them a knowing look; she was still doing it when they'd all said their goodbyes. Hamish obviously wasn't doing nearly as good a job of hiding how he felt about Nadia as he'd thought he was. Maybe it was time to admit it to himself too.

* * *

Mo hadn't even woken up when Nadia had passed him to Hamish and she didn't think she'd have made it all the way back to The Cookie Jar if he hadn't stepped in.

'Is that Freddie?' Nadia peered at the man sitting on the bench outside a shop three doors down from the café, trying to see if it was Genevieve's husband, but he had his head in his hands so it was hard to tell.

'I'm not sure, but whoever it is, they look upset.' The worry in Hamish's voice mirrored her own. The prospect of Ginny or Freddie getting any more bad news made her feel sick.

'Hello my angel, did you enjoy going ice skating again?' Frankie had suddenly emerged from the darkness and swept Remi into her arms. She and Guy had headed off after they'd all watched the Christmas lights get switched on together.

'Mmm hmm.' Remi nuzzled into her grandmother's neck, clearly almost as tired as her little brother. 'Daisy was really good too.'

'I bet you both were.' Frankie smiled down at Hamish's little girl.

'Can I ask you a huge favour please, Mum?' Nadia met her mother's gaze.

'Of course, sweetheart, what is it?'

'We think that's Genevieve's husband on the bench and he looks upset. Could you take the kids up, while we have a quick chat with him?'

'No problem at all.' Frankie put Remi down. 'I'm just going to take Mo from Mummy, darling, and we can all go inside. Once we've got him in bed, I can read you and Daisy a story if you want one.'

'Yay!' Remi and Daisy responded in unison, seeming to get a new lease of life at the prospect of some one-to-one time with Frankie and a minute later they were all on their way upstairs to the flat.

'What are we going to do, just go straight up to him ask if he's okay?' Nadia whispered the words to Hamish.

'The simple approach is usually the best.' By the time they were halfway towards the bench, there was no doubt it was Genevieve's husband sitting there.

'Hi Freddie, we just wanted to check you were okay.' Hamish sat down next to him and the other man's head shot up, his eyes swollen and bloodshot even in the half-light of the streetlamp further down the street.

'I found Ginny's wish list.' Freddie looked from Hamish to Nadia and back again. 'For her funeral and after she's gone.'

'Oh Freddie.' The look on his face made Nadia want to cry, but the last thing he needed was for her to hijack his pain.

'She's chosen the songs and readings, and there's a long list of things she wants me to do for the baby. Everything from the school she wants her to go to, to the Christmas traditions she wants replicated from when she was a kid. It's like she's already accepted she's not going to be there and I'm terrified she's giving in to this.'

'That's not what she's doing.' Hamish put a hand on Freddie's shoulder. 'She wants to be there, even if the worst happens and she can't physically be with you. That's the opposite of giving up, but I know how hard it is to read that sort of thing.'

'Ginny told me about your wife.' Freddie let go of a shuddering sigh and Nadia suddenly felt like she was eavesdropping on a very personal conversation she could never be a part of. It didn't surprise her to learn that Hamish had decided to share his story to help Ginny and Freddie. Neither of them needed her there and yet she couldn't tear herself away. 'How the hell did you get through it?'

'The only way was to take it an hour at a time, even trying to take it a day at a time was too much at some points. I know being able to talk through everything she wanted for me and the girls, if she didn't make it, helped her a lot. I didn't realise it at the time, because I couldn't accept that I was going to need to carry out her wishes, but it helped me so much afterwards too.' Hamish shook his head. 'Genevieve's prognosis is so much better than Sara's, though, and her wish list is much more likely to be something you'll work through together, rather than on your own. But if that helps her to face up to the operation and any treatment she might need, feeling a bit less like it's all out of her control, I promise you it can only be a good thing.'

'Do you know what the worst bit was?' Freddie's eyes filled with tears as he looked at Hamish. 'She'd written about how she wanted me to find someone else, but asked me to make sure it didn't happen too soon so that I wouldn't forget about her or let the baby forget about her. Then she asked me to promise I'd never love another woman as much as I love her. She wanted to die knowing she'd been the love of my life. How can I have done such a shitty job of being a husband that she doesn't already know that?'

'She does. The way she talks about you, from the first moment I met up with her again, has made that obvious.' Nadia might still feel like she was intruding, but she couldn't let Freddie think that way.

'She can't really know though, can she? Not if she thinks there's even a chance I'd ever love someone as much as I love her.' He turned back towards Hamish. 'Did your wife make you promise that?'

'She told me she wanted me to find someone one day, but mostly it was about the girls and putting them first and finding someone else wasn't something I could picture happening.'

'She must have known you'd never feel that way again. You only get one love of your life and if Ginny doesn't realise she's mine, then I've failed.'

'Have you talked to her about it?' Hamish waited, as Freddie shook his head.

'She doesn't even know I've found the list.'

'You need to talk to her and say all the things you've said to us.' Hamish still had a hand on Freddie's shoulder. 'It wouldn't matter even if she wasn't dealing with cancer, because I've seen enough people lose loved ones suddenly to know you shouldn't leave things unsaid. Speak to her, tell her how much you love her and talk about all the things you want for your baby's future. I wish I could have a million more conversations with Sara, but just one would be fantastic. I'd love to ask her how to handle things with our eldest daughter now that she's about to leave home for university, but at least I can be certain she went knowing just how much I loved her. Talk to Ginny like that every day for the next fifty years, if you get the chance, and I really think you will.'

'Thank you.' Some of the torment etched on Freddie's face seemed to lessen. He and Hamish understood each other in a way almost no one else could, because they'd both been forced to face up to the prospect of losing the love of their lives, although Freddie was still struggling. Nadia couldn't even pretend to understand what that felt like, and what Hamish had been through broke her heart. But it wasn't just his loss that made her chest ache, it was the realisation that he was still completely head over heels in love with his wife and probably always would be. Any future there might be with him had only ever been in her imagination, but now there was a ghost lurking in the shadows. Sara would always be there and that didn't leave a lot of space for anyone else. Hamish didn't deserve to lose the love of his life and neither did Freddie. So Nadia would happily pray to any deity listening that Ginny's husband would never have to carry out her wish to find someone else. Some wishes weren't meant to be granted.

19

✉ Message from Ginny
It's Freddie here. Ginny's in labour. Thought you'd want to know. I'll be in touch as soon as there's any news.

Nadia stared at the message for a moment, trying to think how best to reply. Usually, in moments like this where her patients had chosen a hospital delivery, she'd fire off a good luck message and wait to hear more once the baby had arrived. But in Ginny's case everything seemed more loaded somehow. Good luck needed to encompass much more than just the delivery. Ginny would be staying in for an operation, which would more than likely involve a full mastectomy. Then they'd begin the wait to find out if the cancer had spread to the lymph nodes and what follow-up treatment she might need. Ginny had told Nadia that she'd refused the biopsy to find out if there was any cancer in the lymph nodes before she had the baby, because she didn't want the consultant to use the results to keep pushing her to have the operation and chemo straight away.

With all of that, good luck felt completely inadequate and if she didn't need to be at Hamish's house in half an hour to try and finish the costumes for the nativity play, she'd have been tempted to jump into the car and drive to the hospital to wait for the news in person. Daisy and Remi had both been invited to a party at the soft play centre at Thunderhill Farm, and Frankie was taking Mo to a playdate with Riley and Guy. Finishing a donkey costume might not be the most relaxing way to spend a Sunday afternoon, but she was running out of time because the nativity play was less than twenty-four hours away. All of which meant that heading to Truro wasn't even a possibility, so she'd just have to settle for a message instead.

✉ Message to Ginny

Hi Freddie, thanks for letting me know. Thinking of you both and you're going to be such amazing parents. I can't wait to hear the news and please give Ginny a big hug from me once the baby is here X

'Come on sweetheart, we'd better get going or we're going to be late for the party.' Nadia grabbed the present for Remi's friend and the bag with the half-finished donkey costume in it. Based on the state of her attempts so far, it was going to take nothing short of a Christmas miracle to get it finished in time for the play, but if a Christmas miracle was on offer she'd much rather it found its way to Ginny and Freddie.

* * *

'Are you still going out to meet Jamie?' Hamish glanced at his watch. Saffron had said she was leaving at 2 p.m., but it was twenty past already and she still didn't look like she was in any particular hurry and Nadia would be here any minute.

Not mentioning to Saffron that Nadia was coming over might

have been a cowardly decision, but there didn't seem any point in upsetting his older daughter for no reason. He'd talked to her about crossing the line after the incident at the dance competition, but there was no need for Saffron to think a new relationship might be on the cards when it came to Nadia. She clearly wasn't interested in being anything other than his friend and he'd already come to the conclusion that he'd much rather have her in his life as a friend than not have her in it at all, which would have been a definite risk if she'd been interested in taking things further. It meant that telling Saffron a friend was coming over should have been easy, but instead he was trying to get her out of the house so she wouldn't find out. This must be what it was like to have an affair.

'There's no hurry, he'll wait.' Saffron flicked back her blonde hair and Hamish felt a surge of sympathy for Jamie. He could still remember being that age and following his then-girlfriend around like a lovesick puppy. No wonder Saffron wasn't in any rush to leave.

'I thought you two were going to the cinema. What time does the film start?'

'Three, but there's always loads of adverts beforehand.'

'Here.' Hamish took two twenty-pound notes out of his wallet. 'You hardly had anything for lunch, why don't you grab something to eat beforehand.'

'Forty pounds?' Saffron eyed him suspiciously.

'Concession stands are always expensive. Go on, take it, or you'll be starving later.'

'Anyone would think you were trying to get rid of me.' If Saffron was still undecided about her future, she should seriously consider a career as a detective. She was a natural.

'I just want you to have some fun, that's all and I've got to get on with finishing Daisy's outfit for the nativity.'

'Jeez, if there's anything guaranteed to get me out of the house it's that thing. It looks like roadkill, and you nearly burnt the end of my finger off when you made me hold it together while you attacked it with the hot glue gun.'

'I could always use some more help if you've really got that much time on your hands?' He raised his eyebrows.

'Okay, I'm going; in fact, I'm gone.' Grabbing her bag, she kissed his cheek and shot out of the door. Letting out a long breath, he glanced at his watch again; he was just in time because Nadia would be here any minute. God knows how anyone had an affair and didn't drop down dead from the stress, because his heart was racing and he wasn't even doing anything wrong.

* * *

It was the third time Nadia had glued her fingers together and if this carried on, both hands were going to be completely webbed.

'Do you think these costumes will last through the performance?' Nadia looked at Hamish, who could have been performing a surgical procedure given the concentration on his face. He was using a cotton bud dipped in acetone to try and dissolve the glue between her fingers, which he'd already done twice before. Anyone would think her subconscious was doing this on purpose, just so he'd hold her hand again.

'Based on how well the glue has stuck your fingers together, I think the costumes should last a couple of hours.' He looked up at her and smiled, and suddenly the tingling on her skin where he was touching her had nothing to do with his attempts to remove the glue. 'And if that doesn't work, I've bought the biggest box of safety pins you've ever seen in your life.'

'Can you imagine Saskia's face if our girls turn up with their costumes held together with safety pins, after they were given main roles. You can bet your life that Portia's angel costume will be perfect and then she'll have even more to say about Remi being given the role as the donkey.'

'If I didn't think it would worry Daisy, I'd be tempted to do that on purpose, just to show Saskia how ridiculous this whole thing is.' Hamish set down the cotton bud and gently separated her fingers. 'There you go and that should be the last time, now we've finally finished gluing.'

'You do realise you're talking to someone who could make being clumsy into an Olympic sport, don't you? So anything could happen!' She laughed and he looked as though he was about to say something when her phone pinged. Grabbing it, she took in a sharp breath.

✉ Message from Ginny

It's Freddie again. Neviah's here, safe and well, and weighing in at eight pounds two, with crazy blonde hair like Boris Johnson... Not sure if I should be suspicious! Ginny did brilliantly and they're hoping she can have her op as early as Tuesday. I know she wishes you could have been here and hopefully you'll get to meet Neviah really soon. Thanks for everything X

Nadia read the message and then passed it straight to Hamish. 'It's Freddie but he sounds totally different, much more upbeat and I'm so glad everything that's going on hasn't stopped this being a really joyful day for them.'

'He's absolutely thrilled, you can tell and so he should be.' Hamish's eyes were glassy when he looked up from the phone, but he was smiling too. 'I can remember the moments when my girls were born like they happened yesterday. I cried like I was the newborn when we had Saffron, but Daisy's birth was bittersweet. I was so glad that Sara hadn't followed the advice to terminate the pregnancy, but I knew by then that I was going to lose her. Freddie's starting to sound like he really believes they can have it all and that's exactly how they should be feeling today. Like life is as close to perfect as it'll ever be.'

'I don't think Ginny will ever regret the decision she made to delay her operation, even if it means things have progressed and I hope to God they haven't. Neviah was everything to her from the moment she knew she was on the way.'

'We were the same. Even though Saff took us by surprise and changed all our plans. I bet you were too?'

'I was and I used to think the kids meant the world to Ryan too, but I've got a horrible feeling that if he could turn the clock back, he would.' An egg-sized lump had lodged itself in Nadia's throat at the thought that Ryan might want to wish their beautiful children away, but she knew there was a good chance it was true.

'I'll say it again: he's an idiot and he doesn't deserve you or the kids. Hey, don't get upset; he isn't worth it.' Hamish reached out as she blinked back the tears, hating herself for making any part of Ginny and Freddie's moment about her.

'They don't deserve him, they deserve a dad who thanks the universe every day that he has them in his life, but I was stupid enough to make it easier for him to justify not being involved at all and it breaks my heart that I might have caused them that pain.'

'None of this is your fault. You're amazing.' Hamish leant closer to her and suddenly she was moving towards him in slow motion, her brain telling her to stop and the rest of her acting on pure instinct. The gap between them must have been less than a few millimetres when the alarm on her phone suddenly burst into life, making her spring away from him as if she'd had an electric shock.

'I need to go and get Remi.' She'd worried she might lose track of time trying to finish the costume and had set the alarm just in case, but she hadn't expected the distraction to be Hamish.

'Nadia—' He reached out to her again, but she was already stuffing the donkey costume into a bag.

'Thanks for this, I don't think I'd ever have finished it without you, but I'd better go. I'll see you tomorrow.' Holding up a hand she cut off any response he might have made. 'I can see myself out. I'll see you at the nativity tomorrow and thanks again.'

Heading to the front door, she'd have had to run to be moving any faster. If there was ever a case of being saved by the bell, this was it, and thank God, otherwise there was no knowing how much of a fool she'd have made of herself.

* * *

Frankie was even more excited than Remi about the prospect of the nativity play. Anna and Ella had arranged the rotas and some extra cover from agency staff, so that both she and Nadia would be able to see Remi take centre stage. It was the sort of thing she'd only been able to dream of when Nadia and the children had been living in New Zealand and she wasn't going to miss any opportunity to be part of whatever they were doing now they were home.

'There are a couple of seats up near the front, next to Hamish.' Frankie had a feeling he was saving them on purpose, but Nadia was shaking her head.

'You can go up there if you like, but I'm going to sit nearer the back in case Mo starts to get fidgety.' Nadia moved to the end of one of the other rows. Frankie had been surprised when her daughter had said she was keeping Mo off nursery to watch the play, especially after she'd said before that the nativity being on one of his nursery days would mean she could enjoy it without having to worry about him getting fed up. Nadia had said something about making sure he didn't feel left out, but Frankie hadn't been convinced that was the reason and now she was almost certain it had something to do with Hamish. It wasn't the time to ask, even if Nadia had been willing to talk about it. A few minutes later, Remi marched on to the stage to start the play and Frankie forgot about everything else for the next half hour.

'She was brilliant, I mean they were all good, but she definitely stole the show.' Frankie had laughed and cried her way through it and she could see the emotion on her daughter's face too.

'She was amazing.'

'And it's great there's a videographer.' The headteacher had announced that there was no need for audience members to video the show as one of the dads, who was apparently a professional cameraman, was filming it and copies would be sold to raise funds for some new playground equipment. 'At least Remi won't have to keep worrying about Ryan missing out now.'

'It's a shame he couldn't care less.'

'Are you okay sweetheart? You look—'

'Well, wasn't that fantastic?' The headteacher, Mrs Croft, raised and lowered her hands repeatedly, with the palms facing downwards, to indicate that the audience needed to quieten down. 'The children all did so well and we're lucky enough that Reverend Noah Andrews was able to come along today. Reverend Andrews has been a part of the school community since coming to Port Agnes in the summer, and we are delighted to learn that he has now agreed to take over at St Jude's on a permanent basis, following Reverend Sampson's decision to retire. Let's all welcome Reverend Andrews to the stage, where he'll tell us a little bit more about why the story of the nativity is such an important one and why telling it from the animals' point of view can help us to get an even better understanding of the true meaning of Christmas.'

'It's great that Noah's staying on, isn't it?' Frankie's stage whisper to her daughter, as Noah walked on to the stage, barely seemed to register, but she grabbed her phone anyway to snap a quick picture for Izzy. Just at that moment, a message alert flashed up on her phone.

✉ Message from Advik
We need to talk about Hari.

Suddenly it wasn't just Nadia who had a lot on her mind.

20

Nadia had been pretending, even to herself, that she wasn't actively trying to avoid Hamish. He'd texted her after the nativity play, to say how relieved he was that the costumes had held up, how impressed he was with Remi, and how he was sorry he hadn't seen her as he'd been saving seats for her and Frankie. She sent a brief response thanking him and saying Daisy had been great too, but that she'd had to sit at the back because of Mo. It didn't explain why she'd asked Frankie to collect Remi after the play, so that she could disappear before there was any chance of Hamish finding her. Or why she'd hung back the next morning, until she'd seen his car drive away, before walking Remi into the playground.

If she was forced to admit it, she'd have to confess she was hoping to avoid Hamish for the next few days until the girls broke up for Christmas. One heat of the moment kiss could have been explained away, but the fact they'd been so close to another one couldn't have passed him by. It must have been obvious how attracted to him she was and she hated the thought of becoming another woman who'd end up failing miserably to match up to

Sara. Keeping her distance felt like the safest option, but then came the day of Ginny's op.

✉ Message from Hamish
Just spoken to Ginny's consultant at the hospital and she gave her permission to share an update with us both. They managed to remove the tumour with a lumpectomy, so there doesn't seem to have been any further spread from the delay. They've taken biopsies of some of the lymph nodes, so it's a case of waiting for the results now, but she's doing great otherwise. It definitely sounds like news to celebrate and I wondered if you wanted to come over with the kids on Friday, after the girls break up, for a Christmas movie marathon and some takeaway pizza?

Nadia's instinct was to come up with an excuse that they were already busy, but she knew how much Remi would want to celebrate the start of the Christmas holidays by hanging out with Daisy. Her children were already having to miss out on spending Christmas with their father, so it would have been really selfish of her to deny her daughter this as well. The truth was, Nadia had missed seeing Hamish, too, and she thought about him far more often than she should. She wanted to see him every bit as much as Remi wanted to spend time with Daisy, but she had to keep reminding herself that crossing the line in their friendship would never be worth it.

✉ Message to Hamish
Fantastic news about Ginny. Pizza and movies with the kids sounds great. Straight from school? What can we bring?

✉ Message from Hamish
Just yourselves. I've got the delivery service at Casa Mia on speed dial!

At least agreeing to go over to Hamish's might get her mum off her case. Frankie seemed to be out most of the time, either with Guy or at work. But whenever they were at home together, her mum would ask not-so-subtle questions about how Hamish was and whether Nadia had spoken to him lately. At least now she'd be able to say they'd be getting together and hopefully everyone could get back to accepting that their relationship was never going to be anything more than a friendship. Including Nadia.

* * *

'You do realise it's just the two of us still sitting here watching *Arthur Christmas*, don't you?' Hamish turned to Nadia, who looked like she belonged exactly where she was – curled up on the other end of the sofa. Or maybe that was just wishful thinking. It had been the simplest of evenings, but Hamish couldn't remember feeling this content for a long time. Saffron was staying overnight at her best friend Bianca's house after a party to mark their own end-of-term celebrations. So he didn't have to worry about her suddenly coming home and throwing a strop because Nadia and her children were there.

'What's wrong with that? I love this film.' Nadia smiled. The two girls had persuaded Mo to go off and play a game they'd made up where he was Santa's naughtiest elf. Usually they'd have started to get tired by now, but filled with pizza, and probably the equivalent of a bucket of popcorn, they didn't seem to be showing any sign of slowing down.

'Nothing; it's what it could lead to. I accidentally got really into the storyline of *Peppa Pig* when Daisy was little.'

'There's a storyline?'

'Oh you'd be surprised; poor old Daddy Pig can never catch a break.' Hamish loved it when she smiled in response to something he'd said. She really did have the most beautiful smile.

'I think I missed the boat on that, but Mo's obsessed with *PAW Patrol*, so thank goodness Santa managed to track down a Mighty Pups Lookout Tower.'

'Santa's obviously been working very hard.'

'Are you all sorted for Christmas?' Nadia looked over her shoulder as she spoke, obviously checking that none of the children had snuck in and were about to overhear something that could change Christmas for them forever.

'I think so. I've got pretty good at getting everything organised since Sara died and the presents are the easy bit, especially with Saff. She just sends me a series of links to click on these days, so the only thing that works hard is my credit card.' Hamish shrugged. 'The food shopping is much more painful. I've got my parents, my brother and his family coming to us for Christmas this year, as well as Sara's parents. Thankfully the girls are going to their godparents on the twenty-third for the night, which will give me a bit of time to get things organised before the family descends on Christmas Eve.'

'Sounds like it's going to be busy.' An unreadable expression crossed Nadia's face and she suddenly seemed keen to change the subject. 'Do you think Ginny will get her results before Christmas?'

'I hope so, but I know from friends who work in oncology that they sometimes wait until after the holidays if the news isn't so positive. I just hope they get the best possible present in time for Christmas.'

'Me too.'

'My head hurts, Daddy.' Daisy had come back into the room

with Remi and Mo following on behind her. 'And my tummy feels bubbly.'

'Does it darling? Let me see if you've got a temperature.' Hamish stood up and put his hand on his daughter's forehead. 'You don't feel hot, but I'll get the thermometer just to make sure. You've probably just eaten a bit too much popcorn or pizza. Do you feel sick?'

'Uh huh.'

'Okay angel, sit down for a minute and I'll get some things to help you feel better and check it's nothing else.'

'I want a cuddle.'

'I'll only be a minute.'

'Please Daddy.'

'I can give you a cuddle until Daddy gets back if you like, sweetheart?' Nadia held out her arms and Daisy didn't hesitate, snuggling up to Nadia as if she'd done it a thousand times before.

'Thank you. I'm sure it's just too much food and probably too much excitement. But the same thing happened after she had too much ice cream when Saff was looking after her, while we were with Beth at the hospital. So I'm starting to wonder if it might be a dairy allergy.' Hamish stroked his daughter's head. 'I'll be right back.'

True to his word, Hamish had got everything he needed and was back in the room within a couple of minutes. Daisy was still curled up in Nadia's lap, with Remi and Mo further along the sofa, happily watching the film they'd abandoned twenty minutes earlier.

'Okay darling, I'm back, let's take a look at you.'

'I feel really—' Daisy didn't even get to the final word before she was sick and Nadia bore the full brunt of it.

'Oh sweetheart, it's okay, you'll feel much better when it's all out.' Nadia barely seemed to register that she'd been in the line of fire; she was too busy comforting Daisy and stroking the little girl's hair away from her face. It was then, at probably the least romantic moment possible, that Hamish was forced to admit the truth. What he felt for Nadia went way beyond friendship and there was absolutely nothing he could do about it. The feelings had crept up on him, from an initial physical attraction that had grown into huge admiration for the care she showed everyone around her. Her selflessness as a mother was a big part of how he felt about her too, not to mention the warmth and understanding she'd shown Daisy. But there was more to it than all of that; when she smiled, he wanted to be the reason, and when she laughed, he wanted to be in on the joke. He couldn't explain how he'd come to feel so much for someone he'd known for such a short time, but it was out there now – even if the only person he admitted the truth to was himself.

* * *

When Frankie and Guy had offered to take Remi and Mo to a pantomime in Port Kara on the day before Christmas Eve, Nadia could have kissed them. In fact, she did. Having the time to finish her stint as Santa Claus and get all the kids' presents wrapped up, without any chance of them walking in and spoiling the surprise, was priceless. By five o'clock she was all done and looking forward to them coming back from the matinee performance and telling her all about it.

✉ Message from Mum
We bumped into Gwen at the pantomime, with some of her grandchildren, and she's invited us all back to hers for dinner. We'll probably all stay at Guy's place afterwards if that's okay, as we can walk there from Gwen's and it'll give you some extra time to get sorted. Maybe you can

even put your feet up for a bit! It's no problem if you'd rather we didn't go, just let me know xxx

She'd just been contemplating her answer, when another text pinged through.

⊠ Message from Ginny
Hi Nadia and Hamish. I wanted to let you both know that I've just had the most amazing news from my consultant and the lymph nodes are clear! I can't thank you enough for everything and it means I'll just be having a short course of radiotherapy, instead of chemo. I can't wait for Neviah's first Christmas with me and Freddie, and hopefully we'll all see you both really soon. Have a wonderful Christmas and thanks again for everything you've done for us! Xxx

She'd barely had time to read the message when her phone pinged again.

⊠ Message from Hamish
Did you see the message from Ginny? I can't stop smiling, I'm so happy! Just wondered if you fancied a second shot at celebrating the good news? I promise there'll be no vomiting children this time. The girls are with their godparents tonight and I thought we could go for a meal somewhere, my treat to thank you for being so lovely when Daisy was poorly. If you've already got plans, no worries, we can take a rain check until the New Year xx

Nadia tried not to read anything into the fact that it was the first time Hamish had put kisses in a message to her. He was just euphoric about Ginny's news and she had to admit the world did suddenly feel like a much nicer place.

✉ Message to Hamish

I did. Isn't it amazing! No plans here. The kids are at Guy's with Mum overnight, but I thought you were using the time while the girls were away to get everything sorted before the rest of the family arrive? X

She put one kiss on, then two, then deleted them altogether in case his had been a mistake, before finally settling back on one.

✉ Message from Hamish

I was up very early this morning and I'm all sorted for the family's arrival. Great that you're free, I'll pick you up at seven xx

That meant she had over two hours to get ready, which was way more time than she needed. So she had no idea why she felt so nervous. The first thing she was going to do was reply to Ginny and her mum, and then she was going to have to try and work out how on earth to stop placing so much importance on an impromptu celebratory meal with a friend.

* * *

'I'm an idiot, it's okay, you can say it.' Hamish made the admission as soon as Nadia opened the door to him, but she didn't miss a beat.

'I'm afraid you're going to have to be more specific than that before I decide whether or not I agree.' He really did love it when she smiled like that. Maybe it was because of the news about Genevieve, but there was a lightness in the air too, a sense that everything was coming right just in time for Christmas.

'I hadn't even thought about the fact that it's Christmas Eve eve today, until I tried to book a table. I called six places and none of them can fit us in, I'm really sorry.' Hamish had wanted to take her somewhere special and celebrating Genevieve's news was only part of the reason why.

'It's not a problem. We can grab a takeaway and bring it back here if you like, or we can take a rain check.' If Nadia was disappointed about not going out somewhere fancy then she wasn't showing it. She looked stunning, in a wine-coloured dress that was far too good for a date with him – if that's what this was – let alone for sitting at home waiting for a Deliveroo. Luckily, he wasn't quite that much of an idiot.

'I've managed to call in a favour, with Casa Mia. They usually only do pizzas as takeaway and, as you know, I'm probably their most loyal customer.'

'That's fine with me. There's never a bad time for pizza.' He couldn't help smiling as she spoke. It was something else he liked about her; she was the opposite of high maintenance. Sara definitely wouldn't have taken the news that he couldn't get a table at a restaurant with quite such good humour if she'd been all dressed up with nowhere to go. It hadn't detracted from how much he'd loved his wife, but she had high expectations of herself and sometimes that had extended to her expectations of others. Nadia had obviously had to deal with being let down far more often than she should have, but he didn't want to add to that.

'Lorenzo did a bit better than pizza. He didn't have a table for us, but he's making us four antipasti dishes, a couple of main courses, some panna cotta and a *croccantino*. All we need to do is to collect them. We can either bring the food back here, or we can go back to my place and eat in the conservatory. I laid the table in there just in case, and you can see the lights on the boats in the harbour from there, which might make it feel a bit more Christmassy.' He kept his tone casual, trying not to make it sound like he was bothered which choice she made.

'I've always loved the way they light up the boats for Christmas, ever since I was a kid, so that would be great, and I can get a taxi back here if I don't feel like walking.'

'I'll drive you back.'

'No way, we're celebrating and we both need to raise a glass to Ginny.'

'We can argue about that later.' He smiled again, knowing there was no argument in the world that would persuade him to let her walk home. 'But for now, we'd better go and pick up the food, otherwise we might have to settle for whatever I've got in the cupboard that isn't already set aside for Christmas. And as much as a Pot Noodle has its place in the food chain, I feel like we'd really be letting Ginny down!'

* * *

There probably wasn't a restaurant in Port Agnes that could have competed with the view from Hamish's house, perched as it was high on the cliff side. The conservatory, as he'd termed it, was a glass extension that ran along the back of the ground floor for the entire length of the house. There was a huge corner sofa at one end that looked as if it could have comfortably seated about eighteen people and when Hamish had said he'd laid the table, he'd undersold it by some way.

There was a fresh garland of holly, ivy and pine fronds in the centre, with tealights and candles that meant the only other lights they needed were the ones on the harbour in the distance. It was the most romantic thing anyone had ever done for her, which was ironic seeing as they'd come to an unspoken agreement to just be friends. It was probably just how Hamish did things. It didn't mean anything.

'Have you heard from Genevieve about how the baby's doing?' Hamish topped up their champagne glasses again as he spoke, although he'd barely taken a mouthful when they'd toasted Ginny's good news. He was clearly determined to be able to drive her home, but Nadia hadn't shown nearly as much restraint. After another unsuccessful attempt to get hold of Ryan and ask him to record a video message for the children, she hadn't felt like eating all day. It meant that the first delicious mouthful of champagne had hit the spot quickly and made it all too easy to drain the glass.

'Really well. Ginny said we might be able to pop in between Christmas and New Year, but I'm guessing you'll be run off your feet with the family. I'm not sure why she wants us to go together anyway.'

'I'd like to go at the same time, if you don't mind? It feels like supporting Ginny is something we started together and I might well need an excuse to get away from the extended family over the holidays, as lovely as they are.'

'I can understand that. I'll be seeing my dad, grandmother and brother at some point, too, and I'm worried we might end up having an *EastEnders*-style Christmas, with far more drama than any of us want, especially if they don't start being more reasonable about Mum and Guy.'

'Maybe we should come up with an escape plan and a secret code?' He grinned. 'If I text you and say the angry albatross flies at midnight, you know you need to call me and say I've got to leave for an emergency.'

'Sounds like a plan.' Chinking her glass against his, their hands accidentally touched and it felt like a jolt of electricity passing through her body. This wasn't how it was supposed to go.

'I think we should seal the deal with some dessert.' Hamish disappeared for a moment to get the next course from the kitchen. Everything they'd eaten, from the *frittura di gamberi* to the risotto *al basilico* had been absolutely delicious. It was just as well she'd eaten as much as she had, otherwise the champagne she'd drunk could have resulted in her saying something she might regret.

'Here we go.' There were two small deserts on each of the plates that Hamish bought in. The first was a panna cotta, with mint leaves and dots of red jus to look like holly leaves and berries. The other dessert – the *croccantino* – was made from semi-frozen vanilla mousse, with hazelnuts and caramel, and the garnish had been moulded from white chocolate coloured to look like mistletoe.

'They look too good to eat. Lorenzo certainly didn't cut corners, even though we weren't eating in the restaurant.'

'I know; he even put a tablecloth in a separate box. He was obviously worried I was going to serve it to you on tray in front of the TV.'

'I can think of worse things.' Nadia tried not to picture what the mundanity of life might be like with Hamish, because it held far more appeal than it should. 'Although I think Lorenzo would offer you a job if he saw how well you'd set all of this up. The only thing he's got that you haven't is mistletoe.'

As soon as she'd mentioned mistletoe, with all its connotations, she wished she hadn't. Hamish was bound to think she was making a reference to the kiss she thought about far too often, but when she finally made herself glance at him, he was watching her intently. 'There was mistletoe in the garland, but I took it out in case it seemed... I don't know, I just didn't want to make you feel uncomfortable after what happened. Your friendship means a lot to me and I'd much rather have that than nothing at all.'

'I thought you wanted to forget what happened at the hospital.' The tension was suddenly so palpable that the space between them seemed to vibrate as he shook his head.

'I couldn't if I tried, but you didn't even acknowledge it and the sensible part of me said that was the right thing to do.'

'What about the other part of you?' Nadia forced herself to keep eye contact and Hamish wouldn't have been able to hide the truth from her if he'd wanted to, it was written all over his face.

'The 90 percent of me that's nowhere near as sensible as it should be hasn't been able to stop thinking about you, or that kiss.'

'It can get exhausting being sensible all the time and I can't help thinking it wouldn't be a bad thing to give in to the not-so-sensible side every now and again.' Nadia could hardly believe the words that were coming out of her mouth, but a force she didn't even recognise was making her bolder than she would have ever thought possible. 'And surely there's no better time for that than Christmas, with or without mistletoe.'

'Do you know what, I think you might be right.' Hamish tucked a strand of hair behind her ear and she all but threw herself at him. Weeks, months, maybe even years of pent-up desire was bubbling over. Meeting Hamish had been like popping a champagne cork and all the stuff she'd been holding in couldn't be stopped. Thankfully he was responding as if he felt exactly the same, and when he kissed her this time, there was no voice inside her head telling her to stop. Even if there had been, she didn't think she'd have heard it. At some point he took her by the hand and led her up the stairs, pausing when they reached the top to ask her if she was sure, and all she could do was nod.

It should have been awkward, with the way she felt about her body and the things Ryan had said that had undermined her confidence and usually played on a loop in her head, even when the only person she was naked in front of was herself. But the way Hamish reacted when he looked at her or touched her, and when she touched him, drowned out the rest of the world. She'd never experienced anything like it and she didn't even know her body could respond the way it did, over and over again.

Lying in his arms afterwards was different too. He was holding her like he didn't ever want to let go, despite the fact that the sex was over. It was the point at which Ryan would have rolled away and started to snore before she could count to ten. Hamish kissed the top of her head as she lay it against his chest, and he was stroking the outside of her thigh. If she hadn't opened her eyes, it would have been perfect. But when she did and they adjusted to the low light of the room, she saw it. The photograph of Sara staring back at her from Hamish's bedside table, reminding Nadia he could never be completely hers because he loved another woman and always would.

21

Nadia and Frankie had got as far as going to see a litter of giant house rabbits, but they'd come away with the same conclusion that living with one in the flat – and even when they moved to the bigger place in January – would be a crazy idea. It probably didn't help that the only thing Nadia really wanted was to get Lola back, but she had to get something from Remi's list, otherwise there'd be a risk that her little girl might stop believing in Santa Claus altogether.

That was how Nadia and her mum found themselves out at Thunderhill Farm on Christmas Eve, ready to collect two of the guinea pigs the petting zoo had found themselves owning an excess of.

'Our latest litter is the result of one of the guinea pigs being mistaken for a male when it was really a female.' Josh, who managed the farm, shrugged. 'Even when we went in there one morning and found out they'd had six babies, my colleague, Liz, insisted they were definitely both males when she checked them. So I said we ought to change their names to Elton and David. They're not quite ready to be rehomed yet, but we've got a litter from the summer who we need to rehome to make room for the new babies.'

'Are you sure the two we've got are definitely female?' Nadia had no idea how easy it would be to make that sort of mistake, but unexpectedly finding out they'd gone from owning two guinea pigs to eight would have been bad enough. The fact that the guinea pigs they were taking home were siblings would only have made it worse.

'Definitely; we got the vet to check them out this time.'

'They're really cute.' Frankie picked up the ginger ball of fluff that would almost certainly end up being Mo's guinea pig. The other one was tri-coloured, exactly as Remi had set out in her list to Santa. 'Once they see these, Remi will forget all about the giant house rabbits.'

'We've still got two to home, but if you ever think you can't cope with them any more, we'd rather have them back here to rehome again than for you to make your own arrangements.' Josh frowned. 'We've had guinea pigs and domesticated rabbits bought from here before that people have released into the wild because they've got fed up with them, or because they've bitten someone's finger. Surviving long enough to make it here means they're the lucky ones.'

'We won't do that, I promise.' Frankie was still stroking the guinea pig's head. 'Once you're a member of this family, you're a member, even if you do end up biting the hand that feeds.'

'I wish everyone had that attitude.' Josh couldn't have had any idea that Frankie was talking about a lot more than a guinea pig mistaking a finger for a carrot stick, but Nadia knew her mother was talking about Hari. She also knew that Frankie and Advik had met up to discuss the situation and that her father had promised to speak to her brother about it again. It had come to something when her father was willing to step in, and Frankie had said that even he thought Hari was being unreasonable. Hari had been actively encouraging Nani to keep up her campaign and she'd started to ring Advik at least once a day, haranguing him to do whatever he could to put an end to Frankie's relationship with Guy. Up until now it had been easy for Nadia's father to say that the end of the marriage had been Frankie's decision, but he didn't want a reconciliation now any more than her mother did. Trying to reason with Nani was never going to be easy, but with Hari on her side it was next to impossible. So Advik had clearly decided that getting Hari to see sense was a far easier battle. Except, just a day before Christmas, Hari was still ignoring Frankie's messages. 'I don't suppose I can persuade you to take all four can I?'

'I think two will do us for now.' Nadia shot her mother a warning look, knowing what a soft touch she was, just as her phone started to ring. 'Sorry, I'm going to have to get this.'

At this rate Nadia was going to end up on Santa's naughty list, because the phone call wasn't an urgent one from a patient, or even from her father, who'd taken the children to see the reindeers at Portreath while she and Frankie were picking up the guinea pigs. Even so, the name on the caller display wasn't one she had any hope of ignoring, as much as she suspected she probably should.

'Hello.'

'Hi Nadia, it's me. Hamish.'

'Uh huh.' She was all too aware that her mother and Josh were both listening to the call, and Frankie had always been able to hone in on Nadia's conversations. She'd stood no chance of keeping any secrets, even as a teenager.

'Are you okay? You dashed off last night and I didn't even realise you'd ordered the taxi until it turned up.'

'I knew you had a lot on today, that's all, and I didn't want to take up your time.' Nadia turned her body as far away from her mother as she could to try and block her from at least hearing Hamish's part of the conversation.

'I've always got time for you.'

'I thought you'd be rushed off your feet all day.' Nadia had pictured him welcoming his own family and Sara's parents into his home. They'd be reminiscing about Christmases gone by and how much they all missed Sara, which was totally understandable, and she hadn't expected him to give her a second thought.

'My in-laws have taken the girls out for lunch, my brother's not arriving until early evening, and my parents are out panic-buying because they've suddenly decided they haven't bought the girls enough gifts!'

'Sounds like a typical Christmas Eve.'

'The trouble is, I think it's contagious and I'm suddenly starting to worry I haven't bought the girls enough either.' Hamish laughed. 'What time are you picking up the guinea pigs, because I know Daisy is going to want one as soon as she sees Remi's, especially as I've decided against a house rabbit too.'

'I'm there now.'

'Right now?' Hamish breathed out. 'Sorry, that explains why you're so quiet. I thought I'd done something to upset you. I had a great time last night and I was worried when you rushed off.'

'So did I.' She'd been determined to act casual and keep telling herself it had probably been a one-off, but that was much easier when she wasn't with Hamish or even talking to him.

'Great, because it's been less than twenty-four hours and I've already had to stop myself from texting to say that the angry albatross flies at midnight.'

'Already?' She couldn't help laughing and it was nice to know he wanted to see her again so soon. 'There are two guinea pigs still looking to be rehomed, but you've got to be sure, because it's a commitment for life. The life of a guinea pig anyway.'

'Sounds perfect, I'm looking for a long-term commitment and we can help each other through it.' She wished she could see Hamish's face, so she could read his expression, but she was taking what he said at face value. She had to, to protect herself, even though it was already impossible to imagine him not being part of her life.

'They've got two boys left and they like company, so do you want me to pick them up for you now?'

'That would be brilliant, if you're sure it's not too much hassle, and I'll come and get them whenever works best for you. I'd bought some food and a cage when we were still planning to get a rabbit, in case we didn't want to leave it running loose when we were out. So that should be fine for now.'

'I'll text you when we're back in Port Agnes. Guy's going to keep our two at his until after the kids have gone to bed tonight, so I'm sure we can work something out.'

'You're amazing, thank you so much.'

'No problem, see you later.' Nadia ended the call and Frankie was giving her a look that she recognised from old. There was no way she'd get away with brushing her mother's questions off, but she was at least hoping not to have Josh as a part of that conversation.

'That was my friend. He's got a daughter the same age as mine and he'd love to take the last two guinea pigs. I've told him it's a serious commitment, but I definitely don't think he's the sort who'd buy a pet just for Christmas.'

'No, Hamish is a great guy.' Frankie gave her a thumbs up. Her mother was getting as bad as Gwen.

'Great, well if you're happy to take the two boys as well, I can put them in separate carriers. I don't want to risk them getting mixed up and you ending up with another unexpected romantic encounter on your hands somewhere down the line.'

'Oh I don't know.' Frankie was smiling again. 'Sometimes unexpected romances can be the best sort.'

'Are we still talking about guinea pigs?' Josh looked confused. The poor man was probably wondering who on earth he was entrusting these animals to and whether Nadia's mother was trying to set him up with her daughter.

'Separate containers would be great, thank you. I'll double the donation, too, and then we can get going. We've taken up enough of your time on Christmas Eve.' Nadia pulled her debit card out of her purse before her mother could say anything else. Frankie would definitely read more into this than she needed to, but Nadia had to admit she was looking forward to seeing Hamish again and now she had the perfect excuse.

* * *

As expected, Frankie had done her best to get as much information as possible out of Nadia about the phone call and exactly how close she and Hamish had become. But even though Nadia shared almost everything with her mother, what had happened the night before was something she was keeping to herself. Seeing Sara's picture, when she had still been lying in Hamish's arms, was a reminder of just how complex things were. She was still married, but it was Hamish who was still in love with someone else. Then there was Saffron, who had no idea that her father was seeing someone new. Nadia wasn't even sure they could call it dating, but it definitely felt like they were sneaking around behind their children's backs and that wasn't something she wanted to sustain long-term, even if Hamish did.

Thankfully, a WhatsApp message had arrived from Beth not long after they'd got back from Thunderhill Farm, which had proved a perfect distraction from Frankie's interrogation. There was a picture of Beth, her parents, and the baby, who she'd decided to call Rex, all wearing matching Christmas pyjamas. Beth's dad, Simon, was beaming as if he'd been given the most wonderful Christmas present ever and the truth was, he had. The accompanying message was upbeat too, and as Gwen always said, the baby had brought his own love. As shocked as Beth and her parents had been by Rex's arrival, it was obvious they wouldn't change it for the world and Nadia felt as if she'd been given a wonderful gift too.

Once it was clear that Ryan wasn't coming over for Christmas, Nadia had decided not to take up her father's offer of using his house. She'd rather be with Frankie.

Handing over the two male guinea pigs to Hamish on Christmas Eve had definitely felt like an illicit assignation between two people who were supposed to be elsewhere. He'd produced a beautifully gift-wrapped present and she'd thanked her foresight for having bought him a good quality bottle of whisky.

'Just don't judge me too harshly for the cheesy card!' It had been the last thing he'd said before he'd kissed her for the third time in the space of their ten-minute meet-up and they'd gone their separate ways, back home to spend Christmas with their families.

When she'd read the card on Christmas morning and opened the beautiful watch that came with it, she'd laughed out loud.

Hoping to spend a lot more time with you and this way you'll be guaranteed to have time on your hands! Love H xx

Nadia wasn't the only one thrilled with her gift; the guinea pigs couldn't have been more loved by Remi and Mo and by the time they all headed over to join Guy, Jess, Dexter and Riley for Christmas lunch, they'd already been christened Kipo and Fluff. Luckily Jess had kindly said she didn't mind the guinea pigs joining them for Christmas dinner, because it would probably have proved impossible to separate Remi and Mo from their two most prized possessions.

Nadia and the rest of the family could have saved a fortune on their other gifts, because they were barely looked at, and they got through the whole day without either of the children asking about their father. Nothing had arrived from Ryan and he still wasn't responding to Nadia's messages, but at bedtime Remi whispered the words that Nadia had been dreading.

'When can I see Daddy?'

'Hopefully soon, darling, but it's very late now and you need to go to sleep so that Kipo and Fluff can go to sleep too.' The move to the new house was more urgent than ever, now that the three of them were also sharing their bedroom with a guinea pig cage. Thankfully there was less than a month to go and Nadia didn't even care that she hadn't had a chance to see the place yet. Frankie had told her how lovely it was, but she and Guy were being a bit mysterious about it all and she had a good idea why.

When she'd asked how much her contribution to the rent would be, Guy had fobbed her off and said he was barely paying anything for it. After she'd questioned what sort of place could possibly have two separate properties *and* such a low rent, both of them had been cagey and told her that she'd just have to wait and see. She knew they were just trying to help her out, but she'd find a way to make sure she paid her fair share. It might seem crazy that she'd agreed to move somewhere she hadn't even seen, but she trusted her mum's judgement wholeheartedly and all that mattered was that the kids would have a garden to play in, and that it was close enough to the school and nursery to mean they didn't have to be uprooted again. Anything else she could live with.

'Can we go to a party like Jess?' Remi's question brought her back to the present. Her daughter didn't miss a thing, even when she was busy petting Kipo, and she'd obviously been listening when Jess had been talking about the party she and Dexter had been invited to on the Sisters of Agnes Island, to celebrate New Year's Eve. It was probably the mention of fireworks that had piqued Remi's interest; she'd been obsessed with seeing them again since the bonfire party at Ella and Dan's.

'I'll see what I can do; maybe we can have a little party here.'

'Can we have fireworks?' Nadia had known that was coming. 'And can I ask Daisy to come?'

'We'll talk about it in the morning, sweetheart. Night night.' Planting a kiss on her daughter's head, Nadia went back out to the lounge to join her mother and Guy, and that's when she saw the text.

✉ Message from Hamish

The angry albatross flies at midnight, but as much as I want to see you I think it's going to be hard to make it work for a few days. Family are here until the 28th and then I'm back at work for a couple of days, but I was wondering if you had plans for NYE? XX

They'd already exchanged texts earlier in the day, when she'd thanked him for the watch and wished him a happy Christmas. He'd responded to say that he was looking forward to a well-earned whisky once Christmas dinner was over and had wished her the happiest of days too. She hadn't expected to hear from him again until the festivities were over. It was a nice surprise, especially if he wanted to meet up.

✉ Message to Hamish

Nothing yet and I'm on call for the next few days, so off properly on NYE, but Remi's just asked if we can have a party... xx

✉ Message from Hamish
Perfect. Daisy said the same thing, anyone would think they'd been
colluding! Early child-friendly NYE party it is then. Can't wait to see
you XX

Nadia typed a response – *What about Saffron?* – and had almost
sent it, before deleting it instead. How much Hamish decided to
tell his older daughter, or to keep from her, was up to him and it
wasn't like this was anything serious. She had to remember that.

✉ Message to Hamish
Looking forward to it. It's our turn to host and, if the kids can last out,
we can go down to the harbour and watch the fireworks on the Sisters
of Agnes Island. Have a great week xx

Frankie and Guy had already been invited to Gwen and Barry's
house for New Year's Eve, so Nadia, Hamish and the children
would have the flat to themselves. It might not be the grandest of
venues, but she hadn't looked forward to a New Year's Eve as much
in a long time.

22

Nadia was on the rota for home visits on the twenty-ninth of December and there was one she was looking forward to even more than all the others. Ginny had been released from hospital after five days, once she'd had the chance to recover from her operation and for baby Neviah to be treated for the mild jaundice she'd been born with. Both mother and daughter were now doing brilliantly, according to Izzy and Jess, who'd already been out to check on them whilst Nadia had been on call. All being well, this visit should be the last one the midwives had to make before handing over to the health visitor team.

'Come on in and join the chaos!' Freddie opened the door with a smile. Despite the shadows under his eyes, which all new parents wore with pride, his sheer joy at having his wife and daughter at home would have been obvious even if he hadn't said it. 'I can't tell you how happy I am to be able to have my girls here and know they're both going to be okay.'

'Best Christmas present ever, eh?' Nadia returned his smile and followed him into the house. Ginny was propped up against a small mountain of cushions with a very contented-looking baby asleep in the crook of her arm. 'Hello you two. I'm about to do the meanest thing ever and wake her up so I can check her over. I'd feel even more horrible about it if I wasn't desperate for a cuddle.'

'I think she'll forgive you.' Ginny smiled. 'After all, if it hadn't been for you, she might not be here at all.'

'She's absolutely beautiful and she looks the picture of health, too, so I'm sure she'd have been fine whatever you decided about your treatment.' Nadia looked at Freddie for a moment. She hated the thought that the perfect family he and Ginny had strived so hard for might be tainted by any trace of conflict about the choices they'd made. It didn't matter now, because fate had been kind and there was every chance they could put it all behind them one day soon.

'She's incredibly strong; she tries to hold her head up already, even though it's much too soon.' Freddie couldn't contain his pride. 'The paediatrician said she's one of the most alert babies she's ever seen.'

'And boy is she greedy.' Ginny exchanged a smile with Freddie that made Nadia want to do a happy dance. They were both so in love with their little girl, there was no chance of the past couple of months blighting that. 'I'm almost glad the decision to feed her was taken out of my hands. I'd have needed 40DD boobs to stand a chance and this way I get to let Freddie take some of the night feeds.'

'If I keep indulging in midnight snacks after I've done a feed and eating junk in the day to combat the exhaustion, it's me who's going to end up with 40DDs.' Freddie laughed. 'But it'd be worth it and it would certainly give Neviah a comfortable place to snooze.'

'It sounds like the pair of you have taken to parenthood really well. How much paternity leave have you got?' As happy as Nadia was to see how brilliantly everything seemed to be going, she knew from experience that new parents could sometimes hit a wall of exhaustion – even when they hadn't had half the stuff to deal with that Ginny and Freddie had. She also knew from friends who'd had cancer that even good news didn't quite lift the cloud that was always lurking once they'd heard the words: *I'm sorry, it's cancer.* People were often amazing at pushing it to the backs of their minds, but there'd be triggers for Ginny and Freddie along the way, and it was important they had the support they needed to deal with that alongside new parenthood.

'Work has been great. They gave me four weeks holiday, as a combination of paternity and annual leave, but they've said I can work from home indefinitely after that. I think they realised after Ginny was diagnosed that they got more out of me when I was here with her, than when I was in the office worrying myself to death about how she was.'

'I just hope I don't get sick of him!' Ginny laughed, but her expression changed as she looked down at her daughter. 'I know I won't though, because I've got everything I ever wanted and I'm not going to take a single second of it for granted. Hopefully I'll have as long with Neviah and Freddie as any woman my age could expect. But if the worst happens... I don't want to look back and wish I'd made the most of every moment.'

'I think that's a philosophy all of us should live by, but you've been through so much and I want you to know I'm always here for you, even after your care is handed over to the health visitor team. If you're ever worried about anything, just give me a call. Any time.' Nadia sat down next to Ginny on the sofa. 'I just hope you're right about Neviah forgiving me, because I'm planning to demand cuddles on a regular basis and I don't want us to get off on the wrong foot.'

'Don't worry, she's going to hear all about what you and Hamish did to help me and Freddie get through these last couple of months, so you can both have as many cuddles as you want and hopefully next time you might even be able to come together.' Ginny seemed to be waiting for Nadia to agree, as if she and Hamish visiting together was the norm. But they weren't a couple in any official sense, so she couldn't promise Ginny anything on his behalf.

'That would be nice, but neither of us could bear to wait any longer than we had to to meet Neviah for the first time, and you might get sick of me dropping by to see her whenever I'm passing.'

'There's no way that will happen. It means a lot to me to know that you'll still be around if we need you. I wasn't sure if being back in Port Agnes was only temporary.'

'No, I'm definitely here to stay.' Nadia reached out to take Neviah from her mother's arms. Just lately, being in Port Agnes felt more like coming home than ever, but she was determined not to think about how much of that was down to Hamish. Ginny's philosophy of life was spot on; sometimes you just had to learn to appreciate the moment you were in and not worry about what might be just around the corner.

* * *

'Does this mean we've officially lost the plot?' Hamish grinned as he put the last obstacle of the guinea pig assault course in place. Crossing the living room floor was now a major challenge, whether you were a human or a guinea pig, and it would probably go down as the weirdest New Year's Eve entertainment ever planned. But the guinea pigs had been well-handled in their six months at Thunderhill Farm and they seemed to be very confident in their new homes already. Hamish had said that Saffron was at a party with friends, which was just as well given how unlikely it was that she'd have enjoyed an evening of guinea pig agility; especially with Nadia for company.

'You tell me; you're the doctor.' Nadia returned his smile. It was getting harder and harder to stop herself from developing strong feelings for him. When he'd turned up with Daisy's guinea pigs, which they'd named Turner and Hooch, as well as the guinea pig agility course that had made Remi squeal with delight, she'd wanted to kiss him there and then.

'I think we're safe for now, but if we start wandering around Port Agnes wearing matching I 🩶 guinea pigs T-shirts, then I'd say we've crossed the line.'

'More magic!' Mo marched over towards Hamish carrying a banana from the fruit bowl, demanding a repeat of the performance that Hamish had given just after he and Daisy had arrived. All three kids had been amazed when he'd peeled a banana to reveal that it was already sliced and even Nadia had struggled to work out how he'd done it. He also seemed to be able to pass a two-pence piece through the table and it turned out he had an impressive sleight of hand to add to his already extensive repertoire of talents.

'Hamish doesn't want to do more magic right now, darling. We're going to let the guinea pigs have a run, the girls first and then the boys.' Nadia picked up her son who stuck out his bottom lip.

'I like magic.'

'We'll do some more later, but how about for now I teach you all a trick you can show your friends.' Hamish seemed to have unending patience and it was another stark contrast to Ryan. There was no way he'd have spent all that time setting up a guinea pig agility course, let alone grant Mo's wish for another magic trick.

'Yay!' Remi was already squeezing in next to Hamish. She was definitely drawn to him and Guy, and Nadia couldn't help worrying that her daughter was unconsciously looking to fill the gap her father had left in her life.

'Okay, we need paper and some pens, so we can all do this together, and it's probably going to be easiest to sit up at the table.'

'I'll sort the pens and paper.' Nadia went to the bedroom to grab what she needed and by the time she got back, the four of them were sitting around the table ready to get started.

'Right, who knows how to spell the word boy?'

'B O Y.' Remi sounded out the words phonetically.

'Brilliant, now we need to write those letters down but not in capital letters. Let me know if you need me to help, or you can copy me.' Hamish wrote out the word, leaving a bit of space between the letters and made sure all three children were finished before he carried on. Mo needed a bit more help than the girls, but he managed to copy the word really well. 'Okay, now I'm going to show you some magic that you can do for all of your friends, because we're going to turn the word boy into a picture of a boy instead without rubbing any of the letters out.'

'You can't do that Daddy, the letters will be in the way, silly.' Daisy giggled, leaning conspiratorially into Remi, but within a few minutes they all had pictures of little boys in front of them, even Mo.

'I can do magic!' Mo was grinning and Nadia scooped him into her arms.

'You're such a clever boy.'

'I'm going to show Nanny and Guy tomorrow.' Remi was smiling too. It was such a simple thing, but Nadia had a feeling her daughter would never forget learning how to do her first bit of 'magic' and in years to come she might even show her own children.

'Thank you,' Nadia mouthed to Hamish and he reached out to

squeeze her hand, taking it away again before any of the children had the chance to spot the gesture. 'Now who's ready to see whether Fluff and Kipo, or Turner and Hooch are going to be the agility champions?'

'Me!' All three children raised their arms, just as there was a loud hammering on the door to the flat.

'That can't be the pizzas already.' Nadia glanced at her watch, the one Hamish had bought her, which made her smile every time she looked at it. 'I ordered them for eight, they're half an hour early.'

'It might be because there are so many orders on New Year's Eve.' Hamish stood up. 'Do you want me to go and grab them?'

'No it's fine, I'll just put the oven on low to keep them warm until we're ready.' Nadia walked down the hallway, grabbing a five-pound note from her purse to tip the delivery person, having already paid for the pizzas online.

'Thanks, here you go.' Holding out the money, she couldn't see the man's face at first. He had a baseball cap pulled low over his eyes, but weirdly he didn't seem to be carrying any pizza boxes. Even when he looked up, and their eyes finally met, it took a moment for her to register who it was.

'Ryan?' The word sounded strange, but nowhere near as strange as opening the door to see her estranged husband standing on her doorstep.

'Hello Nards. Happy New Year; long time no see.' He held out his arms as if he was actually expecting her to walk into them, but she was still frozen to the spot. She had no idea what he was doing here, but what she did know was that his arrival wasn't going to get the new year off to the start she'd been hoping for.

23

'What the hell are you doing here?' Nadia had to blink several times to make sure she wasn't imaging Ryan standing outside the door.

'What kind of way is that to talk to your husband?' He was smiling, as if this was all some big joke and he'd just got back after popping out for a pint of milk, instead of ghosting his own children.

'I've been trying to get hold of you for weeks with barely any response and suddenly you turn up here, thousands of miles from where you were the last time you even bothered to speak to the children. What's next, is Delilah going to pop out from behind you and announce she's here for a visit too?'

'We split up and that's why I didn't get in touch. I wanted to surprise you and the kids. I was planning to get here in time for Christmas, but I had a few things to sort out.'

'What, like trying to worm your way back into Delilah's bed and when that didn't work you pulled together plan B? She obviously came to her senses and kicked you out.' Nadia was trying desperately not to raise her voice too much; the last thing she wanted was for Mo or Remi to come hurtling down the hallway to see what was going on.

'I was the one who ended things with Delilah. Look, I know I've been an idiot and you've got every right to be angry, but I can admit when I've made a mistake. It wasn't just the affairs, I should never have made you go back to New Zealand with me. I knew you didn't really want to go and I could tell you weren't ever happy there. I suppose I felt guilty, but rather than facing up to that it was easier to bury my head in the sand and drift back to the life I'd had before we even met. I'm a prick, I know that, but I want to put things right and the reason I couldn't get here for Christmas was because I was sorting out the paperwork to bring Lola over with me too.'

'Lola's here?' It told Nadia something when the biggest rush of excitement she got from everything Ryan had said was that he'd brought their beloved dog with him.

'She had to go straight to the vet's at the airport after the plane landed, so they can check over her paperwork and vaccine record. If it's all okay, they'll issue her with a pet passport and we can go and get her and bring her home. We're both ready to make a new life back here, with you and the kids.'

'You think we're going to live here, *together*?' Nadia could hardly believe what she was hearing, but there wasn't a trace of irony in Ryan's words.

'Well maybe not here, exactly, I know you said your mum's place is tiny, but we can find somewhere else.' Nadia had only told him how cramped the flat was in the hope it might make him develop a conscience about paying maintenance, so she could find somewhere decent for the kids to live, but it had been left to Guy to find a solution for that.

'Do you really think it's going to be that easy?'

'It can be. The people renting our old place are interested in buying it, so we'll have the money to start again, over here, like you always wanted to.'

'You're going to miss the start of the inaugural guinea pig agility contest.' Hamish came up behind her, smiling as she turned to look at him, but the expression on her face must have made up for the fact she appeared to have lost the power of speech. 'What's wrong?'

'What's wrong is that I've come to see my wife and kids on New Year's Eve and there's some bloke here, sounding very much at home, which explains why she hasn't even let me across the threshold.' Ryan barged past her and for a moment she thought he might launch himself at Hamish.

'You're Ryan?' There was something so disarming about the calmness of Hamish's response that Ryan stopped in his tracks. 'I'm Hamish, Nadia's friend.'

'Is that what they call it these days?' Ryan might not have got physical, but his tone was still aggressive. 'Well, if you really are a friend, I suggest you do the decent thing and make yourself scarce so I can talk to my wife.'

'Don't you dare!' Nadia's shock had given way to barely contained rage. It was only the thought of upsetting the children that was stopping her from screaming at Ryan. 'Don't you dare come into my house and act like you've got any right to dictate who else is here with me. If you want to stand any chance of rebuilding a relationship with the kids, you're the one who needs to make themself scarce right now. I mean it, or I swear to God I'll do everything I can to make this as difficult for you as possible.'

'And where the hell am I supposed to go on New Year's Eve?'

'How about the pub? That's always been your go-to.' Nadia let out a breath, still fighting to control the anger bubbling up inside her. 'If you mean what you say about wanting to be a part of the kids' lives, you can meet us in The Cookie Jar, the café downstairs, at 11 a.m. the day after tomorrow. But if I even so much as catch a glimpse of you before then, all bets are off.'

'Brunch with my family, what could be better?' Ryan shot a look in Hamish's direction. 'I'll see you then, beautiful.'

Turning on his heel, Ryan disappeared into the darkness as if he'd never been there at all, but it took Nadia a few seconds before she could look at Hamish again.

'Are you okay?' His eyes were full of concern as he reached out and took hold of her arms.

'Uh huh.' The truth was, there were so many emotions racing through her head and it felt as if her blood was pulsating at ten times its normal rate.

'I take it you had no idea he was coming?'

'None and I wish he hadn't. I've been happier lately than I've been in ages; I don't want any of this. I promise.' She could hear the desperation in her own voice. It wasn't the first time that Ryan's actions had made it feel as though he'd put her life in a blender, but she was determined it would be the last.

'It's okay, I'm not going to put you under any more stress than you already are. I meant what I said to Ryan, I'm your friend and I'm not going anywhere unless you ask me to.' She should have been comforted by his words, and the feel of his arms as he pulled her towards him. So why did the fact that he'd described himself as her friend – twice – make her want to cry?

* * *

If it hadn't been for the prospect of getting Lola back, there was a good chance that Nadia might have stood Ryan up altogether. That would have made her a hypocrite, though, given how insistent she was that Hari find a way to make things right with Frankie. So she could hardly keep Ryan away from his children, despite what a terrible father he'd been over the past few months. Everyone deserved a second chance, but if he blew this one a big part of her would be relieved. Seeing him again proved just how comfortable she'd got not having him in her life, but this wasn't about her. He'd always be Remi and Mo's father, and they deserved to decide for themselves how much space they wanted him to take up in their lives.

She hadn't even told Frankie about him turning up yet. If her mother got hold of Ryan, there was every possibility that the only place he'd be staying was Turro hospital. As it was, he'd texted to say that someone he'd spoken to at the pub on New Year's Eve owned a campsite just outside Port Tremellien and he had rented a mobile home from him for a week. He was already complaining about how cold it was, no doubt trying to get her to agree to him staying at the flat instead. But if that was his plan, he was definitely going to be disappointed.

'Daddy's come to see you, so don't eat too much cereal because he wants to buy you some lovely cake when we go to The Cookie Jar to meet him.' Nadia kept her tone light, not wanting to risk letting any of her own feelings colour how the children might react.

'Daddy's in Zealand.' Mo shrugged, as if the fact that he repeated parrot-fashion, whenever anyone asked him about his father, was all the information he needed. At his age, other people, even the most significant ones in his life, could quickly be forgotten when they were out of sight.

'Are we going back there too?' Remi's eyes were suddenly wide with an expression that looked far more like fear than excitement. She'd mentioned Ryan less and less over the last few weeks, but that didn't mean he hadn't been on her mind.

'No, Daddy just misses you both that's all and he wants to see you more often.' Nadia knew her estranged husband far too well to make the children any concrete promises.

'Can we take Kipo and Fluff to the café?' Getting the guinea pigs out to make a fuss of them was the first thing the children did every morning. They'd laughed more than she could ever remember them laughing, when they'd watched all four guinea pigs attempt the agility course. Somehow Nadia had managed to carry on with New Year's Eve, as if the only person to knock on the door had been the pizza delivery guy. Hamish hadn't mentioned Ryan again that night either, but she'd been sure she could feel him backing off. The kiss at midnight, after the fireworks at the harbour, had been brief and staid. It would have been anyway, with the children standing close by and Nadia mindful that Ryan could be in the crowd somewhere too. But it still felt like something had changed between them.

They'd exchanged a couple of texts on New Year's Day, but nothing more than two friends might have said to one another, and she'd promised to let him know how the meet-up with Ryan went. She'd already told Hamish that there was more chance of her being crowned Fisherman of the Year at the Silver of the Sea festival than there was of any kind of a reconciliation with Ryan.

'I'm sorry darling, but the café won't let you take pets in, unless it's a guide dog.'

'Lola's uncle is a guide dog, isn't he, Mummy? The lady told us.' It was funny the things Remi remembered with such clarity that Nadia didn't think she'd have been old enough to recall. The breeder had told them about Lola's mother coming from a litter where one of her brothers had gone on to be trained as a guide dog. 'But Lola couldn't do it, cos she's chocolate.'

'That's right, sweetheart, but she was good at helping Mo learn to walk.' Nadia smiled at the memory. She'd been planning to print out some of the photos from her phone to frame when they moved to a bigger place. There was one of Mo leaning on Lola when he first started to take a few steps and needed to grab on to any nearby object to stop himself from falling onto his bottom.

'I really miss her.' Remi looked close to tears and it wouldn't have taken much for Nadia to join her, especially when she had no idea if Ryan's story about where Lola was had been true. One thing Nadia knew for certain was that Remi's attitude to her father had changed drastically over the past few weeks. She'd gone from asking about him all the time, to barely mentioning him and now she seemed almost nervous – as if clinging to the memory of her dog, rather than the reality of her father, was more meaningful. Kids could be amazingly adaptable, but a few weeks could feel like forever, and if Ryan thought he was just going to be able to pick up where he left off, he was almost certainly mistaken.

'Me too darling, but Kipo needs lots of cuddles. So eat your breakfast up and you can get her out again for a bit before we get ready to go and meet Daddy.' As angry as Nadia was with Ryan, she was determined not to let Remi see. She wanted her children's relationship with their father to be a positive one, even if that meant biting her tongue until it hurt. This wasn't about her or Ryan, and if he even tried to make it about him, he was going to wish he'd never got on that plane.

Ninety minutes later, Nadia pushed open the door to The Cookie Jar café and spotted Ryan sitting at a table on the right-hand side. There were some gift-wrapped parcels in front of him and he stood up when he saw them, holding out his arms to the children. She'd expected Mo to be a bit shy, but what she hadn't expected was for Remi to grab on to her leg and attempt to disappear beneath the coat Nadia was wearing. Ryan clearly hadn't expected it either.

'Hey, Remikins, it's me, Daddy, don't be silly.' When she didn't respond, he played his trump card. 'Look at these presents I've got you.'

'I wanna sit with Mummy.' Remi was still clinging to Nadia and it was Mo who was emboldened by the promise of a gift.

'I want this one.' He grabbed the biggest one and Ryan had to wrestle it from his grasp, making him burst into tears.

'No, this one's yours, mate. Come on, stop crying now.' When Mo didn't even attempt to take the proffered gift, Ryan sat down with a thud. 'Jeez this is hard work.'

'Parenting can be like that.' Even Nadia's skin felt tight. Every time she was around Ryan she had to fight not to react the way she really wanted to, for the children's sake, and she forced a reasonable tone instead. 'It's been a long time in their world, that's all. We need to take this at their pace.'

'I can be patient. It'll be worth it for us all to be back together.' She wasn't even going to respond to that. Reminding Ryan that there would never be an *us* that included the two of them, unless it came to parenting Remi and Mo, would just have to wait for another time. For now it was all about the kids.

'Come on darling, it's okay, let's see what Daddy has bought you.' Nadia lifted Mo on to her lap, while Remi continued to cling to her as if her life depended on it. 'Look Mo, it's a lovely red train.'

'Choo choo!' Mo stopped crying and clapped his hands in delight. Ryan had managed to curry some favour with at least one of his children.

'I knew he'd like that; you're a chip off the old block, aren't you mate? I loved trains when I was your age.' Ryan pushed the biggest present towards Remi. 'Come on then Remikins, let's see if your old dad has found the perfect present for you too.'

'It's all right sweetheart, you can open it.' Remi looked to her mother for reassurance, before carefully peeling back the wrapping paper.

'It's a Lola dog.' The soft toy beneath the wrapping paper defi-nitely bore a resemblance to Lola as a puppy and Remi looked at her father properly for the first time. 'I love it Daddy, thank you.'

'You're welcome darlin'; you know you're sounding like a proper little pom already.' Ryan laughed. 'And if you love the toy dog, I've got some even better news for you.'

'Ryan, don't—' Nadia knew what was coming but he completely ignored her attempt to cut him off.

'When Mummy lets me move back in with you guys, I'll be bringing Lola with me.'

'Really?' Remi jumped out of her chair and threw her arms around her father's neck.

'Yes, really darlin', I promise as soon as Mummy says I can, I'll go and pick her up for you.' Remi was still clinging to his neck as his eyes met Nadia's, whose fingernails were now digging into the flesh on her palms. She'd happily have slapped the smug smile off his face if the children hadn't been there. But, for now, he had her exactly where he wanted her and she'd never felt more trapped in her life.

24

'Thanks for agreeing to meet up; I just needed some air.' Nadia looked exhausted and if Hamish could have lifted the burden off her shoulders he would have done. Despite the pinched look on her face, she was still beautiful. It was really hard not to just reach out and take hold of her hand, but he didn't want to make her feel like he was demanding anything of her when she was clearly struggling to deal with Ryan's return.

'It's no problem. Saff said she'd pick Daisy up from Aria's party on her way home from the library, so after I'd finished work there was nothing for me to rush off for.' He'd walked from the surgery to the harbour to meet Nadia. It was dark and the ground underfoot sparkled with the promise of the frost turning into ice; their breath hung like clouds in the cold night air.

'Ryan's got Mo and they're picking Remi up from the party too, then going for ice cream. That seems to be his solution to everything; cake, ice cream and presents obviously make up for being a crappy father in his eyes.'

'I take it the kids handled the meet-up okay this morning, if he's got them now?'

'They were shy at first, but he came laden down with presents and then he cornered me by telling them he'll bring Lola home when I let him move back in.'

'He's not averse to blackmail then?' Hamish barely knew Ryan, but he already couldn't stand the man. Nadia had told him all about Lola and how much she and the children had missed their beloved dog. It was a really low move of Ryan's to use that sort of emotional blackmail. Hamish wanted to beg Nadia to tell her husband to take a running jump, but he just had to hope that no amount of game playing would make her consider taking Ryan back.

'He can't even see how damaging all of this will be for the kids when none of the promises he's making them about us getting back together are ever going to happen.'

'They're not?' Hamish's eyes searched hers and she shook her head hard enough to make her hair whip from side to side.

'Not in a million years.' She kept her gaze on his. 'I knew I was over him, but I never realised how utterly and completely over him I was until he turned up again. It's not even about us, because I'm not sure what this is between us yet. But I know how much I like you and how much I've been hoping we can keep trying to work out what this might be. Not wanting to be with Ryan goes beyond that, though. I'd rather die miserable and alone, and not be found until I'd fossilised in my armchair, than even contemplate getting back with him.'

'Now there's a brush-off that leaves no room for doubt.' Hamish couldn't help smiling and not just because Ryan was getting what he deserved. Nadia admitting that she wanted to give the two of them a chance was amazing, because it was what he desperately wanted too. He'd been worried she wouldn't feel ready, but now it felt like they were moving forward – together – and he couldn't wait. 'Are you going to tell him that?'

'Yes, but I need to get as good at manipulating the situation as he is, so the children don't suffer because of any of this, and I've no idea where to start.'

'I've seen men like him before and he'll trip himself up sooner or later.'

'I really hope so, but I think you're right, because he can't keep pretending to be a good guy for long. It's too much of an act.'

'Just hang in there; the kids will see for themselves what he's really like and they know how much you love them. That's obvious to everyone and it's one of the things I lo... really like about you.' He'd caught himself just in time. It was too soon to say he loved her, but the truth was there was already a long list of things he loved *about* her and he could see that, before too long, loving things about her could add up to loving her full stop. 'I'm here if you need me, but I know you've got other priorities right now, so I'll give you all the space you want until you're ready.'

'Why can't every man be like you?'

'Because then I wouldn't be special!' He winked, and her smile – just one more thing on the list of things he loved about her – lit up the night.

'No you wouldn't, but you definitely are. Very special.' When she leant forward to kiss him, his whole body was screaming at him just to say the words. If he was going to stop himself from translating the list of things he loved about her into a declaration, far earlier than he should, then Nadia wasn't the only one who was going to need some space.

* * *

Nadia looked at her watch. If she went straight back to the flat she'd have enough time to write a letter to Ryan that told him everything that needed to be said, without having to do it in front of the children. She could give him the details of the new solicitor she'd spoken to earlier in the day about moving ahead with the divorce and selling the house, the same one her mother had used when she'd left her father.

Guy sorting out the rental property for them meant Nadia had another six months to save up to move to a place of her own, so she could afford to make Ryan a very generous offer to more than cover what it had cost to fly Lola over, and compensate him for whatever he felt was his loss. He'd hadn't been remotely interested in the dog when they'd had her. It had been Nadia who'd been desperate for the companionship that Lola brought her, when the kids were in bed and Ryan was God knows where. Setting it all out in a letter had been Frankie's idea, so that Nadia wouldn't forget any of it, the way she might in the heat of an argument.

She was moving along the pavement quickly, with so many thoughts rushing through her head, that she didn't see the figure step out of the shadows until she knocked into them.

'I saw you.' Saffron's face was only inches away from hers and the hostility in her eyes made Nadia recoil.

'I didn't see you, I'm sorry. I wasn't looking where I was going, I was thinking about something else. I didn't hurt you, did I?'

'It's not me you've hurt.' Saffron's tone was steely too. 'I bet I can guess what you were thinking about, sticking your tongue down my father's throat again. I nearly threw up when I saw you. So much for what you said at the dance competition; I knew you were a liar.'

'Oh God... I'm sorry, it's not...' She couldn't finish anything she was trying to say, because there was no point in pretending. Saffron had obviously seen them kissing and she was every bit as horrified by it as Hamish had clearly known she would be. It was why he'd been so careful to keep Saffron and Nadia out of one another's way.

'It's not what? You're out with my dad, while your husband is looking after your kids. You make me sick.' Saffron had obviously registered the look of shock on Nadia's face. 'Yeah, that's right. I met Ryan when we were picking the girls up from Aria's party. Daisy wanted to go with Remi, so Ryan said he'd take them all to Moretti's and he's waiting for me there. He told me all about you looking for a new place to move into together. Don't you think my dad has been through enough losing Mum, without you messing him about?'

'I don't know what Ryan told you, but none of it's true and we're not getting back together. I brought the kids over from New Zealand because he'd more or less decided he'd had enough of being their father.' Nadia couldn't stop her voice from rising. She was sick of being everyone's punchbag, but she couldn't let herself take out everything that was happening with Ryan or Hari on this young girl, even though she was perilously close to the edge.

'So you took the kids away from their dad too? Jesus Christ, it gets worse.' Saffron shook her head, naked disgust in her eyes as she looked at Nadia again. 'I'd give anything to have Mum back again, and Dad would do anything to make that happen, but neither of us will ever get the chance. You could give Remi and Mo their dad back with a click of your fingers, but you're too bloody selfish.'

'I know you're angry and upset, but there are things you don't understand, it's complicated.' Nadia's jaw muscles were so tight from holding back everything she wanted to say that she could barely open her mouth.

'What, because I'm just a kid?' Saffron laughed, but it was a bitter, hollow sound. 'At least I'm not desperate. Doesn't it make you embarrassed to keep throwing yourself at my dad, because it makes me cringe. He's not interested in you or any of the others, and he doesn't need anyone apart from me and Daisy.'

'And what about in ten years' time, when Daisy is where you are, heading off to university? You might well have a partner or even a child of your own by then. Is that when your dad will be allowed to find someone else, or does he have to be on his own forever?' Nadia locked eyes with Saffron, not even trying to keep the sharpness out of her tone any more. She was suddenly more aware than ever of the parallels between Saffron and Hari. It was time for some home truths for Saffron's own good. There was a danger that Remi and Mo might end up holding the same views too, if Nadia didn't stand up for herself. 'Of course, you and Daisy will always come first, but your dad deserves the chance to fall in love again, because whatever happens you'll always have the biggest space in *his* life, but one day you might struggle to make room in your life for him. I think stopping him from having the chance of finding someone special is what's really selfish.'

'You don't know anything about my dad, so just shut up.' Saffron's face twisted as she shouted her response, but she still had a killer blow to deliver. 'If you think my dad is ever going to be with you, then you're even more stupid than I thought. He loved Mum, he still does, and no one is ever going to live up to her, least of all someone like you! I feel sorry for your kids with you as a mother.'

For the second time in the space of a week, Nadia lost the power of speech, as Saffron turned and ran into the darkness and all her resolve crumbled. Standing up for Hamish and for herself had just made things worse. Somehow Ryan had won, because even if she wrote him the letter and pushed on with the divorce, he'd made sure that Hamish was out of her life, because Saffron was never going to accept her. Especially now that Ryan had fed her a string of lies. Nadia would always be the woman who'd chosen to cut her children's father out of their lives, when all Saffron had ever wanted was to have her mother back.

25

It was definitely the coward's way out to send a text, but if Nadia had to see Hamish, or even talk to him, there was a good chance he'd be able to tell she was lying. Cowardly or not, it would be easier on all of them this way.

✉ Message to Hamish
I've been thinking about what you said, about space, and I think we both probably need it. It's not the right time for either of us to be dating, if that's even what we were doing. Things are complicated with Ryan and I don't know how it's going to work out. You need to focus on the girls, especially with Saffron off to uni soon and I know you want to make the most of the time you've got with her. Let's put it down to bad timing and wish each other luck. I really hope you find someone who can make you happy.

Making herself press the send button, Nadia had been relieved when a woman in labour had turned up at the unit, and she and Bobby had been kept busy supporting her for the next three hours. It meant there wasn't any opportunity to check her phone to see whether there was a response. When she eventually had a chance to look, there was a message waiting.

✉ Message from Hamish
I know it's tough at the moment, but let's not rush into anything. I can imagine the last thing you need is to think about 'us' in the midst of what you've got going on, but at the very least I want to be your friend. If you're going to the talk at the primary school tonight, let's have a chat then and you can tell me the latest if you want to. Or we can just have a good moan about how much mathematics has changed since our day! H xx

The talk at the primary school was aimed at helping parents to support their children in getting to grips with the maths curriculum, and it was definitely the sort of thing that was only bearable if you went along with a friend. If they really could find a way to stay friends, maybe she didn't need to take such drastic measures after all. If Saffron saw that's all they were, she might be able to cope with the idea. Eventually. It was funny how easy it was for Nadia to persuade herself of something, when it turned out to be what she really wanted.

✉ Message to Hamish
You're right, sorry. I'm overreacting to everything right now. Will there be wine at this thing tonight? Maths is only bearable when accompanied by a good red! See you later X

Sending the text was like a weight being lifted, which had to mean something. She still had no idea if she was going to tell Hamish about her confrontation with Saffron, but wiping him out of her life altogether was definitely something she didn't want to do. Friendship was better than nothing, but it also meant they wouldn't be slamming the door altogether on what might have been. By the time Saffron was at university, Nadia's divorce would be finalised, too, with any luck and both she and Hamish would be in a much better position to decide if they wanted more than friendship. The fact she already knew she wanted more would just have to be put to one side for now.

After she'd finished her shift, Nadia had just under half an hour to get to the school to meet Hamish and there was almost nothing that would stop her. Almost.

'Oh Nadia, thank God.' Freddie sounded breathless with relief when she picked up his call. 'It's Ginny, she's found another lump and she's absolutely hysterical. She wouldn't let me call Hamish or her consultant, because she's terrified of what they might say. And you're the only person she's willing to talk to.'

'Is the lump in her breast?'

'Yes, but not the one she had the surgery on. They told us she could try and feed Neviah from that breast, when they decided she wouldn't need chemo, but she didn't like the idea because of the radiotherapy on the other side. So she let her milk supply dry up. But now she can feel a lump and we're both terrified of what it might be.'

'I know you are, but I'm sure it's nothing to worry about, not so soon after getting the all-clear on her lymph nodes.'

'Do you think you might be able to rule it out just by looking?' Freddie sounded as if his whole future was pinned on her response.

'I don't know, but I'm coming straight over.'

'Thank you; nothing I say seems to be getting through. She's convinced it's got to be more bad news.'

'I'll be there as soon as I can.' Nadia grabbed her bag, only hesitating to send a brief text.

✉ Message to Hamish

Ginny's found another lump. Hopefully it's nothing, but she needs some support. Sorry if I don't make it. I'll call you later X

* * *

'How's she doing?' This time, when Freddie opened the door, there was no hint of the broad smile he'd greeted her with before.

'Crying non-stop and she won't put Neviah down. She keeps saying she won't get to hold her for much longer, so she's not letting her go.'

'Oh Freddie, this must be so hard.' Nadia touched his arm, suddenly wondering if she was way out of her depth. She'd called Anna on the way over and asked for some advice. Anna had told her to try and calm Ginny down, and whatever she thought the lump might be, to try and persuade her to ring her consultant at the hospital. And that's what she was going to do.

'I'm just hoping she'll listen to you.' Freddie led the way down the hallway. Ginny was sitting in the same spot as she had been on Nadia's last visit, but this time her face looked deathly pale and her eyes were rimmed with red.

'It's back and I'm not going to get to see my baby grow up. After everything I did to try not to lose her, she's going to lose me.' Ginny started to sob and Nadia knelt down in front of her.

'Oh sweetheart, I know you must be really scared, but there are lots of other things this could be, and if we can find out what, we might be able to rule out cancer.'

'It hurts so much. I kept trying not to think about it after I put my hand where the pain was coming from and felt the lump, but even my T-shirt brushing against the skin there makes me want to scream. I just wanted to pretend it wasn't there, to have a bit more time with Neviah, but the bastard thing won't even let me do that.'

'Does it feel warm or look red where the lump is?'

'Yes and I'm terrified that means it's about to break through the skin. When I first got my diagnosis and I looked online, there were some horrible pictures of what happens when the cancer does that.'

'Is it okay if I take a look, Ginny? Because it's sounding more and more to me like you might have mastitis.'

'Is that a type of cancer?' Freddie looked every bit as terrified as his wife had done moments before, but it was Ginny who answered him.

'It's an infection, isn't it? I remember my mum getting it not long after she went through the menopause.'

'That's right and it causes a painful inflammation, which can happen if milk or other debris gets trapped in the breast ducts. It can cause redness and heat, as well as swelling or what might feel like a lump in the infected breast. If I take a look, I should be able to be fairly confident if this is what we're dealing with.'

'Is it dangerous?' Freddie looked at Nadia and she shook her head.

'Not unless it's left untreated. If it is mastitis, and Ginny gets the antibiotics she needs to clear it up, she should make a full recovery within ten days.'

'Thank God for that!' Freddie's whole body seemed to slump with relief.

'We don't know if it is yet.' Ginny was still clutching Neviah in her arms.

'If it looks like a duck and quacks like a duck, then it's probably a duck.' Freddie smiled for the first time and Ginny's face lost some of its tension too.

'Here then, take Neviah, but if I lift up my top and my boob starts quacking then I'm blaming you.'

'Now that really would be a new one.' Nadia returned her smile and it was definitely the first time she'd felt like crying with happiness at the sight of an obvious mastitis, when she finally examined Ginny. Her breast was bright red and hot to the touch, and the shape of the swelling had all the markers of the infection. 'If I had a house, I'd bet it on this being down to a blocked milk duct.'

'So it's definitely not cancer?' Ginny pulled her top down and Nadia shook her head.

'Not unless it's wearing the best disguise ever. I still think you should phone your consultant just to let him know, in case he wants to adjust your treatment anyway, and I'll give Hamish a ring to see if he can issue a prescription for your antibiotics.'

'If I wasn't already married, I'd propose to you right now, or at the very least give you a great big hug.' Ginny blew her a kiss. 'But with my boobs the way they are, I daren't risk it, so you might have to settle for a hug from Freddie and Neviah instead.'

'They call that a booby prize don't they?' Freddie grinned and hugged Nadia, with Neviah wedged between. 'Sorry, stupid jokes are one of the ways we've got through all of this.'

'My mum always said our stupid sense of humour was a sign we were made for each other.' Ginny leant back against the pillows and Freddie put Neviah back in her arms. They might have been terrified when Nadia had arrived, but it was obvious it was because they were each other's whole worlds, along with baby Neviah. Even if there'd been the tiniest chance of Nadia getting back with Ryan, he'd never be able to offer her that. Suddenly it was clearer than ever that she wanted more, for her children and for herself.

* * *

Going back out to the car, the first thing Nadia checked was her messages. There were two, one was an alert saying that her text to Hamish had failed and the second one was from him.

✉ Message from Hamish

I might be a try-hard, but even I can get the message eventually. I said I'd give you space and then I immediately ask you to meet me, straight after you told me that's exactly what you need. You're right too, that I should be concentrating on Saff, not chasing something that clearly wasn't meant to be. I hope we can be friends at some point, but I obviously find it hard not to keep crossing that line. For now at least, I think it's best we don't try for friendship, but I really hope it all works out the way you want.

There were no kisses this time and no real way to respond without making things more complicated that they already were. Maybe the universe was trying to tell her something when the text to him had failed. She'd promised herself she wouldn't come between Hamish and his daughter, but she'd been willing to back down the moment he'd asked her to. It was easier this way – on all of them – so she had no idea why it felt so hard and she couldn't stop herself from hitting the steering wheel or screaming into the silence inside the car. Just because some things weren't meant to be, it didn't make them any easier to accept.

26

After Hamish's text, Nadia had telephoned the out-of-hours doctor at the surgery to ask if they could prescribe some antibiotics for Freddie to collect to treat Ginny's mastitis, without the need to liaise with her consultant first. After that she'd gone home and carried on with the rest of the evening as if nothing had happened, but there was no fooling Frankie, who'd asked every three minutes or so whether everything was okay. She'd managed to fob her mother off with the explanation that she was just fed up with the situation with Ryan. It wasn't as if that was a lie and her estranged husband was still acting as though she'd agreed to making a go of things again, instead of setting out the parameters of their co-parenting relationship very clearly.

If Ryan had even read the contents of the letter she'd agonised over and had given him the night before, then he was playing his cards very close to his chest. She'd worded it so carefully, putting the kids at the centre of everything and expressing the hope they could find a way to become friends, which would make life so much easier for everyone. It was ironic that the person she'd fallen out of love with was now insistent they should be much more than friends, while the person she could easily imagine falling for had even dropped her from the friend zone.

When Frankie had eventually accepted her daughter's explanation for the air of melancholy she was wearing like a scarf, Nadia had finally felt able to make eye contact with her mother. But what she saw brought her up sharp. She'd been so busy wallowing in her own unhappiness that she hadn't seen just how much Frankie was struggling.

'Never mind asking if I'm all right, are you okay? You look like you haven't slept in weeks.' Nadia put an arm around her mother's shoulder. She was quite a bit taller than Frankie and it was almost like hugging a child. Her mother had always been able to make any crisis somehow okay, and now it was her turn to step up.

'Hari's still not replying to any of my messages. It's been weeks and not a word, even at Christmas. I don't think I'd have got through if it wasn't for you, Guy and the kids. Now New Year has come and gone and he's still ignoring me. What if he never forgives me?' Frankie's eyes filled with tears when she looked up at her daughter and Nadia wanted to cry too. But her tears would have been of frustration at how monumentally stupid her brother was being. Frankie had championed them both their whole lives, fighting their corner and standing up for them and this was how he repaid her?

'There's nothing for him to forgive you for, because you haven't done anything wrong.'

'He thinks I have and if he won't give me a chance to explain, I'll never be able to make him understand.'

'He needs to come to his senses himself. It should be blindingly obvious that he's the one in the wrong. The best thing you can do is stop messaging and make him realise how much he's got to lose.'

'I tried that before Christmas, when I said I wouldn't come to the wedding if he didn't want me to. He didn't even reply and I managed not to message him again for a couple of days, but in the end I just couldn't stop myself. If I don't message him, he might think I don't care.'

'And it might scare him into finally waking up to what an idiot he's being. I could honestly knock his and Nani's heads together, but maybe what they need is to know how it feels to be treated the way they've treated you.'

'I don't know if I can just stop trying.'

'Give it a go for a week; what have you got to lose?'

'It feels like I could lose everything.' Frankie wiped her eyes with the back of her hand and took a breath so deep it seemed to change the whole atmosphere. 'If you think it might work, I'll give it a try. Like you say, what've I got to lose?'

'It's going to be okay Mum, just give him enough space to see what he's missing.' Even as Nadia spoke, she couldn't help picturing Hamish. Maybe space really was the solution for everything that was going on. One thing she knew for sure was that if Ryan didn't give her some space soon there was going to be trouble.

* * *

It felt like ages since there had been this many of the team in the staffroom all at once. Christmas and New Year had meant a hiatus from the non-essential clinics and antenatal classes, and only three women had elected to give birth at the unit over the holiday period, with most of them choosing to travel to Truro for hospital deliveries instead. There'd been a handful of home births, but most of Nadia's shifts had been check-ups on mums-to-be at the unit, or out in the community, as well as some home visits to see new mothers and their babies before the health visitor team took over.

It meant there were some of the team she'd barely talked to in weeks, so it was great to have the chance to catch up with almost everyone again. Only Emily and Ella were missing. Emily had gone to a tutorial meeting at the university for part of her midwifery degree studies and Ella was on leave, helping out a friend who'd been struggling to care for her husband, after an accident that had left him paralysed. Between running the unit with Anna, and planning her own wedding only a month away, Ella had been rushed off her feet even before she'd needed to help her friend out.

'Right I need an update on what everyone's been up to before I start doing some hours here next month.' Toni had arrived to pick Bobby up at the end of his shift, bringing baby Ionie with her. Her maternity leave was almost over and she'd be re-joining the team on a part-time basis while she and Bobby went ahead with their plans to try for baby number two. Both Anna and Ella had insisted they'd rather have Toni back for a little while, than not at all. It was Anna who'd suggested that Toni join the impromptu team meeting they'd managed to arrange, because for once, none of the delivery rooms were occupied. 'I don't want to put my foot in it, when I'm back, by asking Izzy if she's still seeing Noah, only to discover they've split up and she'd sprayed Deep Heat into all of his underpants.'

'Remind me never to upset my wife, Izz, won't you?' Bobby rolled his eyes.

'I think we'd all better steer clear of upsetting Toni.' Izzy grinned. 'But the good news is I won't have to borrow your can of Deep Heat, because things are going really well with Noah. He's decided he's definitely staying on permanently at St Jude's and he's been so amazing at helping Pops get through his first Christmas without Nonna. Put it this way: I think he's a keeper.'

'That's great.' Toni smiled. 'And I already know what you've been up to Gwen. I've seen the evidence online.'

'It might not have turned out how we expected, but I'm not going to pretend it wasn't entertaining.' Gwen tapped the side of her nose. 'A man called Jasper contacted Nicky to see if anyone from the Quicksteppers could help as he was planning to propose to his girlfriend. Her favourite film is *La La Land* and he wanted us to help recreate one of the dances. Of course, me and Barry were the first to volunteer, along with most of the rest of the group. What none of us expected was for his brand-new fiancée's sister to turn up, just after the proposal, and announce he'd been sleeping with her too. It was all over the internet by teatime.'

'Only you could get involved with something like that!' Toni laughed. 'What about you, Jess, any chance you've been caught in any dramatic love triangles while I've been away?'

'I'm going to sound very boring compared to that, but Dexter and I have decided once and for all that this will be the year we try IVF.' Jess blew out her cheeks. 'We're not pinning all our hopes on it, but I know I'll regret it if I don't at least try. And if Nicole and James can be brave enough to have another go after losing Gracie, then so can I.'

'That's brilliant news and about as far removed from being boring as anyone could be!' Anna took the words out of Nadia's mouth. 'Now if you want boring, you'll have to come to me and Brae, because we've made absolutely no goals for the new year; we just want things to stay as they are.'

'I think that's lovely.' Frankie was smiling, but Nadia didn't miss the wistful look on her mother's face. 'Nadia and I are both moving. We're renting two properties on the same plot for six months, which Guy has organised through a friend of his. It'll give us all so much more space. It's in Port Agnes, but I can't tell you exactly where yet, as we're keeping it a surprise for Nadia and the kids.'

'That must be really exciting for you and Guy too.' Gwen gave her friend a nudge.

'It is.'

'You might want to tell that to your face.' Gwen was never one to pull any punches, but even she clamped her hand over her mouth when Frankie burst into tears. 'Oh, I'm sorry love, I didn't mean to upset you.'

'It's not that; it's Hari.' Frankie shook her head and Nadia put an arm around her shoulder, just like she had the day before, feeling protective of her all over again.

'My brother's acting like a spoilt child and ignoring Mum because he hasn't got his own way for once. He'd better hope I don't see him before he sorts things out, because my patience with men who have an over-inflated sense of entitlement is in very short supply right now.'

'I don't blame you with Ryan being back.' Gwen tutted. 'My Barry says if he bumps into him he'll be giving him both barrels, so he'll happily join a posse to run him out of town for you. And if I see him, I'll be giving them full frontal too.'

'I don't think you mean full frontal, do you?' Bobby was clearly trying not to laugh, but Gwen nodded.

'Oh yes I do, because the sight of me full frontal will make Ryan run himself out of town!' Gwen laughed. 'And as for Hari, I love that boy – I delivered him for heaven's sake – but he needs a damn good talking to too.'

'Have you spoken to Dad about it?' Jess touched Frankie's arm. 'Maybe if Hari had the chance to meet him properly, he might feel a bit reassured?'

'Guy's been great and he's convinced that Hari just needs time.

But Hari's like my mum in a lot of ways and she'd rather die than admit she was wrong about something.'

'I think Guy's right. My brother might be pig-headed, but he's not an idiot and I know he loves you, so he must be missing you too. And if you keep apologising for something you haven't done, he'll never have to admit to himself that this might all be down to him.'

'They sound like words of wisdom to me.' Toni shifted a sleeping Ionie slightly in her arms. 'And I'm glad I got the lowdown on what you've all been up to, but I suppose I better share mine and Bobby's big news. Promise you won't kill me, Anna, for messing up the rotas... but things have happened even more quickly than we hoped and Ionie's going to be a big sister in July.'

'Kill you? That's the best news I've heard in ages!' Anna led the congratulations, but everyone was joining in and even Frankie had a smile back on her face. Good news like that, and Jess's plans for the future, made it feel like the tide was turning for a lot of the Port Agnes midwives. As much as Nadia was missing spending time with Hamish, the thing she most wanted for herself and the children was for there to be calm waters ahead. But then her phone started to ring.

* * *

When the school secretary called to let Nadia know that Ryan hadn't shown up to collect Remi from her after-school club, all sorts of scenarios had run through her mind. After she'd called Mo's nursery and been told that Ryan hadn't collected him either, and that they'd been just about to phone her, Nadia's emotions had swung between anger and panic. Surely Ryan, who was currently trying to pass himself off as father of the year, wouldn't just forget to collect his children. Something had to have happened; and as much as she didn't want Ryan in her life, she hated the idea of the children losing their father for a second time.

She'd tried calling his mobile at least ten times on the way to collect the children, but it just went straight to voicemail.

'Where's Daddy?' They were Remi's first words after Nadia had screeched to a halt outside the school, having already picked her son up from nursery, and run with Mo clinging to her hand to collect her daughter from the after-school club. Miss Renfrew looked as if she'd sucked a whole lemon grove and Nadia couldn't get out of there fast enough. It was going to take a lot more than an end-of-term gift of a bottle of wine to smooth this one over. 'Mummy, I'm talking to you. Where's Daddy?'

Any other time Nadia might have laughed, hearing some of her own words echoing back to her from the countless times she'd urged Remi to listen to what she was saying. But right now the last thing she felt like doing was laughing. 'Something urgent came up and I know he's really sorry, but you'll see him later.'

'When? Tonight? He said I could get a new scooter and he was going to take us to the toy shop.'

'I'm sure he'll take you as soon as he can.' Nadia caught her breath as an ambulance, with its sirens wailing, raced past them, just as they turned into a road two streets up from The Cookie Jar, which was the closest place they could park. If Ryan had been involved in an accident, it would have been her fault for wishing him gone.

'Nee naw, nee naw!' Mo clapped his hands together in delight and Nadia watched her children in the rear-view mirror. Mo clearly had nothing other than the passing ambulance on his mind, but her daughter looked deep in thought. Remi had struggled with missing her dad when they'd left New Zealand and she'd finally seemed to completely adjust when Ryan had landed back in her life. If she lost him again now, Nadia was terrified it would scar her for life.

'Can we have pizza? Daddy was going to take us for pizza.' Remi could see Nadia watching her.

'Of course darling, whatever you want. Just don't undo your seatbelt until I come round your side and get you out.' Nadia had just reached out for the door handle when the text alert pinged on her phone and even before she opened the message, her skin started to prickle.

✉ Message from Ryan

Catching the evening flight home. U said we R never gonna work so u can't kick off. Delilah's pregnant & we R gonna give it a go 4 the baby's sake. Tell kids I'll call.

Ryan wasn't dead, he was heading back to New Zealand without even saying goodbye to his children, because the woman he'd left them for was pregnant and he needed to be with her for their baby's sake. Funny how he'd never thought about his first two babies in any of this. Nadia swallowed hard, three times in a row, determined not to cry in front of her children about how little regard their father had shown them. Ryan might not be dead, but she'd never wished he was quite as much as she did in that moment.

27

Nadia and Frankie had sat up until past midnight trying to work out what on earth to say to the children about where Ryan had gone, but even the wonders of the internet weren't equipped to answer this one. When Nadia had googled: *What do you tell your children when their father leaves them for someone else?* none of the results would have fitted their situation, even if she'd been able to read them properly through the blur of tears that kept welling up every time she thought about how Remi might react. She wasn't as worried about Mo, who was still so young. And even when they'd still been living in the same house, he'd never had the same attachment to his father that his sister had.

The only thing all the self-help advice sites had in common was a determination that Nadia needed to be honest with the children. Telling them he'd had to go back to New Zealand for work would just be deferring the pain when the truth finally came out, and if Remi decided she couldn't trust either of her parents the consequences could be disastrous.

Frankie had offered to be there while Nadia told them, but that would just have made things more complicated. If it was possible, her mother hated Ryan even more than Nadia did right now and there was a risk she might say something about their father that would hurt the children even more. Nadia might struggle to keep her own feelings in check, but she'd have no chance if she was trying to manage her mother's emotions, as well as her own.

In the end, Frankie had agreed to head off to work early and Nadia had tried and failed to swallow half a slice of toast while she waited for the children to eat their breakfast, rehearsing in her head what she wanted to say to them.

'Do you remember when you had those sentences to write for Miss Renfrew last week, Remi? Nadia's pulse was beating in her ears as Remi nodded. 'Well you found those really difficult didn't you?'

'I'd rather just do colouring, But Miss Renfrew makes us do boring stuff.' Remi had a delightfully simple view of life sometimes and Nadia hated the thought that she was about to chip away at that.

'And Mo finds it really hard when he tries to put his shoes on by himself, don't you darling?'

'Wanna wear my wellies.' Mo's solution to the problem was even simpler and it made her want to laugh and cry all at the same time.

'There are things that we all find it hard to do, and right now Daddy's finding it hard to be a daddy.'

'That's easy. Daisy's daddy does it and he doesn't even have a mummy to help him.' Remi furrowed her brow. 'Has Daddy gone to live with his friend again?'

'Yes darling.' Nadia had agonised over what to tell the children when Ryan had walked out the first time around, and telling them he'd gone to live with his friend had seemed the least damaging. She'd been determined that they'd understand the reason he'd left wasn't because he didn't love them, but because he didn't love their mummy any more and that wasn't because of anything they'd done. Back then, she could never have imagined Ryan turning his back on his children with the callousness that he had. But now he had form, and it was no good pretending to the children, or herself, that he was going to be in their lives to any significant extent. She needed to tell them something, but she didn't want to overwhelm them either and any talk about the new baby could definitely wait until another time.

'In New Zealand?'

'Yes sweetheart, that's right. Daddy should have come to see you to tell you that he was going and he should keep his promises, but because Daddy finds it hard he makes a lot of mistakes. Like when you sometimes get the words the wrong way around in your sentences, or when Mo puts his shoes on the wrong feet. Daddy needs to try harder at being a good daddy, but he might always find it difficult and you must never think that's got anything to do with you. Daddy has to decide for himself if he's going to work hard at getting better, just like you have to keep working hard on your sentences and Mo has to practice putting on his shoes. But even if Daddy decides he's not ready yet to work as hard as he needs to, there's nothing for you to worry about, because I'm always going to be here and I'm always going to try as hard as I can to be the best mummy possible.'

'You're the best mummy already.' Remi's grin took Nadia by surprise and revealed the gap in her teeth where the tooth fairy had taken her first haul. 'Daisy says she wishes she had a mummy like my mummy.'

'That's nice darling.' Nadia couldn't allow that piece of information to infiltrate her heart. It was breaking enough for her own children, without adding Daisy to the mix. 'Are you sure you're okay?'

'Uh huh.' Remi nodded sagely, like a six-year-old with the

wisdom of someone ten times her age and in a way it was almost more heart-breaking that her father leaving could seem so routine. 'Can Lola still come to live with us in the new house?'

'Hopefully we can bring her home really soon.' Nadia offered up a silent prayer that Ryan wouldn't be even more of a disappointment and stand in the way of the children getting their beloved dog back. The vet, whose details had been on the paperwork Ryan had given her, had told her that if Ryan was happy to sign Lola over to Nadia, they could release her. There was a considerable bill waiting to be paid, which was definitely one thing in their favour, because Ryan would do just about anything to avoid parting with his money.

'I hope she still wants to sleep by the end of my bed.' The prospect of having Lola home seemed to more than make up for Ryan's disappearance in his daughter's eyes, but Mo still hadn't said anything.

'And what about you Mo? Are you okay?'

'Can I wear my wellies?' He gave her a hopeful smile and she couldn't resist the urge to pull both of her children into her arms for a moment longer. They were going to be okay, they always had been, and as long as they had each other, nothing else really mattered.

* * *

Despite the calmness of Remi's reaction to Ryan leaving, Nadia was glad she had the day off to process things. She wasn't naïve enough to expect that there wouldn't be some bumps in the road, or times when Remi and Mo might miss their father – or the idea of what their father should be – but for now it was enough to take things one day at a time. They had the excitement of the house move and Guy had already been there several times, getting things ready and building Fluff and Kipo a guinea pig palace of their own. It had become a bit of a game with the children that seeing the house for the first time was going to be a surprise and Nadia had been happy to join in when the children had asked if it was going to be a surprise for her too. It just added to the sense of anticipation and the chance to spend the day preparing for the move was a very welcome one.

Frankie was out on home visits. Making the transition from MCA to qualified midwife might have been a long road for her mother, but everyone who'd ever been cared for by Frankie would know she was going to make a brilliant midwife when she finally completed her training.

With her mother using the car, Nadia got stuck in to the task of boxing up more of the contents of the flat. Some of the stuff she'd had shipped back from New Zealand was still in storage, but just the kids' belongings alone had filled up twelve boxes already. It was amazing to think that the three of them, and all of their most essential possessions, had somehow fitted into the bedroom they'd been sharing since they'd arrived back in Port Agnes. There was a part of her that would happily have dumped the lot and left the memories from New Zealand at the bottom of a landfill site, but facing up to them was part of moving on. They were the children's earliest memories, too, and she was hoping that one day she'd be able to separate the good bits from the bad bits far more easily than she could right now.

It seemed silly when she'd lived in Port Agnes for the majority of her life that so many places triggered a memory of the brief time she'd spent with Hamish, and every time she turned a corner she expected to see him – half of her hoping she would and the other half scared of how she might react if she did. The way Ryan had left had just made her admire Hamish all the more.

He was a man who prioritised his children without even

thinking about it, but he'd made her feel incredibly important too. He'd made her feel beautiful and even though it obviously wasn't meant to be, he'd still managed to mend something she'd thought was broken forever.

It was crazy to worry about how long it might take her to get over a relationship that had been so short-lived, but the intensity of supporting Ginny had bonded her to Hamish, and if it was stupid to miss him this much, she couldn't help it. She was still glad it had happened, even if it meant there were unwanted reminders as she walked around Port Agnes. It was a price she was more than willing to pay.

'Nadia!' She recognised the voice straight away.

'Hari? What on earth are you doing here?' Watching her younger brother as he walked towards her, Nadia could see he was stressed. He had a tell of pinching his right earlobe and his jaw looked like it was set in stone.

'Where's Mum?'

'At work.' Nadia wasn't going to volunteer any other information until she knew whether Hari was in Port Agnes to try and fix things, or to make more trouble.

'She hasn't rung me or messaged me in days.' Hari looked genuinely shocked and Nadia had to suppress the urge to smile.

'Do you think that might have something to do with you ignoring all her messages asking to talk to you, after you acted like such a prat about Guy?'

'She should have told me; I shouldn't have to find out that she was seeing someone by catching them snogging in the street like they're in *Love Island*.'

'Doesn't it worry you how much like Nani you sound? Mum is in love with Guy and people who are in love have been known to kiss, sometimes even in public. If that makes you uncomfortable then I suggest you learn to suck it up, because she spent years putting herself last wanting the best for us.' Nadia could happily have given her brother a dead leg, like they were ten and twelve again, but it was time for at least one of them to be a grown-up. 'She finally gets to put herself first and you can't stand it. What gets me most about all of this is that you and Nani don't seem to care that Dad's girlfriend started staying over before Mum even met Guy. The double standard is breath-taking.'

'But Mum left—'

'Would you really rather she'd stayed? They're both so much happier and even Dad admitted he's glad Mum finally had the courage to do what one of them should have done a long time ago. If it's a bit inconvenient for you to have a complicated family set-up, then you should just count yourself lucky that both your parents are still around and want to see you, despite the fact you're a total idiot sometimes.'

'That's not—'

She held up her hand when her phone started to ring, determined to answer it, even if was someone offering to get compensation for an accident that wasn't her fault. It would do Hari good to know he wasn't always everyone's number one priority.

'Is that Nadia?' The voice on the other end of the phone sound young, male and more than a bit panicky.

'Yes, who's this?'

'It's Liam, Anne-Marie's son. She said the baby is coming and I can't get hold of Dad. It's nearly two weeks late and she was supposed to go into the hospital tomorrow to be induced; they only left if that late because of them being short staffed over Christmas. But now it's started happening really quickly. I've called an ambulance, but they don't know how long it's going to take to get here and they said I need to call back if the baby starts to come.'

'Have you tried the midwifery unit?'

'Mum did, but there's no one available. There are already some other women having their babies at home and no one can come out to us yet. It was them who told us to call for an ambulance and Mum really doesn't want to have the baby at home, but I dunno what I'm going to do if the baby starts to come and it's just us here. I can't drive her to the hospital either, cos Dad's got one car and the other one's in for its MOT. Even if I could, I don't think she'd let me, she's too worried that the baby might come on the way.'

'Okay sweetheart, I'll come up to you now and we can wait for the ambulance together, just in case, but I'm sure it'll get here before your baby brother or sister arrives.'

'I hope so. Thanks, I really didn't know what else to do.'

'No problem, I'll be there as soon as I can.' Ending the call, Nadia looked straight at her brother. 'Where's your car?'

'At the end of King's Street. Why?'

'Because you're driving me to a home delivery whether you like it or not.'

* * *

When Liam came to the door, his whole body seem to sag with relief at the sight of Nadia, which was a stark contrast to Hari who'd begged to stay in the car and who looked like he might still make a bolt for it at any moment. Nadia had insisted he had to come in, to see if there was anything he could help with.

'Like what?' He'd looked more horrified than ever at that point and Nadia had been tempted to hand him a pair of surgical gloves, just to teach him a lesson for being such a selfish pig, but she'd managed to resist.

'I don't know, make tea? Talk to Liam to help him keep calm, ring the ambulance again to see what's going on. I won't know until we get in there, but if this baby really is coming then the chances are I'm going to need you for something. And for now, you can help me carry in the stuff I picked up from the unit on the way up here.'

'You always were a bossy cow.' Hari might have protested, but he'd followed her to the house anyway and stood sheepishly behind her, holding the carry case with a cannister of gas and air, while Liam filled them in on the latest as they went inside the house.

'I just phoned the ambulance again to ask what's happening and it might still be another forty minutes before they get here.'

'Has your mum had the urge to push?'

'That's what the man on the phone asked me, but if she has, she hasn't said so.'

'I think you'd be able to tell if she was getting to that stage.' Nadia's tone was gentle. 'You're doing brilliantly and you've done all the right things for your mum.'

'I'm just really scared of what might happen to her or the baby if the ambulance doesn't get here soon.'

'Don't worry, even if the ambulance doesn't make it in time. I've done this lots of times before and so has your mum.' Nadia was determined not to show even the tiniest hint of nerves that might reveal to Liam that this time was different. She'd never delivered a baby without any other medical staff for support, and if she was honest, she wasn't all that keen to add it to her list of life experiences. She'd left messages to see if any of the other midwives who weren't already on shift might be able to meet her at Anne-Marie's place, but there were no guarantees that any of them would make it before the ambulance did.

'I feel a lot better now you've arrived. She's through here in the lounge. I asked her if she wanted me to help her up to the bedroom, but I think she's worried about being able to get down again quickly enough if the ambulance shows up.' Liam pushed open the door to the lounge and Hari was still hanging back halfway down the hallway.

'Hi Anne-Marie, this wasn't quite what you had planned was it?' Nadia smiled, hoping she sounded as relaxed as she was trying to.

'Not exactly. I was hoping to be drugged from the waist down at least by this stage.' Anne-Marie grimaced. 'But I've got to admit I'm glad to see you.'

'Liam tells me the ambulance is on the way, but you haven't been able to get hold of Greg?'

'We weren't having much luck getting hold of anyone.'

'Right, this is where you can come in useful.' Nadia turned to look behind her. 'This is my brother, Hari, I had to rope him in to give me a lift up here, but he's up for helping out however he can. If you give him Greg's number, he can keep calling until he gets a response.'

'You can have my phone.' Anne-Marie thrust it towards a still reluctant-looking Hari. 'We've left Greg about ten messages already, but he still hasn't rung back.'

'Hari, go outside and keep trying Greg while I take a proper look at Anne-Marie and see how close this baby might be.' Nadia wasn't giving her brother any room to hesitate. 'Liam, if you can put the kettle on sweetheart and make us all a cup of tea please, hopefully I'll be able to let you know when you come back in whether or not I think we need to try and hurry the ambulance up again.'

'Okay.' Liam was already on his way out, with Hari close behind him, neither of them wanting to risk being anywhere nearby when Anne-Marie was examined.

'What's the code for your phone if I need it?' Hari turned back as he reached the door.

'It's eleven ten zero three, Liam's birthday.'

'It's always the favourite child whose birthday is used for stuff like that.' Hari smiled for the first time and gave Liam a gentle nudge. 'My birthday was the code on our burglar alarm, but they did use Nadia's for the padlock on the bin store.'

'Just go and do something useful!' Nadia could still hear Hari laughing as he headed back down the hallway and she couldn't help joining in. 'I thought my annoying little brother might one day drop the annoying bit, but it doesn't look like it's ever going to happen.'

'I'm just glad he was here to drive you up.'

'Me too.' Nadia squeezed her hand. 'Now if you're ready, shall we have a proper look and see what's going on.'

'You might have to wait because I've got another contraction coming.' Nadia held Anne-Marie's hand until the pain passed and her whole body relaxed again. Positioning one of the blankets from the back of the sofa so that Anne-Marie would feel less exposed, Nadia carried out the promised examination. She was sure Liam and Hari wouldn't risk bursting into the room without knocking, but having the blanket over Anne-Marie's raised knees should hopefully help her to stay more relaxed. Thankfully it seemed to do the trick, even when the landline started to ring and there was no way either of them could get to it in time. A few moments later, there was no doubt, this baby was well and truly on its way.

'You're ten centimetres dilated.' Nadia looked at Anne-Marie as she spoke, but she couldn't tell whether the other woman thought this was good news or bad.

'How come I don't want to push yet?' Anne-Marie shuffled back into a sitting position putting both feet on the floor.

'Sometimes it can take up to an hour from being fully dilated to wanting to push. Gwen, who I work with at the unit, always calls it the rest and be thankful stage, but I know you're probably at the point where you just want this to be over.'

'I'd be past that point if I was in a lovely well-equipped delivery room at the hospital.' Anne-Marie managed a wry grin before Liam suddenly burst through the door without checking if the coast was clear.

'Are you done?' He had an arm across his eyes as he walked in.

'We are.' Nadia turned to look at him as he dropped his arm away from his face.

'Thank God for that, because the call was from dad. He was using someone else's phone and he could only remember the home number. The car broke down just outside Port Tremellien and the battery on his phone was dead. He started walking back and when he passed a couple of walkers he told them what had happened, and they offered to let him use their phone. It's going to take him another half an hour to get here though.'

'Do you think the baby will wait that long?' Anne-Marie's eyes were round with concern and Nadia wasn't in the habit of making promises she couldn't keep. Ryan had been the master of that.

'I can't honestly say and he needs to get here before the ambulance does. But if you go and find Hari' – Nadia turned to look at Liam – 'he'll drive you to pick up your dad. You might just need to give him directions.'

'Are you sure he won't mind?' Liam looked doubtful.

'Not if he values his life.' Nadia grinned and then turned her attention back to Anne-Marie. Hari might have been acting like an idiot for the last couple of months, but he was a secret softy really and she'd been almost certain he'd come running back if he thought there was genuinely a chance of Frankie cutting contact with him. She just had to hope Hari wouldn't let her down when it came to getting Greg back in time to witness the delivery of his baby.

* * *

'Oh my God. I'd forgotten how much this bit hurts!' Anne-Marie's face twisted as she pushed her bottom down into the sofa. 'Talk about feel the burn; why did I ever think I wanted to do this again?'

'Baby's crowning now, but once you've got the head out some of that sensation is going to go and I promise you it'll start to feel easier. Are you sure you don't want to try the gas and air again?' Nadia had already administered pethidine and Anne-Marie had been having some Entonox, but she'd kept pushing the mouth-piece of the gas and air away from her.

'It makes me feel too sick; I just wish Greg was here.'

'I know you do sweetheart, and I'd offer to hold your hand for you, but I need to be ready to get the baby out. You're doing brilliantly and it won't be long now.' Anne-Marie was sitting on the edge of the sofa with her feet on two dining room chairs, which she'd insisted was helping. Although she'd clearly had enough of labour.

'Stuff holding his hand, I want to tie his bits and pieces in a very tight knot, so there's no chance of this ever happening again.'

'I think there are less painful ways of ensuring that doesn't happen!'

'But they wouldn't be nearly as satisfying.' Anne-Marie growled the last word and dropped her chin to her chest, as the pain intensified.

'Baby's head is out; well done sweetheart. You're really close now, I'm just going to check the position of the cord before the baby's shoulders turn, so if you get the urge to push again I want you to try and pant through it.'

Feeling for the umbilical cord, Nadia let out a sigh of relief once she was certain it wasn't wrapped around the baby's neck. Dealing with that on her own would have been even more terrifying, but both Anne-Marie and her baby were doing everything by the book so far. Thank goodness.

'The shoulders have turned and baby is in the right position for the rest of the body to come out as easily as possible. So I want you to go with the next push and give it everything you've got, like this is the last time you'll ever do it.'

'It bloody well is!' Anne-Marie gritted her teeth and dropped her chin to her chest again, just as the door to the lounge flung open for a second time.

'I'm so sorry love, I—' Greg stopped in his tracks at the sight of his wife so close to giving birth. Thankfully there was no sign of Liam or Hari.

'The baby's nearly here. You've just got time to hold Anne-Marie's hand and watch the final member of your family come into the world.' Nadia glanced up as she spoke, and Greg grabbed hold of his wife's hand. Anne-Marie didn't break concentration for a second; she really was determined to make this her last ever push and barely a minute after he'd arrived in the room, Greg was a father of six.

'There you go sweetheart.' Nadia lifted the baby straight onto Anne-Marie's chest for skin-to-skin contact, the youngest of the Hudson clan letting the world know they'd arrived with a hearty cry. 'Have you seen what you've got?'

'It's another girl.' Anne-Marie rested her head against Greg's as they looked down at their daughter.

'Do you still want to call her Mila?' Greg looked at his wife, who nodded in response. 'You know you're the most amazing woman who ever lived, don't you?'

'Yes, and I know something else too.'

'What's that?'

'If you don't get your vasectomy booked in after what I've just been through, you'll be getting a DIY one in your sleep!'

28

'That's a nice name. Did they say why they chose it?' Hari hadn't been able to stop smiling since he'd been allowed in to meet baby Mila, just after her big brother Liam had held her for the first time and about two minutes before the ambulance had finally arrived. Nadia recognised the look of euphoria that came when you'd played a part in the safe arrival of a new life, no matter how small that role might have been.

'Anne-Marie said it's Italian for miracle and they were looking for a name that captured how lucky they feel to have such a beautiful family, but they wanted Mila because it's an anagram of Liam's name.' Nadia stretched out her legs in the passenger seat of Hari's car as they headed back into Port Agnes. 'He was the start of their family and the beginning of their miracle, and Anne-Marie said she never wants him to forget how important he is to them all. I think it's partly because he's going off travelling and she's terrified he might decide to settle in some far-flung place, instead of coming home for uni. But it's also because he's her stepson and getting to the point where he calls her mum, and knows that's exactly who she is, hasn't been an easy ride.'

'What happened to his birth mum?' Hari glanced at her for a second, before refocusing on the road in front of him.

'She's been next to useless from what I can gather, but it took Liam a long time to come to terms with that.'

'We're lucky to have the sort of mum we've got.' Hari was still looking straight ahead, but even from that angle, it was obvious there were tears in his eyes.

'We're really lucky. The question is what are you going to do about it?'

'I suppose I ought to tell her.'

'And apologise?'

'Yes, I just don't know what to say. You're right, I've been an idiot and I know it's not the first time, but I'm worried I've pushed it too far lately.'

'You might be an idiot, but you're her idiot.' Nadia nudged his arm. 'So we both know she's going to forgive you. Just get it done, or I might not be nearly as forgiving.'

'God, you really are bossy.' Hari grinned. 'But I still love you.'

'I love you too, even though you are an idiot.' She gave his arm another nudge, their affection for one another cemented in a lifetime of sibling squabbles and shared memories. With Ryan gone and Hari planning to patch things up with their mum, almost everything was falling into place, just in time for their move to their new house. If it was greedy to ask for more than *almost* everything, Nadia couldn't help it. Sometimes almost just wasn't enough.

* * *

Saffron had offered to make cupcakes with Daisy and, if he hadn't already done so, Hamish would have happily bought his older daughter a car for her act of sisterly devotion. Anything that stopped Daisy asking for the tenth time that day when they were going to see Nadia again. It was bad enough that he thought about Nadia hundreds of times every day, without having to deal with the fact that Daisy was clearly pining for her too. He wasn't sure if Saffron had picked up on it as well, or whether she was just doing her bit to keep her little sister entertained on a rainy January day, but either way he was grateful.

Hamish had fully intended to leave them to it, but as he'd been on the way to the utility room with another load of washing he'd scooped up from Saffron's floor, he'd paused by the kitchen door to listen to them chatting.

'I wish we could see Nard-ya today.' Daisy was standing on a kitchen chair that Saffron had pushed up to the work surface, flicking a wooden spoon backwards and forwards in a haphazard motion that sent some of the cake mix sploshing over the side of the bowl with each movement.

'She's got her own kids to look after, I told you that.' Saffron's tone was sharp and at odds with how she usually spoke to her sister.

'She doesn't come here any more cos I was sick on her top.' Daisy sniffed loudly. 'And now she doesn't like me.'

'Don't be silly.' Saffron had snapped for the second time in a row and Daisy started to cry.

'And you don't like me either.' Daisy howled and Hamish had been a split second away from dropping the washing and rushing in to comfort his younger daughter, when Saffron beat him to it.

'Of course I like you, Daisy-boo, I love you to the moon and back.' Saffron wrapped her arms around her little sister. 'I'm sure Nadia likes you too and you being sick has got nothing to do with her not coming over.'

'How d'you know?' Daisy's voice was muffled as she cuddled into her big sister's neck.

'Because I told her not to come here any more.' It was such a clear statement, but Hamish still couldn't believe what he was hearing and he seemed to be frozen to the spot, just out of view of both of his daughters.

'Why? I love Nard-ya; she's really nice.'

'She's only nice because she wants Dad to like her and he still loves Mum. He's always going to love Mum and us the most, so we don't need anyone else.'

'We don't?' Daisy pulled back from her sister, her little brow furrowing with confusion. Hamish still didn't move. He wanted to hear what Saffron had to say.

'No, we don't. You'll understand when you're bigger, but I promise you that it's better if Nadia doesn't come here again.' Saffron sounded so convinced of her vision for the future that suddenly Hamish had never been less certain of his.

* * *

Waiting until Daisy had gone to bed had been agonising. Hamish kept looking at Saffron and trying to imagine her having a conversation with Nadia where she'd told her not to spend any more time with her father. After the way she'd reacted with Camilla and at the dance competition, it was all too easy. The conversation he'd had with her, where he thought he'd managed to set her straight, obviously hadn't had any effect.

She was sitting with her legs curled under her on the sofa when he came downstairs after reading Daisy a bedtime story. He hated the thought that his little girl might be blaming herself for not seeing Nadia, but he couldn't say anything until he'd spoken to Saffron.

In the end, he just came out with it. Saffron had clearly been straight to the point in the way she'd spoken to Nadia, and he was going to follow her lead. 'When did you speak to Nadia about not coming here any more?'

'Did Daisy say something?' Saffron immediately stiffened, her tone tight and defensive.

'No.'

'Oh, so it was Nadia then? I bloody knew it.' Saffron was up on her feet and her high horse in an instant. 'Look, all I told her was that she was wasting her time and that she wasn't going to get any further than any of the others did, because she'll never compare to Mum and not even you can deny that.'

'I don't want to compare her to your mum; they're two different people. I loved your mum and nothing is ever going to change how much she meant to me, but she's gone.' Hamish sighed. Trying to navigate territory like this was almost impossible, because he had no idea what he was doing, or whether anything he said might make things worse. 'And for the first time since I lost her, I've met someone I could imagine having another life with, someone who loves her children every bit as much as I love mine and who understands why you'll always come first. I know I made some mistakes with the others, but Nadia's different to them and, yes, she's different to your mum too, but it's possible to love more than one person in a lifetime and not have to compare them, or to say one of them is better than the other.'

'How can you say you love her, when you've only known her five minutes? And I can't believe you don't think Mum was a better person than she is, when it's obvious to anyone with half a brain! Mum gave you me and she died to give you Daisy, surely that's enough to prove it to you?' Saffron was crying now and Hamish had to fight the urge to comfort her. But there were things that needed to be said first, no matter how difficult they might be.

'What your mother gave me is priceless, and you and Daisy

mean more to me than you'll ever understand, at least until you have children of your own.' Hamish held his daughter's gaze. 'But you had absolutely no right to talk to Nadia the way you did and as much as you've sometimes taken on far more of a motherly role than you should have done, you aren't Daisy's mother and you're certainly not mine.'

'Funny that you've been acting like a typical teenage boy then, isn't it? You're like a dog on heat whenever she's about!' Saffron's tears had given way to anger again. Maybe it was easier for her that way, but it didn't mean Hamish could let her get away with it.

'Saffron, stop it now, I'm warning you.' He was determined not to shout, but it was getting more difficult every time his daughter spoke about Nadia as if she was something she'd scraped off the bottom of her shoe.

'Or what? Are you going to start hitting me now?' Saffron was lashing out, saying the most outlandish things she could think of. She knew as well as Hamish did that what she was saying was ridiculous, but he was beginning to wonder if he'd ever be able to make her understand what he was trying to say.

'I'd never do that, but I need you to know something.' He waited until she finally looked up at him, firing a sullen response in his direction.

'What?'

'I love you and Daisy so much, but that doesn't mean I don't want to have the chance of falling in love again too. It's completely different to what I feel for you and I know the last thing you want to think about is your dad having a girlfriend. I promise nothing will ever change how I feel about you girls, but having another person in your life who loves you too wouldn't be a bad thing and Daisy loves being with Nadia. I think if you gave her a chance, you'd be able to see that and you might even grow to like her too.'

'Do you really think it's going to be that easy?' Saffy's eyes suddenly filled with tears again. 'And what if she hates me now because of all the things I said, but she loves you and she loves Daisy? You'll all be glad when I go away to uni, but when I come back you'll be wishing I wasn't here.'

'Oh sweetheart, I'll never be glad when you aren't here. If it was my choice, I'd keep you here forever, but I know I've got to let you go at least a little bit. It would be really selfish of me not to let you have a life of your own.'

'I suppose it's selfish of me not to want to let you have a life of your own too!' Saffron thumped a fist on to the table. 'It's like the two of you have rehearsed a script. I bet she couldn't wait to tell you everything I said, so she could use it against me.'

'She didn't tell me anything.' Hamish sighed again. He was getting nowhere fast. He'd tried being gentle with Saffron and he'd tried being hard on her too, but she still seemed determined to see Nadia as the bad guy. 'I heard you talking to Daisy about confronting Nadia, otherwise I wouldn't have known anything about it. All she said was that she didn't think it was the right time for us to take things further and that you and Daisy needed me. She's got no idea I even know, let alone the things I've said to you. This is all me, Saff. The way I feel about you hasn't changed and it never will, but I can't change the way I feel about Nadia either.'

'She didn't tell you?' Saffron was staring at him wide-eyed, and it was almost as if Hamish could see the cogs of his daughter's brain turning – the moment of clarity when she realised that Nadia had not only honoured her wishes, but had protected her relationship with her father by not telling him what had happened. He'd rarely seen Saffron lost for words, but she was still staring at him long after he'd shaken his head.

'She's nothing like Kate and it's part of the reason why I like her so much.' Hamish swallowed hard, knowing he was about to make a promise that was really going to hurt, but he'd made another promise years before which meant he didn't have a choice. He'd told Sara when she was dying that he'd always put the girls first, so unless he could find a way of helping Saffron to accept his relationship with Nadia, he was going to have to give it up. It might break his heart, but better that than breaking his daughter's. 'If you don't want me to see Nadia again, I won't, but I'm going to need you to help me find a way to convince Daisy that none of this is her fault and at the moment I don't think she believes what you've said.'

'I'm not even going to be here soon, so I can't exactly stop you seeing her, can I?' Saffron's tone had relaxed a bit, but it was still grudging and Hamish could hardly believe the words she was saying. Five minutes ago she'd seemed to think that him seeing Nadia again was the worst kind of betrayal possible.

'Are you saying you don't mind if I start seeing Nadia again?' He was watching her intently, but she still wasn't giving much away and all she offered was a non-committal shrug.

'I s'pose if she can put up with Daisy being sick on her and not blab about what I said, she can't be all bad, but just don't expect us to suddenly be some kind of happy family.' She sniffed, wiping her eyes with the back of her hands. 'And for God's sake please don't kiss in front of me again.'

There was still bravado in Saffron's attempt to push him and Nadia away to protect herself, but she was right too. There was no chance of things changing overnight, even if Nadia was willing to see him again. But just the possibility of some kind of future between them made him smile and sharing a joke with his daughter was more than enough for now. 'The ability to put up with vomit is always a quality I go for.' Hamish looked at Saffron again and just a hint of a smile was tugging at the corners of her mouth.

'You should text her then. Ask her to come over tomorrow

when I'm out with Jamie. You know, before it's too late. She's very pretty, so you can't afford to hang about.'

'So now I've got to take dating advice from you too?' Hamish dropped a kiss on his daughter's head and tried to laugh off what she'd said. The trouble was, Saffron was right again and he had a horrible feeling it might already be too late.

29

Nadia's phone had pinged several times whilst she was on the long drive home, but she hadn't bothered to stop and check the messages. Anyone who wanted to speak to her urgently would call her, so it wasn't until she pulled up two roads from The Cookie Jar to park Frankie's car, that she checked her phone. There were three new messages.

✉ Message from Hamish

How have you been? Daisy keeps saying she misses you and so do I. Do you think we could meet up to try and start again, like nothing happened? Take care, H xx

✉ Message from Hari

I bought Mum thirty-two yellow roses, one for every year she's had to put up with being my mother! I met her and Guy to apologise too. He seems like a great guy... God, that's like one of Dad's jokes. Thanks for

being my bossy big sister, you know I need it sometimes. I'm going to
speak to Nani later and try and set her straight too. Wish me luck! X

✉ Message from Ginny
Thank you so much for coming to see me when I had my meltdown.
The mastitis has completely cleared up and I'm having some counselling now to help me process everything that's happened. We want to
have a celebration for Neviah, now that the treatment is almost over.
We're going to have a naming ceremony and we'd like you and Hamish
to be guide parents, but no pressure. I'll give you a call when you've
had a chance to think about it. Speak soon xxxx

By the time she'd got to Ginny's message, it was obvious why
Hamish had been in touch. He wanted to wipe the slate clean
between them and start again, as friends, so it wouldn't be
awkward if they were both going to be Neviah's guide parents. She
understood why, and it would be a hell of a lot easier if she could
just do that – wipe the memories of the time she'd spent with
Hamish from her mind – but feelings couldn't just be turned off,
no matter how much you might want them to be. She could put on
a show to get through the naming ceremony and any other time
they might need to meet, like when the girls had play dates. But as
for any kind of meaningful friendship, she just wasn't that good an
actress.

'Come on girl, we've got more important things to do than sit
here thinking about text messages.' Nadia reached across to the
footwell of the car and patted Lola's head. It was time to bring a
missing member of the family back home and this time there was
no danger of the children waking up to discover they'd disappeared all over again.

* * *

If the flat had felt crowded with two adults, two children and two guinea pigs, the arrival of Lola pushed it to bursting point. She was every bit as excited to see the children as they were to see her and she followed them around as if she was worried about letting them out of her sight for an instant. That suited Mo and Remi just fine, because they were constantly stroking her and they'd lie on the floor with her whenever she stretched out, their heads resting up against her side. If guinea pigs were capable of jealousy, there was a good chance that Kipo and Fluff would be feeling some. They were probably safer staying out of Lola's way for a little while anyway. Not that Nadia thought the gentle Lab would try to hurt them, but she was clumsy – trampling on things that shouldn't be trampled on and wiping out whole shelves of stuff with one swipe of her tail. The move to the new house couldn't come soon enough, and with just forty-eight hours to go, they wouldn't have to wait much longer.

'Can we take Lola up to see Daisy and Hamish? She'd love it at their house and she could play with George!' Remi clearly hadn't pictured quite how much damage Lola could wreak in their beautiful home, especially if she ended up tearing around in hot pursuit of George, Daisy's little dog.

'It might be better if Daisy comes to us after school one day. Maybe next week when we're all settled in the new house; you can show her your new bedroom then too.'

'What about Hamish?' Remi had a way of furrowing her brow when she looked at Nadia, which narrowed her eyes, and it was as if she could see into her mother's soul.

'I'm sure he's too busy to have time to come and meet Lola, but I'll bring her up to school to pick you up some days and if he's there, he can see her then.' Nadia was keeping her fingers crossed that they'd be at pick-up together as infrequently as possible, and having the dog with her would be a good excuse to hang back.

'Don't you like Daisy's daddy any more?' Remi really was an old soul, but there was no way Nadia was getting into this sort of discussion with a six-year-old.

'Of course I do, he's just busy, that's all.'

'Can we get the 'gility course out for the guinea pigs again when they come to see us at the new house?' Remi could very well grow up to be a politician, with her ability to completely disregard any responses she didn't want to hear.

'We'll see. Right now we need to box up some more of your toys. You can leave two out, but the rest need to be packed so we can move everything.'

'Four?' Remi gave her an innocent wide-eyed look and all she could do was laugh. That girl was going to go far.

* * *

The whole team were going out for dinner after the end of the day shift. There were a few things to celebrate, and the first was Izzy's engagement. It might have been a bit of whirlwind romance, but with Noah being the newly installed vicar of St Jude's, Izzy had joked that she'd have to say 'I do' before she could move into the beautiful eighteenth-century vicarage that came with the job. It was obvious she was head over heels in love with Noah, though, and the details of the wedding were already being eagerly discussed in the staffroom. Izzy's beloved grandfather would be giving her away and she'd be using the ring her late grandmother had worn throughout their long and happy marriage.

The second cause for celebration was the news that Toni and Bobby's twelve-week scan with baby number two had gone perfectly. The sonographer had even been willing to confide that she was 60 per cent certain of the baby's gender and if she was right, in six months' time, baby Ionie would be getting a little brother.

The team were also welcoming Ella back to work after some extended leave supporting her friend, Jemima, and helping her husband, Leo, adjust to paralysis following an accident. Both Ella and Dan had accompanied their friends on the first holiday they'd had since Leo's accident and from what Ella had shared it had been an emotional time for them all.

There'd no doubt be some glasses raised to wish Jess good luck, too, as she took the next steps in her IVF journey, and Gwen had already told Nadia and Frankie that the team had bought them both house-warming gifts for their upcoming move. Gwen being Gwen had also joked about coming up with ideas for Frankie's hen night, given that her engagement to Guy was bound to be the next thing. With so much to celebrate, it sounded as if it was going to be a night to remember, so Nadia was grateful to Guy and Dexter for looking after the children. They were even taking Lola over to Jess and Dexter's place, so that Riley could meet her. Nadia just hoped that nothing irreplaceable got broken. With Lola and Mo on the loose, she'd had to warn Jess it was a possibility, but her friend had just laughed and said that as long as the kids were happy there was nothing that couldn't be replaced.

The door to the staffroom was open as Nadia approached it and she heard two very familiar voices drifting down the corridor. It was her mother and Gwen.

'Are you getting excited about moving in with your very own silver fox?' Gwen's tone was teasing. 'I must admit I can see the attraction. Guy could definitely get my motor racing if Barry wasn't still tinkering about and keeping it ticking over, even after all these years.'

'Is that what they call it now, tinkering about?' Frankie laughed.

'Guy will be thrilled to know he's got your seal of approval and yes, I can't wait, especially now Hari seems so happy for us. I did wonder if I'd feel apprehensive about us moving in together, after how things ended with Advik, but we just weren't right for each other. Everything feels different with Guy.'

'I bet it does!' Gwen nudged her friend and Nadia couldn't decide whether to breeze in, or wait for them to move on to a new topic. One thing was for certain, she definitely didn't want to overhear any details about her mum and Guy's sex life, or Gwen and Barry's come to that. Not that Gwen really gave anyone a choice.

'You're incorrigible, you know that, don't you?' Frankie shook her head. 'I'm glad Nadia and the kids are going to have their own space too. It's been so lovely having them home, but I know she wants to start afresh now that things with Ryan are definitely over for good.'

'Well it's certainly a lovely place to make a fresh start. You two are going to be my posh friends now, living in the Gatehouse and Lodge at Ocean View. That's got to be the most upmarket postcode in the whole of Port Agnes and isn't it where the town's most dishy GP lives too?' Gwen couldn't be right about that. There was no way they could afford to rent two properties on Hamish's road, whatever kind of deal Guy claimed to have got for the next six months. Frankie was going to put her right any second.

'I know. What are they going to think about having riff-raff like us living up there?' Frankie laughed again. 'Although if they're all as lovely as Hamish, there won't be any snobbery. I just can't wait to see Nadia and the kids' faces when we drive up and tell them where home is going to be for the next six months.'

If Frankie had turned around at that point, she'd have seen a very unwelcome expression on her daughter's face. There was no way she was moving to Ocean View and being Hamish's next-door neighbour. If she did it would be impossible to pretend that nothing had ever happened between them or to tuck her feelings away in a dark corner where they belonged.

* * *

'You're very quiet tonight and you've been checking your phone every five minutes. Are you waiting on a booty call?' Gwen might be heading towards the latter end of her sixties, but she could still take Nadia's breath away with some of the things she said.

'I'm just expecting a text back from the landlord of the flat. I thought I might see if there was any chance of me and the kids staying on.' Nadia spoke as softly as she could without whispering, hoping she could avoid anyone else overhearing.

'Why on earth would you want to do that?' Gwen was incapable of being discreet even when she wanted to, but on this occasion she wasn't even trying.

'I just think it could be a better long-term option than the six months tenancy with Guy's friend, and it would give him and Mum their space too.'

'They'll have plenty of space; you've got separate houses for goodness' sake and there's a beautiful garden there for the kids. You won't have that at the flat.'

'I know, but they've had so much upheaval. It might not be perfect, but I'd just like us to be settled somewhere we could stay for a bit longer.' She was trying to justify the decision to herself every bit as much as to Gwen, but it wasn't working on either of them.

'Your mum said that the woman who owns the flat is talking about selling to the couple who run The Cookie Jar. So it hardly sounds like a long-term proposition.' Gwen turned towards the rest of the group seated around the table, some of whom were already looking in their direction. 'Someone tell Nadia she's being ridiculous please.'

'About what? I can't imagine Nadia being ridiculous about anything.' Anna, who was one of the sweetest people Nadia had ever met, smiled in her direction.

'She doesn't want to move to the new place in case she cramps Frankie's style.' Gwen threw her hands up in the air in exasperation.

'Is that true?' Frankie widened her eyes. 'We won't even be in the same house. But even if we were, I'd rather have you with me than anywhere else. It's me who doesn't want to suffocate you. I'd happily have you and the kids living with us forever and so would Guy. Come to that, if we won the lottery, I think he'd buy a massive place and try to insist that Jess, Dexter and Riley moved in too.'

'Hey, if it's got a pool you can count me in!' Jess grinned.

'And me come to that.' Emily raised her glass.

'Blimey, we'll have a commune of midwives at this rate.' Gwen turned back to Nadia. 'Now can you see how ridiculous you're being?'

'It's not that simple.' Nadia had never wanted the ground to open up and swallow her quite as much as she did at that moment. This wasn't a conversation she wanted to have in front of the whole team and luckily she didn't seem to be the only person to realise how uncomfortable it was.

'I'm sure Nadia doesn't want us all to be discussing this and trying to make the decision for her.' Ella reached over and touched her hand. 'I for one want to hear more about Emily's plans for Izzy's hen night.'

'Me too.' Anna nodded. No wonder she and Ella ran the team so successfully, they both had the emotional intelligence it took to manage people and build friendships in what was often a high-pressure environment. Right now, Nadia was definitely feeling more pressure than she wanted to and she hated being the centre of attention.

'It's not because you've got a problem with Guy is it?' Frankie looked close to tears and no amount of changing the subject was going to help. Nadia was just going to have to tell the truth in front of everyone. Perfect.

'I can't live at Ocean View and be Hamish's neighbour. Not after what happened between us.'

'What did happen?' Gwen almost leapt on Nadia's lap in her haste to get the details.

'Not now, Gwen, for heaven's sake.' Anna rarely had a sharp word for anyone, but thankfully it had the desired effect and Gwen sat back.

'We were seeing each other and then we weren't, that's all. The ending was a bit tricky and his older daughter thinks I'm the most awful person in the world. It's already awkward and I don't want to ramp that up by risking bumping into him or Saffron when I'm out walking Lola. Or have Hamish thinking I've moved in with some sort of motive.'

'I kept thinking it might be a mistake not to tell you we were moving to Ocean View.' Frankie bit her lip. 'But I really don't think Hamish is the sort of person who'll want to make things awkward and Remi's going to be in heaven living next door to Daisy.'

'Some of us around this table know all about awkward situations and I promise you can get through it. Me and Bobby had to work together after we'd split up.' Toni leant against her husband. 'And look how it turned out, we'll be a family of four in the summer.'

'And you know what they say, new house, new baby.' Gwen really did live in another world sometimes.

'I think that's taking things a bit far.' Jess gave her a warning look. 'But it would be a shame if you and the kids had to miss out because you're worried about it being awkward with Hamish. Why don't you talk to him before you decide? You're going to be guide parents for Genevieve's baby anyway, aren't you? So it's worth clearing the air and seeing how you feel after that.'

'I suppose so.' Nadia still wasn't convinced, but Jess was right, she wasn't going to be able to avoid seeing Hamish forever. Maybe when she saw him again, none of the feelings she'd had for him would be there any more. There was always a chance and even if it was as likely as Gwen managing not to put her foot in it again for the rest of the night, it had to be worth taking.

30

Taking Jess's advice to meet up with Hamish had been as simple as pinging off a text, before her evening out with the midwives was even over. He'd responded straight away to say he was happy to meet up any time that suited her, and she'd been brave and arranged it for the next day. She was taking Lola, as a distraction and a reason to have to get home if things got as awkward as expected.

'It's so good to see you.' As soon as Hamish smiled, Nadia knew her feelings for him hadn't gone anywhere. The plan was already going awry.

'I thought it was probably a good idea to meet up and clear the air before we go to Neviah's naming ceremony.'

'That's not why I wanted to come.' He was standing so close to her that moving forward a single step would have meant they were touching and every fibre in her body wanted them to be.

'Then why did you?'

'Because I missed you. I told you that. I haven't felt this way about anyone since Sara and I didn't want to throw that away, not without trying everything I could to change your mind.' His voice was gentle but firm. 'I know what Saffron said to you.'

'She told you?'

'Yes, but she's really sorry. It was Saff who told me not to waste time, because you're too pretty to wait around for someone like me!' He laughed.

'Really?' It was almost too much for Nadia to take in and it would have been so easy just to lean into him and kiss him, forgetting the rest of the world. But she'd made that mistake more than once. 'The thing is, she was right about some things she said. She told me that I'll never compare to Sara and that you'll always love her. I know it's probably pathetic, but having spent most of my marriage to Ryan feeling like second best, I don't want to go through that again.'

'You don't have to compare yourself to Sara, you're two different people. Yes, I'll always love her, but it doesn't change how I feel about you or what we might have the chance of being to each other. My story with Sara was cut short, but ours doesn't have to be.' Hamish reached out and took her hand and she was incapable of pulling away. 'Do you remember what Freddie said to Ginny when she admitted to being worried about the things she'd experienced with her ex-husband making it taint what they had? He said they'll have a whole lifetime of experiences that are theirs alone. Who knows, if things work out, we could have that too. It doesn't change what happened with Sara, but this would be our story and there's no reason why it couldn't be the most amazing one we've ever been a part of.'

'There's also a chance it could burn out in weeks and then what happens? Maybe we can deal with that, but what about the kids? Remi's always asking after you as it is. What happens if we date for a few months and then want to end it? Remi and Mo have already had Ryan walk out on them twice; I can't put them through that again.'

'So you're going to stay single forever, just in case it doesn't work out?' His tone was still gentle and Lola was already looking up at him adoringly; just one more member of the family who'd fallen under his spell.

'It's even more complicated with the girls being friends. I can't risk you breaking their hearts too.'

'You're worried about me ending things?' Hamish waited until she looked up at him. 'I haven't been able to think about anyone but you since the first time we met and I saw how far you went to protect Ginny. I know you'd never do anything to hurt my girls and I feel the same about Remi and Mo. We can take this as slowly as you want and tell the kids we're just friends, at least until you're as sure as I am. But when Saffron asked me if I was in love with you, I had to admit to myself that I was. I'm not expecting you to feel the same, I just want to spend enough time with you to give it a chance.'

'You don't need a chance.'

'I do, I know it feels like a huge step, but—'

'No.' She looked into his eyes, cutting off what he'd been about to say. It was time to take a risk. 'You don't need a chance because I already feel the same. Even if it's crazy and reckless and not what I planned, somehow it just happened.'

'You do?' He was smiling and so was she, and when he kissed her the last bit of fight left her body. They were already immersed in each other's stories and however it turned out, she couldn't pretend she didn't want to find out what the next chapter held.

'I think even Lola's trying to give you a kiss!' Nadia laughed when they finally moved apart and she looked down to see the Labrador licking Hamish's hand, still gazing up at him in admiration.

'I'm just glad I've got the seal of approval from the newest member of your family.' He stroked the dog's head. 'So where do we go from here?'

'How about a walk along my new road? We're moving into the Gatehouse in Ocean View, and Mum and Guy are moving into the Lodge. So we're all going to be neighbours.'

'That's absolutely brilliant news.' Hamish had such a kind and open face, and his genuine joy was written all over it. He really was as delighted as he sounded.

'I hope you still think so in a few months' time, because I'm definitely the sort who'll be over to borrow sugar on a regular basis.'

'I'm counting on it.' Hamish took hold of her hand as they walked up the street in the direction of Ocean View. They were making the journey together and somehow she knew that the road ahead was going to be a beautiful one, they just had to take it one step at a time.

ACKNOWLEDGMENTS

I can't start expressing my gratitude without giving a huge thank you to all the wonderful readers who have chosen one of my books. I am more thankful than you will ever know. I hope you have enjoyed the sixth novel in *The Cornish Midwives* series. Sadly, I am not a midwife or a doctor, but I have done my best to ensure that the medical details are as accurate as possible. I am very lucky that one of my close friends, Beverley Hills, is a brilliant midwife and, as always, she has been a source of support and advice in relation to the midwifery storylines. However, if you are one of the UK's wonderful midwives or maternity care assistants providing such fantastic support for new and expectant mums, I hope you'll forgive any details which draw on poetic licence to fit the plot.

Some of the storyline from *Mistletoe and Magic for the Cornish Midwife* is particularly close to my heart and I have drawn inspiration from personal experiences in relation to some aspects of the plot, including Ginny's miscarriage and cancer diagnosis. My heart goes out to all those going through similar traumas and in particular my beautiful cousin Viv, to whom this book is dedicated.

The support for *The Cornish Midwives* novels remains beyond anything I could have hoped for. I can't thank all the book bloggers and reviewers, and Rachel Gilbey, who organises the blog tours, enough for their help. To all the readers who choose to spend their time and money reading my books, and especially those who make the time to leave a review, it means more than you will ever know and I feel so privileged to be doing the job I love. An extra big thank you goes to Jan Dunham, Beverley Hopper, Tegan Martyn, Anne Williams, Ian Wilfred, Debbie Blackman and Scott from @bookconvos.

My thanks as always go to the team at Boldwood Books for their help, especially my amazing editor, Emily Ruston, for lending me her expertise to get this book into the best possible shape and set the scene for the next book in the series. Thanks too to my wonderful copy editor, Cari, and brilliant proofreader, Candida, for all their hard work. I'm really grateful to Nia, Claire, Laura, Megan, Jenna and Kate for all their work behind the scenes and especially for marketing the books so brilliantly, and to Amanda for having the vision to set up such a wonderful publisher to work with.

Thanks too to my good friend Jennie, from Dunwrite Author Services, for helping these tired eyes out with a final read through!

As ever, I can't sign off without thanking my writing tribe, The Write Romantics, and all the other authors who I am lucky enough to call friends.

Finally, as it always will, my biggest thank you goes to my family – Lloyd, Anna and Harry – for their support, patience, love and belief throughout the journey that got me here. And to baby Arthur, who is a constant source of inspiration and motivation when the going gets tough.

ABOUT THE AUTHOR

Jo Bartlett is the top 10 bestselling author of many women's fiction titles including the Cornish Midwives series. She fits her writing in between her two day jobs as an educational consultant and university lecturer and lives with her family and three dogs on the Kent coast.

Sign up to Jo Bartlett's mailing list for news, competitions and updates on future books.

Visit Jo's Website: www.jobartlettauthor.com

Follow Jo on social media:

 twitter.com/J_B_Writer

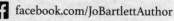 facebook.com/JoBartlettAuthor

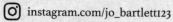 instagram.com/jo_bartlett123

ALSO BY JO BARTLETT

Boldwood

Boldwood Books is an award-winning fiction publishing company seeking out the best stories from around the world.

Find out more at
www.boldwoodbooks.com

Join our reader community for brilliant books, competitions and offers!

Follow us
#BoldBookClub